YAL BOROUGH OF GREENWICH

twitt

Joss Wood loves boo... ...wild places of Southe... ...She's a wife, a mum to ... ...cats. After a career in local economic development, she now writes full-time. Joss is a member of Romance Writers of America and Romance Writers of South Africa.

Katherine Garbera is the *USA TODAY* bestselling author of more than ninety-five books. Her writing is known for its emotional punch and sizzling sensuality. She lives in the Midlands of the UK with the love of her life; her son, who recently graduated university; and a spoiled miniature dachshund. You can find her online on at www.katherinegarbera.com and on Facebook, Twitter and Instagram.

SECOND CHANCE TEMPTATION

JOSS WOOD

ONE NIGHT, TWO SECRETS

KATHERINE GARBERA

MILLS & BOON

First Published in Great Britain 2019
by Mills & Boon, an imprint of HarperCollinsPublishers,
1 London Bridge Street, London, SE1 9GF

Second Chance Temptation © 2019 Joss Wood
One Night, Two Secrets © 2019 Katherine Garbera

ISBN: 978-0-263-27199-7

1119

Printed and bound in Spain
by CPI, Barcelona

SECOND CHANCE TEMPTATION

JOSS WOOD

One

Levi Brogan hurt.

Everywhere.

That's what happened when you leave your dirt bike for a make-out session with a gravel road lined with rocks.

His ass was now welded to a chair, partially because his leg was in plaster from above his knee down to his ankle, but mostly because moving anything more than his eyelids hurt. He'd not only broken his patella but also managed to pull a muscle in his left rotator cuff, so using crutches was like stabbing himself repeatedly in the shoulder.

Wah-wah-wah...

God, he was so over himself and his injuries, but he was rapidly coming to the conclusion he could do with some help.

Someone who wasn't his mother or his sister. He loved them but, God, they never shut up. Ever. And if they weren't talking about wedding guests or honeymoons or babies or flowers, they were fussing over him.

By the time he'd kicked them out earlier this morning, he was close to overdosing on estrogen. Levi now deeply regretted his show of independence and there was a good chance that, by nightfall, he might swallow his pride and send out an SOS.

Levi pushed his hand through his hair, feeling utterly frustrated. His world was now confined to the bottom level of his home. Working out in his state-of-the-art gym in the basement was, obviously, not possible. He wasn't able to climb the stairs leading to his master bedroom, so he was sleeping on the sofa in the media room and using the downstairs bathroom to clean up. He would kill for a hot shower, but he needed help to get in and out of the bathtub. And right now, the kitchen was a million miles away.

And he was hungry.

Levi looked at his crutches, not sure if he had the energy to make the trek to find food, and checked the pain level in his shoulder. It was still screaming from walking the ten yards to the bathroom. Food was, unless he took another painkiller, out of the question. And every time he took a painkiller without food, he tossed his cookies.

Rock, let me introduce you to hard place.

Levi heard a knock on his front door and frowned. His family used the back door leading into the kitchen. And they all announced their presence. The extended Brogan family was not a quiet bunch. The Murphy guys were also frequent visitors and they also used the back door, knowing it was rarely locked. Business associates who needed to see him would've called to make an appointment and the rest of his small circle of friends were at work. And if they had a day off, they would've given him a heads-up via a text message.

End result: Levi had no idea who was knocking on his front door. A reporter? A photographer? The press had ambushed him when he left the hospital, the camera flashes making his headache a hundred times worse. He hadn't responded to any of their nearly indecipherable questions, and neither had his mom or his sisters. His dad had loved the press, but Levi and his mom and siblings didn't.

Despite the Brogans shunning the limelight, the tabloid press paid him, and his sisters, far too much attention, all because they were the children of Boston's most successful businessman and bon vivant, Ray Brogan. And, because those bottom-feeders loved drama, there had been a few articles about Levi's accident, reminding the residents of Boston that he and his father had had a volatile relationship. The press took great delight in telling the world he'd spurned Ray's offer to take over Brogan LLC , a holding company that owned and operated companies in many different sectors and that Levi, reserved, private and taciturn, wasn't the man his father was.

He wasn't as charming, as exciting, as loud or as volatile. Thank God.

Levi didn't make rash decisions, never made promises he couldn't keep, didn't take huge risks, causing the people he loved anxiety. Ray got off on risk and adrenaline—betting every cent on huge deals that might or might not come off. He made impulsive decisions—buying companies without doing due diligence—and calling people who suggested caution—mainly Levi—unimaginative and boring.

Ray's successes had been stratospheric, his failures equally impressive. Levi's mom had ridden the roller coaster; Levi, on joining the family firm after college, couldn't handle his father's volatility and resigned after a year.

His father called him dull and a coward, not cut out for a high-stakes world. Levi had never understood his father, who never felt embarrassed or chastised. He just blustered and BS'd his way through the criticism, and the world seemed to love him even more for his confidence, his brashness.

Levi was the exact opposite; he was not, and never would be, a fan of failure, not privately or publicly. He preferred to be the master of his own ship, avoiding storms rather than sailing directly into them. He liked to be in control. But the world expected him to be like his famous father, so whenever he showed even a hint of his father's impulsive nature—and apparently crashing his dirt bike qualified—he made the news.

Levi used his crutch to lift the drape covering the window of his study, through which he could see the road and his driveway. An unfamiliar SUV sat in his driveway, too expensive to belong to an intrepid reporter.

He hoped.

The knock came again and Levi bellowed a quick "Come in!" But, honestly, if he could persuade his visitor to make him a sandwich and a hot cup of coffee, he'd listen to a pitch for an interview, or from a salesman.

He was that desperate.

"I'm in the media room. Down the hallway, second door on your left."

Levi heard the front door closing and, judging by the hesitant steps, knew his visitor wasn't someone who had constant access to his house.

"For God's sake," Levi muttered, impatient. "Second door on the left."

"I heard you. I'm not deaf."

The words hit his ears at the same time she appeared in his doorway, and Levi stared at her, not sure whether his incredibly strong pain pills were causing hallucinations.

Black jeans and a thin, mint-colored sweater hugged her curves under a thigh-length leather jacket. A multi-colored scarf held back curls and her face was thinner, older and, God, so beautiful. Levi gripped the arm of his chair, physically grounding himself, fighting the instinct to rush her, to pull her into his arms and bury his face in her neck, in her lustrous hair. He needed to inhale the scent of her skin, to know whether it was as soft and creamy as it looked.

He wanted to strip her naked, to finally feel her round breast in his hand, to find out whether her nipples were as luscious as he imagined, her core as warm, as spicy, as the rest of her.

So much time had passed and Levi felt shocked at how much he wanted her. Unable to stop himself, he drank her in. Those light green eyes fringed with long, thick black lashes fascinated him and he'd loved running his thumbs across those high cheekbones and that round, stubborn chin. He'd been addicted to her wide, sexy mouth, with its full lips, and he'd adored her curly, black-as-coal hair. Tanna's skin, thanks to her Bengalese grandmother always made her look like she'd recently returned from a six-week holiday in the hot Caribbean sun.

Tanna was warm island breezes and hot beach bonfires, with a body made to wear a bikini, or better yet, nothing at all. She was a hot sun, a shooting star, blue skies, happiness.

Or she had been…

Before she screwed with his life and made him look like an idiot in front of his family and the world. Before she'd left and his world spun out of control.

He didn't need to see her again, didn't need to hear whatever the hell it was she wanted to say. He'd worked damned hard at surviving her, creating a life he loved and enjoyed, and he'd made a conscious effort to forget her. Like Ray, she'd caused chaos in his life and he never again wanted to feel like he was falling out of an airplane without a parachute.

He was over her.

He had to be.

"What the hell are you doing here, Tanna?" he demanded in a low growl.

"I need to talk to you," Tanna said, advancing into the room and standing next to an easy chair, a twin to the one he was sitting in. He saw her eyes flitting to his leg and an exquisitely arched eyebrow lifted. "What happened?"

"My dirt bike and I parted ways," Levi responded curtly. He jerked his head, hoping she didn't notice the fine tremor in his hands. "You know the way out."

Tanna ignored his order and sat down on the chair, placing her tote bag on the floor next to her. She rested her forearms on her knees and clasped her hands together. "We need to talk, Levi."

Did he want to hear anything she had to say? Hell no. And hell yes.

Hell no, because her walking out on him shortly before their wedding without an explanation made him reluctant to indulge in a rehash ten-plus years later. And hell yes, because, dammit, this was Tanna. The only woman who'd ever caused his lungs to stop functioning, blood to drain from his brain, his heart to beat erratically.

Self-reliant and reticent, Levi didn't make friends easily and, before Tanna Murphy, had never been in love. For months after her leaving, he'd felt like his ribs were broken, every breath he took hurt.

He'd loved her, craved her, would've moved heaven and earth for her. And, because of who he was, his nonmarriage had made all the papers on the East Coast. And on the West Coast too.

God, he'd been the village idiot.

"Just walk your pretty ass out of here, Murphy."

Tanna tipped her head and Levi noticed the determination in her eyes. Dammit. He recognized her look; he'd seen enough of it when she was injured in an accident of her own, before their engagement. Tanna didn't take no for an answer. And since he couldn't forcibly remove her from his house, he was stuck listening to her.

Levi scowled at his right leg resting on a small ottoman. She pretty much had a captive audience and that annoyed the ever-loving crap out of him.

But if he was going to listen to whatever drivel she was about to spout, he'd get something out of it. He narrowed his eyes at her. "You can have five minutes if you make me a cup of coffee."

"Fifteen minutes."

"Ten minutes, but for that I want coffee and a sandwich," Levi countered.

Tanna had the audacity to smile at him. "Or I could do neither and just sit here and stare at you until you give in."

Levi picked up his phone and waved it. "Or I could call 911 and charge you for trespassing."

He saw her hesitate and heard the silent curse on the tip of her tongue. She opened her mouth to speak, hesitated and snapped her mouth closed.

"I thought you'd see it my way," Levi said as she stood up. "You'll find everything you need in the kitchen. And do not think you can fob me off with a PB&J. There's deli meat, salad stuff and an array of condiments. Pile it on, princess."

Tanna stiffened at the use of her old nickname, the one he used to murmur with affection. Now it was coated with sarcasm and a whole lot of annoyance. He'd made sure of it.

Levi watched Tanna walk out of his study and pushed both his hands through his hair. He really wanted a sandwich, mostly so he could take a pain pill, but he was willing to put up with the pain if it meant her walking out of his house and his life.

Tanna Murphy had a way of complicating the hell out of everything and all he craved was simplicity.

Tanna Murphy found the kitchen off the hallway and immediately walked up to the overlarge fridge and rested her forehead against the cool double doors, trying to control her breathing. Her rental car was parked in his driveway and she fought the urge to walk back through the house, out the front door and drive back to Beacon Hill or, even better, to Logan International Airport.

You promised yourself you would do this, Murphy.

She'd sworn to herself she'd do anything to combat the PTSD symptoms that had suddenly flared up before she left London. It was easy to identify the trigger; she'd been the first responder to a car accident where a dark-haired, dark-eyed teenager had caused a multicar pileup. The girl had looked like Addy, and Tanna had frozen. After a minute, her colleague had yanked her off the patient and provided the medical treatment necessary, and Tanna, from that minute, started suffering from anxiety attacks and flashbacks to her own car accident.

She was put on medical leave and, on the advice of her London-based therapist, she'd returned to Boston to face her past. But to her friends and family, she was taking a break from work. Her overprotective brothers didn't need to hear about the demons she was fighting.

Tanna walked across the black-and-white tiles of the kitchen to pull out a chair at a big wooden table. She'd sit here for a minute, gather her courage, because, damn, she needed it. She had to confront the past in order to return to work, to do her damn job. Nobody needed an EMT who hyperventilated in a crisis.

Tanna had only been back in Boston for a week and her local therapist, located in the very trendy area of Back Bay, already had her talking through her memories of the accident. She'd accompanied Tanna on her visit to the scene of the fatal crash, and wanted her to talk to the people impacted by the accident. Isla, having lost her only child, Addy, in the same accident, had been the first person on Tanna's list.

Their conversation had not gone well.

Tanna blinked away her tears. Addy had been bright and beautiful and so damn conscientious. She'd been working her way through college, juggling two jobs and her studies with grace and humor. The night of the accident was the first night in months she'd allowed herself to have some fun.

And, yes, it was stupidly unfair that Addy, completely sober, the most mature and responsible person in their group of friends, was the one who'd lost her life in the crash. And Isla felt the same. Tanna could see Isla's point—Addy, poor but proud, had been studying to be a social worker and worked at soup kitchens and no-kill animal shelters in her spare time. Tanna, a trust fund baby, paid little attention to her studies but was completely devoted to all-night partying with her friends. Addy had been driving Tanna's car because Tanna was drunk, and Addy, an inexperienced driver, hadn't been able to handle the powerful convertible.

Tanna didn't blame Isla for being angry; the useless society girl survived when sweet Addy hadn't. And Tanna'd not only survived, but in the hospital she'd fallen in love with the guy who'd been driving behind them, who'd held her hand while they waited for medical assistance to arrive. The same guy who also happened to be the son of a famous billionaire.

And then Levi had slid a diamond onto her finger.

She'd been told she was exceptionally lucky to be alive, even luckier her family had resources for her recovery.

Because, as Isla had pointed out, she was the lucky one, the girl who'd cheated death, who'd come out of a terrible situation with a couple of scars and a gorgeous man on her arm.

Hell, Isla was right…

And that was why she'd run away from her privileged lifestyle and her wonderful fiancé ten years ago, because the only way she could deal with the guilt of surviving when Addy hadn't was to be anything but that party-loving, credit card flashing trust fund baby. She owed it to Addy to be better, to be more, to contribute…

To suffer.

Tanna sighed, digging both sets of fingers into her hair. Her conversation with Isla had been brief and unpleasant but it was over. Now she needed to talk to Levi…

He looked good, Tanna admitted. If she ignored his pale face and his dinged body, he looked…wonderful. At twenty-four he'd been tall and built and, sure, conventionally handsome with his deep brown hair shot with auburn and his ink-blue eyes. But somehow, and unfairly, Levi Brogan looked even better a decade later. He seemed a lot more muscular and more masculine, with heavy scruff on his face and messy hair.

Unfortunately, her ex-fiancé, even battered and bruised and a little broken, was wildfire hot.

So unfair.

Tanna rubbed her hands over her face and tipped her head back to look at the wooden beams running across the ceiling. Running out on Levi, hurting him, still shamed her, it was her biggest regret.

She'd left his engagement ring on the hall table of the house in Beacon Hill, along with a letter addressed to him in a sealed envelope. She could've explained she was debilitated with guilt, having second thoughts about getting married so young, that she wasn't ready to be anyone's wife.

That she had a debt to pay, that she needed to do more, be more. For Addy.

She could've said she was wondering if she was confusing gratitude with love…

She could've written any or all of that, but she didn't. Through tears, and with her heart breaking, she'd just said she was sorry and she couldn't marry him.

Tanna didn't regret not getting married, didn't regret, not for one moment, the last ten years, but she did regret hurting Levi, for running when she should've had the guts to face him.

But she'd been scared…

Scared she'd never be anything more than her brothers' adored, overly protected sister, Levi's wife, a socialite with ample funds who loved art and designer clothes.

She'd wanted to be more…

More grounded, more real. She'd wanted to be a person who gave rather than took.

And, in time, she'd hoped to feel less guilty. But that had yet to happen.

Tanna doubted it ever would. So, she would work at what she could control and that included facing the past, dealing with her PTSD and getting back to work…

"Hell, Murphy, are you baking the damned bread? What's taking so long?" Levi bellowed.

…and making Levi a damned sandwich.

Two

Standing in his light-filled office, Carrick Murphy, the oldest of the four Murphy siblings, looked across his desk to his two brothers. Finn, as per usual, was on his smart-phone, occasionally sipping from his *Nerd? I prefer in-tellectual badass* coffee mug, a gag gift from their sister, Tanna, many Christmases ago. Carrick transferred his gaze to Ronan, who was staring out the window, his thoughts a million miles away.

Carrick ran a hand through his dark hair and rubbed his hand over his jaw. He knew many Bostonians looked at them, three bachelor brothers—rich and reasonably good-looking—and their beautiful little sister, and thought they lived charmed lives. From the outside look-ing in it was easy to forget they'd lost their parents when they were young, that the brothers had jointly raised their younger sister and they'd all lived through Tanna's near-fatal accident. Carrick's marriage had imploded,

Ronan's wife died, Finn and Beah divorced, and Tanna left Boston…

People seldom looked behind the wealth and success…

Carrick, annoyed by his introspection when he had work to do, rapped his knuckles on the desk. Two sets of Murphy green eyes focused on him. "Before we get to work, let's discuss Tanna."

"Something is up with her," Ronan said, turning around.

Carrick nodded. "I think so too."

"I have to wonder why she's really back in town because Tanna doesn't do vacations." Ronan walked over to the coffee machine. He placed a cup under the nozzle and pushed the start button. Carrick drained his cup and passed it to Ronan for a refill. "And why does she have to live in London? She can save lives here as easily as she could there."

"We can't pressure her to move back to Boston. That'll just make her run in the opposite direction," Finn said, placing his forearms on top of a stack of paper folders. "She's more stubborn than all of us put together."

Stubborn and determined. Those two traits were the only reasons she was walking after the best specialists in the country had given her a ten percent chance of regaining her mobility. A decade later, nobody would suspect their fit and active sister had spent five months in the hospital after the ball of her right femur shattered her pelvis and her left ankle splintered into what they called a fountain break. The only clues to the hell she'd endured were a few livid scars and a barely there limp.

"Does Levi know she's back?" Finn asked.

Carrick raised his shoulders. "I don't know."

"Should we give him a heads-up?" Ronan asked, thinking of their close friend.

Levi and the Murphy brothers had stayed friends after his breakup with Tanna, but Levi never spoke about their vibrant and gorgeous sister, refused to look at the many pictures of her in the Murphys' Beacon Hill house. By the way he now acted, nobody would suspect that, at one time, Levi had loved Tanna.

While they were all tight with Levi, he and Carrick had the closest relationship. And as Carrick was the eldest, being the bearer of news, both good and bad, was his responsibility. "I'll tell him." He picked up his phone and dialed his friend's number. Putting the call on speaker, he waited for Levi's terse greeting.

"Yo."

Carrick exchanged a wry smile with Ronan. Levi was taciturn and abrupt and never used three words when one would do.

Carrick opted to shoot from the hip, the way Levi preferred. "Just a call to let you know Tanna is back in town and she'll be here for about six weeks or so."

Levi waited a beat before he responded. When he did, his tone was colder than an Arctic blizzard. "Too late. She's here."

Carrick heard the call disconnect and shook his head. He took the coffee Ronan held out to him and sighed. "Levi should really stop wearing his heart on his sleeve."

Ronan smiled at Carrick's sarcasm. "Yep. And he really shouldn't be so open and forthcoming." Ro leaned back against the credenza and crossed his foot over his ankle. "Well, he's been told. That's all we can do."

"I have news…" Finn stated after a moment's silence. "And it's big."

Happy to get off the subject of his sister's and best friend's nonrelationship, Carrick turned his attention to Finn. His younger brother was normally the definition of cool and collected, so the excitement on his face was strange to see.

"As you know, Isabel Mounton-Matthews left her entire estate to Keely Matthews and to Joa Jones, whom she took in when Joa was fourteen. Keely and Joa have decided to sell most of Isabel's extensive collection to raise funds for Isabel's foundation and we are handling the sale."

The company they'd jointly inherited, Murphy International, was one of the most exclusive auction houses in the world, renowned for the quality and rarity of the pieces of art passing through their hands. The sale of Isabel's well-documented art collection would be one of the biggest in the past decade and the items were causing a stir in their wealthy art and auction circles. "I've been cataloging the collection and I've come across three paintings I think might be sleepers—"

Carrick exchanged a quick, excited look with Ronan. A "sleeper" was an artwork whose real value or attribution had been missed by either the owner or art dealers.

"Keely said that Isabel thought it was painted by Winslow Homer. Two are iffy but there's one that makes me think it might be."

"Provenance?" Ronan asked. In their world, provenance was everything.

Finn shook his head. "There's nothing but Isabel's suspicions. But, damn, the painting I saw, stylistically, looked like it might be one of his depictions of African American rural life."

"A lost Winslow Homer?" Homer was one of the country's most revered artists and a lost painting by him would set the art world on fire. Carrick would get excited but he also knew fraudsters loved to fake Homer. And they were good at it. "It sounds too good to be true."

Ronan looked at Finn, who was their resident art historian. "Are you going to chase this down?"

"I'd love to but I'm slammed. And I think we need an

expert in nineteenth-century American painters." Finn gestured to Carrick's phone. "If the paintings are by Homer, it would have to be authenticated by you-know-who."

You-know-who, she-who-should-not-be-named, Satan's Bride.

Also known as his ex-wife.

Tamlyn had written the catalogue raisonné, the definitive work detailing all of Winslow Homer's work. If Tamlyn didn't believe the paintings were by Homer, the canvas wouldn't be worth diddly-squat.

"We need a specialist art detective, preferably someone Tamlyn trusts, to run the tests, to track down any provenance," Finn stated. "Tamlyn takes every opportunity to smear your name, Carrick. She's vindictive enough to dismiss these paintings just because you brought them to her attention. But if we hire someone she respects, someone she works with regularly, we might have a shot of getting a decent result."

Carrick and Tamlyn's marriage had been brief. It was a relationship he now deeply regretted. They'd both been ridiculously unhappy and when, after a year, he'd asked for a divorce, Tamlyn punished him by dragging his reputation through the court of public opinion. Since he'd never, not once, publicly defended himself, Carrick, in certain social circles, was still considered to be a bad husband at best, an adulterer at worst.

Good thing he didn't give a crap what people thought.

At least his reputation as an honest art dealer and auctioneer was still intact, and that was all that mattered.

"Okay, point taken." He looked at Finn. "Find me an art detective whose opinion Tamlyn Smith respects."

"I'll find someone," Finn told him and then his mouth curved into a smile. "And that's Tamlyn Smith-Murphy to you, son."

Carrick resisted the urge to punch his youngest brother. Finn was yanking his chain and he'd learned not to respond. But he wished Tamlyn would stop using his surname, dammit. Yeah, she was an art appraiser and in the art world using the name Murphy added gravitas. But surely, when you'd screwed a guy six ways to Sunday—physically, emotionally, financially and mentally—you forfeited the right to use his name?

Carrick looked at Finn and ignored his building headache. "Find someone with impeccable references and unimpeachable references. The sooner we establish provenance, the more publicity we can generate for the sale."

Ronan nodded. "This sale is going to be huge."

Carrick agreed. "And profitable."

Tanna put the plate holding two thick sandwiches on the small table next to Levi's chair and picked up a state-of-the-art tablet to make way for his large mug of coffee. Levi immediately lifted the cup to his mouth, his low groan reminding her of the sound he'd made the few times they kissed.

For two people who'd been about to legally and morally bind themselves to each other for the rest of their lives, they hadn't indulged in a lot of public displays of affection. Or even private displays of affection.

For the first few months of their relationship, she'd been in too much pain, and when she started to feel better, Levi had treated her like spun sugar. On leaving the hospital, she'd still needed time to recover and when she regained most of her mobility, she was so confused about what she was feeling she'd asked Levi if they could wait until their wedding night to make love.

He'd gently teased her for being old-fashioned and she'd felt guilty because her morals had nothing to do with her decision. She was having enough doubts about her future without sex complicating her thought processes.

Not making love to Levi, not having him be her first, was one of her most profound regrets.

Pulling her attention off the past—she'd have to address that soon enough—she looked around the room.

She'd visited this house a few times between leaving the hospital and running out on Levi. His parents—lovely Callie and charismatic Ray—had lived in it back then and Tanna had fallen in love with the open plan, light-filled, spacious mansion.

Callie had filled the rooms with a mishmash of contemporary and family pieces, effortlessly combining old and new into rooms that felt both lived in and cozy, comfortable and sophisticated. While this was now Levi's home, it still held traces of his mom's creative flair.

Tanna couldn't help thinking that if she'd stuck around, this might've been her home too, stamped by her style. There would be photos of her siblings on the walls along with his, artwork she'd loved and bought, pieces of furniture she'd inherited from her parents. But everything she owned was in her flat in London, Levi's stuff was here and they hadn't had the chance to combine their lives and possessions.

Because she'd run…

"I like this room," she said, ignoring his deep scowl.

"It's not filled with priceless pieces of artwork like your childhood home but it's okay."

As auctioneers and fine art dealers, her family, going back generations, had amassed an incredible collection of art, most of which adorned the walls of the house in Beacon Hill. Her bedroom held a sketch by Degas and a watercolor by Georgia O'Keeffe.

She'd grown up surrounded by incredible art, textiles

and ceramics, and had planned to follow her brothers into the family business at Murphy's, joining the auction house's PR and publicity department. But she hadn't been back to Boston in years and hadn't, not since her accident, been back to Murphy's. She'd avoided it because it had once been her second home, a place she adored...

Murphy's was the one place in Boston where she'd felt completely at ease and happy. She adored art, in all its forms, loved talking about it and promoting it, and being around people who loved it as much as she did. On every visit home, Tanna knew that if she stepped into Murphy International she'd start questioning her decision to become an EMT. So she avoided the family business. And, as much as she could, Boston.

Tanna sighed. "I should've just stayed in London," she said, mostly to herself.

"I absolutely agree. Feel free to go back."

She would if she could but that wasn't possible until she had her PTSD symptoms under control. And who knew how hard she'd have to work or how long it would take her to achieve that goal? Tanna's stomach clenched and the muscles in her neck contracted.

Relax, Tanna.

Concentrating on her breathing, she pushed away her negative thoughts.

She'd just hit a bad patch and she needed a little time to get her head sorted. Her accident had been a long time ago and she was fit and healthy. She was done being hostage to her fears. She liked emergency medicine, and the notion of helping others as she was once helped was important to her.

She owed those paramedics for saving her life—her heart had stopped twice en route to the hospital—and the only way she could show her gratitude for walking away from the crash with nothing more than a few scars was to pay it forward.

Unfortunately, paying that debt came with panic attacks, flashbacks and cold sweats. She just needed to control her reactions at work. She'd live with her PTSD symptoms if she could save lives. The symptoms wouldn't, after all, kill her. Sometimes it just felt like they would.

They couldn't sit here in silence, so Tanna attempted to initiate conversation. "I'm sorry about your dad, Levi. I know it happened years ago, but I'm still sorry."

"As you said, it was a long time ago."

Okay, then. She'd try again. "And I read somewhere your family sold your dad's company when he died. It must've been difficult losing your dad and the company."

"Not really."

She hoped he was referring to the loss of the company and not his father's death. The Levi she remembered was private and reticent but he'd never been a jerk.

"Is there a point to this inane conversation? Since you walked out on me, I didn't think you particularly cared about my life. And I, in turn, don't care how you've spent the last ten years, Tanna."

"I'm an EMT." Seeing the quick flash of surprise in his eyes, she blurted out a question and immediately regretted letting the words fly. "You didn't, just once, ask my brothers where I was, what I was doing?"

"You bailed on me, bailed on the life we planned, so I didn't feel the need to keep up with yours," Levi shot back. So that was a no then.

"Sit down, say what you want to say and then leave."

His casual order, and his expectation that he would be instantly obeyed, annoyed her. Unless she was at work being paid to take orders, she took umbrage at being told what to do.

Tanna took her time walking to a wingback chair, crossing her legs, making herself comfortable. Levi placed his plate on the arm of his own chair and picked up his sandwich. "Talk. Make it quick."

Tanna stared down at her hands. She'd imagined this meeting so often, had practiced what to say, but now those carefully crafted words wouldn't come. Seeing Levi's impatience building, she forced them across her tongue. "I didn't leave you at the àltar, but it was close."

"You left straight after the rehearsal dinner. A scant twenty-four hours before," Levi said, dumping his hardly touched sandwich back onto the plate and putting it on the table. Tanna forced herself to meet his eyes, a deep blue that defied description. Sometimes they were cobalt, sometimes ink. Sometimes, like now, they held more than a touch of ice.

"I should not have left without talking to you, without a goodbye. Without an explanation."

"No argument from me."

"Levi, from the time we got engaged, I had my doubt—"

"Did I ask you for an explanation? Do I want one? I have a one-word answer…no."

Well, okay then. Tanna wasn't sure what came next, so she sat quietly, wondering how quickly he'd ask her to leave. The words were on his lips; she could see them hovering there. She needed to speak before he kicked her out.

"I was wrong, and I should've had the courage to face you, to explain. It was easier to run, to leave you that letter."

"Yeah, after watching you fight to recover from your injuries, watching you learn to walk again, I was surprised by your lack of bravery. And decency."

Ouch. Tanna felt the knife in her back, felt it turn. But she couldn't argue with his statement. How she wished she could tell him the truth. That she couldn't talk to him face-to-face before she left because if she had, she knew he would have brushed off her fears as prewedding jitters. He would've dismissed her concerns, persuaded her they were doing the right thing, and she would have listened. Then she'd have been miserable. And furious with herself for not standing up to him.

"My mom canceled the wedding, called everyone and returned the presents. Christmas was pretty crap that year." Levi's words drove the knife in deeper and harder. "But we did make headlines, day after day, week after week. All of us—me, my parents, your brothers and my sisters—lived with the press following us everywhere, shoving cameras into our faces, demanding an explanation, a comment, something. Yeah, best Christmas ever."

Tanna winced. She'd asked about the press attention but Carrick told her not to worry about it and she hadn't. Because she'd been trying to find a new life, a new normal, she'd done as he suggested.

"Maybe one day you will let me explain…"

"Don't hold your breath," Levi told her, his expression reminding her of the Bering Sea in the dead of winter.

Tanna nodded and rubbed her damp hands on her thighs. "Well, I am sorry. I wish there was something I could do to make it up to you."

Levi stared at her and she could see his agile mind working, spinning a hundred miles a minute. He was cooking up something and Tanna looked at the media room door, her inner *oh-no* radar telling her to leave, now. Whatever Levi was going to say next was going to flip her life on its head.

"Carrick said you are in town for six weeks. Is that right?"

She was due to go back to work on March 1. "Give or take," Tanna replied, wondering where he was going with this.

Levi's smile was full of sarcasm. "You say you want to make it up to me?"

Yeah, and she'd meant it, kind of. She'd meant it in an it's-the-right-thing-to-say way, not in an I'll-do-anything-to-make-it-up-to-you way.

"Uh…what do you have in mind?"

Levi picked up his coffee mug again and looked at her over the rim. "It pains me to admit this but it's become abundantly clear I need help. I'm mobile but walking hurts like hell—"

"It should if you broke your patella."

"The cast I can handle. It's annoying but manageable. But I can't hobble around because using the crutches hurts like hell. So, it would help to have a runner, a gopher. Someone at my beck and call. Someone I don't mind ordering around—" Levi bared his teeth "—because she owes me."

Oh, crap. She'd walked right into that one.

Three

Damn right, she owed him.

Tanna owed him for walking out on their engagement, from running away from their wedding, leaving behind the life they'd planned. He didn't care about the hours he'd spent by her bedside, holding her while she cried—from pain and from frustration—

Those were his choices and he lived by them.

But it had been her choice to say yes to his proposal, to agree to a Christmas wedding, to say yes when she really meant no.

The weeks and months after their nonwedding had been hell on so many different levels. He'd shrugged off the embarrassment factor and ignored the subtle comments about his young bride's flight, the fake sympathy in the eyes of people who cared more about gossip than they did about him. He'd hated the media attention for making him, as intensely private as his father was extroverted, a public spectacle.

And he never gave the money he spent on the wedding another thought.

But Tanna damn well owed him for encouraging him to take a chance on her when he knew how risky taking chances could be.

She owed him for the sleepless nights he'd spent questioning his own judgment, for making him think asking her to marry her wasn't a smart decision. For the months and years he'd spent second-guessing himself. For whipping the entire situation out of his control…

She.

Owed.

Him.

And yeah, he could freely admit he really wanted to sleep with her, still. Maybe more now than he ever had before. A decade had transformed her from an eager-to-please girl into a fully confident woman and he didn't feel the need to rein in his responses, to choose his words.

Tanna could give as good as she got.

And, hey, she was stunning and he was injured, not dead.

Levi rubbed his hand over his face, conscious of his throbbing shoulder, leg and, yeah, cock. In the past, he'd never allowed their physical interactions to go much beyond a couple of light kisses. It wasn't that he didn't desire her; he'd been twenty-four years old and a vibrating hormone, and she'd been a beautiful, striking girl.

But she'd also been broken, and every time he'd wanted to take their physical relationship deeper, he remembered her pinned to that crumpled car seat, her green eyes wide with shock and pain, her thin voice asking him if she was going to die. He clearly recalled telling her not to look at Addy, sitting in the driver's seat, slumped over the wheel, bloody and unresponsive.

During the weeks and months following that god-awful

night, he'd found himself falling deeper and deeper, entranced by Tanna's fierce courage. He'd loved her, craved her and promised himself he wouldn't push her for a physical relationship. He was a big guy, he outweighed her by a hundred pounds and a part of him was terrified he'd inadvertently do something to hamper her recovery. So, he'd pushed down his desire and banked his lust. Things would change when she left the hospital…

But they hadn't. When she was finally discharged, sporting his ring, she asked for more time, to delay intimacy until they were married.

In hindsight, that was a pretty big clue all was not well.

Tanna wasn't weak now, or fragile. And the lust he'd felt for her back then was a baby version of the hot, needy, roiling emotion coursing through his system today. She was toned, healthy, vibrant and he knew she could handle him…

Physically, emotionally, mentally.

Unlike a decade ago, she was whole. And strong. And challenging. And, God knew, he could never resist a challenge.

Payback wouldn't be a bitch, it would be a delight. Revenge would be supersweet.

Levi watched as she tried to find a way to say no, to wiggle out of her obligation. She opened her mouth and the lame excuse he expected failed to materialize. Instead, she posed a question. "How long will it take me to work off my debt?"

"Is that a yes?"

"No, it's a question," Tanna replied. "How long?"

As soon as he could use his crutches, he'd be able to fend for himself, to move about. But he still wouldn't be able to drive. And he needed to get to his businesses—his marinas, the shipyard and the extensive corporate interests he ran on behalf of the Brogan Family Trust. Yes, he could take time off work for as long as he wanted. Hell, he could retire tomorrow if he wanted to. But he didn't want to do that. Work kept him sane and by staying involved, he kept control and control was essential to his peace of mind.

"I'm not allowed to put any weight on my leg for six to eight weeks," Levi replied. "I need someone on call for another two weeks, part-time for at least another four weeks after that."

"Your sisters and mom aren't prepared to help you?" Tanna asked, looking for an escape.

"Of course they are, but I like them. I don't see why they should have to put up with my foul mood when you can."

"Because I owe you," Tanna said, sounding miserable.

Yep, she did. And also because he couldn't imagine her walking out of his life again until he knew every inch of her luscious body.

Because he wanted revenge, a little payback.

And her.

Remember that, Brogan. Sex and revenge were the only two reasons he was pushing her to stay.

Levi looked at her again and swallowed, wondering why his mouth was so dry. His heart was also slamming against his rib cage—a pissed-off prisoner demanding release—and his stomach was joining in the rebellion.

What the hell was wrong with him?

So much. He was sore, he was horny and he was, not that he'd ever admit this to anyone, a little scared. Nobody had ever affected him the way Tanna Murphy did.

Damn.

Right, enough BS, Brogan. Get your head on straight.

He was attracted to Tanna. This grown-up version of the girl he'd loved was as sexy as hell.

It was okay, normal even, to be a little carried away thinking about how she'd feel, naked and soft, and so intensely feminine, in his arms. But sex was all he'd take from her, all he had to give her. He wasn't fool enough to give her more. Not again.

"I don't think so, Levi." Tanna shook her head. "It's really not a good idea and I don't see why I should give up my…vacation time to be at your beck and call."

Why had she hesitated when she said vacation? Why did he suspect a vacation was not the reason she was back in Boston? And why did it matter? All he needed was for her to be around…

"I'm not asking you to glue yourself to my side, Tanna. I just need you to move in here, to help with some meals, to drive me to work and back."

"You are not nearly ready to go back to work," Tanna told him, her tone as bossy as hell. Levi raised his eyebrows at her assertiveness.

"But I will be, soon. I heal fast," Levi retorted, not willing to get into an argument about something that wasn't going to happen today, or even tomorrow. "Anyway, as I was saying, I need you for a couple of hours a day, to be on call if I need you. The rest of the time will be your own."

"Good of you."

Levi refused to let her see his quick smile. Assertive and sarcastic. Better and better. And he was glad. If Tanna was the same timid, eager-to-please girl she'd been, he probably wouldn't be making this offer, wouldn't be half as interested in that version as he was in this.

At twenty-four he'd been happy to have his ego stroked; at thirty-four he liked women who pushed back, who weren't afraid to speak their minds.

He was surrounded by strong, gutsy, opinionated women and if he ever came to the point of considering another relationship—an exceedingly remote possibility—he wanted someone who could stand on her own two feet, who was prepared to make her own mistakes and live with them.

Being the voice of reason when his dad's ambition outstripped his common sense, Levi couldn't remember a time when he hadn't felt responsible for protecting his mom and sisters. When his dad died, Levi oversaw the sale of Brogan LLC and he personally managed the billions in the family trust.

He did, he admitted, have a strong rescue gene. But his mom and sisters were perfectly able to look after themselves and while they were happy for him to manage their family money, he'd been told, repeatedly, he didn't need to worry about their emotional well-being.

They had their own alpha men doing enough hovering, thank you very much.

He still felt protective of them; he probably always would. But he was smart enough not to tell them that. But they were his blood, a part of his psyche. Tanna—or any other woman—did not warrant that much of his soul. It hurt far too much when they handed it back to him, battered and bruised.

God, enough with the melodrama, Brogan.

This was a straight-up deal. He needed someone. Tanna owed him, and while he'd never be verbally abusive to her or any other woman, with her he wouldn't have to pretend he wasn't in pain, frustrated or pissed off. He could just be because, dammit, there was nothing she could do to hurt him again.

"A couple of meals, a couple of rides, a little light housekeeping, that's all I need you for." Levi shifted in his seat and pain barreled through him, digging its claws into his body, and it took everything he had not to allow her to see how weak and miserable it made him feel. He'd been vulnerable once with her. He'd never allow her to look beneath his surface again.

A tiny frown appeared between her eyebrows. "You're in pain."

Dammit, what had happened to his impenetrable mask? Not wanting to give her an inch, he made a sound he hoped sounded like a scoff. "Please."

"God save me from stubborn men," Tanna muttered.

"I'm fine, Murphy." Such a lie.

Dropping his head back, Levi fought to keep his eyes open, cursing himself for feeling so tired. Sometimes he managed to ignore the pain and drift off and he felt this might be one of those times. His battered body needed sleep to recover but he didn't want to fall asleep now, not in front of Tanna. If he did, she'd leave and he might never see her again.

He wouldn't get any payback if she did that.

Levi forced his eyes open and gripped her wrist. "Will you be here when I wake up?"

Tanna shook her head. "Probably not."

Disappointment, hot and sour, rocketed through him. Why did he care? She meant nothing to him, not anymore.

Tanna didn't try to pull her wrist from his grip and her skin was so soft, so smooth. He thought he heard her sigh and her voice, when she spoke, came from a long way away. "I have things to do. I need to talk to my brothers, explain what I'll be doing here. I'll be back in a couple of hours."

"Promise?"

"Yeah. Sleep now, Levi."

Levi hoped, for the first time in a decade, he'd see her again. But only because, he sternly reminded himself as he drifted off, he needed help and she owed him.

And because he really, really, really wanted to see her naked.

* * *

Like that other famous auction house on the other side of the pond, Murphy's boasted a canvas portico in front of its main entrance with Murphy International written in white across the bloodred canvas. It was simple, effective and attractive, and Tanna felt the familiar kick of pride as she stared up at the letters spelling her surname.

Her great-grandfather started the company, passed it on to her grandfather, then to her father and now her brothers were running the world-famous auction house with satellite offices across the world.

She was the only Murphy who'd ever stepped away, who was working in a completely different field.

The thought made her sad.

Tanna jammed her hands into the pockets of her coat, conscious of her heart beating out of her chest. Just like always, she'd planned to avoid Murphy's, but she needed to talk to Carrick and he was, if she remembered correctly, leaving for Tokyo shortly. She needed to tell him she was moving out of the Beacon Hill house, moving in with Levi…

But only to help him, of course.

She definitely could not tell her brother she hoped, as insane as it sounded, that somehow, some way, she and Levi would finally get naked and she'd find out what making love with her ex-fiancé felt like.

She'd spent many nights imagining the way his hands would feel on her skin, how strong and hard he'd be when he pushed into her, filling up those empty and desperate spaces no man had ever managed to fill.

She needed to know because, honestly, her sexual education was incomplete.

She and Levi were done, over, their time had passed…

But, not having slept with him, Tanna was convinced

there was a puzzle piece missing, like she'd never quite seen the complete picture. Like she'd never read the last chapter in a sad but compelling story.

Tanna heard the incoming message on her phone and pulled it out of her pocket. She swiped the screen and read the text from Carrick.

Security just warned me about a suspicious-looking woman casing the joint. Get your ass in here before you get arrested.

Tanna grinned. She knew Murphy's security firm employed facial recognition software and she'd been identified within a few seconds of arriving at the entrance. Carrick was just yanking her chain.

Tanna greeted the doorman and walked inside the iconic building, her boots echoing on the polished concrete floor. In front of her was the concierge, and to the left and right were the main viewing rooms.

Tanna was a frequent visitor to Murphy's website and knew there was an upcoming auction of Henry Moore sculptures and a collection of vintage clothing and accessories. She wanted to lose herself in both exhibitions but she knew she couldn't afford to step inside either room—there were too many memories here that she wasn't quite ready to deal with.

Tanna watched as a young woman wearing a black pencil skirt and sky-high red heels half ran up the marble steps leading to the private offices on the floors above. She pushed down a wave of envy. How lucky that woman was to be working here, to be interacting with art lovers, with collectors, with the beautiful objects. How fortunate she was to be immersed in art, surrounded by beauty.

She could be you. You worked here, before you left. You chose to leave, Tanna Murphy, nobody chased you away.

Tanna had left because she didn't have a right to live her dream life, the life she'd been born to. Addy'd never had that chance and it was Tanna's fault. For Addy she had to do more, be better, be useful.

Art was lovely but it wasn't important...

She shouldn't have come back here. She should've just called Carrick...

Feeling sad and emotional and teary-eyed, Tanna ran up one flight of stairs, through a security door and up another flight of stairs. Her feet took her down the hallway to Carrick's large, third-floor office and after greeting Marsha, Carrick's PA, she knocked on his partially open door.

Carrick looked up at the knock and his smile broadened as he waved her in. Standing up, he kissed her cheek and shook his head, bemused.

"Why are you looking at me like that?" Tanna asked him, dropping her bag onto one of the chairs on the opposite side of his desk.

"Just happy that I've finally gotten you to come into Murphy's. I'm also thinking about how much you look like Mom," Carrick replied, his voice gruff. Tanna appreciated the observation but she knew she couldn't hold a candle to her obscenely beautiful mother.

"I know I don't talk about her often, Tan, but I still miss her. I miss them both."

Tanna's eyes misted over. "I do too. But I don't remember them as well as you do."

Carrick gestured to his messy desk. "I could do with Dad's help today," he admitted, slapping his hands on his hips.

Tanna dropped into the other chair and crossed her long legs. "Problems?" She couldn't help asking the question.

She might be completely devoted to her career but Murphy's was, and would always be, a huge part of her.

Carrick walked around his enormous desk and rested his butt against the edge. "When are there ever not?"

"Tell me."

Because, just for a minute or two, she wanted to pretend she was still part of this business, still a Murphy. Tanna never got the chance to talk art with her colleagues. For the most part, art didn't interest them and they were also too damn busy saving lives.

But she wasn't at work now and she could spend time talking about Murphy clients and collections with her elder brother.

It didn't mean anything…

"For someone who professes to have no interest in the family company, you still ask pertinent questions and make sensible suggestions," Carrick said later, sending her a sly grin.

"I could still use you here at Murphy's, in public or client relations. You enjoy people, love art and you're naturally warm and charming, just like Mom. Do you still enjoy being an EMT?" Carrick asked her before she could think of a suitable response.

Tanna crossed her legs and stared at the tip of her leather boot. "It's an important job, Carrick. I make a difference."

"You didn't answer my question," Carrick persisted. "Do you enjoy it?"

She didn't *hate* it.

She looked at the painting sitting on the easel in the corner of his office and lifted her chin. She wasn't going to spoil her trip to Murphy's by fighting with her brother over her return, something she couldn't consider. So she changed the subject. "Is that a Homer?"

Carrick, thank God, didn't push.

"We're not sure," Carrick said, looking at the painting of two children and their African American mother.

"It's an intensely powerful painting and if it isn't a Homer, then it's a superb fake."

"I have an appointment shortly with an art detective we are hiring to chase down provenance and run tests."

"I thought you employed art detectives. Isn't that what Finn does?"

"Finn is checking and double-checking the provenance of all the paintings we are putting up for sale at the Mounton-Matthews auction. It'll be the biggest sale of the decade and we've been working on it for months. Finn is slammed. We also need to use an art detective Tamlyn trusts because she'll be the one who will eventually decide whether it's a genuine Homer or not," Carrick continued.

Tanna's eyes cooled at the mention of his ex. She and Tamlyn had never jelled and neither made any bones about the fact. "You're dealing with that witch?"

It was Carrick's turn to change the subject and he did it by tapping the face of his watch with his index finger. Tanna couldn't complain; what was good for the goose and all that.

"I have an appointment in five and I need to leave for the airport in an hour so was there a reason for this visit or did you just drop in to say hi?"

Tanna scratched her forehead and wrinkled her nose. "Talking of revisiting the past…"

"Yeah?"

"So, as I said, I'm in Boston for about six weeks…" Tanna nibbled at the corner of her mouth. *Get it out, Murphy.* Her words rolled out in a rush of syllables. "I went to see Levi this morning. I wanted to apologize to him, see if I could make things right."

Carrick winced and Tanna didn't blame him. They both

knew a couple of words wouldn't make it right. "How did he respond?"

"It didn't go well," Tanna admitted. "I apologized. He was dismissive."

Tanna looked past her brother's shoulder to his incredible view of the Downtown Crossing neighborhood and Boston Common.

Carrick folded his arms, tipped his head and waited for more. Because, somehow, he knew there were at least ten thousand things she wasn't saying. "He's still angry at me."

"Uh-huh?"

"He says I owe him and there's something I can do to repay him."

When Tanna didn't speak again Carrick frowned.

"You going to tell me what Brogan wants, Tan?" Carrick demanded, not bothering to hide his curiosity.

"He wants me to move in with him. He needs someone to run errands for him, cook and clean." Tanna pulled a face. "He says he can be rude to me and not care."

"Uh-huh," Carrick said and Tanna didn't appreciate his lack of effort to hide his amusement. "And you believed him?"

"He was pretty damn rude," Tanna muttered.

She couldn't see anything funny in what she'd said. What was wrong with her oldest brother?

"So, are you going to agree to his demands, clear your debt?" Carrick asked.

"You think I should?"

"I think you should help him out, Tan."

Tanna narrowed her eyes. "You're just saying that in the hopes something will spark between us again, so there might be a chance of me moving back to Boston."

"I've never made a secret of the fact that I want you back in Boston and that I want you to be part of the family business again, part of this family. We've missed you intensely and you've barely spent any time with Ronan's kids. London is a hella long way away. Levi sat by your bedside for months. The least you can do is help him out when he's in a jam."

Yep, Carrick wasn't above playing the guilt card. Tanna muttered a curse. "Ugh."

"Is that a yes?" Carrick asked.

"Actually, I'd pretty much made up my mind to help Levi before I got here." Tanna glared at him. "But I'm not happy about it."

Carrick started to speak but was interrupted by another knock on his door. Marsha opened it and behind his middle-aged, short and ruthlessly efficient PA stood a tall blonde.

"Carrick, your three o'clock appointment is here. This is Dr. Sadie Slade." Marsha stepped aside to allow a tall, modern Cinderella look-alike to walk into his office. Tumbling honey curls framed a triangular face dominated by big, round blue eyes holding more than a trace of violet. Tanna looked from the *Sports Illustrated* model to her eldest brother and her eyes widened at the look of profound— Was that shock on his face?

It was either that or Carrick was having a heart attack. Since she knew her brother was a workout junkie, she figured she didn't need to call for an ambulance. Thank God, because the thought of giving him mouth-to-mouth made her want to gag.

Then again, the blonde—judging by her flushed face and her inability to pull her eyes off Carrick's face—wouldn't hesitate.

Chemical reaction.

Tanna looked past Carrick to where Marsha stood in the doorway and she caught Marsha's eye, fighting not to return her grin. So, she wasn't the only one who'd caught the zings between these two.

Ha ha, karma is a bitch, Carrick.

He'd laughed at her for her Levi predicament. She couldn't wait to watch him dealing with Dr. Sadie Slade, acting like the cool, reserved CEO of one of the premier auction houses in the world while fighting his fierce attraction.

Tanna had no idea how he was going to act cool with his tongue on the floor.

Four

Tanna, leather tote over her shoulder, rapped briefly on Levi's front door and stepped inside. Pulling her suitcase into the hall, she dropped her duffel bag to the floor and looked up to see Levi shuffling down the hallway.

He stopped, stood on his good foot and relaxed his arms, regarding her with eyes that instantly made her want to spill her secrets.

Even dinged and dented, you are so hot.

I've missed you.

It's weird and wrong and right to be here.

"Hi." *Scintillating opening line, Murphy.*

"I didn't think you were coming back," Levi said, his voice extra growly. And, strangely, extra sexy.

"Miss me?" Tanna asked, aiming for jokey but hitting breathless. Honestly, what was wrong with her? She just had to look at Levi and her brains, and ovaries, exploded.

Not good.

"I survived. Just I like I survived the past decade," Levi

replied, but his words didn't hold the bite she expected. He just sounded tired.

Tanna glanced at the antique, freestanding clock in the corner, wincing when she saw it was later than she'd realized. "Yeah, I'm sorry I'm a bit late. I meant to be here earlier, but I had to go see Carrick, tell him I was moving out of his house into yours—"

Alarm skittered across Levi's face. "Ah, I meant to call him, to explain the situation, but I fell asleep. How did he take the news?"

Tanna thought about her brother's reaction. She couldn't forget his amusement.

"Strangely, he said that I should help you. He, kind of, agreed that I owed you. But he didn't say very much on the subject at all."

She really hoped her big brother wasn't trying to play matchmaker. That ship had sailed.

And sunk.

Levi frowned and instantly looked suspicious. "That doesn't sound like Carrick."

"I thought so too."

Levi ran his hand over the scruff on his jaw. "Huh. Should I call him and ask?"

Tanna shook her head. Why borrow trouble? "No…hell no. Let sleeping dogs, or noncommunicative brothers, lie." She glanced down at her bags. "Where can I dump these?"

"There's a guest bedroom up the stairs on the right. I have a cleaning service. They come in once a week and they keep it in a state of readiness."

"And I supposed your overnight guests stay in your bed and don't use the guest room."

Tanna winced when the words left her mouth and she wished she could haul them back. Dammit. His sex life had nothing to do with her, nothing at all. But if he did have a live-in or a steady girlfriend, why wasn't she here, tending to her man?

And if he did have a girlfriend, how would she react to Tanna's presence in his house?

But if he *was* seeing someone, Tanna would have the perfect excuse to leave. She could just pick up her bags and walk out the front door. There was only one way to find out and Tanna bit the conversational bullet. "So, should I be worried about some girlfriend showing up here, ready to scratch me stupid?"

A smile touched Levi's mouth. "Jealous?"

She was not going to dignify that with an answer. Mostly because, yes, she was. But she was allowed to be. This man had once considered spending the rest of his life with her. But she'd left him, bailed out in a spectacular fashion. She'd forfeited her right to feel jealous.

Or any other emotion.

Tanna, because she knew she was digging a hole for herself, just lifted her chin and waited for him to answer her question, and Levi finally put her out of her misery...

Correction...to satisfy her curiosity.

"No, no girlfriend, steady or otherwise."

Her inner twelve-year-old did a happy dance. Ridiculous. Not wanting him to see a hint of her relief, she bent down to pick up her duffel bag.

"And you?"

Tanna straightened, blinked and frowned. "Me what?"

"Are you seeing someone?"

Not for a long, long time. When last had she even been on a date? How sad was it that she didn't have the foggiest idea?

"Not that it has anything to do with you but...no. Not currently."

Levi's eyes burned with dark blue intensity. "Good."

"It's not good! Why is it good?" Tanna demanded.

Levi half smiled again and gripped his crutches. "You and I, Tanna Murphy, have unfinished business, and that business would be complicated if other people were involved."

Unfinished business? What was he talking about? Was he talking about sex?

Please, please let him be talking about sex.

Levi turned his back to her and Tanna couldn't help her eyes dropping to his butt, perfectly outlined by a pair of straight-legged track pants. Utterly distracted, Tanna appreciated the way his long-sleeved T-shirt hugged his broad back and showed off his wide shoulders and skimmed over his big biceps. Man, he was as delicious going as he was coming…

As for the other type of coming, she'd like to see that too.

Levi stopped, half turned and looked back at her. Their eyes clashed and held, and Tanna watched his eyes deepen and darken. His hot gaze bounced from her eyes to her mouth and back up again.

It had been far too long since she'd kissed him. She'd forgotten what his mouth felt like, how he tasted. She needed to know…

She couldn't wait for a second longer. Tanna didn't hesitate, moving closer to him so she could place her hands on his wide chest. Keeping her eyes on his, she stood up on her tiptoes to allow her lips to touch his.

His lips felt cool under hers, firm and so damn masculine. Tanna moved her hands from his chest to hold his strong upper arms, the muscles unyielding. She wanted to pull his shirt up his chest, find hot, warm skin, but she just dug her fingertips into his flesh, disappointed he'd yet to respond to her kiss.

She was out of practice, so maybe she hadn't seen lust

in his eyes, maybe she'd read him wrong. Sinking back to her toes, she dropped her hands and felt her face blaze with humiliation.

"Okay, so I misread you, this… Sorry." Tanna rocked on her heels. Embarrassed beyond belief, Tanna turned, but Levi grabbed the hem of her jacket, stopping her flight.

Tanna tossed her hair back and lifted her head, forcing herself to meet his eyes. Before she could, he hauled her into him, his flat hand on her lower back pulling her close. His hand was strong, his erection felt like a shaft of pure, hard delight and his mouth—finally—was on hers and doing what his mouth did best.

And that was kissing her…

She remembered his banked and restrained kisses from long ago, but this was a different Levi kissing her. This Levi wasn't polite or thoughtful. His mouth demanded she respond, that she step into the fire with him and burn.

Tanna was all too happy to feel the flames. His tongue pushed past her teeth to swirl around hers and Tanna whimpered, feeling hot and scratchy and wonderful and uncomfortable, all at the same time.

This was a grown-up kiss, sexy, raunchy, demanding. It was a kiss shared by a man and a woman, different but equal. It was an I-want-you kiss, a this-will-only-get-better kiss. It was bourbon and ice, deep midnight, the shock of a dip in icy water, the thrill of free diving.

It was Levi let off his leash.

Tanna felt his fingers on her neck, skimming the shell of her ear and traveling over her cheekbone. Then his hand dropped, and he returned his grip to the crutch he'd tucked under his arm. Tanna stepped back, pushed her fingers into her hair before dropping her hand to hold his crutch, needing a little support of her own.

Only Levi Brogan could make her feel unsteady.

"What the hell was that?" she demanded, the words husky.

"That was the unfinished business I was talking about," Levi told her, his tone now brusque. "And, just so we are clear, part of our unfinished business is having you under me—or more likely, given my busted leg—on top of me."

"Uh…uh…" Tanna felt her head whirl, the moisture in her mouth faded. God, she wanted that. Now, immediately.

Not making love with Levi all those years ago was, along with handing her keys to Addy, one of her biggest regrets.

Tanna released a long breath. "Wow, tell me what you really think, Levi."

A small smile touched his lips. "I shoot from the hip, Tanna, and you should be prepared for that."

He lifted his hand to rake back his dark brown hair, which contained those flashes of auburn she loved so much. Tanna was also happy to see the fine tremors in his fingers, showing her he wasn't as controlled as he wanted her to think.

Levi cleared his throat and Tanna made herself look at him. "Ten years ago, I treated you like glass and you ran. This time around, I'm going to tell you what I want from you. I'm going to be as up-front as possible."

She could live with that. "Okay."

"As much as I'd love to pick you up and carry you to the nearest horizontal surface, that's not going to happen today." Humor flashed in his eyes and Tanna caught her breath as his brief smile upped his sexy factor a thousand percent.

"But in a week or two, hopefully a helluva lot sooner, I am going to ask you if you want to sleep with me and I sure as hell hope you say yes." He looked past her to the front door and his expression turned hard and remote. "A decade ago I gave you my heart. That's not on offer anymore. But my body sure as hell is." Levi adjusted his crutches under his arms. "And, no, before you ask, this is a completely separate issue from you helping me out, the debt I said you need to repay."

A million thoughts buzzed through her but one dominated: if they never made love, Tanna knew she would regret it. She would always wonder how he'd taste, feel, move.

Whether he'd fill her as wonderfully as she'd imagined or whether he'd be a letdown. If she didn't make love with him, just once, she'd regret it for the rest of her life.

He wouldn't pressure her, coerce her or nag her. No, that wasn't Levi's style. In his direct way, he'd just stated his position and thrown his offer on the table. It was hers to pick up.

Or not.

It would be easy to say yes, to allow her hot blood and the taste of him on her lips to influence her decision. Sure, she wanted this but now that her blood had cooled and she was thinking more clearly, she was a little scared and a lot uncertain.

Was she ready for this? Did she really want to reopen the door to the only man who'd ever touched her heart?

Shouldn't she think about this a little more?

Tanna jammed her hands into the pockets of her leather jacket and hunched her shoulders in what she hoped was a casual shrug.

It wasn't a yes to sex; neither was it a no. Her nonresponse left her some wiggle room.

"I won't give you my heart again either, Levi." She knew that for sure. Her heart was permanently off-limits.

Levi's cold smile held no amusement. "Tanna, you never did."

In the white-and-sunshine-yellow guest bedroom upstairs, Tanna unpacked her clothes and placed them in the closet, her toiletries and makeup in the minimalistic but pretty en suite bathroom. All the while she wondered if she'd completely lost her marbles.

Levi wasn't an idiot. He knew her nonanswer wasn't a solid no and there was a strong possibility that she'd sleep with him. Not tonight obviously, or tomorrow, but sometime in the near future.

She might as well start wrapping her head around the concept.

At some point, she'd see whether his long body was as muscled as she imagined. She'd know how he tasted, how he liked to move. Judging by the kiss they'd shared, Tanna had no doubt Levi was a skilled lover, and at the very least, she expected an orgasm. Maybe, if she was very lucky, two.

It had been a while since she'd felt comfortable enough with a guy to allow him in her bed.

Levi might be terse and abrupt, but she trusted him with her body. She had no intention of handing over her heart... because she wasn't the heart-handing-over type and also because he didn't want it.

She'd had her chance and she was fully aware she'd never get another.

Their time had passed and sex, and their insane attraction, was all that was left.

Their history couldn't be changed but when she and Levi did make love, her curiosity would finally be satisfied, and she wouldn't have to live with any more *what if?* thoughts.

Tanna looked out of the guest bedroom window onto a small lake that was part of the Lockwood Country Club's golf course. As she always did when she felt out of sorts and needed a strong dose of what was, not what she wanted to be, she called Padma.

Her godmother specialized in step-into-the-light talks. Although it was nearing midnight in London, Padma answered on the second ring, sounding alert and focused. "Baby girl."

Her mom called her baby girl and Padma's greeting created a link between her and her mom. "Hey, fairy godmother."

Tanna heard the flick of a lighter, Padma's long inhale. How she wished Padma'd give up smoking, but despite her nagging, and Tanna had done plenty, Padma had yet to give up her pack-a-day habit.

Tanna opened her mouth to pester but Padma beat her to it. "Don't start, darling. Rather, tell me why you are calling in the dead of night."

How did she explain the unexplainable? Tanna decided it was better just to give it to her straight. "I've got myself into a bit of a pickle."

Padma had been married five times and always had a man, or three, hanging off her every word. She was a master at digging herself out of deep holes. "Ooh, sounds promising. What did you do?"

Tanna smiled. Padma was the type of person who appreciated drunken mistakes, dancing on bars, protest action and fast cars. She couldn't abide mediocrity or, as she called it, "sheep behavior."

"I'm not at the Beacon Hill house with Carrick."

"Please tell me that you have found a hot man to have an affair with," Padma replied, sounding delighted. Then she hesitated, remembering Tanna wasn't the fall-into-bed-on-a-whim type. "Darling, if that's not the case, then feel free to lie. Because, as you know, I've been telling you for months and months that you need a good rogering."

Honestly, who was Roger and how did his name come to be associated with sex? Only the English...

"Well, I didn't move in because I was offered sex. That came a few hours after I barged back into his life."

It only took Padma a moment to connect the dots. "Oh, for the love of baby Jesus! You went to see Levi, didn't you?"

It was a rhetorical question since Padma knew there was only one man who could make Tanna feel so out of control.

"I presume you threw yourself at his feet and demanded forgiveness?" Padma's question was scathing.

"I wasn't subservient! I asked him for forgiveness, he told me I owed him, that I needed to help him and that he wanted to sleep with me." Tanna wrinkled her nose. Those were the highlights, weren't they? So much had happened today.

"Oh, my God, you are too much."

Okay, that wasn't a compliment. Not waiting for Padma, Tanna quickly explained the situation. When she was done, Tanna heard Padma light up another cigarette and waited for her pronouncement. "Sounds like a bad idea, darling girl."

The hell of it was that she was right.

Tanna transferred her phone to her other ear, lifted her foot up onto the seat and hooked her elbow around her knee.

"I saw him, and I knew I needed to be here, needed to do this," Tanna admitted. "It was the same feeling I had ten years ago. Back then, my gut instinct told me to run, to leave Boston. This time it's telling me to stay here with Levi. But only for the next six weeks, that's all," she quickly added. Because there was no way she'd considered returning to Boston, living here, with or without Levi.

In London she wasn't Tanna Murphy, a trust fund baby, heir to one of the oldest businesses in the city. In London she was just Murphy, another EMT trying to save lives, earning a paycheck and paying off her debt to the universe for letting her live.

For sparing her when Addy died.

"You told me, when I arrived in London, sobbing and scared, that my intuition was the most powerful part of me. It was my soul talking. You have even suggested it can be our connection to feminine wisdom, to people who have passed before us," Tanna gabbled. "I can't just dismiss what I am feeling."

"Yeah, yeah, sounds like me," Padma admitted, irritated. "In my defense, I probably had four too many G&Ts at that stage."

Tanna grinned. Padma would move heaven and earth for her but hated it when she got sentimental and mushy. And Padma loathed it when Tanna became overly emotional or verbose.

"So, you are going to stay with him?" Padma asked.

"Yeah."

"Did you call me to ask my permission?" Padma demanded. "Last I heard, you were an adult and made your own decisions. Decide what you want to do and then do it, Tanna. Stop overanalyzing it to death."

And that was why she'd called. Right there…that. Padma always said something to clarify Tanna's thinking and the words were exactly what she'd been waiting for.

So, to break it down…what did she want?

She wanted to give Levi a hand—she did owe him for leaving so abruptly and the chaos she'd caused—and she wanted to sleep with him. She'd satisfy her curiosity about sex with him and then she'd move on, back to London, back to her real life.

There! Sorted. Tanna closed her eyes and wished she could hug her godmother. And her best friend. "Thanks, Pad. Love you."

"Yeah, yeah, whatever."

Tanna heard the emotion under the irritation and decided

to ramp up her godmother's annoyance. "I love you to the moon and back. I miss you so—"

Click, call disconnected.

Tanna grinned and tossed her phone onto the huge double bed. Linking her arms around her bent knees, she remembered Padma asking her why she'd run out on her wedding, Levi, her family and her hometown. All she could tell Padma at the time was that she knew she needed to leave, that staying was impossible.

She couldn't tell her that living the pampered and protected life Levi and her brothers had mapped out for her was impossible, knowing Addy was dead.

Had she stayed and married Levi, she probably wouldn't have been miserable. She would've been a young wife with a husband who adored her, living a lovely life as one only could when one had access to enormous wealth, both his and hers. They would've been fine for a year, two, maybe three or four. But, at some point, she would've started to question her actions, to look back on her choices and wonder if marrying Levi was the best choice she could have made.

She'd made the right choice to run. She had.

Despite the fact that she been confused and guilt-ridden, and so sad, leaving Boston had been the biggest gift she'd given herself. In running, she'd discovered who she was, or could be. She'd left Princess Tanna behind and become a different person, had many different experiences—both good and bad—and looked at the world through her own lens and not one tinted by her family's or her partner's views and expectations. She'd experienced the highs and lows of life, stood on her own two feet, made her own way. Ignoring her massive trust fund, she lived on her salary, counting pennies when her bank account didn't stretch as far as she needed it to.

She'd compromised on where and how she lived, made friends and lost others, but through it all, she'd made choices for herself without taking a man's opinion into consideration. Some of those decisions had been smart, some not… but they were all part of her steep learning curve.

If she had married Levi, her Boston-based learning curve would've been gentler, softer, not as dramatic. And possibly not as much fun. It would've also been drawn by Levi, by her brothers. And, had she stayed in this city, she wouldn't be half as confident, and she'd be far less assertive.

Levi, then and now, was strong-willed, and she now realized he needed a strong woman, someone mentally tough, someone who could stand up to him, argue her point. He needed an equal partner, someone who challenged him. Young Tanna had not been that person and, if she'd stayed, would not have grown into the type of woman Levi, deep down, wanted. Needed.

Despite having hurt Levi, despite leaving a mess behind her, not getting married had been the correct thing to do. Oh, maybe she could've handled the breakup better, maybe she should've stuck around and cleaned up her own mess, but she hadn't and that was on her. She'd apologize for how she did it but not for the action itself.

So, what was she expecting from Boston this time around? To face her past so she could heal. Good sex, at some point, would be a bonus. To pay off her debt to Levi by helping him out.

But nothing else had changed.

She was only going to stay in Boston as long as it took her to put her past into perspective and deal with the PTSD symptoms. She could not go back to London still fighting her demons. She needed to get them, once and for all, under control.

Because HART—Hazardous Area Response Team—

was a vital service and she and her colleagues took on the worst cases and the trickiest situations. But she couldn't return to the unit if she wasn't a hundred percent psychologically healthy. She owed that to herself and to her colleagues but mostly to her patients. She'd had the best care possible when she was injured and she believed that her patients deserved the best of her. So she needed to stay in Boston, confront her past, see her therapist. Help Levi out and clear her debt. Then she'd go back to London and her demanding, important job.

That was her plan and she was sticking to it.

After washing her face and refreshing her lipstick, Tanna headed back downstairs, and as her foot hit the bottom stair, she heard feminine voices in the kitchen. If she wasn't mistaken, and she didn't think she was, Levi's sisters were in the room, ready to ambush her.

Tanna bit her lip, debating whether to face his family or run upstairs and hide. Uncertain as to what she should do, she froze in place, her mind whirling. She hadn't spent much time with the twins when she and Levi were together. His sisters had been away at college and only came home for their brother's engagement party. Jules and Darby, and their friend DJ, were outwardly friendly but Tanna wasn't a fool. She'd immediately realized she would have to work hard to prove to them she was worthy of their brother.

The problem was that by the time she met them she wasn't sure whether she wanted to prove anything to them. And she wasn't sure she wanted to face them now. Tanna, hoping no one had heard her clattering down the stairs, turned around to run back up to her room when she heard a throat clearing.

"Chicken."

God, she was so busted. By Callie Brogan of all people. "I thought you had more gumption than that, Tanna."

She'd thought wrong. Her back to Callie, Tanna pulled a face and gathered her courage to face Levi's mom.

Tanna scrunched her eyes closed, took a deep breath and felt every muscle in her body contract. She regretted running out on Levi, she really did, but she also felt bad for never contacting Callie again.

Levi had brought his mom to the hospital, maybe two or three weeks after Tanna's accident, and ten minutes after meeting her, Tanna fell in love. Callie, blonde and blue-eyed and so tiny Tanna couldn't believe she'd produced the big and burly Levi, took her hand, kissed her cheek and looked around her hospital room.

"How much longer are you going to be in here, darling?"

At that point they hadn't been sure, so Tanna had shrugged, fighting back tears. "They said a least a few months."

"Then we have to make it look less like a jail cell," Callie had declared.

She'd returned that evening with potted plants and soft linen, cut flowers in a crystal vase and the picture of her parents that sat on Tanna's bedside table. Magazines and her tablet were in easy reach, as were sparkling water and notebooks.

Due to work constraints, Levi and Tanna's brothers could only visit her in the evening, but Callie made friends with the nursing staff and often visited Tanna out of the official hours. During those long months in the hospital, Tanna and Callie became exceptionally close and getting Callie as a mom-in-law, as a mom—something she hadn't had for the longest time—had been an enormous tick in the reasons-to-marry-Levi column.

Tanna, knowing she couldn't stay on the stairs and that running away was impossible, turned slowly and, with

heavy feet, made her way down to where Callie stood waiting, looking not a day older than she had a decade before.
She wore a pair of dove-gray slacks, a black cashmere jer-
sey and diamond studs the size of pigeon eggs in her ears.
On her finger rested a pink diamond and platinum ring
fully able to outshine the sun. Her blond hair hit her chin in
a classic bob and bold red lipstick covered her mouth, and
Tanna remembered this was the woman who'd once been
the most popular hostess on Boston's A-List social scene.

Expecting to see censure in Callie's eyes and a frown
on her face, Tanna was shocked when Callie held out her
hands with a warm and welcoming smile.

"My darling girl." She pulled Tanna into her arms. "I've
missed you so."

Tanna felt tears burning as she returned Callie's hug,
unable to believe she was getting such a wonderful welcome from the woman who, she was sure, had wanted to
eviscerate her for jilting her son.

"Why are you being nice to me?" Tanna asked as Callie
pulled back. "I mean, don't get me wrong, I appreciate it,
but jeez, I never expected such a warm welcome."

Callie cupped Tanna's cheek with a cool hand. "Oh, don't
get me wrong. I was very cross with you for a long time.
But you're back and I am thrilled to see you."

Tanna needed to say something about Ray, Levi's father.
He'd died a few months after she'd left, and she'd sent flowers. "I'm so sorry about Ray, Callie. He was a lovely man."

Callie nodded and grief gently touched her face before
wafting away. "Thank you for the white lilies. They were
lovely."

Holy crap, Callie had a good memory.

Callie tucked her hand into the crook of Tanna's elbow
and steered her toward the kitchen.

"I have a new partner and he keeps me on my toes."

Callie flashed a brilliant smile. "He's ten years younger than me, is seriously ripped and has quite a few tattoos."

Tanna laughed at the excitement in Callie's voice. It was obvious her new man was making her very happy, in all the ways that counted.

Callie patted Tanna's hand and kept her feet moving forward. "We have so much to catch up on. I want you to meet Mason. He's so lovely and makes me so happy. But first, you have to give the girls a chance to take a bite out of your very pretty hide."

Fabulous.

"They are interrogating Levi in the kitchen. They want an explanation about why you are back. I wouldn't mind one myself."

Callie was sweet and gracious and altogether lovely but Tanna heard the note of steel in her voice. The Brogans were a tight bunch and Levi once told her that, while they argued like crazy, they were loyal to the nth degree. If you fought with one, you fought with all.

Tanna braked, not wanting to fight with anyone.

"You might as well get it over with," Callie said on a light laugh. "Pull up your big-girl panties, darling."

"But what if I don't want to?" Tanna wailed. "What if I don't own any big-girl panties?"

"Then suck it up, sunshine," Callie said cheerfully before placing her hand between Tanna's shoulder blades and propelling her into the kitchen.

Five

Levi sat at the scarred wooden table, his hand around his coffee mug, his head angled toward the doorway, expecting Tanna to appear any moment. He knew she was on her way because there was something about how the air changed when she was near. It was almost as if the atmosphere held its breath, waiting for her to arrive.

Or maybe that was just him.

Tanna stepped into the kitchen, her hands tucked into the back pockets of her jeans. She'd shed her thigh-length leather jacket, and her thin, light-green-colored silk sweater clung to her small breasts and slim curves. With her ballerina's body, she wasn't voluptuous by any means, but to him, she was as sexy as hell.

And he couldn't believe she'd agreed to sleep with him. Well, not in so many words, but yeah, she was still here, wasn't she? Her presence in his kitchen was proof she accepted that sleeping together—having hot, raunchy sex— was a definite possibility.

Hoo-damn-ray.

Levi leaned back in his chair and watched Tanna's glance bounce from one twin's face to the other and he was impressed by her composure. He admired her calm attitude and her courage to face his sisters.

Because his sisters could be pretty damn scary. They loved hard and they loved deeply, and hurting someone they cared about—even if he was their annoying brother—made them want to do some ass kicking.

He'd never let them tag team Tanna, but he appreciated their willingness to do so.

Levi transferred his attention to his mother, caught the speculation in her eyes and immediately dropped his gaze. Callie had a fully functioning mom-dar. She'd always been too intuitive for his own good and he didn't want her seeing anything that might give her hope there was a second chance for a happy-ever-after for him and Tanna.

There would be a happy ending, for both of them, several if he had his way. But a happy-ever-after? He didn't believe in those anymore.

Tanna broke the awkward silence in the room. "Jules and Darby, it's nice to see you again."

Such a lie, Levi thought. If she could've she would've avoided this conversation. Hell, if he'd had the choice, they wouldn't be having this conversation either, but while this house was now legally his, it was also their childhood home and the home they had all shared up until a few months ago.

Frankly, he'd need a nuclear bomb to dislodge them.

"Tanna," Darby responded, making her name sound like week-old trash.

Such fun.

Levi looked longingly at the cupboard containing his ten-year-old whiskey and wished someone would pour him a shot, or two. But he couldn't drink alcohol with the pain meds, more's the pity.

Well, if he couldn't have whiskey, he wished one of the many women in his life would get him another cup of coffee.

He opened his mouth to ask for a refill, but Darby responded before he could speak.

"I wish we could say we were happy to see you," Darby said, as forthright as ever. Jules had more tact than her twin, but probably because he was as straightforward, Levi liked Darby's shoot-from-the-hip style. He always knew exactly where he stood with that sister. "Why are you back, Tanna?"

"And if you're back only to mess with Levi's head, then we'd like you to leave," Jules interjected, folding her arms across her chest.

"He broke his knee, not his head, so he won't be taking you back," Darby continued.

Levi started to tell her she didn't talk for him, but before he could speak, Tanna held up her hand in a silent plea. When she was sure she had the floor, she straightened her shoulders and lifted her chin. "Are you two done?" she quietly asked the twins.

Jules nodded and Darby shrugged.

"Thank you," Tanna said, her voice smooth but holding a don't-mess-with-me edge. "I'm back because I had something to say to Levi—"

"What?" Darby demanded.

Levi considered responding but decided Tanna was doing a fine job dealing with his sisters on her own.

Tanna raised her eyebrows at Darby's interruption and Darby flushed. "Sorry," she muttered. "Go on."

"Thank you," Tanna said again. After a moment of silence, she continued, "What Levi and I discussed has noth-

ing to do with his family. That's between us. As is our
arrangement. While I appreciate your protective streak, I
can assure you there is no chance of a reconciliation between us—"

Her declaration was a sharp-tipped blade, stabbing him
in the stomach. What the hell was the matter with him?
There was no way in hell he'd give Tanna a second chance,
even if she wanted one…

Which she obviously didn't.

"—but I have agreed to help him out while he recovers.
The reasons behind our decision have nothing to do with
you," Tanna said, moving over to the coffee machine behind
where Callie was sitting. She turned her back to him and
reached for a mug in the cupboard above. They all waited
while the machine dispensed hot black coffee and Levi was
surprised when she swapped his empty cup for the full one.

"Thanks," Levi murmured.

"Hungry?" she softly asked.

"I ordered pizza. It should be here soon," Levi told her,
embarrassed when his stomach released a low growl. He
was hungry for the first time since his accident and not
just for food.

He wanted this woman…

Now, here. Immediately. How soon could he get his family to leave?

"That's all very well, Tanna, but you must understand
your returning to Boston sounds fishy," Darby said, breaking their stare.

Levi blinked at Darby's statement and shook his head.
Right. He loved his sisters but enough was enough. Injured
or not, he could fight his own battles.

He cleared his throat. "While I appreciate your concern—"

"No, you don't," Callie interrupted, laughter in her voice.
Not helping, Mom. Levi scowled at her and looked back

to the twins. "I don't need you to protect me. Or to interfere in something that has nothing to do with you."

Jules and Darby both rolled their eyes. In that moment, in their disbelief, the fraternal twins looked the same.

"Our love lives had nothing to do with you but that didn't stop you from interfering," Darby pointed out.

"I never interfered," Levi stated, knowing he was on thin ice. It was true. No good deed ever went unpunished.

Damn, but he longed to feel in control again. In the past week, he'd injured himself, was housebound and his ex-fiancée was not only back in his life, but in his home. What was next? A meteor strike? A swarm of locusts?

"Pfft. What about the time you took Matt outside and threatened him if he messed with DJ?" Jules demanded.

The ice cracked. "I'm not arguing with you about this, twins." Levi lowered his voice so they had no doubt he was losing his patience. "Tanna and I have come to an understanding and I'm asking you to respect that. And her," he added.

Both Jules and Darby looked mutinous, so Levi spoke again, his tone suggesting he wasn't interested in any of their opinions. "Tanna came back and she apologized. The fact that she was willing to do that is worthy of respect."

Levi ignored the surprised look on Tanna's face, the gratitude flashing in her eyes. He didn't want her gratitude, he wanted her mouth under his, their legs and arms tangled. He wanted her naked, preferably immediately.

And the sooner his interfering family left, the sooner that could happen. He started to lift himself to his feet and just managed to swallow his yelp of pain. Yeah, damn, he'd moved too fast. And if he couldn't move, then he certainly couldn't make love to Tanna the way he wanted to, the way their first time deserved.

He wouldn't be making love today. Probably not tomorrow either...

Hell.

"Girls, it's time to go," Callie said, sending him a you-can't-fool-me look. No matter how old they were or how independent, when Callie used that tone of voice, they all made haste to obey.

Jules and Darby rose and they both, as they always did, dropped a kiss on his cheek. Callie, surprisingly, ignored him to wrap her arms around Tanna, who still had her back to them. Levi saw Callie's squeeze and wondered what his mom whispered into her ear.

Sometimes, back then, he'd arrive at the hospital and find Callie lying next to Tanna in her hospital bed, Tanna's head on Callie's shoulder, talking or watching a movie. His mom and Tanna had become close very quickly, and he'd been a little jealous at their easy camaraderie. His relationship with his mom had been collateral damage in his ongoing fights with his dad; she'd been caught in the middle, her loyalty torn in two.

Levi's warnings, his doom-and-gloom prophecies about Ray's risk-taking, had caused tension and a hundred arguments, and then Ray died. Levi was still the only person who knew that Ray, at the time of his death, was about to acquire new cell phone technology that he said would revolutionize the industry. He'd handed over personal and business sureties and had been on the point of signing away everything they owned...

The technology, as Levi discovered after the funeral, was a dud. It didn't work.

They would've lost every damn thing they owned had the deal gone through...

And people wondered why Levi liked to be cautious,

why he needed to be in control? His father had taught him how dangerous freewheeling could be...

Callie turned away from Tanna and stood in front of him, waiting for him to meet her eyes. He finally did and Callie shook her head, looking a little amused.

"There's nothing to worry about, Mom," Levi told her, hoping she'd believe him, that he'd start to believe himself.

Her mouth tipped upward at the corners. "Oh, I know there isn't." She bent down and dropped a kiss on his forehead. "I'm not worried at all. Are you?"

Hell no. Even if he was, he'd never admit it to the Grand Interrogator.

Callie's smiled broadened at his negative response. "But I do know that, from tonight on, my darling, your life is never going to be the same again. And I, for one, am thrilled."

Levi watched her walk across the room and resisted the urge to call her back, to try to convince her that she was letting her imagination run wild. That she was seeing stuff that simply wasn't there.

He wanted to explain that he and Tanna were just two people who no longer had anything in common other than their mutual wish to strip each other down and put their hands and tongues to work.

But there were some things you couldn't say to your mom, even if she was one of the coolest people you knew.

"Bye, Mom."

Callie, and her great smile, walked out.

Tanna dropped the pizza crust onto her plate and wiped her fingers on a napkin, thinking it was going to be a very long six weeks if she and Levi couldn't get past their awkward silence.

She took a sip of red wine and tucked her feet under her bottom.

Levi sat in his easy chair, his busted leg resting on a leather ottoman, his hand wrapped around a glass of water and his expression pensive.

"I went to Murphy's today," Tanna said and watched as his eyes flew up to meet hers.

"Yeah?"

His expression was interested so Tanna nodded. "When I left Carrick's office, I couldn't resist popping into the viewing rooms. They are holding a vintage dress and accessories auction soon and the items on display are amazing, one-of-a-kind pieces from some of the most iconic designers of the past. And they are also auctioning off a collection of Henry Moore's work, so I spent some time in the viewing room."

Levi pulled a face. "Remind me who Moore is?"

Levi still wasn't an art connoisseur. "Twentieth-century sculptor? English, best known for his huge bronze sculptures. He dabbled in abstractions of the human figure, often depicting mother-and-child figures. He was a little obsessed with the female body—"

"Aren't we all?" Levi murmured. Okay, she wasn't touching that comment with a ten-foot pole.

"—and his forms often contain hollow spaces," Tanna continued.

"Thank you, Wikipedia," Levi stated, his voice dry.

As she always had before, she provided far too much information when Levi asked her about art. She couldn't help it; art facts stuck in her head like lint stuck to Velcro. She adored art and loved to share her knowledge.

"Did you ever finish your degree in art history?" Levi asked her, his index fingers tapping his strong thigh.

Tanna shook her head. "I got…distracted."

"But I bet your bedside table is still stacked with art books."

Tanna smiled at his observation. It was. Her bedtime reading was catalogues raisonnés and autobiographies of artists.

"It's the first time I've been back to the business since I left when I was nineteen," Tanna said softly, thinking about her visit to Murphy's. She felt Levi's eyes on her face and wondered why she felt the need to tell him something so personal.

Levi put his plate down on the table next to him and tipped his head to the side. "Really? Why haven't you been back?"

Tanna looked down into her glass, gently swirling the liquid so it stuck to the sides of the crystal. How could she explain this? Should she even try?

"Tanna?"

She wrinkled her nose and met his inquisitive gaze. "I've only been back to Boston a handful of times and I didn't want to go back to Murphy's because I was scared it would be too hard. And that I would question my choices about my education and my career."

"And did you?"

She sent him a small smile. She wasn't ready to admit to Levi that it had been hard, a little.

"I watched this woman walk up the stairs. She was wearing an amazing pair of red heels and I followed her up. She was talking to a client about a Schiaparelli dress—"

"English, Murphy."

"Elsa Schiaparelli was an iconic Italian designer. Coco Chanel was her greatest rival, and she was big between the two world wars. She was influenced by surrealists like Salvador Dalí."

Levi groaned and Tanna knew she'd provided too much

information again. "Anyway, this woman was talking about this vintage dress and doing a really poor job of selling it. I wanted to rip the phone from her and take over the conversation."

"I presume you managed to restrain yourself?" Levi asked, amused.

Tanna pulled a face. "Barely. She wasn't enthusiastic about the product, didn't respect the process. You've got to have a passion for the product if you're going to sell it effectively, Levi."

"You aren't short of passion, Tanna."

Tanna ignored the obvious double entendre. "Maybe, but that's not my field anymore, Levi. It was something else I gave up when I left."

"It was your choice to walk away, Tanna. That's on you," Levi said, dousing her with a hard dose of reality.

Of course it was, but surely she was allowed to reflect on what she'd given up? She could've had a career at Murphy's; she could've married Levi, be living in this house and having a totally different life. Surely it was normal to wonder what it would be like working with her brothers, indulging her deep love of art, textiles and ceramics, and sharing her passion with collectors?

She could see herself leaving Levi's bed, maybe after some fun in the shower, kissing him goodbye as she left this beautiful house, driving into Boston central. She'd have her own office at Murphy's and she'd spend her time working with the PR department, promoting upcoming sales and meeting with collectors all over the world. She'd travel internationally, visiting clients in Hong Kong and New York, Paris and Dubai. If she had time, she'd visit the Louvre or the Met, the antiques shops and the art dealers.

Pop into a perfumery in Paris, a spice market in Delhi, a boutique on Rodeo Drive.

But she'd always come home to Levi…

Tanna yanked herself out of the daydream, distraught over how real it felt, how natural. In the daydream, she wasn't nineteen, she was the age she was now.

But it wasn't possible and it certainly wasn't real…

Her imagination, sparked by her visit to Murphy's, was just working overtime, playing tricks on her.

So why did it feel more—she searched for the word— *normal* than her current London-based life?

Ridiculous!

She needed to pull herself together, to remind herself what was important. Working at Murphy's had been her dream, her destiny, but everything changed when she put Addy behind the wheel of her car and handed her a death sentence. By giving Addy the keys, Tanna set in motion a train of events that not only led to Addy's death, but also Isla's lifetime of mourning and Tanna walking away from everything she thought she deserved.

And Levi had been collateral damage.

Boston wasn't her city and this wasn't her life anymore. She'd taken a step out of time, that was all. She could only do what she could today, here and now, and that meant clearing her debt to Levi and sorting out her PTSD so she could return to London and her job.

That was real life. This wasn't.

Standing up, Tanna placed her glass of wine on the side table and gave Levi a tight smile. "I'm turning in."

"You're upset." Levi frowned at her, obviously confused. "It couldn't be anything I said because you hardly gave me a chance to speak."

Tanna nodded, taking his point. "It's me, not you, Brogan. Just as always."

Tanna walked out of the room and ran up the stairs, desperately trying to outrun the past.

SECOND CHANCE TEMPTATION

Six

They made it to the end of the third day by gritting their teeth and trying, really hard, to be polite. But on Wednesday afternoon, Tanna left Levi's house mid-afternoon, telling him she'd be back shortly, but it was two hours before he heard her footsteps on his wooden floor. Two hours, ten minutes and fifty-three seconds.

Not that he was counting.

Sitting in his father's old wingback, his leg propped up on an ottoman, his heart kicked up a beat when he saw her standing in the doorway, holding a shopping bag in her right hand.

"Where have you been?" he demanded.

Tanna raised her eyebrows at his tone and it took all he had not to apologize.

She was here to help him and they had a deal. She was paying off a debt. This was about a little light revenge.

But that didn't mean he had to act like a jerk.

"Sorry." Levi ran his hand over his face before moving his eyes back to her lovely face. "What's in the bag, Tanna?" he asked her, feeling infinitely weary.

"Give me ten minutes and I'll show you."

Before he could question her further, she disappeared into the house and Levi wished he could follow her out the door but moving quickly wasn't a skill he currently possessed. He swallowed down a surge of panic at being confined and, very deliberately, breathed deeply.

Suck it up, cupcake.

"Levi?"

Levi lifted his head at Tanna's call. "Yeah?" he responded, raising his voice.

"Come here."

Levi hobbled to the doorway, walked down the long hall and caught his breath outside the half-closed door to the small bathroom at the end. He pushed the door open with the tip of his crutch and was rewarded with an amazing view of Tanna bent over the bath, her perfect ass in the air.

Levi's cargo shorts tightened as his cock told him, in the only way it knew, how much it appreciated the view. Levi wanted to grip those slim legs, explore the soft skin of her inner thighs, see if his hands could encircle her tiny waist. He wanted to twist her long hair around his hands, plunder her mouth.

He wanted Tanna more than he wanted the use of his leg back, and since he was comprehensively frustrated at his lack of mobility, that was saying something.

"The reason I am here?"

Tanna sat back on her heels, pushed a silky curl the color of midnight off her cheek and turned her head to look at him. She gestured to the bathtub. "I thought you might want a shower."

He'd freakin' kill for a shower but that wasn't going to happen since he couldn't get his cast wet.

"I'm an accident waiting to happen, Tanna," Levi brusquely told her, hating, as always, to admit weakness.

"That was when you didn't have me." Tanna gracefully climbed to her feet and when she stepped away, he saw two stools in the bathtub and a handheld shower attachment. For the first time in days, possibly since his accident, his mouth turned up in a genuine smile. This could work.

Except...

"I can't get my cast wet. And plastic bags don't work."

Tanna picked up a long plastic sleeve and a roll of duct tape. "This is a cast cover and—" she held up the roll of tape "—this is waterproof tape. I guarantee the cast will stay dry. Strip off and I'll help you into the bath."

Yeah, no. Because, while he was a guy who had a lot of control—a man who prided himself on it—this was Tanna, the girl he'd never had and always wanted. The woman who haunted his dreams. And if he stripped down, she'd see how much she affected him and that wasn't acceptable.

"Problem?" Tanna asked him.

"I'll shower but I'll keep my shorts on."

Tanna rolled her eyes. "I have seen naked men before, Brogan. I'm pretty sure you have the same bits they have."

A red mist danced across Levi's eyes at the thought of Tanna being naked with another man, her hands on his body, her mouth on someone else's... *No, can't go there. Not ever going there.*

Tanna placed her hands on her hips and her gaze ping-ponged between him and the tub. "So, are you going to do this or not?"

Hell yes, he was going to shower. And he'd deal with the embarrassment factor when it came up. And it would come up. Levi hobbled into the bathroom and wished they were in his newly renovated master bathroom upstairs. In that ample space, he could have put some distance between himself and Tanna; they'd have room to breathe. But this bathroom was minuscule, and he could smell her perfume, feel her heat, see her pulse beating in the cord of her neck.

So, she wasn't as unaffected by him as she liked to pretend. Good to know.

Levi placed his crutches between the commode and the basin and pulled his T-shirt up his chest, catching the appreciation on Tanna's face as she looked at his body. He worked hard to stay in shape and seeing her desire made all those long gym sessions worth it.

Keeping his hands off his onetime fiancée while he got naked was going to be damn difficult.

"Let's get this plastic cover on," Tanna said, her voice sounding brisk.

Before he could protest, Tanna dropped to her haunches and started to slide the cover over his toes and up his shin. Her hands moved up and under his shorts and he silently implored her to go a little higher, to cover his balls, to stroke his…

Get a grip, Brogan.

"Hold the plastic in place, please," Tanna said, her voice husky. She had to be aware of the effect she was having on him, his cock was a steel rod tenting his pants. He didn't reply, mostly because his brain didn't have enough blood to power his mouth.

"I'm going to tape it down." Tanna looked up at him, her green eyes large and compelling. This was how she'd look if she was actually going down on him.

Holy crap.

"Do you want me to shave your leg?"

Okay, what? "Why?" He croaked the one-word question.

"It's going to hurt when we take the tape off unless I shave your hair."

Not happening. Not in this lifetime. "I have a busted patella. I can handle a little hair pulling."

Tanna's mouth twitched. "So says every man who thinks he can endure a wax. Okay, your call."

Tanna taped the plastic to his thigh and rested on her heels, pushing her hair back with her wrist. "Sit down on the edge of the tub and let's get your shorts off."

Not wanting to shock her, Levi reached for a washcloth before sitting down. He flipped the button of his shorts open, undid the zip and pushed the washcloth under the fabric, hoping it would keep him moderately decent.

Tanna arched her eyebrows. "Don't bother on my account."

His hand stilled, and their eyes clashed, and Levi saw the passion in those green depths. And curiosity.

To hell with it. He pulled the washcloth out, tossed it away and met her gaze with defiance. "I was trying to be polite."

"You've never been polite in your life," Tanna scoffed. "And you have a beautiful body. You shouldn't be ashamed of it."

"I'm not ashamed of my body," Levi retorted, annoyed.

"And you shouldn't be," Tanna told him, sounding patronizing.

Annoyed by her cool tone, Levi gripped her chin with his fingers. "I have a hard-on from hell. I was covering it up."

Tanna's tongue flicked out to touch her top lip. "I noticed," she replied, her voice husky.

"It wants what it never had."

"I figured that out too."

He couldn't help it; he needed to taste her. He needed to know whether her mouth was as warm as he remembered from their first kiss, whether she could still make his head swim.

Levi curled his fingers into the band of her jeans and tugged her to stand between his legs. He rested his forehead between her breasts, trying to calm his breathing. This was a bad idea. Once they went down this slippery slope, they wouldn't be able to stop the ride. Kissing her, fully clothed, was one thing. His being half-naked was a lot more dangerous.

"I want you, Tanna," he growled, resisting the urge to pull one of those nipples pushing against the fabric of her shirt.

Tanna didn't reply but her hand stroked the side of his neck, pushed into his hair.

"I don't want to want you. I'm over you," Levi informed her, wondering whether he was trying to convince her or himself.

Levi lifted his head and his eyes clashed with hers, deep blue smacking into her green. Tanna nodded. "Got it. But… just one taste," Tanna murmured, bending down to brush her lips across his. But instead of taking it deeper, Tanna made a gentle exploration of his mouth and Levi relished the getting-to-know-you-again kiss.

It was simple and sexy and…yeah, sweet.

Then Tanna slipped her tongue past his teeth to tangle with his and Levi waited for the bathroom to catch alight, for the walls to blow apart. Fireworks danced across his skin as they fought for dominance of the kiss, both taking and demanding and giving and feeding…

Levi banded his arm around her butt. This was all that was important; feasting on Tanna was all he needed. As long as she was kissing him, he could forget everything else.

Levi heard her mutter his name against his lips and thought he'd never liked the way it sounded until now. He wanted to hear it as he stripped her down, his lips on her breast, on her stomach, tasting the sweet honey between her thighs.

He needed her to yell his name as she shattered on his tongue and again when he pushed inside her...

"Okay, this can't happen."

It took Levi a few moments to make sense of the words, to realize her hands on his shoulders were trying to put some space between them. He licked his lips and looked at her, disconcerted. Why was she stopping?

Tanna pushed her hair back as his hands dropped from her body. She took a step back, then another, and he could hear her ragged breathing in the small room.

Or was that his breathing? Who knew?

"You need to shower, and I know you are in pain."

Well, yeah. But they could still have some fun.

"Wrong time, wrong place."

Her suggestion was sensible, but he didn't want to be freakin' sensible. He wanted to be naked, with Tanna wrapped around him.

Levi placed his hands on her hips and drew circles on her hip bones. "Bend down so I can kiss you again."

Tanna slapped his hands away. "Brogan! Concentrate!"

The moment, it seemed, had passed. *Dammit.*

"Right, let's concentrate on getting you into the tub," Tanna said, sounding remarkably brisk and nurse-like. And, because he was a guy, the image of Tanna dressed in a tiny, revealing nurse outfit—displaying a deep cleavage, wearing fishnet stockings and red heels—flashed on his retinas. Levi groaned and tipped his head back to look at the ceiling.

Since he wasn't about to get lucky, he'd take a shower.

Levi, with Tanna's help, got his pants off and they both ignored his erection. Well, as much as they could ignore a hard-as-hell, wanting-to-play cock.

Levi swung his legs over the side of the tub and settled himself on the stool. Tanna helped lift his injured leg onto the other stool and quickly and efficiently placed soap, a loofah and shampoo in easy reach. She tossed the wash-cloth and it landed on his crotch, which wasn't, he was sure, a mistake.

Tanna flipped open the taps and hot water hit his shoulders as she gave him the handheld showerhead.

Levi directed the hot water at his face, at his neck. God, it felt amazing. But not nearly as good as kissing Tanna had.

"Call me when you are done," Tanna said, walking toward the door.

Levi opened his eyes and called her back. When she turned, he saw confusion in her eyes and, beneath it, still-bubbling desire.

"Thank you for doing this. For thinking of this. I was so tired of washing up in the basin."

Tanna handed him a soft smile, flipping his heart inside out. She nodded before walking through the door and closing it behind her.

Levi dropped the showerhead and looked down at his still hard erection. He could, easily, take care of the problem, but he didn't want to do it solo.

He wanted female hands, a feminine mouth, a gentle touch.

He only wanted Tanna...

Dammit.

Tanna heard Levi's crutches hitting the wooden floor and shook her head. She'd left clean underwear, shorts and a T-shirt on the bathroom cabinet earlier but she'd expected him to call for her to help him out of the tub.

But the man was too damn stubborn to ask for help.

Levi shuffled into the kitchen and Tanna cast an eye over his body, appreciating his wide, muscled chest, the light body hair narrowing into a thin line bisecting a mus-

cled stomach and disappearing beneath the band of his
shorts. He held the black T-shirt in his hands and his leg
still sported the plastic cast cover.

He was battered and a little dented but, God, he was
gorgeous. Masculine, sexy, big and bold. Tanna felt warm
as she recalled his big hands on her butt, his tongue in her
mouth, demanding more, wanting everything.

Levi wouldn't be a gentle lover—oh, he'd never hurt her,
but he'd demand everything from her. He'd wring every
drop of pleasure from her. In his arms, she knew, she might
find herself, sexually.

And, she was pretty sure, he'd be the one to finally—
finally—give her the orgasm she'd never experienced
from a man's touch.

But sleeping with Levi was a bad idea. A terrible idea.
Because if it was as good as his kisses suggested it would
be, it would make leaving him, leaving Boston, hard. She
had a career to salvage, people to save, her PTSD symptoms to conquer. She had a bigger debt to repay than the
one she owed Levi.

She couldn't afford to be distracted by the still-gorgeous
Levi Brogan.

She would *not* be distracted…

Tanna pushed her hair off her shoulders and reminded
herself Levi didn't want anything from her…

Nothing but sex.

Strangely, and very irrationally considering her need to
leave Boston, the thought made her sad.

Levi stopped at the chair next to the big, well-used
kitchen table. Gorgeous skin, dotted with freckles and covering bulging, rippling muscles—Tanna swallowed, looking
for the smallest hint of moisture in her mouth.

Nope, nothing.

Tanna looked at the dish towel in her hands and remembered a time when it had felt natural to step up to him, to place her mouth on his.

Levi cleared his throat and Tanna jumped, embarrassment coloring her face. Refusing to meet his eyes, she knew he'd be wearing a know-it-all smirk. She looked down at the floor, and when she raised her head again, Levi was dressed.

"Feel free to take it off again if you like," Levi suggested, gesturing to his shirt.

Annoyed by his smirk, by his complete faith that she was crazy attracted to him—she was but he didn't need to rub it in her face!—Tanna felt the need to do something to remind him who he was messing with…

She wasn't nineteen anymore and desperately eager to please…

Without giving Levi any warning, Tanna caught the corner of the piece of tape on his thigh and yanked it super hard. Levi yelped as the tape separated hair from his skin and he immediately gripped his leg, stopping her from pulling the rest of the tape away.

"What the hell are you doing?" Levi demanded, his eyes glistening.

She couldn't help teasing him. "I thought you said you could handle a little waxing."

"I was wrong. So, so wrong," Levi told her, his hands not moving from his leg.

Tanna laughed. "Stop being a baby. Millions of women, me included, do this on a regular basis."

"There are these things called razors," Levi grumbled.

"I offered, remember?" Tanna peeled his fingers away from the plaster cast. "The only way to get this off is to go hard and go fast. I'm going to count to three and then rip it away, okay?"

Levi nodded, locked his teeth and Tanna held the tape tightly. "Okay, here we go… One."

Tanna ripped the tape, and Levi gasped, and the plastic sleeve fell down his thigh. Tanna stood up, clapped her hands together and grinned. "Done!"

"You are truly evil," Levi told her. "What happened to counting to three?"

Tanna shrugged. "Lightweight."

Tanna tossed the tape, folded the plastic sleeve and washed her hands. Then she walked over to the counter and picked up the vine tomatoes she'd been slicing and tossed them into a skillet on the gas stove. The insanely good combination of basil, garlic, tomatoes and olive oil filled the room.

"What are you making?"

"Pasta and vegetables in a tomato sauce," Tanna replied, leaving the stove to look for spices.

Levi looked disappointed. "Please tell me there's protein in there, somewhere."

"Chicken breasts are baking in the oven."

"There is a God," Levi murmured, pulling his shirt halfway up his chest to scratch a spot just under his ribs. Tanna noticed his ripped stomach, that fine happy trail and his warm, tanned skin.

"You okay?" Levi asked her, dropping his shirt, and Tanna nearly whimpered her disappointment.

No, I want sex. With you. Now.

I'll even go on top...

"Fine."

Liar, liar, thong on fire. Tanna walked back to the stove, stirring the contents of her pan. Needing wine, and to cool down, she opened the fridge and jammed her head inside.

"How was your shower?" Tanna asked, pulling out a bottle of merlot. She also took out a jug of iced tea and poured Levi a glass.

Levi's smiled flashed and Tanna was sure the earth

sighed in appreciation. "It was amazing. It's so nice to feel properly clean."

"So, is dirt bike riding a new thing?" Tanna asked, tossing the pasta into a pot of boiling water.

"Within the last eighteen months or so," Levi replied. "Finn introduced me to the sport." Levi winced and pulled a face. "Uh, you do know Finn is a bit of adrenaline junkie?"

Tanna shrugged. "I do. I've told him I will kill him if he hurts himself doing something stupid."

His smile tilted the world off its axis again. Tanna tipped her head to look at him. There were fine lines at the corners of his twinkling eyes and his lips stretched into a we-can-melt-steel smile.

Hot. So hot.

"You should smile more often. You've got a great smile," Tanna said, her words falling into the silence of the kitchen.

Tanna felt the urge to backtrack, to tell him she didn't think their sleeping together sometime in the immediate future was a good idea. Because, oh, too many things...

He was too much, too masculine, too attractive, too able to make her feel things she couldn't, or didn't want to, deal with. He made her want, and worst of all, he made her question.

Her past. Her present. And her future.

"Sauce is burning, Murphy."

Levi's prosaic statement cut through her panic and Tanna whirled around to see smoke coming off the pan. Cursing, she quickly stirred the sauce, relieved she'd caught it in time.

Now, if she could save herself from falling under Brogan's spell again, that would be an even better result.

Seven

Tanna topped off her coffee cup and, glancing over her shoulder, saw Levi's attention was still on the screen of his laptop. Rimless wire glasses made his blue eyes seem darker, look more serious and older than his years. A frown pulled his strong eyebrows together and she smiled as he lobbed quiet insults at his state-of-the-art machine.

After picking up her coffee, she leaned her butt against the marble counter. "Problem?"

Levi lifted his head to look at her. "Payroll, company accounts."

"For the marina?" She knew Levi owned a majority share in a marina downtown with Noah Lockwood and she recalled one of her brothers telling her he'd revamped the business so it was one of the best, and most technologically advanced, marinas on the East Coast.

"And for the boatyard, and my other two marinas."

So, how to ask this without causing offense? Everyone knew Ray left the family billions, that neither Levi, Callie nor his sisters needed to work if they didn't want to. Hell, she was pretty sure their kids and grandkids wouldn't need to work either.

"Um, I didn't think you were so hands-on. I thought you had people to take care of the day-to-day stuff."

"I do have people who are very capable at running my businesses but I'm a control freak, hadn't you noticed? I don't hand over control easily and I like to know what's happening, every day."

"I definitely remember the control freak aspect of your personality. I remember you having very definite ideas about what you wanted for our wedding."

Not meaning to rake up the past and the unpleasantness that went along with it, she waved her comment away. "But I didn't know you owned so many businesses."

Levi lifted his uninjured shoulder. "I have a few but it's a fraction of what my father owned."

Judging by his flat, offhand comment, Tanna knew there was a story behind his hard statement. "Do you *want* to own as many businesses as your dad?" she carefully asked.

Levi released an irritated sigh and leaned back in his chair. "My father was a multibillionaire, one of the most successful businessmen in the state. I have a long way to go before I hit such illustrious heights."

He hadn't answered her question and his tone oozed sarcasm. She still didn't understand his subtext. "But do you want to be as successful as him?"

"I'm the son, his heir. He expected it. The world expects it."

Again, an answer that wasn't an answer. "But is that what you *want*?"

Levi glared at her, and without replying, returned to his screen. Okay, so that was his tender spot. She wondered if he had others.

She'd only met Levi's father a few times after their engagement and she remembered a charming man, with a personality as big as the sun. He walked into the room and immediately dominated it with his loud voice, his raucous laughter and his inimitable charm. His light shone bright and Tanna distinctly remembered Levi's mental withdrawal with every passing minute they spent with his dad.

The louder Ray got, the quieter Levi became.

Levi wasn't naturally ebullient; he was, fundamentally, reticent and reserved. Ray had tossed question after question at her, asking her about her accident, her family, how it felt to lose her parents at a young age, whether she thought her brothers had done a good job raising her. Ray didn't have any boundaries and no tact and she'd been grateful when Levi, with a few words quietly uttered, had shut down the interrogation.

At the time she'd been grateful Levi removed the spotlight from her and had gone on to enjoy her lunch. Now, with a little maturity and hindsight, she could look back on that lunch and see that Levi spoke and Ray had listened. And obeyed.

Tanna wondered if Levi knew how much his father had respected him...

"Tell me about your relationship with your dad," Tanna said after blowing air across the surface of her hot coffee.

"Trying to work here, Murphy," Levi retorted and stared at his screen. After a minute, he threw down his pen and leaned back in his chair, his red Henley pulling tight across his biceps as he folded his arms across his wide chest.

Classic defensive pose, Brogan. What are you hiding?

"He was my dad. What's there to say?"

Behind those glasses there was so much pain in his eyes, and a whole lot of unresolved emotion. And, because this was Levi, it was all covered by a solid layer of don't-go-there.

"I liked your dad. He was charming. A bit over the top but, yeah, charismatic," Tanna quietly told him. "But he wouldn't be the person I ran to in a crisis."

Levi linked his hands behind his head, looking interested. "Why do you say that?"

Tanna lifted one shoulder. "Because I sensed that, in geology terms, Callie was the rock, the foundation of your family. Ray, to me, was the pretty streaks of gold or the flash of quartz, the trace of platinum. He provided the flash while Callie provided the stability."

Levi sent her a hard stare before releasing a long, steady sigh. "Wow. That's pretty astute of you."

Tanna half smiled at him. "You want to know what else I think?"

She could see the doubt in his eyes, and wondered whether he'd change the subject, push their conversation in another direction. Years ago, Levi always, always avoided emotional discussions.

He surprised her when he gestured for her to continue. "I think you made your dad feel uncomfortable…"

Levi jerked back, shocked. "That's not possible, Tanna."

"I'm sure you did. I think your dad saw something in you he didn't have."

"And what would that be?"

Tanna tapped the side of her mug with her finger. "When he said something controversial, he looked at you, needing to see your reaction. It was like he was looking for your approval."

Levi shook his head. "Nope, my dad never listened to anything I had to say, especially in business. If I said black, he said white."

Maybe that was because Levi always seemed so happy in

his skin, so totally and utterly in control. Little rattled him and maybe Ray, who commanded attention from everybody else, wanted his son's attention more than anyone else's.

"I think he wanted you to be proud of him."

Levi rolled his eyes. "If he wanted that, he shouldn't have taken such enormous risks, shouldn't have gambled every cent he owned on crazy propositions."

Surely Levi couldn't hold that against him? "Your father made billions doing that, Levi."

"Luckily they panned out. Possibly, I think, because God looks after the stupid." Levi rested his arms on the kitchen table, his frown pulling his strong eyebrows together, blue eyes troubled.

"Everybody sees him as being this incredible business-man and he was, to a point. But he got lucky more often than he should've. There were times, during some of his biggest deals, when I was on the edge of my seat, waiting to hear if we'd lost everything."

They'd had a lot to lose. "You would've still had this house, the cars, personal bank accounts."

Levi's smile was cold. "You don't understand, Tanna. On *all* of his deals he risked *everything*. He put everything on the line to raise the cash he needed—this house, all the houses, the investments, our college funds. Everything got tossed into the pot."

"Wow. That bad, huh?"

"That bad," Levi confirmed. "That's why I stopped working for him. I couldn't make him see reason and I couldn't control his wild impulses. He was gambling with the company and I could see it going south. I needed to get out and start up something new, so we'd have a source of income when we lost everything."

Tanna winced. "You were sure that was going to happen?"

"Oh, hell yes. Absolutely positive. When he died…" Levi stopped talking, cursed and waved his words away.

Tanna cursed too when he didn't continue his explanation, wishing he trusted her enough to complete his sentence.

When he returned his attention to his laptop, Tanna continued to stare at him, her mind whirling.

"So, that's why you like to be in control, why you like your ducks in a row. Because your father's ducks were drunk and at a rave."

Levi lifted his head, frowning until he made sense of her words. Then he smiled. "I suppose that's a good way to describe him. My dad thrived on chaos. I do not."

Tanna returned to her earlier thought, that Ray wanted approval from his son. "Maybe he wanted to impress you and he kept doing that by launching into bigger and riskier deals. Maybe he wanted to show you he could do it."

Levi sighed. "Then he didn't know me at all. I'm not impressed by flash."

"Maybe that was all he knew how to be," Tanna murmured. This was the first time Levi had ever said something this personal, had cracked the door to what went on behind his implacable facade. She wanted to know more, she wanted to know everything.

So when she heard the sharp rap on the kitchen door, she nearly howled in frustration. Tanna darted a look at Levi and he, not surprisingly, looked like a French aristocrat who'd been spared a meeting with Madame Guillotine.

The kitchen door opened and Tanna smiled as Carrick walked in, closely followed by the stunning blonde she'd met at Carrick's offices.

After giving her a quick hug, Carrick gestured to the blonde. "Meet Sadie. She's working with us to authenticate what we think might be a lost Winslow Homer. Levi Brogan and my sister, Tanna."

Tanna sent Carrick an exasperated look. "You introduced Sadie to me at Murphy's, Carrick. Don't you remember?"

Probably not since she was convinced his blood had left his brain on seeing the sexy PhD.

Tanna watched Levi's reaction as Sadie walked over to him to shake his hand. Tanna waited for the flash of attraction in his eyes, the slow smile she knew could melt panties at fifty paces.

Well, huh. Nothing, zip, diddly-squat. They shook hands, exchanged polite smiles and she didn't even pick up a hint of zing. They were two spectacular-looking humans. How could they *not* be attracted to each other?

Tanna turned her attention to Carrick and, yep, there she saw what she'd been looking for in Levi's reaction to Sadie. Carrick's green eyes, so much like hers, flickered with possession, a hint of jealousy and a healthy dose of irritation. The latter was probably directed at himself for allowing himself to be distracted by the gorgeous blonde.

Well, well, well…this could be interesting.

"Did you come to see me, or Levi?" Tanna asked Carrick.

She was his sister but Levi was his best friend.

"Both of you."

Tanna gestured to the empty seats at the table. "Can I get you coffee?" They both nodded, shed their coats and took seats next to and opposite Levi, who closed the lid of his laptop. Levi asked Sadie about her career as an art detective and they were soon engaged in a lively conversation about Sadie's attempts to track down the painting's provenance.

It all sounded wonderful, and interesting.

"You should document the process, Carrick. Show your clients how you go about authenticating a work of art. They'd be interested, I'm sure. You could do it as a series of vlogs." Tanna grinned. "It helps you are both pretty."

Carrick sent her a penetrating stare. "That's a really good idea. I'll run it by the owners of the painting and the PR department." He tipped his head to the side. "When are you going to come and head up our PR department?"

Tanna pretended to think about it. "Uh…never?"

"Damn." Carrick pulled a face. "Talking of PR, I came up with an idea of my own I'd like your help with. It's why I'm here, actually."

Now that sounded intriguing. Tanna, coffee forgotten, gave him her full attention. "I'm listening."

"Next Friday night, Murphy's is hosting a cocktail party to promote next week's sale of, mostly, vintage haute couture and high-end fashion. We have jewelry, accessories and, obviously, some of the once-in-a-lifetime gowns by the most prominent and feted designers of the twentieth century."

"I know. I saw the collection at Murphy's. It's wonderful."

Carrick cleared his throat. "You might not know this, Levi, but Tanna's mom, my stepmom, collected amazing ensembles from the twenties through to the eighties."

"Is Mom's clothing collection part of the sale?" Tanna demanded, horrified. As a child she'd played dress-up with her outfits and when she was sad, mad or needing her mom, she'd often gone into that spacious closet located in the dance studio at the Beacon Hill house to feel closer to her mother.

Carrick shook his head. "Of course not. It doesn't belong to me."

Tanna frowned, confused. As the eldest son, Carrick

had inherited the family home and all its contents. When they all became adults and moved into their own places, Carrick had offered to split the contents between the four of them but they all wanted the house to remain the way their parents left it.

"Yes, it does."

Carrick shook his head. "The collection is yours, Tan. She would've wanted you to have it. Besides, I'd look silly wearing a Coco Chanel."

Tanna blinked back her tears, thinking that it had been too long since she'd seen the collection. As soon as she could, she'd go home and see what she owned.

Carrick cleared his throat and adjusted his already perfect tie. "Anyway, we're having a cocktail party to show off the sale collection to a very select handful of collectors and fashion editors and Jane, our head of PR, suggested putting up some photos of Mom dressed in some of her designer gowns. I wanted to run it by you first."

Tanna placed her hand on her chest and sighed. "Aw, I love that. It's such a great idea."

"An even better idea would be for Tanna to wear one of her mom's vintage gowns to the party," Levi suggested.

Tanna's surprise was reflected in Carrick's eyes and on Sadie's face.

"That's a really excellent idea." Carrick quietly agreed.

Levi immediately looked grumpy. "I have them occasionally." He pushed his hand through his hair and rubbed the back of his neck before continuing. "Tanna looks a lot like Raeni and if she changed a few times during the cocktail party, showing off different gowns, she would, together with her mom's photos wearing the same gowns, make a hell of an impact."

Carrick smiled at his friend. "Want to come and head up my PR department since my sister won't?"

Levi looked horrified. "I'd rather shoot myself in my already injured foot."

Carrick grinned at his sarcastic reply and looked at Tanna. "What do you say, Tan?"

He was asking her to wear her mom's stunning gowns and her amazing jewelry, drink champagne, and talk art and fashion with some of the best minds in the business? Oh, yeah, she was so in.

Attending the event didn't mean this was her life anymore. It was just one night of pleasure. Surely she was entitled to a little fun before returning to London?

It would be a night to remember. "Sure."

"Excellent. I'll get Jane to email you Mom's photos and you can choose the gowns you want to wear." Carrick stood up and pulled out Sadie's chair as she rose with him. "We don't have time to get anything altered so keep that in mind."

Tanna nodded. "I'll liaise with Jane and we'll get it sorted."

Carrick, his hand on Sadie's back—interesting—bent his head to kiss Tanna's cheek. "Thanks, Tan. Later, Levi."

"Later," Levi replied, flipping open the lid to his computer.

"Don't kill each other," Carrick told them as he ushered Sadie out the back door.

Tanna grinned. "We'll try."

At the marina, Levi settled himself into the passenger seat and glowered through the windscreen as Tanna pulled into traffic, heading for Carrick's house in Beacon Hill.

He hated not being able to drive his own vehicle, Levi decided. Handing over control, even something as simple as driving, annoyed him. Levi felt relieved when Tanna pulled up to her magnificent childhood house in Beacon

Hill and parked his luxury Lexus SUV under the magnolia tree. He'd been concerned about how she'd handle his super-expensive car, but she hadn't seemed intimidated and she handled the large vehicle like a pro.

After Carrick and Sadie left, Tanna told him she had a two-hour appointment in the city and her closed-off expression suggested he not ask any further questions, which, honestly, just made him want to know who she was meeting and why she wanted to keep it a secret. Her reticence intrigued him; the Tanna he used to know couldn't keep a secret to save her life.

But Tanna was no longer the girl he'd loved. She was now a fully independent woman who marched to the beat of her own drum. He'd adored his fiancée but this version of Tanna was, in many ways, even more intriguing. Tanna-today had an edge to her he found exciting and whenever he thought he had her pegged, she moved the goalposts and kept him guessing. Tanna-today was exciting, mysterious and more than a little addictive.

Levi—understanding she wouldn't share any personal information with him until she was good and ready to do so, which might be never—had asked her, since she was headed in the same direction, to drive him to the marina so he could touch base with his staff and see how his business was faring in his absence.

So, after arranging for Tanna to collect him later, he'd spent an hour in his office with his manager before taking a tour of the marina.

He was paying for his physical activity now, but he couldn't regret his actions. He wasn't a rule-from-the-office boss. He liked to get down and dirty, and he worked the business from the ground up. He greeted his staff, approved some requisitions and checked on his maintenance crew. Levi was very aware winter brought many problems to the marina; with the recent winter storms, he was worried his staff wasn't monitoring the snow loads, especially on the finger piers. The weight of the snow could push the piers under the water, taking the electrical connections with them.

It had happened before, and it wasn't a scenario he ever wanted to repeat. Winter at the marina was quiet but it was also a never-ending ball ache. And that was without him being incapacitated.

But his staff had everything under control and he hadn't been needed. The thought both pleased and terrified him.

"Are you sure I can't take you home?" Tanna asked.

"Stop fussing, Tan," Levi told her and he heard the irritation in his voice. "I know you are itching to look at your mom's collection of dresses. We can order lunch. From previous visits to Carrick's house, I know that there's an awesome Chinese place around the corner and they will deliver."

He'd been watching her eyes earlier when he made the suggestion about her wearing her mom's clothing—where the burst of inspiration came from, he had no idea—and quickly realized he'd never seen such a spark of excitement in her eyes, that particular expression on her face.

It was part sadness, part delight, all enthusiasm.

He wasn't sure if she was eager about wearing her mom's clothes, or the exhibition, or thrilled to be involved in Murphy International's business again.

In the hospital, all those years ago, she'd spoken about the PR role her mom played in the business and often told him that when she graduated with her degree in art history, she wanted to follow in her mom's footsteps.

Her mom had been a PR wizard and it was her hard work that made Murphy's one of the most prominent and visible auction houses in the country.

But then Tanna left and took a completely different path, forging another career in emergency medicine. A career she didn't talk about much. Or at all.

Tanna pushed her sunglasses onto the top of her head, pulling back her black curls to reveal her beautiful face. "I really do want to look at her clothes. I've been racking my brain trying to remember what the collection contains since it's been over twelve years since I last saw it."

Tanna stared at the oversize black front door in front of her. "I used to go and hide out in her closet when I was a kid."

Levi nodded. "You probably scuttled in there when times got tough, when you needed a connection to your mom. When you needed *a* mom."

Tanna turned to face him, surprised. "How do you know that?"

Because he knew her, just as she knew him. Despite spending so much time apart, they were still, somehow, in sync. He with her and she with him.

Levi thought back to their earlier conversations and Tanna's reflections about his dad. Her observations had been remarkably astute, and it was funny she easily looked past his dad's charisma to the man beneath. Just like she looked past Levi's reticence and self-sufficiency to find the pieces of himself he kept hidden from the rest of the world.

Seeing Tanna was still waiting for an answer, Levi shrugged. "Good guess."

Not wanting to get into it, Levi opened his door and sighed at the blast of frigid air swirling in through the open door. Tanna took the hint, hopped out of the car and ran around the hood. Opening the door behind him, she pulled his crutches off the back seat and handed them to him before taking a dayglow yellow beanie from her coat pocket and pulling it over her ears.

"Hey, that's my hat!" Levi protested. His favorite, in fact.

"I found it in the laundry basket." Tanna didn't look remotely fazed. "And you don't wear hats."

"I do when I'm skiing."

Tanna cocked her head, her smile a touch smug. "Are you skiing now? Are you going to be skiing soon?"

She had him there. Levi shook his head and jammed his crutches under his armpits. "Were you always this annoying?"

Her laughter cut through the icy winter air. "Oh, I've honed my skills over the years. And, scarily, I'm making a concerted effort to be polite."

God help him.

Eight

Levi settled himself in Carrick's library, grateful to get off his feet. He accepted Tanna's offer of a cup of coffee and after dialing in their lunch order, he pulled out his laptop and booted it up.

He had work to do—specifically, Brogan Family Trust work—and could do it as well here as he could at home. After telling Tanna, for the third time, that he was fine, he asked her to get the door when their lunch arrived before waving her away.

Time passed quickly, the doorbell rang and a minute later he saw Tanna's long, bare legs—her butt barely covered by something looking like a black bandage—as she streaked past the library door.

What the hell was she wearing?

"Tanna!" he bellowed.

Two seconds later she stood in the doorway and Levi snapped his teeth closed so his tongue didn't hit the floor.

She wore the smallest dress he'd ever seen, made from

a slinky fabric clinging to her every curve and showing off her finely muscled, long, smooth, tanned legs. Her feet were slender, ending in red-tipped toes. On the inside of her left foot she had a tattoo of a starburst and a gold ring encompassed the third toe on her right foot.

He forced his eyes up… The dress was comprised of various slits and rips, revealing a large portion of her tanned stomach and most of the right cup of her bright red bra.

"What the hell are you wearing?" he croaked.

Forget getting a little revenge, this woman was going to kill him.

Tanna picked up the tattered hem of the ripped skirt. If he could call the strips a skirt. "It's a grunge dress, from the eighties. I'm not sure who the designer is. I'd have to look that up, but it's exquisitely made."

It was a pile of rags. And it was probably worth a freakin' fortune.

This…this was a great example of why women were so difficult to figure out.

The doorbell rang again and Tanna started to turn. He yelled at her to stop and threw up his hands at her puzzled expression. "You cannot answer the door wearing that dress. Do you want to give the delivery guy heart failure?"

Tanna looked down, grimaced and met his eyes. "Dammit. Okay, I'll get changed."

Levi reached for his crutches and hauled himself onto his feet. "I'll get it. You…" He closed his eyes, bemused. Dammit, how could something so…okay, ugly—he wasn't brave enough to say the word out loud—look so good on her?

It was an enigma.

"Go get changed, Tan." *Please, for the love of God, put something decent on before I do something stupid. Like rip that so-called dress off your body…*

Then again, he doubted anyone would notice any damage to the dress, or whatever the hell that thing was.

Tanna left and Levi told his heart to hang in there. Taking a couple of deep breaths, he ambled down the hallway to the magnificent foyer, where a Jackson Pollack dominated the one free wall. Years ago, Carrick had taken him on a tour of the historic house, casually telling him about the Vermeer in the sitting room and the Dalí in the dining room. In one of the reception rooms there was a credenza once owned by the Sun King. It had, apparently, started its life at the palace at Versailles.

And he'd thought his dad was rich. He was, in money and in assets, but in art and collectibles, the Murphys had him beat. Not that it was a competition…

After paying the deliveryman and tipping him well—it was cold and windy and the guy had been cheerful—Levi took the food to the kitchen and walked back into the hall. Calling for Tanna, he was surprised when her voice came from a room two doors down.

On his crutches, Levi walked down the long hallway and stopped at a partially open door. He pushed the door open and saw Tanna standing in front of a mirrored wall in a room holding a ballet barre and a wood parquet dance floor. Floor-to-ceiling mirrors covered three walls. Food forgotten, he stared at her, entranced.

He wasn't a guy who knew a lot about clothes but he had been raised in a house filled with girls so he could, just, describe the gown Tanna wore as a black tulle dress in a series of layers. It was as tame as the previous outfit had been crazy, but this dress, concealing most of Tanna's exquisite body, was sexier, more intriguing.

He stepped into the room and rested his back against the barre, trying to ignore his reflection in so many mirrors. "I think Carrick skipped this room when he took me on the tour all those years ago."

"My mom was an accomplished ballerina. I took lessons all my life and we both used this room to practice," Tanna explained. She gestured to a plain door across the room. "There's the built-in closet, if you want to take a look."

"Yeah, dresses aren't my thing," Levi replied, his tone dry. "I wouldn't know what I'm looking at."

Tanna turned and smiled at him. "Fair enough. To educate you, the dress I'm wearing is a Jean Patou, circa 1930." She stroked the fabric like it was the soft coat of a well-loved cat. "Confession time. I love clothes. I especially love old clothes. I'm a design nut and I love what clothes say about a certain time in history. It's crazy I spend my days in a very practical, very unflattering jumpsuit."

Her eyes clouded over, and she stared off into space for a minute.

Levi wanted to know what was going through her very agile brain. "Tell me about your job."

Tanna lifted the top layer of the dress and examined the hem, giving it far more attention than it deserved. "I respond to emergency calls. I treat the patient and I get him, or her, to a hospital. Nothing much to say."

Wrong. There was so much to say, to discover.

"Did you decide on emergency medicine because of your accident? Do you enjoy your job? When did you realize emergency medicine was what you wanted to do?" Levi asked, seeing the crack in her psyche and pushing his way through.

He caught the panic in her eyes and saw her tense. Why was she feeling uncomfortable? Why did talking about her career—the one thing that should be easy to discuss—make her close up and shut down? What was he missing?

Tanna gestured to a couple of garments bags draped

over the barre, a clear indication she was about to change the subject.

"Jane, the PR person, and I decided on three garment changes. I can't decide between a wool dress by Pierre Cardin which is adorned with vinyl from the late sixties, a Karl Lagerfeld and a Grès."

When he didn't respond, Tanna sent him an uncertain look and flicked her thumbnail against her chin. She looked at the closet and flushed, and Levi lifted his eyebrows, intrigued. What was she up to now? What was she about to ask?

"Out with it, Murphy. My Chinese is getting cold." He didn't give a rat's ass about food but he was desperate to know what made this gorgeous woman blush.

"There's a dress that's amazing but…"

"But?" Levi prompted her when she stopped speaking.

"It's pretty daring. That doesn't bother me. I'm happy to show some skin…" He was okay with that too, actually. Her skin was amazing. "But I'm not sure if it suits me." Tanna cleared her throat. "If I try it on, will you tell me what you think? Will you be brutally honest?"

"Have you ever known me to be anything but honest?" he asked her.

Tanna released a small laugh. "True. Hang tight. I'm going to change as quickly as I can. Then we can eat."

Levi leaned against the wall, easily imagining Tanna moving across this floor, dressed in pink leotard and tights, her skin glistening from the exercise. Great, another fantasy to keep him awake at night. And since he already had a thousand, he really didn't need any more.

Switching mental gears, Levi wondered how long she'd danced before she gave it up. Despite spending so many hours with her while she was in the hospital, there was still a lot he didn't know about her.

He hadn't known she loved the history of fashion as much as she loved art, that she could cook pasta like an Italian mama or that her out-of-tune singing made his ears ache.

He wanted to know more. Sometimes, when he allowed his defenses to drop, he wanted to know everything.

You asked her to stay because you wanted a little revenge, some payback. Seems like the tables have turned here, Brogan.

Levi sighed, reluctantly admitting he wanted to know everything, including the noise she'd make when he slid into her and whether her skin still smelled of wild cherries, and he was desperate to discover if any other tattoos adorned her incredible body.

Tanna released a small cough and Levi pulled his eyes off the floor and onto the vision standing in front of the built-in closet in the corner of the sparsely furnished room.

Basically, her dress was a series of folds, covering the tops of her thighs and falling to the floor in a cascade of heavy cream. The top consisted of two triangles, plunging to her navel. Acres of warm, sun-kissed skin were on display and Levi, needing to hold on to something because he felt like the world was teetering, reached behind him to wrap his fingers around the barre.

Then Tanna turned around and he nearly died. Right then, his vision tunneled, and his functioning knee buckled.

There was no back to the dress and Tanna held up her heavy curls, stretching her spine, and through the gap in the side of the dress, he saw the profile of her pretty right breast.

It was official; he was down. If his leg wasn't in a cast, he'd have been on his knees, panting.

"You're killing me here, Tanna," Levi said with what was left of his breath.

Tanna dropped her hair and it tumbled down her back as she slowly, oh, so slowly, turned. "Do you like it?"

Like it? *Like* was too tame a word…but he couldn't explain his inability to speak, let alone find adequate adjectives.

"It's not vintage but there is an amazing photo of my mom in this dress and I wanted to know whether I could pull it off as well as she did," Tanna babbled. "I mean, I know I won't look as good as her, my mom was stunning, but if I can wear it, I'd like to. But I'm repeating myself… So…what do you think?"

Was she kidding him? He couldn't think, that was the goddamn problem! "Come here, Murphy."

A small frown pulled Tanna's finely arched brows together, but she collected the long skirt in her hands and lifted it halfway up her shapely calves to walk toward him.

When she was in touching distance, Levi traced the edge of her bodice with his index finger and smiled when she shivered. Still unable to speak—would he ever be able to again?—he reverently touched her collarbone and ran his fingers up her neck before pushing into those heavy curls, his hand cupping the back of her head. Her small hands rested on his chest and he watched her sexy mouth lift up to his.

Yeah, this…

He didn't understand dresses or vintage or ballet or why she was back in his life, but he didn't care. This he understood.

Levi's brain shut down when their mouths crashed and clashed. He tasted the flavor of her lip balm and swallowed her tiny moan when his tongue twisted around hers. Needing to feel her, he dropped his crutches and then his free hand was on her back, covering a good portion of her creamy, exposed skin. He danced his fingers up and down her spine, pushing under the fabric to palm her butt cheek.

God, he loved this dress.

Tanna pressed closer to him and he relished the feel of her, chest to thigh. She was a fragrant armful, a taste of heaven, the temptation of sin. Her lips were soft, her smell divine, her ability to make him as hard as titanium was a revelation.

He needed her, he wanted her…now. In this room, surrounded by mirrors where he felt overwhelmed by her, but in the best way possible.

Levi, reluctantly, pulled his mouth off hers and his hand from out of the band of the skirt. He cupped her face with both hands, his thumbs tracing the ridges of her cheekbones.

She offered him a tremulous smile. "I take it you like the dress?"

"I do." He pulled the words up, wanting to reassure her. "You're naturally stunning, Murphy. You don't need a fancy dress to look great."

The smile grew bigger and brighter, and Levi's chest tightened.

"Trust me on this, you can pull off the dress, Tanna." He sighed and rested his forehead on hers. "It feels like I've been fighting the urge to rip the clothes off you since we stepped into this house." Another sigh. "That's a lie. I've wanted to strip you down since you walked back into my life a couple weeks ago… It has been two weeks, right?"

So much had happened and it felt like the weeks had been condensed into thirty-six hours.

Tanna's green eyes turned wicked and her mouth curved sensuously. "I'll make you a deal…"

Oh, God, his brain didn't have enough red blood cells to negotiate with this sharp-brained Murphy. He was probably about to be fleeced but he'd seen Tanna in this dress, kissed the hell out of her and could die a happy man.

"I strip for you—no ripping because this dress is, after all, couture—and then you can do whatever the hell you want with me."

Holy hell.

Levi watched as Tanna carefully removed the ivory-colored dress, revealing her wonderful skin inch by inch. The silky fabric fell down her chest and he saw, for the first time, her beautiful breasts, her taut nipples a deep, dark, rich pink, touched with spice. The fabric skimmed slim hips and as Tanna stepped out of the skirt, he noticed she was wearing a black thong. His eyes skittered over her hip and his thumb traced the long, wide scar.

"It's so ugly," Tanna whispered.

Levi shook his head. "It's your survival badge, baby."

Tanna gave him a grateful smile. Gripping the barre behind him, Levi watched through slitted eyes as Tanna draped the dress over the barre next to them before coming to stand in front of him, her hands on his hips. She stared up, and up, into his eyes and it took everything Levi had not to drag her into him, to take control of what was about to happen.

Because this had to be her decision, every step of the way.

"Do you know how often I've thought of this over the years?" she asked him, her voice, low and sensuous, sliding over him. Not as often, surely, as he had.

"I deeply regret not making love to you, Levi," Tanna said, her voice husky. "I need to know if the reality is as good as my imagination."

He did too.

Tanna played with the buttons on his shirt and he wished

she'd get on with it and rip it off him. "Can I make love to you, Lee?"

It had been years since she'd called him that and it sounded good on her lips.

Maybe too good.

Levi released his grip on the barre to push a curl behind her ear. "I'll cry like a baby if you don't."

Tanna nodded but made no motion to get this show on the road. He arched an eyebrow at her. "Problem?"

"Well, yeah. You have a busted knee and a strained shoulder," Tanna said, sounding worried. "How are we going to do this? All the beds are upstairs but there are a couple of couches close by."

He didn't want to wait that long; in fact, he couldn't wait another minute. But, because he was touched by her concern, he smiled. "You don't weigh more than a feather and if you grip my hips with your legs, and I hold you with one arm, we should be able to get it done."

Levi winced. *Crap, so romantic. Try harder, Brogan.* This was Tanna, not a quick fling who was well aware of his no-commitment policy.

Instead of taking offense, Tanna giggled. "It'll have to be quick."

Levi's voice dropped to a smoky rumble. "Honey, I've wanted you for so long and so hard that being quick won't be a problem for me."

Tanna's smile flashed and then she turned her attention to his button-down shirt, slowly pulling it apart to run her hands over his chest. Levi sucked in his breath when her fingers explored his flat nipples, surprised by how sensitive they were to her touch. Inspired, he lifted his hands to her breasts, rubbing his thumbs, slowly and deliberately, across her nipples. Her eyes, still connected to his, fogged over and her breathing quickened.

Yeah, this first time wouldn't take long at all. He was already as hard as a brick and he could feel the heat wafting up from between her legs. Every inch of skin he could see was tinged with the heat of desire, her nipples were hard points begging to be touched and her eyes were full of *take me now.*

He'd done that. Levi felt awed and proud, ridiculously masculine and strangely humbled that this woman, this amazing, strong woman, was falling apart in his arms.

And they hadn't even gotten to the good part yet.

Levi hooked his finger under the thin cord around her hips and pulled her thong down her legs. When the lace lay on the floor, he looked at her perfect form and sighed. He could see her reflection in all the mirrors and each version of Tanna was better than the last. This was a memory he'd never forget.

He couldn't take the time to get properly naked. He wanted her right now; he couldn't wait a second longer.

He pushed down his pants and underwear, and Tanna immediately reached for him, but he caught her hand before she could make contact. "Don't. If you touch me, I'll blow. I'm that close."

She nodded and gripped his hip, her eyes wide with impatience. "So, what now?"

"This." Levi banded his good arm around the backs on her thighs, lifted her up and groaned when her hot mound dragged over his penis. He gritted his teeth and forced himself to concentrate. "Lock your legs behind my back and rest your calves on the barre."

Tanna did as he asked, and Levi kissed the corner of her mouth. "I'm going to slide into you and when I am deep inside you, I'm going to kiss you senseless."

Tanna's eyes flashed with hot, potent desire and a little mischief as she wound her arms around his neck, her breasts pushing into his chest. It was so hot that she was naked and he was not.

"Hell of a lot of talk happening, Brogan, not so much action."

Goaded, but also amused, Levi positioned his cock at her entrance and scraped his knuckles over her feminine folds. He saw the shock ricocheting through her eyes and she pressed down on his hand, sliding her core across the head of his penis. So…

Damn…

Good.

First times together could either be awkward, tentative or hesitant—or a combination of all three—but nothing in the way they touched, in the way they took, suggested any of that. Tanna moaned and pushed his hand away, and Levi groaned as he pushed into her warm, wet heat. God, she felt so amazing, a million times better than he'd imagined.

Reality kicked imagination's ass. And if this was revenge, he'd have more of it, thank you very much.

Needing to kiss her, to have her as close as he could get her, Levi trapped her mouth beneath his and, to hell with his shoulder, held her tight and close. He couldn't thrust, his balance was too precarious, but Tanna, obviously on the same wavelength, took control, making tiny hip movements devastating to his self-control.

He didn't need much friction, didn't need a lot of foreplay, just holding her like this, being so deeply embedded in her was enough to make his balls contract, for concentrated pleasure to build at the base of his spine.

He'd spoken the truth—this was going to be quick.

Levi gripped Tanna's butt, pushing his fingers into her soft skin. He moved from her mouth to her neck to her shoulder, sucking on her perfect skin. "Please tell me you're close, Tanna, 'cause I'm not going to be able to hang on much longer."

"Me neither."

Tanna lifted her hips, dropped back down and released a tiny scream. Her internal muscles rippled, and she clenched around him, pulsing against him. Levi lifted his head to watch her face, to watch her come, thinking he'd never seen anyone as beautiful in his life. Her skin was flushed, her lips were red from his kisses and her eyes were the fiery green of a Mogul's prize emerald.

She was utterly exquisite.

Then Tanna's channel clenched again and her small movement was it all took to release his contained pleasure, allowing it to rocket through his system, up his spine and to blow his head apart. He released a roar, angled his hips, drove deeper and smiled when Tanna orgasmed again, harder and faster than before. Yeah, he'd thought that making love to Tanna would be good, but he hadn't expected dissolve-his-knees spectacular.

Levi held her as she trembled in his arms. As his orgasm faded, his shoulder and knee were quick to remind him he'd just had sex after surgery, not even three weeks after his accident.

He didn't care.

He'd have sex, with Tanna, anytime and anywhere.

That was why they made kick-ass painkillers.

Nine

"Relax, Murphy. I'm not dead yet or even close to it."

Tanna, sitting on a chair with her elbows on her knees, immediately straightened. She hastily picked up a magazine off the floor and waved it around. "I was just reading an article on French gardens."

Levi opened his eyes to glance at the cover of the magazine. "Funny, last I heard they don't have French gardens on yachts."

Tanna looked down at the yachting magazine and silently cursed. She was so busted. Yes, she'd been watching him sleep, embarrassed by her brazen behavior in the dance studio and terrified he'd reinjured his shoulder. Or his knee. Or pulled another muscle. She didn't, after all, weigh nothing.

When they'd left the house and returned to Levi's home on the Lockwood Estate, she could see he was in pain. Instead of his normal swinging style, he'd shuffled to the car.

It was her fault. She was the medical professional. If she had been thinking straight, she would've put his rehabilitation above her sobbing libido.

"Don't you dare apologize," Levi warned her, his deep blue eyes flashing with irritation. "I was an active participant in that madness, and I could've, at any time, called it off."

Tanna sucked in her right cheek. "Why didn't you?"

"I needed to have you." Levi touched her cheekbone with the tips of his fingers, his touch light but reassuring. "Stop feeling guilty, Tanna. It doesn't suit you."

Maybe, but she and guilt were best buddies.

"But your shoulder, your knee…"

"Are fine," Levi reassured her. He must've seen the doubt in her eyes because he released a frustrated sigh. "Okay, I'm in pain, but I know I didn't do any more damage."

"Maybe we should take you to the ER to make sure?"

Levi's wicked smile turned her stomach to mush. "And how are you going to explain how I reinjured myself? Yeah, Dr. Bryce, we had wall sex."

Tanna blushed and Levi's smile widened. "Stop fussing, Murphy. I'm fine. Let's move on to another consequence of our unforgettable actions."

She wasn't sure she could deal with much more. "Okay, shoot."

Levi folded his arms across his massive chest. "We didn't use protection."

It took a few moments for his sentence to make sense. When it did, her mouth dropped open and heat rolled over her. She closed her eyes and cursed.

"I'm judging, from your reaction, that you aren't on the pill."

Tanna shook her head. "Nope."

Levi nodded, looking remarkably sanguine. "So, you could, maybe, become pregnant?"

Tanna ran through her cycle and lifted her hand to rock it back and forth. "I think I'll be okay. We're just out of the window."

"So, there is a chance?"

"A small one," Tanna conceded. "But, if your sperm is already charming my egg, I'm up the river without a paddle." Panic flashed in her eyes, chased by fear.

"Okay, the look on your face is starting to scare me," Levi said.

"I can't be pregnant, Levi. I don't want a baby! If I'm pregnant, I'll be tied to you, tied to Boston."

Wow.

He didn't think he could still be hurt by Tanna, but yep, apparently he was wrong about that.

Levi tipped his head to the side. "Is being pregnant really the worst thing that can happen, Tanna? Being a mother, living in Boston…"

Being around me? Seeing where this is going?

What the hell was wrong with him? Why was he walking down this road again? Tanna had made her feelings clear a decade ago and nothing had changed.

He hadn't understood her then, and ten years on, he was still fumbling around in the dark.

"Maybe I should explain," Tanna quietly stated and it was only then that Levi realized he'd spoken out loud. "I need you to understand…it wasn't you but me."

This crap again? "Isn't that the standard line?"

Tanna spread her hands. "Maybe. But, in my case, it's pure truth. When I left Boston, I flew to London and I moved in with Padma, my godmother. I was a bit of a wreck." Tanna paused. "I know you won't believe me, but leaving was hard for me, Levi."

Yeah, he didn't believe it. Or maybe he didn't want to believe it. Who knew?

Tanna started to speak, stopped and pushed her hand into her long hair. She stared at the TV set on the wall opposite and he waited for her to continue.

They might as well get this done and out of the way.

"So, I was in London, missing you, missing my brothers, missing my home. After a week of crying, Padma, who is as tough as she is sweet, told me I couldn't just lie about, I had to do something. So, I went traveling. When I returned to London two years later, Padma sat me down again and demanded to know what I wanted to do with the rest of my life, where I was going, what I was going to do when I got there," Tanna said. "You never met Padma but I know you'd love her. And she'd flirt with you."

Her eyes met his and her smile pushed his world off its axis, shifted magnetic north. God, that was another thing he'd forgotten…the way her eyes lightened, her face brightened, how her smile dimmed the power of the sun.

"I knew I couldn't return to Boston or join Murphy's."

"Couldn't? Why not?"

Tanna took a long time to answer. "It felt frivolous. It *still* feels frivolous. Back then, I couldn't see myself going back to Murphy's when everything else had changed. I also couldn't stop thinking that, if you hadn't called 911 when you did, if the EMTs weren't as quick as they were, I might have, like Addy, died that night. It really worried me that I didn't know what to do in an emergency if someone needed my help. So I decided to do a first-aid course. I loved it, so I did another. Within a few years, I was pretty highly qualified."

Levi listened, fascinated by her story. He'd had firsthand experience of her determination, so he could easily imagine Tanna applying her mind to her studies. "I finally felt like I was contributing, like I was doing something important, and then I joined HART."

"Heart?"

Tanna enunciated the individual letters. "*H-A-R-T* is the Hazardous Area Response Team. They recruit and train selected emergency personnel who respond to major incidents."

Levi frowned. "What sort of major incidents?"

"Train crashes, large-scale motorway accidents, building collapses or significant fires. Terrorism incidents, bomb blasts, that type of thing. HART doesn't respond to your normal, run-of-the-mill accident," Tanna explained. "Basically, we go into all the hot zones."

His worst nightmare. Levi couldn't think of anything worse than one of his loved ones constantly walking into danger and being unable to protect them. Thank God, and all his minions, he and Tanna weren't together anymore.

He'd wouldn't be able to function knowing she was walking into a situation out of his control.

"I was the youngest, and least experienced, recruit in fifteen years. They looked at my injuries and told me there was no way I'd pass the fitness exam, but I did. They told me they doubted I'd pass the psychological exam, given the trauma I experienced, but I did. The survival drills were the toughest—white-water rafting, abseiling, crawling through a tunnel in the dark with my kit—but I got through it."

He could see she was waiting for him to say something, to praise her efforts, and he should; her achievements were incredibly impressive, especially given how broken she'd been just a few years before. But he couldn't form the words because the urge to pick her up and shake her, to demand to know why she was putting herself at risk—after barely surviving a bad accident—was like a hot, violent river of lava.

How dare she play with her safety? How dare she place herself in danger again?

Levi opened his mouth to blast her but knowing he didn't have the right—his ring wasn't on her finger—he dropped his head back to stare at the ceiling. His sisters were always on him about being too protective and he knew that if he ripped into Tanna, she'd shut down and this conversation would end.

Knowing it was smarter to keep his mouth shut, he gritted his teeth. It was hard but he managed it. Just.

He folded his arms and dug his fingers into his biceps. "Okay, so you joined this specialized team…"

"I finally felt like I was where I was supposed to be. I started in emergency medicine because I wanted to give something back and I joined HART because I felt like I had a bigger part to play, because the work is relevant. I guess I needed to prove to myself I was more than a PR person, that I was more than a broken body lying in that hospital bed," Tanna added.

"Of course you were more," Levi protested, unable to believe she'd felt that way.

"No, you don't understand!" Tanna pushed both hands into her hair and gripped the long strands in her fingers. "Before the accident, Levi, I lived this charmed life. Sure, I lost my folks young, but I had three gorgeous, strong, dedicated brothers who made me their entire world. School was easy for me. I was pretty, rich, smart and popular. I got into an Ivy League college without trying very hard."

"You also had an accident that nearly took your life."

"But it didn't," Tanna said, her eyes bubbling with raw emotion. "I should've died but I didn't. I should not have been able to walk, but I did. I even, somehow, managed to find a handsome, gorgeous man, who stood by me and then proposed marriage. Who does that happen to?"

"You, apparently," Levi pointed out.

"I realized I've never really been challenged, that everything came to me so easily."

She'd nearly died and had endured months of pain after many surgeries. Why did she keep forgetting that part?

"Before the accident I'd never stood on my own two feet, never had to make a hard decision, never faced anything difficult at all."

Wasn't the trick to life to enjoy the good times and avoid the hard? Or had he missed something?

Tanna put her hands into the back pockets of her jeans and rocked on her heels, looking young and vulnerable. "Becoming an EMT was tough. There were so many times I wanted to give up. But it's good work, Levi, important work."

She stared at her feet, her face pale. "And I think Addy would like the fact that I'm doing something worthwhile, contributing."

Levi leaned forward, seeing something in her eyes suggesting deep sadness and an ocean's worth of guilt. "What do you mean by that, Tan?"

"She'd appreciate the fact that I'm no longer some little rich girl who needs her burly brothers or sexy fiancé to take care of her. Addy was so independent, she'd applaud me for making my own way. That I'm doing something important, something to make the world a little better. After all, she's not here to do it herself."

Levi held up his hand, shocked by the suspicion forming in his brain. "Tan, it's not your fault she died."

Tanna glared at him. "Oh, please, of course it is. She was driving my fast, powerful car because I was drunk. Because I had too much of a party, too much fun. She died because of me, Levi."

It had been an accident, an unfortunate series of events,

and if Tanna had gotten behind the wheel drunk, she could've killed herself and a dozen other people. His heart ached for her; she'd thought she was doing the right thing by not driving under the influence, but the evening still ended in someone dying.

How utterly, profoundly sad was that?

"Honey, you've got to give yourself a break."

"Life didn't give Addy a break so I'm not entitled to one either."

Tanna took a step back and Levi knew she was regretting her words, that she'd said too much. Before he could push her for more, to talk this through with her, to make her see how tough she was being on herself, she abruptly spun around and left the room. Thirty seconds later he heard her footsteps running up the stairs.

He started to go after her but quickly remembered he couldn't follow her up the stairs.

He was so over being injured. If he could, he'd rip his cast off with his bare hands.

"Can I get you something to drink?"

Thankfully, Tanna wasn't one to sulk and she was back downstairs in thirty minutes, her eyes red but her expression composed.

Levi rubbed his hands over his face, wishing she had a bit more color to hers. He'd do anything to strip the exhaustion from her expression and the haunted look from her eyes. She wasn't as together as he'd thought she was, and neither was he.

His plan for revenge, a little payback and keeping his distance had gone to hell.

And that might be because they were digging too deep, picking at sores long healed. The past was the past and couldn't be changed or fixed, and he wasn't the type to look back. Neither was he the type to look forward, not when it came to relationships.

He had to remember he and Tanna had a past but they had no future. They only had the present and he didn't want to spend their time together arguing about things that couldn't be changed.

He—they—needed control and they needed it now. It was time for a reset.

"Come here, Tan."

Tanna crossed the room and when she was close enough, he reached for her arm, gently wrapping his fingers around her delicate wrist and tugging her toward him. Tanna looked down at him and he smiled at her defiant, proud expression. "Honey, I don't want to fight with you."

She didn't look convinced.

Levi's thumb traced the soft skin of her inner wrist. "You're here for another few weeks and I don't think re-hashing the past is a productive use of our time."

Amusement tinged with relief touched her eyes and her lips, and Levi knew he was gaining ground.

"And I suppose you have a couple of ideas of how productive we can be?"

He patted his thigh. "If you sit down, I could show you what I had in mind."

Tanna flipped her legs over his hips to straddle him, her hair falling down the side of her face and tickling his chin.

"Looks like you have some ideas of your own," Levi said, his hand tucking her hair behind her ear.

Tanna nibbled the side of his jaw, her teeth scraping his three-day beard. "Oh, I have a few."

"I'm happy to consider them." Levi ran his hand down her back, cupped her butt and squeezed. This was all that was important, the here and the now of being able to touch her. He wanted slow, he wanted sexy, he wanted to wring every ounce of pleasure from her.

But, like before, they didn't have any condoms. They'd taken a hell of a risk earlier and he wasn't about to spin the barrel of that loaded revolver again.

He also couldn't, wouldn't, let there be any misunderstandings between them. Gripping her biceps, he gently pushed her up and back, to sit her on his thighs.

Confusion flashed in Tanna's eyes. "Problem?"

"We need condoms."

Tanna slapped her hand against her forehead, obviously embarrassed she'd forgotten about protection again.

"What the hell is wrong with me? Okay, condoms." She wrinkled her nose. "I don't have any. Do you?"

Yeah, he had a box upstairs. Levi told her where to find them but, as she started to climb off him, he gripped her hips to keep her in place.

Tanna sighed her frustration and lifted her eyebrows to give him a *what now?* look.

When she'd strolled back into his life with her lithe body and gorgeous face, he'd wanted revenge, payback, for her to beg for his forgiveness. Now all he could think about was protecting himself, making sure he didn't start to fall for her again.

Because he could only be that stupid once.

Levi stroked her arm from shoulder to wrist, making sure to keep eye contact. "We always found it easy to talk to each other, Tan, but it's not a good idea."

She immediately caught his drift. Nobody could ever accuse Tanna of being slow. "Because it feels a bit too real, huh? Too much like what we had?"

Levi nodded. "I can't go back there, Tanna."

Tanna's shoulders slumped. "Me neither."

"I want you, but I don't want you thinking we can go anywhere with this," Levi added.

"I know. I'm the one who is leaving, remember? As soon as I—" She stopped talking abruptly and stared past him.

As soon as she what? Levi started to ask and cursed himself when he remembered what he'd said not a minute before. He had to stop asking her questions that led to deeper conversations.

Tanna waved her comment away. "Forget it. It doesn't matter."

It did. Everything she thought or felt was important. He didn't want it to be, but it was.

"I still want to sleep with you," Levi said. Sex was all they could have.

He expected her to retreat, to slide off his lap, but Tanna just looked at him with clear eyes. "I still want that too."

Levi released the breath he'd been holding when Tanna finally climbed off his lap. Okay, good, still on the same page.

At the door, Tanna turned and her smile was a brain-stopping combination of sweet and seductive. "You said the condoms are on the top shelf of your bathroom cabinet?"

Thank you, baby Jesus. Sex he could do, but this emotional BS? Not so much.

Or at all.

Ten

Carrick stood at the entrance to the viewing room and watched as Tanna directed the maintenance staff on how to hang the huge photographs of Raeni in dresses very similar to the ones on sale. He had to admit that Levi's idea to link the sale with his stepmom and have Tanna wear Raeni's dresses was fantastic. Murphy's was now expecting a bigger crowd than before.

Excellent news.

Somehow, without managing to upset his head of PR, Jane, or any other staff, Tanna had taken over all the arrangements for the presale cocktail party. Her antipathy toward Murphy International seemed to have vanished and Carrick often found her about the place, in this viewing room or in Jane's office. Or on the phone to a potential buyer or chatting to a vendor.

When he asked her why she was spending her vacation time in Murphy's, working, she blithely told him she liked being there and she needed to find something to fill her hours while Levi was at work. He might've believed her if she'd been able to meet his eyes while speaking.

Tanna was lying about being back in Boston on vacation and he would, eventually, find out why. And Levi spending more and more hours at work worried Carrick. He was pretty sure Levi shouldn't be so mobile yet.

He was also sure Levi and Tanna were getting naked. If Levi was up for sex, he could handle going to work.

Carrick was glad someone was getting lucky because he as sure as hell wasn't.

Sadie Slade's stunning face flashed into his mind and Carrick closed his eyes, thinking of a math equation to stop him from embarrassing himself.

Damn, now he was getting turned on at work? He'd had a couple of X-rated dreams about the art detective and he'd woken up sweaty and disorientated and needing, literally, to take himself in hand.

That hadn't happened to him since he was in his teens and it annoyed him that Sadie had that much power over him. Until he got his craving for her under control, he was avoiding her.

Because, apparently, he had all the maturity and sophistication of a fifteen-year-old.

Carrick pushed his hand through his hair and, realizing standing around wasn't productive, decided to return to his office where he could, he was sure, still smell Sadie's perfume in the air.

Carrick felt a hand on his shoulder and whipped around to see Levi behind him, still on crutches. He smiled as they exchanged fist bumps.

"Tanna asked if I would send a driver to fetch you," Carrick told him, looking at his watch. "But in an hour or so."

"My orthopedic surgeon had a cancellation so he could see me earlier. I caught a taxi here." Levi nodded to Tanna, who was on a stepladder, holding a huge photograph of her mom. "Is she being as bossy as hell?"

Carrick grinned at the affection in Levi's voice. "She is."

Levi looked around the room, his gaze bouncing off the massive arrangements of flowers, and frowned. "Where are the dresses, the items that are going to be on sale?"

"Ah, well, my bossy sister decided that, instead of using mannequins to display the dresses, she would hire live models to parade the clothes and the jewelry. The clothing is presently being allocated to models and there are about a dozen in the conference room, half naked."

Levi grinned and grabbed his crutches. "Remind me where the conference room is?"

Carrick smiled. "Ha ha. Anyway, Tanna has blown the budget to hell and back."

"I know you and you're not even a little annoyed. Why not?" Levi asked.

"I suppose that's because I'm so damn happy to see her in Murphy's, having fun." Carrick sighed. "And she's also persuaded at least ten of the world's biggest collectors to personally attend the cocktail party and the auction. Because they are coming, we've had a lot more interest in the sale. Their presence will drive the prices up, so how can I complain about her being over budget?"

"Your sister has a way of overturning apple carts," Levi commented.

"Is that what she's doing to you?" Carrick asked.

Levi stared at Tanna, who was still up on the ladder, before turning to face Carrick. He shook his head. "Get that idea out of your head, Murph. It's not going to happen. We're just friends."

Pfft. Sure they were. Just like Carrick didn't want Sadie Slade with his next breath.

And, talking about the good doctor of art history, he

turned around to see her approaching him, dressed in another of her bohemian business outfits. Today she wore a tiny, Aztec-inspired miniskirt and a flame-colored jacket skimming slim hips over a bright cobalt blue silk shirt. Her heels showed off her gorgeous legs.

Yep, tonight would be another long, long, night.

Sadie smiled at him and he was certain his heart stopped, just for a minute. She gestured to the viewing room and, after greeting Levi, asked whether she could look inside.

Carrick stood aside to let her pass and she stared at the large room, disappointment on her face. "I really wanted to see the dresses and the jewelry."

"Come to the cocktail party tomorrow night," Carrick impulsively suggested.

Excitement jumped into Sadie's eyes and Carrick felt heat invade his veins. Yep, it was official; he'd do just about anything to see her smile. After his marriage fell apart, he'd vowed to keep his love life uncomplicated and surface based. Sadie was testing that vow.

"Are you sure?" she asked.

Carrick nodded. "I'll email you an invitation."

"That's great, thanks. I presume it's formal?"

"Black tie," Carrick confirmed, unable to pull his eyes off her sexy, wide mouth. He was vaguely aware of Tanna approaching him and he finally yanked his gaze away, helped by Levi's elbow in his ribs.

"God, you are so pathetic," Levi muttered out of the side of his mouth.

"Pot. Kettle. Black," Carrick retorted as he watched his sister and the woman he wanted to sleep with exchange greetings and knew he was in for a world of hurt.

So, judging by the look on Levi's face, was his best friend.

* * *

On Friday morning, Tanna drained her coffee and turned to Levi, who'd just finished his daily call to his marina manager. Or one of his managers as there were many calls, every morning.

"I have an appointment in the city," Tanna informed him. "Then I have a hair appointment this afternoon so I'm not going to be around a lot today. And tonight is the Murphy cocktail party."

A small frown pulled Levi's eyebrows together. "This is the third appointment you've had this week. Are you sick or something?"

Please don't pry, Tanna silently begged him. *I don't want to lie to you but I'm not ready to talk about this, not yet. Probably not ever.*

"I'm fine."

Levi sent her his patented you're-BS-ing-me look. "What's going on, Tanna?"

Tanna picked up her phone and swiped the screen, hoping he'd take the hint that she didn't want to discuss this further.

Levi's hand caught her wrist and she was forced to look at him. Tense and annoyed, she returned his hard look. "Why are you pushing this, Levi? It's not relevant to...us."

Levi released her and annoyance flashed across his face. "Tanna, you have bad dreams. I hear them. You wake up often and you talk in your sleep. Something is going on with you and I want to know what it is."

After telling her that there was no point in rehashing the past, why was he pushing her? And if she had to answer, what would she say?

I'm suffering from PTSD and my career is on the line. I've been placed on medical leave and I might lose my job— the job I need so I can live with myself—if I don't get myself under control. This isn't something you or anyone else can fix. And I will fix it. I'm not the girl you used to know who needs her big, tough fiancé to solve her problems.

So, no, that was far too personal and she couldn't share any of that.

"Does it have something to do with your job? Why are you taking a six-week break? And don't tell me it's a vacation. I'm not buying that."

He didn't understand; spending time with him and at Murphy's *was* a vacation...

She'd loved every minute she'd spent talking art and design and jewelry. When she went back to London, she'd be faced with injury and death, making quick, hard decisions in an instant. Work wasn't fun, but it was good, *necessary*.

"What part of 'I'm fine' don't you understand, Brogan?" Tanna demanded, annoyed. She made a show of glancing at her watch. "I'm going to shower and get changed—"

"Why won't you talk about your job? About why you are really here in Boston?"

More questions, Brogan?

Aargh, she didn't have time for this. And no, she didn't want to explain that, ten years after her accident, all the trauma she'd experienced then was rushing back to torment her again. She'd had counseling sessions; she'd thought she'd dealt with this emotional mess.

But the flashbacks and panic attacks were from the PTSD. Her therapist had told her that unresolved issues were lingering deep inside her. Those were the issues she'd come to Boston to face.

Reining in her impatience, she made herself smile. "I don't talk about my job because most people don't want to hear about broken bones and heart attacks."

And because every time she thought about returning

to her position at HART, her stomach clenched and her throat tightened. It was ridiculous; she was stronger than this. Not returning to London wasn't an option. She would not let this beat her.

The muscle in Levi's jaw ticked and Tanna knew he was trying to understand. She waited for him to resume speaking and when he did, he surprised her with his next question. "Do you enjoy being a paramedic?"

Tanna looked at him, shocked. Of course, she did. She hadn't studied long and hard for the fun of it. "Yes, of course."

Levi didn't look convinced. "Tell me something you love about your job, something that gives you a kick every time you do it." He held up a hand. "And don't say *when I save a life*. That's too easy."

Saving a life had been the first thing that popped into her head. "I don't understand what you're getting at."

Levi tapped his index finger against the wooden tabletop. "Okay, let me give you an example. It's a little silly but when a yacht leaves the marina, I immediately check the visitor's book to see what they said about their stay. I get some damn good reviews and it gives me a kick. That's one of my many little joys. Tell me one of yours."

Tanna looked at him, askance. Crap, she couldn't remember any of the little joys. Her job was filled with lots of downtime punctuated by sessions of intense concentration and craziness. She'd always been consumed by the feeling she was doing something worthwhile, something important, so she never stopped to notice the joys. She only noticed the successes, and that was decidedly different...

"Can't answer, huh? Okay, then answer me this..."

Tanna forced herself to meet his eyes and they drilled through her, pinning her to the floor. His expression, and his tone, reflected the seriousness of his question.

"Do you actually like what you do, Murphy? Did you ever?"

She couldn't answer him; the question was too big and too direct and too honest. She didn't want to continue this conversation because if Levi pushed her to dig, to question her own motivations, she might not like her answers.

Besides, it didn't matter whether she enjoyed her job or not, it was what she had to do in order to live with herself, to live with the guilt of Addy's death.

It was way past time to shut this down... They weren't supposed to be talking, anyway.

Gathering her courage, she walked around the table and dragged her mouth across his lips, pulling back to see the desire flash in his eyes. She kissed him again, allowing her tongue to slide into his mouth. Levi immediately reached for her and dragged her onto his lap, her legs straddling his hips and his erection settling between her thighs.

Tanna deepened the kiss, grateful men were so easily distracted.

Levi took control of their kiss and soon Tanna had forgotten his question, sinking into his hard body, entranced by his strength and captivated by his kisses. Levi had the ability to pull her into another dimension, a world where nothing existed but their passion and need to make each other feel as good as possible.

They didn't need to talk, they just needed to touch.

Then Levi put his hands on her shoulders and gently pushed her away. Tanna looked at him through passion-fogged eyes and wondered why he'd stopped.

Levi ran his thumb over her bottom lip. "I know you were trying to distract me but I'm not a kid anymore. You didn't answer my question, Murphy."

And she wouldn't. Frustrated and a little annoyed at being called out, she climbed off Levi's strong thighs and sent him a cool smile. "I'm going to shower and then I'm going into the city. I'll see you when I see you."

"You are so damn frustrating," Levi told her as she walked away.

Since she had to live with herself, his statement wasn't even news.

"Mrs. Talbot." Tanna held out her hand to the matriarch of Boston society, her blood so blue it was almost purple, and dropped a kiss on each of her leathery cheeks. "I haven't seen you since I was a child."

Mrs. Frieda Talbot, as old as God, looked at Tanna with eyes that had lived a million lives. "I remember you wearing pigtails, sitting in the corner of Carrick's office while we conducted business."

Frieda was one of Murphy's oldest and wealthiest clients, owning both extensive art and jewelry collections. Addicted to spending money, she received an invitation to every function and auction Murphy's held.

"It's so lovely to see you. Do you have an eye on anything special?" Tanna asked her.

"I rather fancy the flower purse, circa 1930. I think the estimate is a bit high at five hundred dollars."

Tanna smiled, remembering Frieda had once purchased a Willem de Kooning for more than three million dollars. Frieda liked what she liked and was always looking for a bargain.

"I hope you get it," Tanna told her sincerely. "And at a satisfactory price."

Frieda seemed pleased by her statement and, her attention caught by an old friend, abruptly left Tanna. Tanna grinned and turned at the light tap on her shoulder.

Pulling a polite smile onto her face—everybody present wanted to talk to her about her mom's dresses or her mom or fashion in general—Tanna turned and her smile widened in genuine pleasure.

"Sadie, it's so nice to see you. I love your dress."

In fact, with its white bodice and short skirt trimmed with flowers, it looked a lot like the Christian Dior in the sale.

"It's a cheap knockoff," Sadie admitted. "I found it in a little boutique in Paris. The owner slash designer takes her inspiration from the sixties."

"You look wonderful."

"You do too," Sadie replied. "I've loved every dress you've worn tonight but this one is simply sensational."

Tanna couldn't help it; she looked across the room to where Levi stood by the bar, leaning on his crutches and talking to Finn. When she looked down at the ivory crepe, she remembered stepping out of it in the dance studio at the Beacon Hill house, being naked while Levi was still fully dressed.

This dress made her hot...

Oh, Lord, who was she kidding? Levi made her hot. All the freakin' time.

Tanna accepted a martini from a passing waiter and tossed a large portion of the drink down her throat, thinking she'd never had so much sex in her life...

And every single time, Levi made it magical. Even with his limited movement. God help her if she ever got to make love to him when he was fully mobile. She might not survive.

But she'd be long gone before that happened. She had to keep her eye on her goal, on what she needed to do. Her plan was to get healthy and return to her job.

Playing house with Levi wasn't her real life. That had been a teenager's dream and it had been a long time since she'd been a teenager, or a dreamer. Tanna looked at Sadie's flower ring, thinking that leaving Levi, again, was going to be hard, possibly even harder than before. Because, while she knew she had to go back to her job and her life in London, she'd enjoyed playing house with her ex-fiancé. It had given her a taste of how her life could've been had she taken the easy route and married Levi.

And, dammit, a huge part of her felt a little sick about all she'd missed out on with him. The years of sharing his home and his bed, loving and laughing and fighting and making up.

But, had she married Levi, her life, their lives, would've been tainted by her guilt, by her *what-ifs* and her *should haves*. How would she have been able to live such a wonderful life when Addy had been stripped of hers?

And if Tanna got a little carried away, thinking she could easily fall in love with Levi again—had she even stopped loving him?—she still wasn't entitled to live a fairy-tale life.

No, she had to pay for the choices she'd made. And she was paying, dammit.

She was just taking a little time out, having a few weeks of fun and a lot of great sex. In a few weeks, she'd return to her real, gritty, emotionally draining job and her quiet life in London. But for now, yeah, she was going to enjoy the hell out of Levi Brogan.

"Wow, that was a hell of a side trip," Sadie said, smiling. "I want some of whatever put that faraway look in your eyes."

Tanna just smiled, wishing she and Sadie were good enough friends that she could share the truth, that she was overdosing on great sex. Her eyes darted to Levi and he almost immediately turned his head, and their eyes clashed and connected. Even though they were at opposite ends of the room, she could feel the intensity of his gaze, and knew exactly what he was thinking…

Your dress is coming off, sooner rather than later.

Levi jerked his head in a subtle come-here movement and Tanna, liking the adventurous light in his eyes, excused herself from Sadie.

Instead of waiting for her, Levi headed to the door and quickly—man, he could move on those crutches—disappeared through the door leading from the cocktail lounge into the hallway.

Despite trying to dodge people wanting to talk to her, Tanna greeted Murphy's clients, exchanged kisses and hugs, and kept the conversations super short. But it was still more than ten minutes before she slipped out the door into the hallway of the hotel and Levi was nowhere to be seen. Needing a minute to catch her breath, she walked toward the elevators, looking for the ladies' room. Seeing the discreet sign, she headed to the end of the hall, holding her long skirt off the carpet.

She was a few yards from the restroom when a door to her right opened and a strong arm wrapped around her waist and pulled her up against a hard chest.

Levi's mouth covered hers as he stepped back, and she dimly heard the door slam behind him.

Pulling her mouth off his, she noticed they were in a small lounge, perfect for a two-person meeting. Levi leaned against the door and reached behind him to flip the lock.

Oh, God, she'd heard about people who sneaked away from functions for a little naughtiness, but like joining the mile-high club, she'd never expected it to happen to her. Judging by the very hard erection tenting Levi's pants, however, that was exactly what was going to happen.

She was so on board.

"Have I told you how sexy you look tonight? How much I love this dress?" Levi demanded, his lips on her bare shoulder.

No, but since he'd made love to her before leaving the house, carefully removing the dress, she'd gotten the message.

"I freaking *love* this dress."

Tanna laughed. "I got the hint." She looped her arms around his neck and crossed her wrists behind his head. "I was hoping you'd do this."

"Make out with you in an empty room in the middle of a cocktail party?" Levi asked, his tongue tracing the cord in her neck.

Tanna shivered and pushed her fingers into his soft hair. "Yeah. It's…hot," Tanna admitted, blushing. Levi had the ability to make her rocket from zero to about-to-come in ten seconds flat. "Whenever we are together, I feel like I'm permanently connected to an electrical socket."

Levi lifted his head and his thumb rubbed her lower lip. "Is that a good or bad thing?"

"You know it's a good thing, Lee," Tanna whispered. In fact, everything about him was, well, pretty damn wonderful. No matter what limits he'd tried to place on their conversations, in between making love they talked, and unlike before, they connected on the same intellectual wavelength. There was a balance now…

"Do you want me to touch you?" Levi asked her, his voice rough with need.

He always asked for permission and never assumed he had the right to make love to her. Tanna knew it was his way of keeping an emotional distance between them, a certain barrier.

Levi was still waiting for an answer and Tanna nodded. "Please touch me, Lee. Make love to me, here. Now. Immediately."

"I want to, you know I do, but you're in the public eye tonight and if I do, everyone—including your brothers—

will know what we did." Levi held her nape, his thumb stroking her jaw. "I'm not going to embarrass you like that, babe."

"Aargh." Tanna dropped her forehead to rest it on Levi's collarbone. "So, why did you haul me in here, then?"

"Because I couldn't stand being across the room and not being able to hold you, kiss you. Acting like we are just platonic friends is killing me," Levi responded. "And if your brothers find out we've hooked up, they will kill me. Though I think Carrick suspects something is going on."

"It has nothing to do with them," Tanna told him, instantly annoyed. Her life, her body, her choice…

"Yeah, trust me, that's not the way brothers work, babe." Levi tipped her face up and his lips touched hers in a kiss as sweet as it was sexy. "Need you, Tan. Again. It's too much, isn't it?"

Tanna agreed. It really was. But she'd take this type of too much.

Holding Levi's face in her hands, her mouth softened under his, and their kiss was languid, lovely, soft and liquid. Passion was there, underneath the sweet, but was banked, and they both knew if they allowed it to run rampant, they'd lose control. So Tanna matched his pace, their tongues tangling softly, their hands moving lightly across each other's bodies. Tanna sighed as his hand slid inside the triangle covering her right breast, his fingers flickering over her nipple, barely touching her but stunningly sexy.

She groaned into his mouth, wanting to take it deeper, harder, but Levi shook his head. "Got to go slow, babe. Got to keep this light."

Right, cocktail party, people outside, appearances to keep up.

Levi's hand skimmed over her hip, down her thigh and

under the high slit of her dress, his hand disappearing under the flowing folds. She sucked in her breath when his fingers found the edge of her panties and she immediately undid his tuxedo jacket, looking for the snap on his pants.

Levi's strong hand covered hers. "Nope. This isn't about me."

What? Her hand stilled, wanting to stroke the large bulge beneath her hand. "But…"

"Slow, sexy and only one of us is going to come. And guess what?" Levi whispered against her lips.

"What?"

"It isn't going to be me."

His words were barely out of his mouth when his fingers pulled down her flesh-colored panties and sank into her folds. Like before, his touch was gentle, soft, and Tanna couldn't believe how turned on she was. He'd just need to flick her, a couple of strokes and she'd be flying.

How? How did he do this?

"Do you want to get off, Tan? Right here, right now? As gently as hell and twice as sexy?"

He didn't need to do anything, he just needed to rumble words against her skin, and she was already there. "Please, Lee."

Levi took her mouth again and his tongue echoed the soft, gentle movements of his fingers as they slid inside her. Only Levi could touch her like this, could make her churn and yearn…

Tanna felt herself building, climbing, pleasure—this time a soft, gentle wave as opposed to a passion-driven tsunami—washing over her.

Tanna pushed down on his fingers and he curled them into her, hitting a special spot she hadn't known existed until Levi taught her it was there. He also ran his thumb over that little bundle of nerves. It was all too much and Tanna stilled, pulled her mouth from Levi's, her entire body focused on what he was doing between her legs.

The wave rose, heated her from the inside out, and she tumbled, falling, spinning, rolling...

All the colors of a spectacular coral reef exploded in her brain and she slapped her hand against Levi's chest, hoping he'd realize she couldn't stand, that she could hardly breathe.

Nothing else, besides what he was doing to her, mattered. Levi banded his other arm around her, held her steady as he pushed her to reach for more, to own her pleasure, to fall into it. She came again, screamed softly and disintegrated in his arms.

Tanna had no idea how long it took her to fall back into reality, a place she didn't want to return to, but she had to return when Levi pulled his hand away. Then his strong arms cuddled her close and she could feel his nose in her hair, his lips against her temple.

"God, Tanna. You're so damn beautiful."

Tanna closed her eyes and let his words wash over her.

"Why do I have to be so damn addicted you?"

Dammit, how the hell was she going to walk away from him, from this again? She'd done it once, but back then she hadn't known the power of his touch, how utterly satisfied she felt standing in his arms. Oh, not just because he gave her amazing orgasms, but because he saw her.

He saw her as she was now, today. Strong. Independent. Confident.

Leaving was something she had to do.

Wasn't it?

"Tanna? Where are you?"

Tanna jerked her head back at the loud shout from the

hallway. She saw the *WTF?* look in Levi's eyes, knowing she hadn't imagined the panic in Carrick's voice.

"Tanna, I need you, dammit!" Carrick's voice was a loud roar outside the door.

Levi spun around, opened the door behind him to Carrick, whose face was ashen beneath his tan.

Tanna placed a hand on her brother's arm, her nails digging in to grab his attention. "Carrick! What's the problem?"

"It's Sadie. I think she's choking. You need to come."

Tanna didn't hesitate; she just kicked off her shoes, lifted her skirts and started to run.

Eleven

The doors to the ambulance had barely closed when the driver accelerated, desperate to take Sadie, who was still breathing via a pen tube jammed into her throat, to the nearest emergency room. Tanna felt Finn's arm around her waist and Ronan's big body shielding her from the freezing wind. Soft fabric enveloped her and Tanna looked down to see Ronan's jacket on her bare shoulders.

Ronan placed his hand on her back. "Honey, you need to get inside. Your feet must be freezing."

Tanna looked down, suddenly realizing she couldn't feel her toes. Coming back to where she was—standing on the cold stone steps leading up to the hotel's front door—she looked around and blinked.

"Where's Levi?" she asked, as Ronan and Finn escorted her back into the lobby of the iconic Forrester-Grantham hotel. Tanna saw the strange looks she was getting and shrugged. Let people talk—what did she care?

She wouldn't be staying in Boston so what people said didn't worry her.

"We're not sure, honey," Finn gently told her.

She looked up into Finn's face and blinked back her tears, not wanting to hurt him by telling him that, while she appreciated his support, she wanted Levi.

Right. Damn. Now.

"I'll go up to the function room and see whether he's still there," Ronan offered.

Tanna watched Ronan walk away and stared down at the grubby, wet hem of her dress and her blue feet. She felt like she was operating outside of herself, like she was watching herself go through the motions.

"Are you okay, Tan?" Finn asked, obviously concerned.

She really wasn't.

She was going to toss her cookies—and her champagne and those delicious canapés—right now.

Breathing through her nose, Tanna counted to ten, then to twenty, pushing the nausea away. Images of the past twenty minutes floated through her brain, Sadie lying on her back, her eyes wide and terrified, gagging from the obstruction in her throat. Her hand fluttered around her neck, silently begging Tanna to help her.

Tanna's training kicked in and she'd started barking orders like a drill sergeant. By the time she was done, she'd performed an emergency tracheotomy and Sadie was breathing again, her blue eyes wide and scared.

Tanna hadn't panicked or seen dots in front of her eyes or battled to breathe. No, she'd remained calm and cool and in control, doing what she needed to do, what she'd committed her life to doing. She'd saved Sadie's life, just like she'd saved other lives in other situations.

Addy was still dead, but Tanna was paying it forward as best she could. This was what she was supposed to do.

Working at Murphy's was lovely, fun and light and fluffy, but it wasn't important, imperative. Saving lives was.

And she'd done it. Without a single PTSD symptom.

Tanna felt Levi's heat and then his big arms came around her, cuddling her close. Tanna turned, buried her face in his chest and wrapped her arms around his waist, wishing she could slide inside him.

"Well done, Tan. You saved her life."

"Can't stop shaking," Tanna told him, feeling tears slip down her face.

"I've got you." Levi stroked her back, up into her hair, his hands and body warming her as Ronan's designer jacket couldn't do. Handing her shoes to Finn, his strong arm around her waist, he led her to a sofa in a secluded corner of the lobby and sat down, pulling her onto his lap. Tanna buried her face in his neck and just cried harder, her sobs coming out as a series of hiccups.

She normally only fell apart when she was alone, when she was guaranteed her privacy. But this was different, she wasn't seeing Addy, she couldn't smell blood, she wasn't back in her long-ago car, her legs pinned by metal.

She wasn't crying because of the PTSD, she was crying because, this time, for the first time, she recognized herself again, as the EMT she'd been for so many years. She'd done what she needed to do, quickly, efficiently.

She'd saved Sadie's life. And maybe, just maybe, her PTSD symptoms had left as quickly as they'd arrived.

Tanna wasn't sure how long she cried. It could've been for two minutes or twenty, but eventually Levi patted her back and commanded her to stop. The combination of his sharp tone and the light grip of his fingers on her shoulder snapped her head up and she stared at him through water-logged eyes.

"I don't understand—this is what you do. This is what

you trained for," Levi said. "You've been in worse situations than this, Tanna, surely?"

Tanna nodded. "Yeah, obviously."

"Then I don't understand your reaction, the tears and the falling apart," Levi said, thoroughly confused.

Tanna wiped her tears away with the heels of her hands, conceding it was a fair point. She slid off his lap and perched on the edge of the sofa next to him.

"Well?" Levi demanded.

She wanted to lie to him, but she didn't have the energy. "For the last few weeks, I've been battling with flashbacks of my accident, with anxiety and a range of other PTSD symptoms."

Levi stilled, his hand tightening on her thigh. "When did this start, exactly?"

Tanna pulled Ronan's jacket tightly across her body. "A couple of weeks before I left London, I attended an accident. A teenage girl was trapped, and they had to cut her out of the car."

"Just like you."

No. Wrong. He didn't understand. "Not me—she looked just like Addy. I felt like I was back there, in the car, with her. At that accident scene, I was the first person to reach the girl, but I froze. I couldn't treat her. I zoned out. My colleague had to take over." Tanna nodded, staring at the wall behind him. "Like Addy, she didn't make it. She stopped breathing and I can't help thinking if I had done something for her sooner, I could've saved her."

She hadn't admitted this, not even to herself. But Tanna knew she had to lance this wound, allow the muck to flow out. "I feel so damn guilty, Lee. About her and about Addy. Since then I've been having flashbacks, anxiety and really bad dreams, and worse than that, I second-guessed myself on the couple of rescues I attended after that. My supervisor sent me to a psychologist, and I was put on medical leave. They strongly recommended I take a vacation and that I use the time to get therapy for my PTSD symptoms. And if I don't get it sorted out, I won't have a job."

Tanna stood up, sliding her arms into the sleeves of Ronan's jacket. She pulled in a long breath, held Levi's eyes and forced herself to speak. "I didn't fall apart just now because I had flashbacks, Levi."

"Okay." Levi frowned, puzzled. "I don't understand what you are trying to tell me, Tanna."

"I fell apart because I *didn't*," Tanna quietly stated. "I saw Sadie and I knew what I had to do, and how. I didn't think about the accident, about Addy, about that night so long ago. I just did my job."

Tanna sent him a small, sad smile. "I think I've conquered my demons, Levi."

She could go back to London, return to her job.

So why wasn't she ecstatically happy?

The next morning, Levi walked into his kitchen, crutches under his arms. Jules and Darby and Callie stood at three of the four corners of the big table, each holding a stack of different colored rectangles. The table was covered by a large piece of paper printed with circles.

The heading Lockwood–Brogan Seating Arrangements was a solid clue they were discussing his least favorite subject.

Again.

"Why does wedding planning have to take place at my house?" he demanded.

"Because Noah threatened to kidnap me and whisk me off to Vegas if I asked him one more wedding-related question," Jules told him, her attention elsewhere.

Noah was getting married and Levi was the one suffering for it? So not fair.

"Where's Tanna?" Callie asked after he gave her a kiss on her cheek. His mom looked amazing, happy and fit. Mason was good for her.

Levi didn't think he was good for Tanna.

Levi rubbed the back of his neck, thinking back to the night before. After her rock-his-world declaration, Tanna had extracted herself from his arms and headed for the restroom. When she returned, she was extraordinarily pale but dry-eyed and composed.

And as remote as a Siberian wilderness.

Instead of sleeping with him downstairs, she'd returned to the guest room and he'd given her the space she so obviously required. He'd barely slept himself, missing her soft breathing, her soft body, her gorgeous, feminine scent. He needed to see her, now. Immediately.

Crap, he was toast.

"So, what actually happened last night?" Callie asked. "I heard Tanna was involved in an emergency rescue at the Murphy cocktail party."

Levi couldn't believe how fast news traveled in Boston. And Callie, once one of Boston's most popular socialites, was still one of the first people to hear anything interesting.

Darby's head shot up. "What happened?" she asked, placing rectangles around a circle on the table.

"Carrick's new art detective choked and Tanna gave her an emergency tracheotomy," Levi told them, heading for the coffee machine. "She saved her life."

Jules's eyes widened. "That is so cool."

It was cool. But saving people had taken an enormous toll on Tanna and nobody realized the heavy burden she carried. And, as much as Tanna wanted to believe she was cured, he wasn't convinced PTSD symptoms came and went that quickly. In a few weeks, months, there might be another trigger and the symptoms could come roaring back.

He knew what she needed, and it wasn't a career that made her relive that long ago, horrible night in all its Technicolor gruesomeness. He'd been so angry with her for so long, but he'd finally accepted and understood why she'd needed to run.

And how naive he'd been to think she was ready for marriage a few months after a serious accident, after seeing her friend die. How arrogant he'd been to think that by pulling her into marriage, pulling her under his wing, he could just make those horrible memories go away.

He'd wanted to protect her, had been so convinced marriage was the way to do that. He'd been so damn determined not to let anything bad happen to her again, to wrap her up in cotton wool, to love the memories of that night away.

But trauma couldn't be wished away, or simply forgotten or camouflaged by a white wedding and good sex. It had to be dealt with, examined, worked through, looked in the eye and wrestled with.

Tanna had been attempting to come to terms with her trauma by choosing a career where she could make a difference, to atone. To give back and lessen the survivor's guilt she lived with.

But Levi knew what she did not: guilt couldn't be assuaged by doing a job she hated.

Okay, maybe *hate* was too strong a word—a job she was good at but didn't particularly enjoy. Because her eyes didn't light up with excitement when she spoke about emergency medicine, her lips didn't curl upward like they did when she was talking about a painting or admiring the design of a dress, the intricate work that went into making Victorian-era jewelry.

He knew what she didn't: she belonged in Boston, at

Murphy's, working in a field she adored, with her family. She'd blossomed since she'd come back to Boston. And her unfurling had nothing—okay, maybe a little—do with him. But any fool could see she was happy here, that Boston was where she needed to be.

Levi stared out the kitchen window, thinking hard. His agreement with Tanna, if they could still call it by that name, had only a few weeks left. Revenge was forgotten and he'd moved past the idea of a no-strings fling. He didn't have much time to persuade her not to go back to London, to start a new life, or a new chapter of her life, in Boston.

With him.

Levi pushed his phone into the back pocket of his faded jeans and stared out onto the snow-covered back garden. They were older, wiser, still crazy attracted.

They worked. Nobody else did, or ever would. She was his person and she belonged in Boston, with him.

And damn, it was time she realized that.

Levi wanted her in his house and his life. He still wanted to marry her, wanted her to be the only one to wear his ring.

His heart lurched into his throat and felt like it was stuck there. He'd tried that once before and it hadn't worked out. She'd bailed.

She wouldn't do that again, he argued with himself.

Or, if she wanted to, he was pretty sure he could talk her out of it.

They'd made no promises, but he could see their connection—it was too early, and he was too scared to call it love—in her eyes. It was in her actions, in her touch, and he sensed it when she curled up into him, pulling his arm around her to hold her close. He saw it in the way she loved to touch him—from soft, gentle, I'm-so-glad-you're-here touches to hot, greedy kisses at night.

It would be okay—it had to be. Life would never be so cruel as to give him a taste of her only to rip her from his life again.

They'd make it this time. They were stronger, wiser, older, more sensible. It would be fine...

"Levi, where do you think we should put Cousin Bob?"

Levi gripped the bridge of his nose with his thumb and index finger. "The point is, why would you invite him in the first place? He's a stepcousin once removed and we only ever see or speak to him at weddings. Or funerals."

"He's family!" Jules protested, but her eyes told him she was willing to be convinced.

"If you invite him, you're asking for trouble."

Jules nodded. She crumpled the rectangle and tossed it at Levi's chest. "Cousin Bob will not receive his formal invitation. That okay with you, Mom?"

"Since the man tried to French kiss me on my wedding day, I'm more than okay with it." Callie smiled, her eyes far away. "Your dad punched him, sent him flying into the cake."

His sisters' mouths fell open and Levi laughed.

"I've seen pictures of your cake. It was beautiful," Jules wailed.

"And it tasted like sawdust. All of Aunt Penelope's cakes did. She was brilliant at icing, but her cakes were revolting," Callie explained. "I wasn't upset."

Weddings, Levi thought. He couldn't wait for this one to be over. But, as soon as it was done, he'd have to listen to DJ's plans, then Darby's. Why was life punishing him like this? And why in his own house?

"Morning."

Levi's head spun around to see Tanna across the room, standing in the doorway, dressed in jeans, boots and her thigh-length leather coat. With a multicolored scarf wrapped around her throat, she looked like she was heading out.

She probably wanted some air, Levi told himself. Maybe she thought they needed supplies—he had to be misreading the *I'm leaving* sign flashing in her eyes.

He was overreacting...

He hoped.

Tanna answered the few questions his nosy sisters threw at her about last night's excitement, her answers becoming more clipped as the discussion progressed. Yeah, she was still upset by Sadie's choking incident and she didn't want to rehash it.

Tanna stepped into the kitchen and put her hands into the pockets of her coat. It was warm in the kitchen. In a second, she'd slip it off, head for the coffee machine, slide into a chair.

Tanna just looked down at the large sheet, her expression curious. "Are you trying to torture Levi with wedding plans?"

He was pretty sure that was their intention. "I don't have any room at Lockwood House," Jules replied.

Yeah sure, he wasn't buying what she was selling. Jules lived at Noah's family estate, Lockwood House, the first house in the country-club community, and still magnificent. Callie and Darby, beneficiaries of the Brogan Family Trust, lived in houses just as big.

"BS," he said.

Jules exchanged a look with Callie and gently shrugged. "Being here makes me feel closer to Dad. It's as if I'm waiting for him to come in from work, just hanging like we used to do. He'd be so involved in the planning, driving me nuts—"

Levi stared down at his coffee cup, wishing he could ignore the jealousy he always experienced when he heard the sad, wistful, loving note in his sisters' voices when they spoke of their father.

His relationship with his father had been so different from the twins'. With them their dad had been softer, more relaxed, kinder. They hadn't seen the extremes of his personality, his drive and his reckless need to push the boundaries.

They had no idea their father took so many risks, that he flew so close to the sun.

Why was Levi so different from Ray? Why did he need to have everything tied up, corralled and controlled? Why did he feel the need to restrain his dad's actions, have this fierce need to protect his mom and sisters? Where had that come from and why was he like that?

He'd always thought it was because his dad took too many business risks, but Levi had been anxious long before he became aware of his dad's business practices.

What had happened to make him feel this way?

Well, huh, so Tanna wasn't the only one who had unresolved issues from her past.

Tanna's shoulder pushed into his biceps and then her hand came to rest between his shoulder blades, her touch reassuring. Suddenly everything inside him stilled and his resentment and guilt retreated as her touch filled him.

He didn't need to be in control; he didn't need to have his life wrapped up in a box, tied with a bow. He didn't need much—hell, he didn't need anything—if Tanna stood next to him, in his house and in his life.

He needed her. Period.

"Are your brothers bringing guests to the wedding?" Jules asked Tanna, her question pulling Levi from his thoughts.

"Ah, that's not something they'd share with me," Tanna

replied, sounding apologetic. "But yeah, I guess they would."

"Okay, so do you and Levi want to sit with us or with them?"

Levi started to tell Jules it really didn't matter, but then he looked down at Tanna and saw guilt infuse her face. He frowned, and panic squeezed his lungs, tightening his throat.

Jules looked from the seating plan to them, her brow furrowed. "Well?"

Tanna bit her lip and her eyes clouded over. Levi's stomach hit the floor and bounced.

Don't do it, Tan. Don't say it.

Don't break my heart again.

For God's sake, don't run.

"Can I get back to you on that?" Tanna replied, her smile forced.

Levi wanted to feel relieved at not hearing the words he knew would change everything, but he couldn't. There was too much happening in Tanna's lovely eyes for him to feel comfortable. Or reassured.

Tanna forced a smile onto her lips and excused herself. Levi frowned, grabbed his crutches and followed her out of the kitchen.

Something was going on here and he wanted to know what the hell it was.

Twelve

Saving Sadie had been a sign from the universe, Tanna decided, walking out of the kitchen.

It was life's way of telling her that emergency medicine was what she was supposed to be doing, how she was meant to operate in the world. That Levi—and a life spent with him, working at Murphy's—wasn't something she could seriously consider, or consider at all.

And maybe she'd needed to come back to Boston to be reminded of that.

She'd grown up surrounded by amazing pieces of art, her childhood home in Beacon Hill was better than most museums. She'd been taught to appreciate the stroke of a paintbrush, a perfectly constructed dovetail joint, the fine placement of micro mosaics, the impact of negative space. She'd come to revere the Old Masters, to interrogate the meaning behind abstract paintings, to look beyond the surface.

Her family made their living from trading beautiful objects, from passing pieces of wondrous art from one collector to another.

But, when faced with death, their bodies battered and broken, people didn't think of Monet's *Water Lilies* or Fabergé's brilliantly constructed, jewel-encrusted golden eggs. Thoughts about furniture made in rosewood or bronze sculptures didn't happen.

Tanna would bet her trust fund Sadie had been more concerned with survival, in taking the next breath, in getting through the next second, the next minute, the next hour than she had been about those fantastic dresses she'd been admiring earlier.

People who were badly injured needed to fight and they needed a chance. Tanna's job, her training, helped them do that.

It was important. It was necessary. It was what she was supposed to do.

Tanna stood in front of the massive windows in the most formal of Levi's sitting rooms and ignored the richly decorated room behind her. If she stayed in Boston, if she continued to live with Levi, she'd slide back into being a Murphy, into the society princess she'd been before. Levi might not be as extroverted or as sociable as his father but he was still a Brogan, still one of the most prominent men in Boston.

And as a Murphy, she was a Boston princess, and if she stayed, she'd be expected to fill that role. If she joined the PR department of Murphy's then attending the social events of rich East Coasters, wearing designer clothes and shoes, would be part of her job.

How could she stand around talking art when she knew she should be out there saving someone's life? How could she live with herself? Within weeks, months, she'd be discontented; within a year she'd loathe herself. Why put herself through that?

And how would Addy feel, knowing she'd sacrificed her life so Tanna could be a woman who stood around drinking champagne, eating canapés and talking through the finer points of a painting with collectors who were wealthy enough to buy a small third world country?

Addy would be disappointed in Tanna and her actions would confirm all Addy's mother's accusations—she would be just another rich girl, her life sprinkled with fairy dust, unable to live in the real world and do a tough job.

The bottom line: Tanna hadn't cheated death to waste her life and her education. Yeah, she'd had a tough time in the hospital after her accident, but she hadn't suffered, not really. She was still alive, wasn't she?

She wasn't unhappy in London. She could cope. Okay, leaving Levi, not waking up with him, sharing his bed and his body, not being able to kick back and relax in his wonderful home, laughing and loving him, would be tough. But she'd left him before and, like back then, leaving Levi was necessary.

Besides, unlike before, this time her leaving wouldn't hurt him. He'd told her, without equivocation, that he'd never trust her with his heart again, that he'd never allow himself to love her again, so while he might miss the sex, he wouldn't miss her.

Her leaving wouldn't break his heart.

It might well break hers.

But she'd still leave.

She had to.

Levi found her in the formal sitting room, the one with the portrait of his father over the fireplace and a Picasso sketch on the wall between the two arched windows. He didn't come into this room often as this was the "formal" room, the one the family used for serious conversations.

These walls had heard more than a few of his discussions—or fights—with his dad. In this room he'd told his folks he banged up his brand-new car, and the walls had been witness to the many fights with Ray over deals Levi thought were too risky, and to Ray losing his temper when Levi told him he was leaving Brogan LLC.

Few conversations in this room had ended well.

He was pretty sure this one wouldn't either.

Tanna stood by the left window, her arms crossed tightly against her chest, staring out the window at the snow falling outside.

Winter in Boston. Cold enough to freeze the balls off any primate.

"Want to tell me what's going on?" Levi placed his crutches against the back of the sofa. He bit the bullet. "Why didn't you answer Jules's simple question?"

When he received nothing from her but heavy silence, his irritation started to build. "What's going on, Tanna?"

Tanna finally turned around. "You know why I didn't answer her question, Levi. I'm not going to be around for her wedding."

And there it was, confirmation of his biggest fear.

She was leaving him, again.

"So, you're still planning on going back to London in a few weeks?"

"No."

His heart soared, she was staying…

"I'm leaving today, flying out tonight. I called them and told them I was coming back."

Levi felt his battered heart, and all his organs, plunge back down to earth.

You're not going to die, Brogan. It just feels like it.

Levi swallowed and rubbed his hand over his face. "Is that a wise decision? How do you know you won't have an attack tomorrow, or next week?"

"Thanks for the vote of confidence," Tanna retorted before lifting and dropping her hands in obvious frustration. "Admittedly, I can't guarantee the panic attacks and the anxiety won't come back, Levi."

She continued to speak. "But they didn't affect me while I was working on Sadie. The tracheotomy was a scary, serious option and I handled myself. That's a huge improvement. I called my supervisor today, told him what happened, and he was impressed. He agreed I could come back on a trial basis, that I still have to go for therapy but if I don't have another attack on the job over the next month, I'll be fully reinstated."

"And what happens if any of your PTSD symptoms return?"

"As long as they don't affect my job, I'll deal."

He didn't want her to deal, he wanted her to be happy. Levi opened his mouth, ready to persuade her to stay. He'd start by telling her Carrick would employ her tomorrow, that she was both needed and wanted at Murphy's.

At the cocktail party, he'd seen the joy in her eyes as she spoke about art, how she loved interacting with their clients, charming both old and new customers alike. He'd listened to her long conversation with Jane about publicity for an upcoming sale of rubies, spinels and red sapphires. They'd been talking about how to publicize the "Red" sale and Tanna had been fully engaged in the conversation, her creative mind running fast and happy.

He knew she'd be so much happier in Boston, working at Murphy's, than in London, providing emergency medicine. But what did that help if Tanna believed differently?

He had to make her understand. "Why do you feel the need to go back, Tanna?"

Tanna shook her head. "I need to be out there, doing something important, playing my part."

Levi sighed. "At what cost, Tanna? How can I let you go back to London, knowing that the PTSD might come back and worrying about you being alone and in a strange place?"

"How can you let me?" Tanna's voice dropped a couple of degrees. "You don't *let* me do a damn thing, Brogan. And London is more my home than Boston."

Bad choice of words. Levi swallowed down his desire to howl. "Why can't you see that your place is here, that Boston is where you are supposed to be? It's so damn obvious. I'm trying to understand why you are being so stubborn, so determined to leave me, to leave Boston again. Work with me here."

Tanna's eyes shot green fire. "My place? Are you kidding me?"

Brilliant time to use misogynistic words, Brogan. You idiot. Maybe he should just keep his mouth shut. But then she'd definitely leave…

And that was unacceptable.

"We'll come back to your crazy notion that you still think you have some sort of power over what I do with my life…" Tanna told him, her face taut with tension. "I'm not leaving, Levi. I never came back."

Okay, then.

"I'm good at my job, Levi. Or didn't you notice I saved someone's life last night?"

"I was there," Levi said, trying hard not to sound snappish. "I also held you as you dissolved in my arms. Do you think I like seeing that happen?"

"Do you think I like having it happen?" Tanna shot back.

"What's important is that I didn't freeze or have an anxiety attack. That's *all* that's important."

"Not to me. Your happiness is important. Doing something you love, every day, is important."

Loving me is important.

"It's the price I pay, Levi, for the life I've had, the life I *have*."

Say what? What the hell did she mean?

Levi walked over to her and turned her so she faced him, her eyes defiant. "No, you don't get to brush me off without an explanation. Talk to me, Tanna. What did you mean by that last statement?"

"Can you please leave it alone, Brogan?"

Not this time. Tanna had been left alone for far too long. "Explain."

"Dammit." Tanna pushed her hair back from her face before unwinding her scarf from around her neck.

"Take off your coat," Levi told her. "You're not going anywhere until we thrash this out."

Wrong move because Tanna just narrowed her eyes at his barked order. "I'm not staying long enough to do that. Do you want to hear this or do you want to nag me?"

Keep it together, Brogan. You're not doing yourself any favors.

Levi tightened his lips and gestured for her to continue.

"Before my accident, I lived a charmed life—you can't deny it."

"You did lose your parents when you were a toddler."

"But I had my brothers who adored me. I was wealthy and protected, spoiled beyond belief."

Levi thought she was exaggerating but at this point he was picking his battles.

"Then I had a brutal accident, but I came through it, thanks to having access to some of the best doctors in the country. I even ended up falling in love with a handsome, rich guy who wanted to marry me."

This was a problem?

"Isla, Addy's mom, called me Little Miss Lucky. She said I lived a charmed life and that I had no idea what reality looked like."

"When did she say that to you and why am I only hearing about this now?" Levi demanded, furious.

"When I left the hospital, I went to visit her. She was not happy to see me. She basically told me I should've died, not Addy."

Levi's temper spiked and he reminded himself the woman had lost her only child. "She was grieving. People say things they don't mean when they are in pain."

Tanna tried to smile. "I saw her recently too, the same day I barged in here, actually. She hasn't changed her opinion."

Levi desperately wanted to hold her. "I'm sorry, Tan."

Tanna tried to look nonchalant but didn't quite get there. Isla's opinions still affected her. "I also overheard quite a few conversations between the nurses, some I'm pretty sure they meant for me to hear. Some of it was nasty, but a lot of what they said was true."

"Like?" Levi demanded.

"I was rich and spoiled and had no idea what it felt like to live in a world that frequently isn't kind and is definitely unfair. After all, only a girl sprinkled with fairy dust could survive a near-fatal car accident and then, during convalescence, find herself a handsome fiancé, making plans to go back to college to finish her degree while he supported her and then work at a cushy job in the family company when she was done studying."

"Sounds like jealousy to me. Why are we discussing this?"

"Because those women poured water on the seeds of discontent I was already feeling. I did feel useless, unsure of who I was and what I was doing. But mostly I felt so damn guilty about being alive. About continuing to live my charmed life when Addy was dead. I felt this urge to do more, to be more."

"And you couldn't do that, in Boston, with me?"

Tanna shook her head. "If I'd stayed, I'd always be your wife, the spoiled and pampered princess. I needed to leave, Levi. I needed—need—to do what Addy couldn't. I need to make a difference."

"You always were more, Tanna," Levi said, his voice growly from all the emotion he was trying to suppress. "You were the one who decided you were going to walk again, the one who refused to give up and give in. You proved everyone wrong. You have no idea how strong you are. And I, for one, am profoundly grateful you didn't die back then, Tanna."

Tanna lifted her fingers to her mouth, her eyes bright with unshed tears. He knew this conversation was hurting her but they needed to talk this through. She needed to understand. "I read somewhere one of the hardest things in life is to let go. Guilt, anger, love, loss, betrayal, it becomes a habit to hold on to it, and it's tough to let it go."

Levi lifted his hand to hold her cheek. "You need to let it go, Tanna."

Tanna stepped back and held up her hands, trying to put a barrier between them. "I need to let it go? That's rich coming from you, Levi."

Levi frowned, not understanding her.

"When are you going to stop trying to control everything because you couldn't control your dad?"

There were talking about her, not him. He was fine.

Well, mostly fine. And his relationship with his dad had nothing to do with her, and his feelings for her.

But, if it helped to move this conversation along, to get the result he wanted, he'd make a tiny concession. "We're both carrying baggage from our past, Tanna, but I'm not the one who is walking away, *again*."

Tanna glared, her jaw tight with tension. "What does that even mean, Levi? Are you telling me you want to start something with me?"

Levi shook his head. "Honey, we don't need to start a damn thing because we never ended it. I'm as crazy about you as I ever was."

Tanna stared at him, shocked. "Please! If you really mean what you are saying, come back to London with me, live in my small apartment, support me as I do my job."

Levi made sure his look was steady, that she saw his determination. "I could agree to that, and I would do that, in a heartbeat. But—"

"And here comes the but!" Tanna mocked him.

God, keeping his temper was killing him.

This would be so much easier if he just tossed her over his shoulder and locked her in his room, naked, until she came to her senses.

"But I don't think my moving to London would solve the problem because you would still be unhappy. You've been unhappy for a long, long time."

"And you think my moving back to Boston would resolve that issue?"

Of course it would! Why couldn't she see it? What was wrong with her? And what was wrong with him that he couldn't make her see something that was so damn obvious?

This was like arguing with his dad all over again.

"It sure as hell couldn't hurt," he muttered.

Levi tried to rein in his impatience and tried to even out his voice. "If I knew you loved your job, that it excited you, that it energized you, I could understand your wanting to return to London. But you don't. You're just going through the motions, trying to assuage your guilt, to make amends for something that wasn't your fault."

"She died, Levi! Because I was drunk and asked her to drive."

He heard the panic in her voice and shook his head. "She died because it was an accident, sweetheart. A horrible accident. Please stop punishing yourself."

Levi jammed his bunched fists into the pockets of his track pants. Although he already knew what her answer would be, he knew he had to ask. Just once.

"Don't go, Tanna. Stay here, with me."

Tanna didn't reply but her silence was answer enough.

He'd argued his position, tried to make her see the situation from his perspective, had been forceful in his opinions. But Tanna had held her position, she hadn't moved an inch.

He'd failed to control the rapidly deteriorating situation...

She was running away, again. From him, today. And he had to let her.

He had to let her leave. The thought hit him with the impact of a punch to his heart and, feeling a little unsteady, he locked his knees.

He knew that keeping her here—even if he could do that, and he couldn't—wasn't fair to either of them. She had to figure this out herself.

He wanted to be her choice; he wanted to be her person. She was his, she always had been, but he was an all-or-nothing type of guy; he didn't want to live with doubt—hers, his, theirs.

He had to let her go.

She'd run the last time, but this time he needed to respect her enough, love her enough, to stop trying to control her.

He'd lived without her once, he could do it again. How, he didn't have the smallest clue, but he would. What other choice did he have?

Levi stared down at the hardwood floors beneath his feet and gathered his courage, prepared to give Tanna the one thing she needed the most, unconditional acceptance, tangible support.

"Tan, baby, look at me."

Levi waited until her tearstained eyes met his and he fought the urge to sweep her into his arms, to love all that pain away.

But he couldn't, not this time. "Tan…go."

Tanna jerked back and her sexy mouth fell open in complete shock. "What did you say?"

Levi knew she'd heard him. "Go back to London, Tan."

"But… I thought…you… Crap." Tanna threw up her hands, obviously frustrated. "I thought you wanted me to stay in Boston, for us to be together?"

He did, as much as he wanted his heart to keep pumping. "You know I do, but I don't want you here if that's not what you want too. I only want you in Boston, back with me, if there's nowhere else you want to be, nothing else you want to do."

"I'll always want to work, Levi."

She wasn't understanding him. "I don't care what you do for work. I just care whether you love it. Whether doing it every day makes you happy. Don't you understand that your happiness is all I care about?" Levi sucked in some air and forced himself to smile. "I'd rather you be in London, doing whatever the hell you want, than being miserable with me, Tan."

"Lee…"

No, damn, he was done here. He couldn't do this any-more, he was done with being strong. She needed to leave…

So did he.

Levi stepped forward, dropped a kiss on Tanna's tem-ple and rubbed his thumb, just once more, over her full bottom lip. "For God's sake, be happy, Tan. That's all I've ever wanted for you."

Levi picked up his crutches, jammed them under his arms and headed for the door.

Levi sat on the expensive leather sofa facing his father's portrait, needing to be in the room where he'd last seen Tanna.

Sometimes he closed his eyes and imagined her stand-ing by the window, the weak winter sun turning her hair the color of a raven's wing. He could still see her perfect profile, smell her subtle perfume.

She was in his thoughts, his dreams, the place his mind went to every minute of the day.

He more than missed her—he craved her, longed for her. Hell, why not just be pathetic and admit that he was pin-ing for her? It was like she'd sucked every shade of color from his life…

Melodramatic much, Brogan?

If he didn't pull himself together, he'd soon find himself reading *Romeo and Juliet* and watching those cry-me-a-river breakup movies.

Levi heard the door open behind him and didn't bother to look around. It would either be his mother or one of his annoying sisters, none of whom he wanted to see. If he couldn't be with Tanna then he just wanted to be alone.

Yep, definitely pathetic.

Levi looked at his father's portrait and ignored his mom

sitting down next to him, shoulder to shoulder, thigh to thigh. Levi felt her concerned eyes on his face.

"I'm *fine*, Mom."

"Physically maybe," Callie conceded. "Your shoulder is healed, and you can move around without pain. Your body heals quickly, Lee."

He knew she was waiting for him to respond, but because he was both stubborn and obstinate, he didn't. He'd bet the contents of his bank account that his mom had more to say. And she would—she didn't need any encouragement from him.

"Your heart takes forever to heal."

Yep, there it was. His mom was trying to get into his head. He was almost too tired, too heartsick to care. "Whatever, Mom."

Callie poked him in the thigh with a rather sharp nail. "Don't you *whatever* me, Levi Ray Brogan."

Callie folded her arms and out of the corner of his eye, he saw her looking at his father's portrait. "Your dad. God, he drove me nuts."

Levi frowned at the hint of annoyance he heard in her voice. He wasn't going to ask, he really wasn't...

Luckily Callie offered an explanation before his pride took a beating. "Your dad was this big, bright, bold force of energy who loved to be loved. And I did love him, Levi."

Levi turned to look at Callie and, seeing her distress, rested his big hand on her knee. "I've never had any doubt about that, Mom. You grieved him for a long time."

Callie nodded. "I did. But when he died, I also grieved the person I was, the person I could've been."

Levi half turned, putting his shoulder into the back of the couch. "I don't understand..."

Callie's smile was soft. "One of the reasons Mason and I took some time to come together was because I didn't know who I was without your dad—there'd never been a me without him. I didn't know if I could be me, without Ray."

"Yet, I could only ever be me. I couldn't be the person he wanted me to be," Levi murmured.

Callie threaded her fingers through his, her eyes sad. "He'd agree his greatest failing was you, Lee. All our fights were always about you."

He'd not known that, and it added another layer of guilt to the heavy load he carried. "I'm sorry, Mom."

Callie's grip on his hand tightened. "Oh, no, that was on your dad, not you. You didn't do anything wrong."

"I was so mad at him, so often. I hated the risks he took, his lack of control. I hated him worrying you, putting everything we had at risk. He's been dead for a long time but I'm still so angry that I couldn't get through to him, that he was so damn impulsive and impetuous."

"But that's not the only reason why you're angry with him," Callie said, her voice low and sad.

"I'm pretty sure that it is, Mom."

Callie turned to face him, her beautiful face tight with tension. "You never forgave your father for nearly killing you all by driving too fast and spinning out."

Levi stared at her, conscious his heart was in his throat and his stomach was tying itself up in knots. He swallowed but his throat didn't clear so he swallowed again.

"I don't know what you are talking about, Mom."

"Yes, you do, Lee."

It was a memory he'd pushed down deep, something he, very deliberately, chose not to remember. He had been young, five or six, and he remembered the music blaring, the huge smiles on the twins' faces and his dad flinging them around the sharp corners of a long forgotten road, speeding up every time the twins yelled for him to go faster.

Levi had screamed at Ray to slow down, begging him to brake and yelling repeatedly that they were going to crash.

His father had mocked him for being a scaredy-cat and told him that his sisters had more guts than he did. His sisters had been too young to realize the danger they were in.

Then Ray lost control of his car and Levi remembered them spinning and spinning and spinning…

Levi scrubbed his hands over his face, recalling the dust, the sharp whine of the car scraping along the barrier, the twins' soft sobs and his father's white face. The long drop below them when they finally, finally came to a standstill.

Ray begged Levi not to tell Callie and he stopped trusting his father that day.

"He nearly killed us, Mom. It was so damn close." Levi croaked the words out. "He said I shouldn't tell you, that it would upset you terribly. After all, we were all fine."

Callie shook her head. "Your father couldn't live with himself and he did tell me, about three months after it happened. I was so mad at him and we didn't talk for weeks, months." Callie rested her forehead on his shoulder. "That's why you are so protective of the twins, why you never, really, trusted your father's decisions, about anything, again."

Her statement made sense. His lack of trust in his dad had been born that afternoon.

"Every time he took a risk, I think I was subliminally reminded of that summer afternoon and I hated him for it," Levi admitted. "And maybe I overreacted at some of the things he did—maybe they weren't as bad as I thought."

"Oh, most were," Callie admitted. "Risk-taking was his nature, Lee. Nothing you did or said would've changed him."

Callie leaned into him, her head on the ball of his shoulder. "For what it's worth and no matter what you think, he was extraordinarily proud of you, Lee."

Levi rested his head on his mother's. "That's good to know, Mom."

"But it's not what's keeping you up at night, right?"

Levi managed to smile. "No, it's not." He shrugged, looking past Callie's sympathetic face to the wet, miserable day beyond the window. "I miss her."

"You never stopped missing her, Lee. And I don't think your heart was healed from the last time she left. Hearts as big as yours don't heal quickly."

Yeah, not what he needed to hear. Levi slid down the sofa and rested his head on the back. "I let her go, Mom. No, I *told* her to go."

Callie was silent for a minute, maybe more. "I think it's amazingly brave of you, Levi. Because staying, or going, has to be her choice," Callie replied. "You can't force love, Levi. You know that better than most. You deserve to be loved completely, unreservedly."

Levi nodded. "But it still hurts like hell." Levi took a deep breath, knowing he could tell Callie this, that she was the one person who'd understand.

"Just for once, Mom, I want to be the person Tanna runs back to, not away from."

Thirteen

Carrick stood in the private viewing space overlooking the sale floor and watched Ronan work the room. His brother, their chief auctioneer, hadn't planned on running this vintage clothing auction but, thanks to Tanna, many of Raeni's old contacts and clients were present and all had expressed the wish to see a Murphy controlling the sale.

Their wishes were his command so his charming, fast-talking brother did what he did best: push up prices with wit and laughter and natural charm.

Carrick lifted his eyebrows when a dress hit the fifty thousand mark and shook his head. God, Tanna would've loved this; she would've been out on the floor, spotting bids or working a phone for a client who couldn't be present. Either way, she would've loved to have been part of the evening.

But Tanna was back in London and Levi wasn't answering his calls so Carrick could only presume they'd messed up their second chance.

Would any Murphy sibling ever find love?

Carrick was divorced from Satan's bride, Ronan's wife, Thandi, had died giving birth to Aron, his second son, and who the hell knew why Finn and Beah had gotten divorced?

He'd had high hopes for Tanna and Levi, but his sister's rapid departure back to London suggested their relationship had hit the rocks…again.

Carrick leaned into the wall as Ronan banged his gavel down, indicating the dress was sold. Next up was a vintage Hermès handbag, an item Carrick knew many of the buyers had expressed interest in. Although he was separated from his well-dressed and very loaded clients by a glass window, he could feel the energy in the room change. He'd been doing this long enough to know a bidding war was about to break out and he smiled; bidding wars were spectacularly good for the Murphy International bank account.

Carrick scanned the room, his eyes bouncing over perfectly made-up faces, coiffed hair, stupendous jewelry. He identified a few of his clients and smiled at Frieda Talbot, sporting a necklace of matched pearls the size of marbles and a don't-mess-with-my-checkbook look.

Along the sides of the room his staff manned the phones and standing to the right of them was a blonde in a rich blue-and-black-patterned wraparound dress and wearing high-heeled boots.

Sadie.

Carrick's heart kicked up and he drank in her features, smiling at the excitement on her face. A small smile played about her lips and her eyes flipped between the big screen on the wall, showing a picture of the next item up for sale, to the bidders in the room. There was a supermodel and a famous dress designer and an A-list Hollywood actress, so maybe she was a little starstruck.

Sadie lifted her hand to her throat and he remembered her doing that the other night as he slid inside her, warm and wet and wonderful.

He'd headed over to Sadie's apartment to see whether she'd recovered from her brief hospital visit but when he knocked on her door, a huge bunch of flowers in hand, she'd grabbed his tie and pulled him into her home and locked her lips on his.

Clothes started flying soon afterward and he'd ended up making love to her for most of the night.

The next morning, they'd both agreed it was a onetime thing…

But looking at her standing there, excitement in her eyes, he wanted her again.

But he'd mixed business and pleasure before and it had blown up in his face.

He'd be stupid to do that again.

But, hell, if he was given the opportunity to be stupid again, in that particular way, he'd jump at the chance.

In her fabulous and luxurious apartment in Marble Arch, Padma dumped a healthy amount of red wine into Tanna's silver goblet and pushed it across the marble kitchen counter that hadn't seen a pot, or a home-made meal, since 1992.

Padma had an arrangement with several Michelin star chefs in London that, if she didn't eat at one of their restaurants, they delivered. Padma—with her dark eyes, scarlet lipstick and complete self-confidence—had no problem bending egotistic head chefs and restaurant owners to her way of thinking.

That amount of self-possession both impressed and terrified Tanna.

"So, how was your first week back at work?" Padma demanded, perching on a bar stool on the other side of the counter and lighting up a cigarette.

Tanna shrugged. "Cold. Wet. Quiet, mostly. We did a couple of training exercises yesterday."

Tanna took a sip of her wine and ran her hand over her hair, pulled back into a tight braid. London was London; nothing much had changed in a month.

Although it did feel like she'd rocketed back a decade as her thoughts were consumed by Levi.

Was he okay? How was his leg? Was he missing her? Furious with her? She hadn't heard anything from him since she left ten days ago and she kept checking her phone, desperate to hear something.

But nope, nothing.

Tanna sighed, ripped the band from her braid and raked her fingers through her hair, wincing as her scalp tingled. If she were with Levi, she'd ask him to massage her scalp and he would, then his hands would move to her neck and her back, his fingers digging into her knots. But within a couple of minutes he'd become distracted and his hands would wander to her breast, between her legs...

Tanna blinked when Padma flicked her hand with a glossy, red-tipped finger. "Earth to Tanna."

Tanna ran the tip of her finger around the rim of her goblet. She couldn't help thinking about Levi. She missed him as much as she would an amputated limb. Had she done the right thing leaving?

She'd thought that when she touched down in London, she'd feel better about her decision to leave Boston, but it never happened. She'd thought she'd feel settled when she walked through the door to her Wimbledon apartment, but…nope.

On the first day back at work, at the end of the first week…

Nothing. Ten days later she was still questioning her decision, was still wondering if leaving Boston was the right thing to do.

"Have you responded to any emergency calls this week?" Padma asked.

Tanna nodded. "A car accident on the A3 the day before yesterday, a bomb threat at a politician's office."

Padma's expression turned speculative and Tanna knew what was coming next. "And how are you?"

"I'm fine, fairy godmother."

Padma's thin fingers encircled her wrist and she squeezed to get Tanna's attention. "Tanna, this is me. Tell me."

Tanna rubbed the back of her neck. "I've actually been fine," she admitted. "I thought the multicar pileup would be a trigger and I kept waiting for the anxiety to strike but nothing. Not when I was treating patients or later, when I was alone at home."

"Nothing at all?" Padma asked, her thin, perfectly penciled eyebrows flying upward.

She sounded like Tanna's supervisor, who kept taking her emotional temperature, constantly hovering. "Absolutely nothing. I think it's gone as quickly as it arrived."

"So, if the trigger was the accident where the young girl died, what made the PTSD symptoms disappear?"

Tanna was scared to call herself cured; she was asking for trouble if she did that. But maybe she had the symptoms under control.

Tanna thought about how to answer Padma's question. "I think it was doing that tracheotomy. I was terrified but

I did it. I cried all over Levi afterward but I think I cried it all out."

Padma sipped her wine before rolling the bowl between the palms of her hands. "Ah, you've finally mentioned Levi. I was wondering when you were going to pull him into the conversation."

Tanna undid the zip on her work coveralls to reveal the black T-shirt underneath. Was Padma preparing to sweat the truth out of her? "Can we turn the heat down?"

"No," Padma replied, putting her wine down. "It's not hot. You're just feeling uncomfortable."

"Anyone would be when faced with your tell-me-everything expression," Tanna shot back.

There wasn't a boundary Padma wouldn't cross, so Tanna waited for the third, or thirty-third, degree. Instead of throwing questions at her, Padma lit up another cigarette and, through the smoke, squinted at Tanna. "Do you love him?"

Of course she did. "I never stopped loving him."

"Uh-huh." Padma inhaled then picked up her wine again. Before taking a sip, she waved the goblet back and forth. "So, that being established, can I ask why you are in my apartment, in London, drinking my wine when you could be with him having great sex?"

It was a question Tanna asked herself often. "My job is here, Padma."

"They don't need medical people in Boston?"

"No, I mean, yes, of course they do," Tanna replied, flustered.

"So, you could be in Boston, with Levi, doing what you do now," Padma said prosaically. She narrowed her eyes and leaned forward. "Let's try that again… Why aren't you in Boston, with the man you say you love?"

Tanna could lie, spin her a line, but she was tired of lying to herself, and to others. "Because I'm scared."

"You should be scared. Love is scary." Padma shrugged, unfazed. "But what, specifically, are you scared of?"

"I don't want to hurt him again," Tanna fudged.

Padma sent her a hard-eyed squint, worthy of one of *Macbeth*'s witches. "Be honest with yourself, Tanna Murphy."

Tanna blew air into her cheeks. "How can I ask for more when I've already had, have, so much, Padma? When I'm alive, breathing, living, for God's sake!"

There it was, in black-and-white.

The crux of what she was feeling. She was fit and healthy and wealthy. Did she have a right to love and happiness, as well? She had her brothers and her trust fund and the means to go anywhere and do anything.

Addy never had the opportunity to live a fraction of the life Tanna had. Who was she to expect or want marriage and babies and great sex when Addy didn't get to experience any of that?

When Tanna finished her bumbling explanation, Padma leaned back in her chair and folded her arms across her Armani silk shirt. Ignoring both her burning cigarette and her wine, Padma pursed her lips. Tanna, who thought she knew Padma well, couldn't decipher her expression.

Whatever Padma was thinking, Tanna hoped she treated her gently. Her heart was split wide-open, her belly exposed, and vulnerability pumped from every pore.

Padma opened her mouth to speak, snapped it closed and shook her head. Hopping off the stool, she paced the area between the island and the kitchen counters, scowling at the expensive marble floor.

Padma, the most languid woman Tanna had ever met,

was expending energy. And that meant she was either upset or…pissed.

"What a lot of horse crap."

Pissed it was, then.

Maybe Padma wasn't the person Tanna should be sharing her inner fears with. Then again, she was one person—apart from Levi—Tanna could trust to give it to her straight.

"I have a question for you…"

Tanna nodded and reached for her wine. This conversation most definitely needed the soothing powers of expensive alcohol.

"Please explain how your living small, not having a relationship, not touching your trust fund has helped Addy."

This again?

"I've helped a lot of people, Padma. I've saved a few lives. I learned how to budget, to live within my salary, the difference between wants and needs. I think I've grown up."

Padma stopped pacing and her dark eyes pinned Tanna to her seat. "Maybe. But you didn't answer the question… How does any of that, how does staying here in London and not being with Levi, help Addy?"

Was this a trick question? "It doesn't. She's dead."

"So, why are you sacrificing yourself, sacrificing your happiness for a dead person? Is that something she'd expect you to do?"

Tanna swirled her wine around in her glass. "Her mom was so mad, Padma. So angry I survived, and Addy didn't. To her, it was just another example of the rich getting everything they wanted and the poor getting the bad deal."

Padma winced. "The woman lost her only child, Tanna. But that's her perception, not yours. You can't make your life smaller, deny yourself happiness because Addy died. In fact, many people would say you should honor her memory by living the best life you can. You've paid back any debt you think you owe, Tanna."

Padma took both Tanna's hands in hers and squeezed. "Nobody is going to forgive you, Tanna. No one is going to say it is okay, to tell you that you are allowed to be happy. No one is going to give you permission to fall in love, to get married, to have babies. No one is going to rescue you from yourself, fight these demons for you, pull you out of this rut of self-flagellation. You've got to forgive your nineteen-year-old self. You've got to accept you made a decision not to drink and drive and you've got to start believing it was the only decision you could've made at the time. Denying yourself happiness is just you punishing yourself."

"I—" Tanna didn't know what to say, how to process what she was hearing.

Padma wouldn't release her grip on Tanna's hands. "Do you want to stay in London?"

Tanna touched her tongue to her top lip. "No."

"Do you still want to work in emergency medicine?"

"No, I want to work at Murphy's, but it's so damn frivolous, Pad. It's not important."

Padma released an irritated sigh. "Picasso said the purpose of art is to wash the daily dust of life off our souls."

Tanna lifted her eyebrows at her godmother, not at the quote but at the familiarity of her use of the artist's name. "You make it sound like you knew him."

"I met him a few times in the early seventies. He was old, I was young. He thought I was beautiful, and I was... Anyway, I'm not going to let you distract me with tales of my wild youth."

And Tanna knew Padma had taken the concept of *wild* to new heights.

"Art…art is important, Tanna. The appreciation of beauty, the creation of beauty, is what makes us human. It makes us look inside ourselves, see the world from different perspectives, challenges us to think deeper. You're allowed to love what you do, darling."

Tann shook her head. "I don't want to go back to being a pampered princess, Padma."

Padma smiled at her. "Darling, you were a princess at nineteen. At nearly thirty, you are now a queen. You have fought battles, gone to war, lived and laughed and wept."

Padma lifted her fingers to push a curl off Tanna's forehead. "Baby girl, you are more than just a queen, you are a warrior queen! Now, straighten your crown and embrace your life, embrace love and be happy for God's sake!"

Tanna really wanted to, but denying herself was a hard habit to break. "I don't know how to do that, Pad."

"Well, I suggest you learn," Padma tartly replied.

A few more weeks and his cast would come off. He couldn't wait.

Levi rolled the elastic band holding the plastic cast sleeve down his thigh and over his cast, taking the cover with it. He hadn't wanted to repeat the duct tape experiment and lose more of his leg hair, so Tanna had suggested the rubber bands and they worked like a dream, allowing him to shower without getting his cast wet.

Levi wrapped a towel around his waist and pushed his dripping hair off his face. Gripping the edges of the basin, he looked up into the mirror and grimaced at his pale face and the strips of blue under his eyes.

He'd been pushing himself too hard, physically and mentally. Unable to sit at home in an empty house, he'd hired a limo and a driver to take him to work, staying there far longer than he should. And when he finally called his driver to take him back to the estate, he dreaded walking into a house that didn't have Tanna in it.

It had been two weeks and he was over feeling like crap. Dammit, he really envied the cavemen of the past. He wanted to go to London, wrap his hand around her hair and drag her back home.

No fuss, no talking… Yeah, those cavemen didn't realize how easy they had it.

That being said, even if forcing Tanna back to Boston had been an option, it wasn't something he'd ever do. He wanted her with him but more than that, he wanted her to *want* to be with him.

Nothing else would suffice.

So, long nights and busy days would be the way he'd be spending his time until he got the hell over her.

As if that was a possibility.

He was so sick of feeling…sick. Heartsore. Incapacitated. Slow. He wanted to walk freely, run, drive his damn car, make love without the discomfort of his cast. He wanted to go to sleep without having to take a pain pill or a sleeping pill or a combination of both, only to lie awake and ache for Tanna.

Man, he hurt. Physically and emotionally.

And, worst of all, he was starting to think she wasn't coming back. Not ever…

How the everlasting hell was he supposed to live the rest of his life without Tanna in it?

But he'd done it once; he'd have to suck it up and do it again.

His life…such fun.

"You look like hell, Brogan."

Levi closed his eyes at the sound of her voice and prayed, begged God, that he wasn't hallucinating, that she was standing in the doorway to his bathroom. Because if he opened his eyes and she wasn't there, he didn't know if he could stand it.

"Hey, Lee."

Levi opened his eyes and saw her reflection in the bathroom mirror, her hair pulled off her face, her eyes dominating her face. She looked pale and tired—someone else hadn't been sleeping much.

The fact that they both looked like ghouls gave him some hope. Levi released his grip on the basin and slowly turned around, allowing his good leg to take most of his weight. Yep, she was back, dressed in faded blue jeans, a red cashmere sweater and her favorite black coat.

Swear to God, he was going to strip her naked and kidnap her clothes. She was never leaving him again.

He didn't give a crap. He was letting his inner caveman loose…

"How's the leg? And your shoulder?"

Like that was important. Levi finally managed to get his tongue to form words. "Come here," he growled.

Tanna tipped her head to the side, as if she was debating whether to obey him or not, but then she started to move. When he could reach her, he placed both his hands on her hips and yanked her into him, his mouth covering hers. God, he needed this; he needed her.

In his arms, melded to him, just like this…

Levi pushed his hands into her thick hair, keeping her head still as he devoured her mouth, reacquainted himself with her taste. There was a hint of coffee on her tongue but mostly he could taste her… Tanna. His head swam.

She was here and he wasn't letting her go. Not again.

He didn't care if he had to beg or grovel or move to bloody London, he was going to live his life with her.

She was his person...the other half of his soul.

Cool feminine hands skimmed down his rib cage and long, elegant fingers fluttered over his stomach and slid over the skin just above his towel. His body was telling her how happy it was to see her again and Tanna's thumb drifted over his erection. Levi groaned.

This would be a good time to sweep her into his arms, carry her up the stairs and toss her on the bed. He wanted to do that, more than he wanted to breathe. "I wish I could carry you to bed."

"In a few weeks, I'll hold you to your wish." Tanna murmured her reply against his mouth. "But for now, let me love you."

The towel fell to the floor and Tanna's hands wrapped around his shaft, setting off red and blue and gold fireworks in his brain.

Wait...what did that mean?

Was she back to stay or was she just going to stay until he was fully recovered?

Levi started to ask her but then she dropped to her knees, covered him with her lips and Levi forgot how to talk. Or think.

He could only grip the basin behind him as waves of pleasure rolled over him.

A little while later, Tanna pushed a cup of coffee across the kitchen table toward Levi, who was still looking at her with a what-the-hell-is-happening expression on his bemused face. Tanna lifted her mug to her lips to hide her smile. She hadn't planned on making love to her man in that particular way as a honey-I'm-home gift, but it was hella effective.

And she rather liked seeing Levi caught off guard.

Levi, now dressed in track pants and a Henley, sleeves pushed above his elbows, looked at her as if deciding whether she was a figment of his imagination or not. To help him along, Tanna pinched the skin on the top of his hand.

"Ow!" Levi glared at her. "What the hell?"

"I'm back—get used to it," Tanna told him, taking the seat opposite.

Levi carefully placed his coffee cup on the table and pushed it away from himself. He rested his forearms on the table too, and sent Tanna a hard look. "As happy as I am to see you, and as much as I enjoyed what happened in the bathroom, I'm going to be brutally honest with you, Tan."

"What? Just for a change?"

Levi ignored her sarcastic quip. "If you're not staying or if you intend to leave again in a few weeks, just do it now. Just walk out and don't come back. I want you, God knows how much I want you, but I can't handle you jumping in and out of my life, Tanna." Levi pushed a shaking hand through his hair and Tanna's throat closed at the emotion in his eyes. "I love you, dammit, but I'm an all-or-nothing type of guy."

"I know, Lee."

Tanna held his eyes, but didn't say anything more. She wanted to tell him she'd packed up her apartment in London, that all her furniture, books and boxes were in a container and were due to arrive in Boston in a week. She wanted to ask him whether she should rent an apartment or move back into the house in Beacon Hill or whether he wanted her here. Whether he'd consider marriage again, children...

With her obviously. But the words, big and hot and scary, were stuck in her throat. Why couldn't she say anything?

Why now, at one of the most important times of her life, was her brain overloading, her tongue not functional?

Because this was so big, so important, so life-changing…

And she was terrified.

Levi pushed his chair back and started to stand up. "Okay, well, your silence is your answer."

Wait! What? No, it wasn't!

Tanna leaned forward and cleared her throat. "Sit down, Levi. Please?"

Levi glared at her, obviously frustrated, but he sat down, his eyes on his mug of coffee. Tanna, knowing it was do-or-die time, cleared her throat. She didn't have time to marshal her thoughts or pick her words, she just had to speak. "I'm a lucky woman, Lee. So incredibly blessed."

Levi narrowed his eyes at her, frustration leaping into them. "Are you really going to spout that BS again?"

Tanna smiled at his irritation. "I *am* lucky, Levi. I had a couple of bad things happen to me but really, in the scheme of things, I was extremely fortunate. I had my brothers when my parents died, I had excellent medical care and I found you. Being loved by you has been the greatest blessing of my life."

"But?"

Tanna reached across the table and placed her hand on his wrist, tracing the raised veins with the tips of her finger. "I'm sorry for the way I left you, Levi, but I'm not sorry for leaving. I needed to do that. I needed to live a different life. I needed to do what I did. I very much needed to stand on my own two feet."

"You're not telling me anything new here, Murphy," Levi growled, impatient.

Tanna stroked the length of his ring finger. "But I'm done with feeling guilty, done with thinking I don't deserve love and happiness because I lived this sprinkled-with-fairy-dust life."

"You lost your parents, you had an accident and you worked your ass off to walk again. Where was the fairy dust while you were in the hospital?" Levi demanded.

"You were my fairy dust, Lee. You and your mom and my brothers, you were there every step of the way. In the midst of my pain, I fell in love—who does that happen to?—and I got a mom at the same time. I fell in love with Callie about the same time I fell in love with you."

Tanna touched her top lip with her tongue. "Back then, and up until recently, I couldn't help contrasting my life with Addy's. I felt guilty and the guilt grew and grew. I needed time to work through it, to work through a bunch of stuff."

"Are you done with that?" Levi asked her, his tone gruff but his eyes, finally, hopeful.

Tanna nodded. "Yep, I'm done. I mean, I feel incredibly lucky but I'm going to just be grateful and not let my past stop me from being happy. From living the life I want to lead."

Levi tangled his fingers in hers, his grip tight. "And what type of life do you want to lead, Murphy?"

Tanna shrugged. "It doesn't matter, as long as you're in it. I'll take anything you can give me." Tears brightened her eyes. "I'm not proud. I just want you, however I can get you."

Levi stared at her for a long minute, maybe two, and Tanna squirmed in her chair, wishing she could figure out what was going on in those dark blue eyes. His were the eyes she wanted to look into for the rest of her life.

"Nope. I'm not buying that. What do you really want?" Levi demanded. "I need to know, Tanna."

Okay, laying her heart on the line here. Fine, she could

do this. She *would* do this. This was only the rest of her life she was fighting for. She'd start with the easy stuff.

"I spoke to Carrick earlier and he wants me to join Murphy's, help out in PR, be the liaison for their wealthiest clients."

Levi narrowed his eyes. "Is working for Murphy's absolutely what you want to do? What about being an EMT? You worked hard to qualify, and it's important too."

His concern over her happiness made her feel all squishy inside. "I'm going to find an organization that can use my skills on a part-time, volunteer basis. Professionally, I think it's a balance that will work for me."

Levi nodded and Tanna saw his agreement in his eyes. Right, now came the hard part...

"Personally, I want to be able to tell the movers to deliver my furniture to this house. I want to move my clothes into a closet next to yours, use your shoulder as a pillow. I want to wake up every day to the sound of your breathing. I want to see your smile, feel your mouth on my skin, make love as often as we possibly can." Tanna broke off, conscious she was babbling.

Levi gestured for her to continue.

"I want to give you babies, fight with you, laugh with you." Tanna looked for a last little bit of courage. "I want the wedding we never had. But wedding or not, I really, really, want to be your wife."

Levi's eyes lightened and hope flared when she saw the humor in his eyes. He shrugged, aiming for casual when she knew he was feeling anything but. "So...ask me."

Tanna frowned, puzzled. "What?"

"I asked the last time. It's your turn now," Levi told her, leaning back in his chair, a small smile on his face.

His meaning sank in. Seriously? He wanted her to do this?

Levi made a circular motion with his index finger. "I'm growing old here, Murphy."

Laughing, Tanna placed both her hands on his forearms and dug her fingers into his bare skin. "Will you marry me, Levi Brogan?"

If he said no, after all this, she'd slap him. Really, really hard.

"And why do you want to marry me, Tan?"

Hadn't she explained all that in her rambling speech earlier? Then Tanna realized what she'd left out and she swallowed, tears clogging her throat. "Because I love you, Lee. So very much."

"Thank God." Levi leaned across the table and touched her lips in the sweetest, sexiest kiss she'd ever experienced. He pulled back, touched her cheek and smiled. "Are you going to bail on me again, Murphy?"

"I promise you I won't. If you say yes, I'm in this for the whole for better and for worse, richer, poorer, death do us part deal."

Levi grinned. "No obey?"

"Nice try, Lee." Tanna rose, walked around the table and plopped herself on his lap. Levi's arms immediately went around her waist to hold her tight, his mouth on her temple. After exchanging tender kisses, Tanna pulled back and stroked his cheek with her thumb. "You didn't give me an answer, Lee."

"You know my answer, baby." Levi placed his hand on her heart and copped a feel while he was at it. "Yes. To everything. To moving in, to babies, to marriage…"

Levi cuddled her close and Tanna felt like her life was starting over, as if she was cracking open a brand-new journal, the white pages begging her to fill the pages with love and beauty.

"I also say yes to spontaneous sex in the bathroom."

And laughter, Tanna thought as she blushed. They'd fill their lives, and the journal, with love and happiness, great sex and a whole bunch of laughter.

It sounded perfect, and best of all, she finally felt like she deserved this very wonderful man, and the life she'd been given a second chance at having.

She wouldn't, she vowed, waste a second of it.

* * * * *

ONE NIGHT,
TWO SECRETS

KATHERINE GARBERA

This book is dedicated to my kids, Courtney and Lucas. I'm so proud of the adults you've become. You know I love you more than words and that you both mean the world to me. Someday I'll have to reveal that my favorite child is… Just kidding! I couldn't choose between the both of you.

One

Throwing up three mornings in a row wasn't unheard-of for an O'Malley. After all, they were a family known to live life to the fullest, and that often involved excess. But Scarlet hadn't been drinking for weeks, ever since her best friend, Siobahn Murphy, lead singer for the hottest girl group since Destiny's Child, had broken up with her fiancé and he'd immediately eloped to Vegas with Siobahn's main rival. The paparazzi had been on Siobahn 24/7, and Scarlet had wanted to keep her wits about her to help protect her friend. She'd had her own experiences being hounded by the press, and wouldn't wish it on anyone.

Now Siobahn was safely ensconced in the guest room of Scarlet's East Hampton cottage, being watched over by Billie, Scarlet's personal assistant.

As Scarlet splashed water on her face, she went through all the reasons she might be throwing up. Food poisoning wasn't the issue. No one else staying here had been sick and her personal chef, Lourdes, was pretty scrupulous about kitchen hygiene.

"Not food poisoning," she muttered aloud as she wiped her face with a muslin cloth recommended by her aesthetician. At twenty-eight, she didn't have many fine lines or signs of aging, but still, her mother had always said it was never too late to take steps to prevent them.

You're distracting yourself from the obvious.

Scarlet looked in the mirror, knowing the voice was in her mind and that she was alone. She'd lost her sister three years ago to a drug overdose, but that hadn't stopped Scarlet from still hearing her voice at odd moments. Usually when she least wanted to hear it.

Tara had been a bossy older sister and apparently didn't want to stop giving her orders. Scarlet sighed and stared down at her stomach. She hadn't had a period in over six weeks even though she'd always been regular as clockwork.

Yup, you're preggers. Wish I was still there to see the old man's face when he hears the news.

"Shut up, Tay. I'm not even sure yet." Scarlet couldn't believe she was talking to herself, and that she was even in this situation to begin with.

If there was one thing the O'Malleys were good at, it was making money, living life full on and making colossally bad decisions. It went all the way back to her mother, who'd died when Scarlet was seventeen. Dying under mysterious circumstances that had been concluded an accident but many believed might have been more deliberate. Her father was on his sixth wife, and that didn't count the mistresses he'd had in between and often during those liaisons. Scarlet's longest relationship to date was twelve days, and honestly, she knew that was because they'd been on her private island and Leon's private plane couldn't land because of high winds.

She couldn't be pregnant.

If she was…

God, this was a nightmare.

She knew the responsible thing would be to give the child up. Everyone said she was spoiled, and she took it as a compliment. Her goal had always been to live her best life.

But a kid?

She had a few acquaintances who had children but they tended to employ an army of nannies to care for them. Her own childhood had shown her how alienating that could be.

She walked into her bedroom and fell back on her bed, staring up at the ceiling that she'd had painted to resemble the night sky. As she looked up at the "stars," Lulu, her miniature dachshund, bounded up the ramp that Scarlet kept next to the bed and hopped on her stomach. She petted her sweet little dog as she lay there trying to ignore the inevitable.

What about the dad?

Tara's voice again.

The dad?

That's right… Mauricio Velasquez. *Texan Humanitarian of the Year.* Other than drinking too much with her and hooking up for one night, he was pretty rock solid. And he'd told her about his large family and how close they all were.

She put her hand on her stomach again. Mauricio might be the best chance this baby had…if there was one. She'd have Billie get Dr. Patel to drop by later on today. If she was pregnant, she'd book a trip for herself, Billie and Siobahn to Cole's Hill. The tiny town might be the perfect place for Siobahn to recover from her breakup while Scarlet checked out her baby daddy.

Four hours later she was sitting on the couch across from Billie and Siobahn, who were both staring at her as if she'd lost her ever-loving mind. To be fair, she might have.

"Texas?" Siobahn asked again. "No way. That's the last place I want to be chased by paparazzi."

"Precisely my point," Scarlet reminded her friend. "They won't follow you there. It's the perfect move. I rented a house this morning in something called the Five Families neighborhood, which has a manned security gate. We'll have plenty of privacy."

"But why Texas?" Billie asked. "I mean, I don't mind going, but it's hot in Texas in July."

Not as hot as it was going to be when she found Mauricio Velasquez. Dang, but the two of them had burned up the sheets during their one night together.

"I need to see someone there, and we could all use a break," Scarlet said. "Trust me. It will be fun, and Siobahn, you'll forget all about Maté."

"I already have," her friend said.

"Liar," Scarlet said in a kind tone. She walked over and sat down on the arm of Siobahn's chair and hugged her friend.

"This will be good for both of us," Scarlet promised.

Siobahn looked up at her, and it broke Scarlet's heart to see her usually bubbly friend's sad, red-rimmed eyes. She would do whatever it took to distract Siobahn, and though she hadn't mentioned it to her friend, Scarlet knew that this pregnancy was going to be a distraction for both of them.

Dr. Patel had confirmed it—she was going to have a child. Scarlet was still reeling from the news but she'd always been the kind of girl who dealt with things by getting busy and moving. She couldn't stay in New York City or the Hamptons. She had to see Mauricio again and then she'd figure out this entire baby thing.

If there was one thing the O'Malleys were bad at it was taking care of someone else.

A baby.

She had always wanted someone of her own to love, but she had promised herself that she'd never have kids. She'd seen firsthand what happened when the wrong sort of people had kids. And she had never been anyone's idea of a "good girl."

She put her hand on her stomach and looked in the mirror. Mauricio Velasquez was a decent guy. He'd won a humanitarian award. He'd be a good father, right?

She'd meet his family and make sure, but she wanted everything for this baby that she'd never had. Two loving parents, and a family support network so that her baby wouldn't turn out like her.

Sunday brunch with the parents was a Velasquez tradition, one that Alec Velasquez had been lucky enough to miss for the last month thanks to various speaking engagements at different technology symposia around the globe. In fact, if he could figure out a way to miss this week, he would do it, as well.

He hadn't been back to Cole's Hill since the fiasco where he'd posed as his twin brother, Mauricio, to accept a humanitarian award on Mo's behalf in Houston and—damn. He'd had the night of his life with Scarlet O'Malley. But there'd been no way for him to contact her again. He'd tried to come up with a plan where he'd go to New York and just casually run into her, but then he kept coming up against how to tell her he wasn't Mo. He knew straight off that no woman liked being lied to like that.

At least he'd spoken on the phone to Mo's girlfriend, Hadley Everton, and cleared things up with her. After initially thinking it was Mo in the tabloid photos with Scarlet from that night, Hadley had been able to sort it out with him. And now they were engaged. That made their mom so happy she'd almost been okay with Alec missing all those brunches.

But she knew he was back in town and she wanted answers. Given that Hadley and Mo were engaged, everyone knew it was Alec who had hooked up with Scarlet O'Malley. Around town, the gossips referred to her as "the heiress." And unless he wanted to deal with the full force of his mother's temper, he'd be at brunch.

He sat down at his laptop and looked at the email to Scarlet he'd saved in his drafts folder. He kept changing it but every time he read it he knew he couldn't send it to her. He should be happy they had one night together and let it go.

He heard the ding of his security system and suspected it might be his twin brother, who had texted him that they could ride together out to the polo grounds where brunch was being held today.

He hid the email window on his computer and stood up just as his brother entered the room. The walls of Alec's home office were lined with leather-bound volumes of books; the interior designer had thought they would make the study look more elegant. But Alec had insisted that the books all be ones he'd read. So there was an entire shelf of Goosebumps and Harry Potter, all leather-bound, right below the Shakespeare and Hemingway.

"Morning, bro."

"Morning," Alec said. They did the one-arm bro hug and then he stepped back. "Where is your better half?"

"There was some sort of emergency with Helena's wedding and she had to go see Kinley this morning to solve it," Mo said. Hadley's sister, Helena, was planning a wedding to her high school sweetheart, Malcolm. They had faced a rough patch recently when Mal had gambled away their wedding fund. But the couple had come back together stronger than ever.

Kinley Quinten-Caruthers was a sought after wedding planner working for the famous Jaqs Veerland. Kinley was a hometown girl who'd moved back to Cole's Hill a few years ago to open a Texas branch to service high profile clients including former NFL bad boy Hunter Caruthers, who became her brother-in-law after she married Nathan Caruthers, the father of her child.

"What kind of emergency? It's a Sunday."

Mauricio shrugged and shook his head. "I have no idea. I'm told it's better not to know."

"Indeed," Alec said. "I guess we should be heading out."

"Before we do…"

"I knew it."

"Knew what?"

"That you were here for something other than to carpool," Alec said.

"Well, you've been shifty recently."

"Shifty?" Alec asked, arching one eyebrow.

"Mom's words. She suggested I use our twin connection to find out what's going on with you," Mo said, pacing over to the bookshelf. "I didn't want to tell her that it's probably a girl problem because that would activate her matrimony radar and you'd never have a moment's peace today."

"Thanks for that."

"You need to come up with something I can tell her," Mo said.

"Yeah, we don't want a replay of what happened when we were kids and you told Mom that I skipped soccer practice to talk to a girl." Alec smiled at the memory.

Harking back to their childhood provided a momentary distraction, but he knew that Mo wasn't going to let this go that easily. While neither of them believed in a psychic twin sense, they'd always been able to perceive when the other brother was in turmoil.

"And still it's a woman causing you problems—wanna talk about it? We have some time before we are due at the polo grounds."

Did he want to talk about it? Hell, no. He wasn't a touchy-feely sort of guy, and to be fair, neither was Mo.

"Not really."

"Okay."

"Okay? Mom would be so disappointed," Alec said.

"No she wouldn't. I suspect that Bianca is going to be the next one to try to figure out what's going on with you."

Alec groaned. Their sister would be a lot more persistent. Even though she was a year younger than the two of them, she'd always had a way of getting what she wanted from all of the Velasquez men.

"I don't think there's anything that can be done about this," Alec said. "It's Scarlet. I can't stop thinking about her but I can't contact her because she thinks I'm you. If I say, 'Hey, I was pretending to be my brother,' I don't think she's going to want to see me again."

There, he'd said it. And saying it out loud made him realize how ridiculous the entire thing was. He and Mo were thirty years old, almost thirty-one. The time for switching places with his twin had long passed.

Mo clapped Alec's shoulder.

"That is a tough one. But if I learned anything from my relationship with Hadley, it's that if you want a woman badly enough, you go after her. Apologize for your mistakes, tell her the truth and then tell her how you feel."

"Ugh. That's a lot of telling."

"Maybe you could write an app that would do it for you," Mo said sarcastically.

"Screw you."

But Alec felt better after talking to Mo. Maybe he

would call Scarlet or even take the jet to New York and see her. It wouldn't hurt. And then he'd have an idea if this obsession was simply because she was out of reach or if it was something else.

When they finally arrived in Cole's Hill, Siobahn decided to stay at the house but Scarlet was eager to find Mauricio right away and talk to him about the pregnancy. She had Lulu in the large bag that she carried her in when they were in a new place and Billie by her side as they drove into town for coffee.

She wasn't sure what kind of man he was; after all they'd spent only one night together and they'd both been drinking and dancing and laughing. When she'd woken up the next morning, he'd been gone, and she didn't blame him after she'd seen the paparazzi pictures from the night before that had ended up on TMZ.

Her life wasn't for everyone, but she'd gotten used to it. Tara used to say they'd been born a goldfish bowl and like good little guppies they'd learned how to preen for the press. There were times when Scarlet wished for a simpler, less public life, but to be honest she loved it most days.

In this town, though, no one seemed to pay her the least bit of attention. She could get used to this. When she stopped into the coffee shop to get her coconut milk latte, everyone left her alone.

"Do you know the Velasquez family?" Scarlet causally asked the barista after ordering.

"Everyone knows them. They're legends in Cole's Hill. I think they'll all be out at the new polo grounds today. I don't follow the sport but there's a former professional scheduled to play today... Dee, do you remember his name?" the barista asked the woman at the espresso machine.

"Bartolome Figueras. He's also a model. Oh, my, he's good-looking," Dee said.

"He is," Scarlet agreed. She had met him and his sister at a polo match in Bridgehampton earlier in the summer. She might even have his number. "I love polo. Do you think that we could attend the match?" Scarlet said, turning to Billie, who smiled.

"I'm sure you could. They've been doing monthly matches to raise money for a housing charity that Mauricio Velasquez runs," the barista said. She pushed a button on her register and some receipt paper came out. She ripped it off and jotted down a website.

"I think you can get all of the information from here," she said, handing the paper to Scarlet. "Have fun."

When they had their orders, Scarlet and Billie walked out of the coffee shop toward the parking lot.

"That was surprisingly easy," Billie said.

"It was. Let's go home and get changed. I bet Siobahn will want to join us," Scarlet said.

"I don't know about that. She's sort of in a funk this morning."

Scarlet stopped walking and turned to her assistant. Billie had been picking up the slack the last few days, looking after Siobahn for her while Scarlet had been trying to figure out this pregnancy thing. She hadn't mentioned the test results to anyone, even Billie. Only she and Dr. Patel knew.

"I should have stopped in to see her. I'm sorry I've been so focused on finding Mauricio."

"It's okay. I'm just saying I don't know if you're going to be able to persuade her to come with you to the polo match."

"Fair enough," Scarlet said.

They went back to the house. While Billie tracked down contact info for Bartolome Figueras's assistant and texted her to put their names on the VIP list, Scarlet talked with Siobahn. She wasn't in the mood to leave the house, so Scarlet left Lulu with her.

The polo grounds were busy when they arrived. Billie went to see if she could find out where the stables were. Scarlet moved through the crowds, searching the men who were dressed in traditional polo shirts and jodhpurs, scanning for the one she'd spent the night with.

She saw Bart first, and heard his sister Zaria's laughter. Scarlet smiled at the sound of it. The Argentinean heiress had a big, bold laugh that matched her personality. Scarlet headed toward them, then noticed Mauricio Velasquez was standing in the same group. He had his arm around a very pretty woman with thick dark curly hair that hung to the middle of her back. She watched them for a minute. Maybe she was his sister. But then he bent to kiss the woman, and not in a sisterly way.

Scarlet had never in her life been a timid person, and seeing the father of her unborn child kiss another woman made her angry. For a split second she realized she'd had a little fantasy of some sort of perfect rendezvous where they'd instantly agree to spend the rest of their lives together.

It was as if she'd forgotten she was an O'Malley and that kind of thing wasn't in the cards for her. She didn't do commitment. She wasn't programmed for long term. She'd seen what that had done to her mother, who couldn't handle being left by Scarlet's father as he'd moved on to someone younger, hotter and a little bit wilder.

Tara had been the same as their father, living fast and hard and burning bright for such a short time. But Scarlet had been confused, caught between two opposites. On the one hand, she had the dream of having the perfect family that at times she saw in old pictures of the O'Malleys taken when she was a child. And then there was the reality that she had never been responsible for anyone but herself.

O'Malleys were better when they only had to look out for themselves. It was what they were the best at... that and doing something outrageous and creating scandal.

Plastering a smile on her face, she strode determinedly toward the group, forcing herself not to look at the woman or Mauricio again. Instead she'd just play it cool and pretend she was here to see Bart. But as she got closer, she couldn't prevent her gaze from straying to Mauricio.

He was still handsome—damn him. For a brief second she wondered if there was a world where the Velasquez good would balance out her O'Malley bad. She'd heard nothing but good things about the Velasquez family and how close knit they were.

And it had created a longing inside her for the family that she'd never had and had always been a little curious about. Even though she wasn't built for commitment, it might be nice to be a part of this kind of thing for real.

"Scarlet," Bart said in his wonderfully accented English. "What a surprise! I'm glad you're here. Please meet my friends Mauricio Velasquez and his fiancée, Hadley Everton."

Fiancée?

What the hell?

She turned toward the man she thought she knew and noticed the set of his shoulders and the scar on his eyebrow. The man she'd slept with didn't have that. What the hell was going on?

"Hello, Mauricio," she said. "I believe we've met. At that gala in Houston."

"Well, actually—" Mauricio began.

"I'm the one you're looking for," a male voice said from behind her.

She turned to face the man and was struck speechless. He was a mirror image of Mauricio. He had a twin? In that moment, Scarlet realized that in true O'Malley fashion this situation had gone from bad to worse. A baby scare from a one-night stand? Sure, it happened. But learning that her baby daddy was an impostor, a virtual stranger whom she knew nothing about... Well, that was the old O'Malley bad luck.

Two

Alec really wished he'd figured out a way to send that email. The look on Scarlet's face as she turned to face him was one of shock, followed quickly by disdain and anger. He'd actually never had a woman look at him like that before and he didn't like it.

He prided himself on being a good guy.

He had always treated women with respect—he had a sister after all. He never wanted to be the kind of man who did anything to incur this kind of look.

In his head words swirled around like computer code when he was trying to figure out a new algorithm. He sorted through them with lightning speed.

But this wasn't the time to really talk. Bart, Mo, Hadley and the others were all staring at him. Mo and Hadley at least knew what was going on, but to everyone else… It had to seem crazy.

He reached for Scarlet's arm, to draw her away and speak privately, trying to ignore the fact that her honey-blond hair, falling in waves to her shoulders, seemed even thicker and more tempting than he remembered. Her gray-green eyes sparkled with temper as she shrugged away from his arm and turned, the full skirt of her flowy dress swinging around her legs. Her shoulders were straight as she headed toward a copse of trees on the edge of the polo grounds. Alec had no choice but to follow her.

She stumbled on the grass and he reached out to steady her.

"Thanks."

He nodded. He couldn't believe she was here. Or that his lie had been found out in such a public way. He knew he'd screwed up.

When they finally reached the shade of the trees, he immediately launched into an apology. "I'm sorry. I should have told you everything that night. Mauricio was sick with food poisoning and he asked me to step in and accept the award for him. For some reason, I thought it would just be easier to let everyone think I was Mauricio, instead of having to explain his absence. I didn't want the organizers to think that Mo had blown them off. It goes back to how we handled things like this when we were young. I should have told you, too, but by the time I realized my mistake, it was too late," he said.

She tipped her head back, lifting the hat that he hadn't realized she was carrying in one of her hands and settling it over her hair. Then she drew out a pair of large dark sunglasses and put them on.

"I don't accept your apology," she said. "Who are you? I don't even know your name."

Shame made him shake his head. How could he ever make this up to her? "I'm Alejandro. Mauricio and I are twins. My friends call me Alec."

"That's good to know, Alejandro. I think you should have told me when we got back to my hotel room."

"We were too busy with…other things to talk at that point," he said in his defense. "But you're right. I definitely should have stopped and told you who I was. I meant to do it in the morning but by then our photo was going viral and I knew my brother was going to be in hot water with Hadley. And I rushed out to try to warn him. Not that you should take that as an excuse."

She crossed her arms under her breasts and his gaze drifted down for a moment. He enjoyed the deep V of the bodice of her wrap dress before he realized what he was doing and brought his eyes back up to meet hers.

"Fair enough. I get why you left," she said.

"I'm sorry," he said. Was it actually that easy? He'd been afraid to let her know and now it seemed his worry had been for nothing. He might actually be able to ask her out and maybe get something started.

She nodded. "Actually, I need to talk to you about that night."

Talking was good. *Right?* He was a practical man. A rational man. But he'd been raised by parents who believed in fate and destiny, and a part of him thought Scarlet's presence in Cole's Hill had to be more than just coincidence. But what was it?

He easily attributed his longing for her to the fact

that one night hadn't been enough for him. It never was. One weekend…maybe. But one night—no way! Now he was standing in front of her and that ache he'd felt when he'd been trying not to think about her for the last six weeks was stronger than ever. So he wasn't going to walk away from it.

He'd learned early on that the more he denied he wanted something, the more he craved it. But Scarlet hardly seemed like she was going to give him a second chance.

And really, did he blame her?

No, of course not.

His smart watch buzzed, warning him he needed to head to the barn to get ready for the polo match.

He scrubbed his hand over his face and wished for once that he had more self-control. Though following his gut had led him to great success in business, this wasn't the first time it had landed him in hot water with his personal life.

"I have about ten minutes before the match starts," Alec said. "My family is having a brunch afterward and I'd love it if you would accompany me. So you can see I'm not a total douchebag."

"I don't think you're a *total* douchebag."

He almost smiled at the way she said it but he knew he was still in hot water. It reminded him of why he'd hooked up with her. She'd been so spot-on with her descriptions of some of the more pretentious people in the room the night of the awards banquet, they'd sort of started bonding over it.

"Will you please come with me?" he asked. "They all know what I did…well, at least that I kissed you while pretending to be Mo. So they will definitely understand you're angry with me."

"My assistant is here. Can she come, too?"

"Yes, of course. I think Bart and Zaria will be joining us, too, so there will be more familiar faces for you."

"Fine. I'll see you after the match," she said, walking past him in a cloud of feminine ire and Chanel perfume. He glanced over his shoulder, watching her retreat and ignoring the spark of excitement that was spreading through him.

She kept her cool until she was sure she was out of his line of sight and then she finally stopped walking like she had all the confidence in the world.

Whom the hell had she slept with?

She'd made some dumb decisions in the course of her life. Heck, who hadn't, right? But the truth was she was usually pretty picky when it came to bed partners. She didn't hook up with just every cute guy who came along, despite what the tabloids liked to print about her. And that night... Well, she'd thought she was connecting with Mauricio Velasquez. As for Alejandro—Alec—she'd had no idea she was being tricked like that.

Ugh.

"You okay?" Billie asked, coming up next to her.

"Yeah. I mean no. I don't know," she admitted to her assistant. "This isn't going like I planned."

Billie laughed in that honest way of hers and Scarlet couldn't help smiling. "When does it ever? What's going on here? You haven't told me a single deet except you wanted to reconnect with that guy you met in Houston."

Scarlet took her sunglasses off and glanced at her friend, trying to find the words. But they still escaped her. This was the kind of situation Tara had always found herself in. Usually Scarlet prided herself on being smarter about her personal life.

"It's complicated," she said.

"I'm all ears," Billie said.

"Well, I can't say too much here," Scarlet said, glancing around at all the people gathering on the observation deck to watch the match. There was a bar set up and a small buffet table. The conversation was about the Velasquez brothers; apparently one of them was married to the British jewelry heiress Phillipa Hamilton-Hoff.

"Later, then?" Billie asked.

Scarlet nodded.

"Do you need me? I thought I'd go back to the house and check on Siobahn and then go grocery shopping. I have two interviews lined up for later this evening with private chefs but I'm probably going to have to cook dinner tonight," Billie said.

Billie was obviously busy, and a part of Scarlet knew she should just let her get on with her job. What was she going to say to Billie?

"Scar?"

She just shrugged and shoved her glasses back on her face and turned away. The quick movement made her stomach churn.

Crap.

She didn't want to throw up here. She couldn't.

But she felt the bile in the back of her throat and put her hand in front of her mouth.

"Bathroom?" she said to Billie.

"Shit. Too far," Billie said, quickly realizing that Scarlet was going to throw up. Billie grabbed her hand and they started running away from the crowd as the first chukka of the polo match got under way. Billie drew her behind the side of the barn in the nick of time and Scarlet was sick while Billie squeezed her shoulder and held her hair out of the way.

When her stomach was empty, Billie handed her a water bottle and she rinsed her mouth and spit before standing up and turning to her friend. She'd lost her sunglasses somewhere and she needed them.

She liked the illusion that she was invisible hiding behind the large-framed glasses. And as she saw the surprised look Billie's brown eyes, she knew she needed to hide. Her friend wasn't going to buy any excuse. She knew for a fact that Scarlet had been on a detox, eating and drinking healthy.

"You're pregnant?"

Scarlet swallowed, her throat dry and sore. "Yes. But it's complicated."

"The father is that Mauricio guy?" Billie asked, taking a few steps away from Scarlet and picking up her sunglasses from the ground.

She handed them to Scarlet and she put them on. "I thought so. But the guy has a twin brother. They switched places that night."

"Okay, obviously we are mad about this. What do you want me to do? I can reach out to our press contacts and start a smear—"

"Not yet. I don't even know this guy. He invited me to join him and his family for brunch after the match. I was hoping you'd come with me," Scarlet said.

"Oh, hell yes, I'll be there. What's his name?" Billie asked, pulling her smartphone from her pocket.

"Alejandro Velasquez," Scarlet said.

"Shit, are you kidding?"

"Do you think I'd joke about that? Why? Who is he?"

"Well, let me do a quick internet search to confirm it but I'm pretty sure he's a tech genius who owns a billion-dollar software company."

"So why would he do something so immature, like pretending to be his brother?" Scarlet asked. "B, what am I going to do? You know my family… I thought—"

"I'll do some research while you watch the match. Then at this brunch thing we can see what kind of family he has, what kind of people they are. Maybe the switching-places thing was innocent. Whatever happens you've got me by your side," Billie said as she hugged Scarlet.

She wasn't alone. Why, then, did she always feel that way? Billie was the best assistant she'd ever had but, in a way, she was just like the nanny Scarlet and Tara had shared growing up. Paid family. Though she knew Billie wasn't with her just for a paycheck.

"Thanks, B," she said. "This has completely screwed with my head."

"That's saying something. Nothing ever rattles you."

She had to smile at that. She had built up a resistance to the kinds of situations that would freak out most people. But this… Maybe it was the fact that Tara wasn't here for her to talk to about it. Tara would be able to make her laugh about it even though a part of her was hurt.

Scarlet couldn't help but think that maybe he hadn't worried about lying to her because of who she was. Because she was the kind of person who'd lived her life going from one scandal to the next. She had a reputation. So lying to her hadn't worried him.

She hoped that wasn't the case.

But then she'd learned that hoping was a waste of time. She'd hoped her dad would stop marrying younger women and actually be a parent to her and Tara. She'd hoped that Tara would stop using and get clean. Now she was hoping that Alejandro Velasquez was a decent guy…

Alec had grown up playing polo with his brothers. The Velasquez family had been horse breeders for generations, and Alec's dad had been playing on a team with Tio Jose and their cousins since they were children. So riding was second nature to Alec. His four-player team generally consisted of Alec, Mo, their eldest brother, Diego, and the youngest Velasquez, Inigo, with either Malcolm Ferris—Mo's best friend—or their dad often subbing for Inigo, who was gone a lot of the time on the Formula 1 circuit. Technically Inigo wasn't supposed to play when he was home because of insurance concerns, but the Velasquez men had a problem with following the rules.

Diego was always number one—the goal striker. He'd always had a good eye for hitting goals, so it made sense for him to play in that position. Alec and Mauricio traded off being number two, the forward, and number three, the pivotal player who switches between offense and defense. Then number four protected the goal. Malcolm was really good at that position and since they'd grown up playing with him, he knew everyone's strengths and weaknesses.

But when the third chukka ended, Alec knew his brothers and Malcolm weren't pleased with his performance. It didn't help that they were playing against Bart and his friends, who'd all played polo professionally at some point in their lives.

Alec hung back from the others trying to search out Scarlet in the crowd. He finally spotted her standing with Zaria and laughing at something Bart's sister had said. Scarlet's head was thrown back and he felt a jolt of lust just seeing her happiness.

"You're not going to be in a state to even talk to her if you don't get your head in the game," Mo said, coming over to him.

His twin was known for his hot temper, but since he and Hadley had gotten engaged, Mauricio hadn't been giving in to it as often. For a while after Hadley and Mo had broken up he'd been getting into fights with everyone in town and drinking way too much. It had been Mo's way of dealing with losing Hadley while not having to admit he'd pushed her away.

"I'm trying," Alec said. "I wasn't expecting to see her today. Why is she here? And how am I going to make up for lying about being you?" he asked his twin. She'd thrown him and he wasn't used to being caught off guard. Part of the reason he was so successful was that he could usually envision all the possibilities in a situation. But this was completely out of left field.

He'd done some research on Scarlet—she was known for moving forward and rarely going back to anything or anyone.

Mo sighed. "Dude, I have no clue but winning the game would probably go a long way to impressing her."

Alec knew the outcome of this match didn't matter to her at all. "I think that would make you happy, not her."

"Maybe your right… But damn, you're in trouble now."

"What?" he asked, glancing over at Scarlet and noticing that his sister, who was almost six months pregnant, and his mom had joined the group Scarlet was in.

Oh crap. That was all he needed: Bianca and his mom over there talking to her. "I wonder if Dad wants to play for me for a minute."

"No. Don't do it. There's nothing you can say to make anything better. Plus, Dad hasn't played in a couple of weeks and he's taking care of Benito," Mo said, referring to their little nephew. "Come on, time to finish the match."

Alec's performance was as crappy in the last two chukkas as it had been in the first four. He gave his twin a wide berth when they were in the locker room, showering and changing. He wasn't looking forward to joining his family, who were up on the second-floor balcony of the main barn area. When Diego and Alec had started designing and developing the polo grounds, they'd known they wanted a place for the family to hang out after matches. In fact, Diego was hiring an event manager to run the space as it had become popular with many of the townspeople in Cole's Hill.

When he left the locker room, he went to the barn instead of up to the balcony where everyone was waiting, including Scarlet O'Malley. He wished he had his laptop with him but instead he leaned against Dusty his polo pony's stall, took out his phone, pulled up the internet and deployed the search algorithm that he'd developed to find all imprints left by a person on the web. It wouldn't help him in time for the brunch he was having with Scarlet and his family, but afterward he'd have a better idea of who she was and why she was here.

One night in her bed had whetted his appetite for her but he'd resigned himself to never seeing her or touching her again. There was just too much explaining to do, so he'd figured that she'd just be one of those women he thought about wistfully from afar. But now she was back and he wanted her, as badly as he had the first time he'd kissed her.

Dusty lifted his head and looked toward the barn entrance. Alec turned and saw Scarlet walking through the doors toward him. He took a deep breath as he pocketed his smartphone.

"Hello."

"Hi, Alejandro. I was waiting for you upstairs," she said.

"Sorry. I wanted to apologize to Dusty for my poor playing today," he said.

She tipped her head to the side and studied him. She didn't say anything, just crossed her arms over her chest and waited.

"What?"

"Nothing. But now I know what you look like when you lie."

He straightened away from the stall and walked toward her. "No, you don't. That's the truth."

"Are you sure? Because you have the exact same look on your face as you did when you introduced yourself to me as Mauricio."

Three

He stood there in the middle of the stables looking more at home than he'd been at the gala in Houston. She wondered if she was glimpsing the real man now. But then how would she know? Since they'd been introduced, he'd done nothing but lie to her.

"I'm sorry I lied to you, Scarlet," he said. "If there had been a chance to tell you the truth I would have, but I got carried away and the last thing on my mind once we got to your hotel room was explaining the rather complicated fact that I had helped my twin out by pretending to be him."

As close as he stood to her she couldn't help but inhale the spicy, outdoorsy aftershave he wore. She closed her eyes. The scent wasn't unpleasant, but she was pregnant and it bothered her the slightest bit.

Damn.

If she got sick in front of him, she was going to throw the biggest, ugliest fit anyone had ever witnessed. She needed the advantage here. She wanted to find out what kind of man he was before she told him about the baby.

She took a few steps back and turned toward the horse stalls that held the polo ponies. She didn't mind horses but hadn't really ever been a great rider. Tara had been the rider in their family. And since their father always insisted on making a competition of everything the two of them had done, they'd quickly decided not to pursue the same passions.

The queasiness subsided as soon as she stepped away from him.

She turned to look back at him over her shoulder. She'd left her sunglasses on when she'd entered the stables and now it was hard to see him. The lenses were very dark, and she couldn't make out his expression.

Maybe that wasn't a bad thing. She skimmed her gaze down his body. He wore a pair of white jeans with a black belt that emphasized his narrow waist and the strength of his legs. He also wore a light-colored button-down shirt and gray blazer. She wished he appeared unkempt or wrinkled. But instead he looked like the sophisticated man she'd thought him to be.

"So you're a tech guy?" she asked.

One side of his mouth lifted in a sort of half smile. "You could say that."

"I just did," she quipped. Something she'd learned from a lifetime of dealing with her father—a man she'd never understood and still didn't really know—was to always stay on her toes.

"Touché."

"What do you do?" she asked.

"I'll be happy to tell you about it over brunch," he said. "Should we go and join the rest of my family?"

"Not yet," she said. "I want to know more about you, Alejandro."

"Fair enough. I want to know more about you as well, Scarlet. I want to know the woman behind the headlines."

She shook her head. No one knew that woman… Well, maybe Tara had, but she was dead. And Billie and Siobahn saw what she wanted them to see. She had never felt comfortable letting someone all the way in. She doubted this man who'd lied to her when they'd first met would be the one.

"That's not how it's going to work," she said. "It's not a tit-for-tat thing. You lied about who you are. I didn't."

He came over and reached out, taking her hand in his. When he lifted it to his mouth and kissed it, a shiver went up her arm and awareness spread throughout her body. Here was a reaction she could understand. Lust. Pure and simple.

"I did lie. I'm incredibly sorry about that. If I could do it over, I would have told you who I was right away. But everything else about that night was me. I wasn't acting like Mo. He's much duller than I am."

He was inviting her to see the humor in the moment and if she hadn't been pregnant, if her family hadn't been the biggest mess on the planet and if she hadn't thought he was a better man, she might be able to laugh. But there was too much riding on this. She didn't want to give birth to another tragic little human who was doomed like Tara or her mom, or to be fair, like herself. And this man had been a ray of hope until she'd realized he wasn't who she thought he was.

"Are you ever going to be able to forgive me?" he asked.

Sincerity radiated from every inch of his body. He might be a great guy. She just didn't know him.

She shrugged. "I don't know."

"At least meet the rest of my family. I think you'll see that I'm not as big of an asshole as you take me for."

He dropped her hand and turned away from her, but she stopped him with her hand on his shoulder. She couldn't help letting her fingers flex against the rock-hard muscles.

"Did you do it because of who I am?" she asked. It was one thing she needed to have answered before she could move forward.

"What are you talking about?"

"Did you and your brother believe that lying to me didn't matter because you think I'm morally bankrupt?" she asked. It was one of the nicer ways her critics had put it over the years.

"*Dios mio*, Scarlet. Mo and I never discussed you until after it happened. I told him you were enchanting, beautiful and the kind of woman who made me forget everything but being by your side."

She caught her breath. She wanted to believe him. When she looked into his dark chocolate-colored eyes, she hoped it was truth she saw there. But she didn't know him.

She could only reserve judgment for now and tuck that sentiment away. Time would tell if Alejandro Velasquez was a man of honor.

* * *

Given that he'd done nothing but think about Scarlet since she'd shown up at the polo match, Alec was glad to be back in the company of his family. Everyone, including Bart and his sister, was milling around by the bar. Normally they'd be seated at the table and eating by now.

They'd waited for him, or more precisely for Scarlet.

As soon as they walked onto the balcony, Bianca and her sisters-in-law, Kinley and Ferrin, turned toward them.

"I should warn you that everyone here is going to be very curious about you," he said to Scarlet. "Also, I'm not sure if you've ever been in a small town before, but it's pretty much like being on a reality TV show without the cameras. Everyone will know who you are in less than a day and they'll want to know why you're here."

"Nice. I'm used to it. You saw how TMZ published those pics of us kissing before we'd even left the ballroom."

"Fair enough. I will say that generally most people are pretty nice here."

"I'll wait and see. I tend to bring out extreme reactions in people," she said.

"What kind—"

"Alec, where have you been? I'm starving but Mom wouldn't let us start eating until you were here with your date," Bianca said, coming up to them. "And it's not nice to keep a pregnant lady away from food."

"Sorry, Bia," he said, leaning over to kiss his sister's cheek. "Have you met?"

"We did earlier. I'm glad you're here," Bianca said

to Scarlet. "Now, how about if we mosey over to the buffet line."

She looped her arm through Scarlet's and drew her toward the food. As the two women walked away, he realized that it might be in his best interest to step back and let his family do their thing. Maybe their warmth and kindness would help convince her that he wasn't a total jerk.

"Mom would scold me if I didn't make sure you're eating, too," he heard Bianca announce as they walked away.

As soon as Bianca and Scarlet were at the buffet table, most of the crowd shifted from their conversations to line up. Mo held back and Alec went over to join his brother.

"So?"

"What?"

"Did you make things right with her?" Mo asked.

"In twenty minutes? It's a wonder that you got Hadley back. I mean you have no clue about women," Alec said.

Mo punched him in the shoulder a little harder than was necessary, but Alec knew his brother was still mad about losing the match to Bart.

"I think I have a bit more than a clue, Alec. After all, one of us will be going home with the woman he loves today, and the other one…"

"Will still be trying to figure out how he screwed up so badly. I don't know what it was about that night," Alec said. "Don't listen to me. I'm tired and have to leave for Seattle in the morning to meet with one of my clients. I'm a little distracted by that."

Mo shook his head at him. "It's not fatigue that made you say that. I get it. It's hard when you screw up. It took me a long time to get past my own anger and realize that I had to change if I wanted Hadley back in my life."

"But you knew she wanted you back," he said.

"Not really," Mo said. "You'll figure this out. Be yourself and see what happens. It's not like all your hookups show up in Cole's Hill. She must be back for a reason."

A reason?

Well, that showed how screwed up he was that he'd never stopped to think about why she had sought him out. Was she in trouble?

She was an heiress with her own reality show and an A-list lifestyle. He doubted she'd come looking for him to solve a problem for her. Maybe she hadn't been able to write off their night together as a onetime thing.

By the time he got his plate of food, there was only one chair left at the table, conveniently between Scarlet and Hadley. He took the seat and noticed that a woman he didn't know was seated across from him. He guessed she must be Scarlet's assistant. She had midnight-black hair that she wore in a ponytail and large sunglasses pushed up on her forehead. When their gazes met, she glared at him.

She was definitely Scarlet's friend. He didn't need to guess how she felt about him. "I'm Alejandro."

"I know," she said.

"And you are?"

"Billie Sampson," she said. "I'm here with Scarlet."

"I guessed," he said. "So are you from New York originally?"

He had learned a long time ago that if he kept asking questions eventually whoever he was talking to would relax.

"No. I'm originally from Maine."

"I have some business interests in Maine," he said. "I need to plan a visit. Can you recommend a time of year?"

"Yes." But she didn't say anything more.

He almost smiled. She was stubborn and he could tell she wasn't going to give him an inch. He respected that. He'd lied to her friend. He liked that Scarlet had someone like Billie in her life.

From what he'd read online, it seemed like her life was a big chaotic mess, but this interaction with Billie and his earlier conversation with Scarlet showed him how little he knew of the real woman.

Billie turned to talk to Ferrin. Alec took a bite of his food before glancing at Scarlet, who was watching him.

"You have a good friend in her," Alec said.

"I know. It takes a lot to tick her off and even more to win her over," Scarlet said.

"Like you?"

"Yes, just like me. It's just that so many people think they know everything about me that I hold my close friends to a different standard," she said. "They really have my back."

"I'm glad to hear that," he said. He wanted to be cool and just make small talk, but he had never been that kind of guy. He was someone who got answers; it was what made him so good at his job. He solved problems and helped companies by researching their digital imprint and finding ways to clean up the bad stuff.

"I'm glad you're glad," she said, a soft smile playing around her lips.

"I stink at small talk," he said.

"You do," she agreed. "What's on your mind?"

"Why did you come to Cole's Hill?"

Her face lost all color and she chewed her lower lip before wrinkling her nose and sort of shaking her head. "I'm not ready to talk to you about that yet."

So it was something... But what?

Scarlet enjoyed meeting the Velasquez family and their friends. During the lunch, Alec took a lot of good-natured ribbing from his family members about pretending to be Mo. Scarlet wished she could laugh about it but she wasn't there yet.

After they were done eating, Alec's nephew, Benito, and Penny, the daughter of Kinley and Nate Caruthers, wanted to ride the ponies, so the group went back downstairs so the kids could ride. Billie was deep in conversation with Ferrin Caruthers, the daughter of illustrious college football coach Gainer.

"Hey, Scarlet, come over here," Hadley called out.

She sat down next to Hadley, who was engaged in an intense conversation with her sister and her sister's fiancé. Hadley leaned closer to Scarlet. "So, I figure you and I are the only ones who don't think the fact that Mo and Alec switched places is funny."

"Yeah. I mean I get that this family likes to joke but it was kind of a dumb thing for grown men to do," Scarlet said.

"I agree. Do you know why they did it?"

"No. Alec has promised to tell me when we're alone," she said.

"Well, it's totally Mo's fault. You should know that to begin with. He got sick with food poisoning and didn't want to cancel. So, he asked Alejandro to accept the award for him, and read the prepared speech."

"It sounds so reasonable when you say it like that," she said softly, almost to herself.

"It does. But, of course, I saw the photo of the two of you kissing and I thought it was Mo. He and I have some history, so it caused problems for us. Once we talked, I got why they did it, but it still hurt to see his name and yours linked together everywhere on social media," Hadley said. "I think… I can't speak for Alec but once he realized the photo was everywhere, he rushed to Mo to try to fix things. Still, I know that doesn't make him a good guy in your eyes."

Scarlet leaned back in the chair and tipped her head up to stare at the summer sky. It was hot, and she felt sticky and tired. Hearing Hadley's explanation of the lie didn't make her feel better. She was more confused than ever.

Alec should have said something to her at some point that night.

"Thanks for sharing that with me," she said, realizing that Hadley was waiting for a response from her.

"It didn't help, did it?"

"No. I'm still ticked."

"Me, too," Hadley said. "Half the town thinks I took Mo back after he kissed you."

"They think we just kissed?" Scarlet asked.

"Well, probably more, but I'm not giving them any

of my time. The thing with Mo and me is more complicated because we have a long relationship. So, I've definitely seen the real guy behind the hottie that everyone in the town thinks he is. I've seen him angry and sad and apologetic. He's real to me. I don't think that Alec is that way for you yet."

"He's not," Scarlet admitted. "I don't know that he ever will be."

"If you need someone to talk to," Hadley said, "I'm here. In fact, I'm hosting book club at the Bull Pen on Friday night if you want to join us."

"What's the Bull Pen? What book are you reading?"

"It's a bar and music hall on the outskirts of Cole's Hill. We never read a book but just call it book club so our moms won't be on us about going out too much. Funny how a weekly book club is fine, but drinks aren't."

Scarlet had to smile at the way Hadley said it. "Who will be there?"

"Let's see. My best friends, Zuri and Belle, and Helena if her fiancé, Malcolm, is working late," Hadley said. "You can bring Billie if you want."

"Let me talk to her and see if she wants to come. My friend Siobahn is here with me, as well," Scarlet said. "Your book club sounds like her kind of thing."

"Great. So, I'll put you down as a maybe." Hadley reached for her phone. "What's your cell? I'll text you, so we can keep in touch."

After Hadley sent her her number, Scarlet realized she was starving. She hadn't been able to eat at the buffet mainly because everyone at the table had been asking her questions and her stomach was in knots. But now she wanted to eat.

"Do you know where I can get something to eat here?"

"I'm heading there now."

"Scarlet, this is my sister, Helena," Hadley said. "Hel, this is Scarlet O'Malley."

"Hello, I love your show. And I have to be honest— you're gorgeous in person," Helena said.

"Thank you," Scarlet said. "Your fiancé is playing with the Velasquez team?"

"Yes," Helena said. "He grew up hanging out with the Velasquez brothers."

"There was tons of food left from the brunch. Come on, I'll show you the kitchen." She followed Hadley and found Bianca was already in there eating a plate of enchiladas.

"Busted," Bianca said. "I'm going to be on a water and carrot stick diet after I give birth but right now I don't even care."

Hadley, Helena and Scarlet laughed with Bianca as she took a huge bite of her food. Scarlet made herself a plate.

Hadley left the kitchen to take a call. Bianca wiped her mouth as Scarlet and Helena sat down next to her and started eating. She was so hungry she ate too quickly, and she didn't realize it until she felt the food start to come back up.

Crap.

Glancing around trying to find the bathroom, she got out of chair, pushing it back too forcefully. Bianca glanced over at her as she tried to be cool and walk out of the room, but she felt the bile in back of her throat and no amount of swallowing was going to keep this down. She looked around and saw the sink. She ran toward it, getting there just as she threw up. This was the worst. She rinsed her mouth and straightened, taking the towel that Bianca was holding out to her and Helena had gotten her a cup of water.

"So... How far along are you?" Bianca asked.

"What are you talking about?" Scarlet knew there was a slim chance that Bianca was going to let her get away with pretending she wasn't pregnant.

"Okay. I guess it was the pork. Sometimes it doesn't agree with me. Especially when I'm meeting new people," Helena said.

"No," she said, not wanting to add another lie to her life right now. "You were right. I'm six weeks...maybe seven. When was that gala in Houston?"

"No wonder you were so upset when you found out he lied," Bianca said.

"Yeah. I'm not sure if I should tell him or not," Scarlet said. "I know you don't know me, but would you mind keeping this between us for now?"

"You have my word," Bianca said. "And my ear if you need a friend."

Scarlet nodded. She hadn't expected to find women like the ones she'd met here in Cole's Hill. No one wanted her social connections or felt the need to be catty; instead they seemed to just accept her as she was.

For the first time in her life, someone else was really depending on her. Not for a paycheck or entrée into another world, but for something way more important. She needed all of the emotional support she could get as she tried to figure out what kind of man Alec was and if he'd be a good father to their unborn child.

Four

This day wasn't going at all the way he planned. And when he felt someone tugging at the hem of his blazer and looked down to see Penny, his five-year-old niece, he knew the surprises weren't over.

"What's up?" he asked as he stooped down to bring himself to her eye level.

"Tio, can girls play polo?" Penny asked.

"Yes, they can," he answered her. "Why do you ask?"

"Daddy said girls can't."

Oh. Polo was a dangerous sport and he could understand why Nate wouldn't want his daughter to play, but he had a feeling Kinley would lose it if she heard that Nate had said *girls* couldn't play.

He figured Nate for a smarter man than that.

"Let's go find your daddy and I'll show him some of the safety equipment that's available. I think he just wants you to be safe," Alec said, standing and taking Penny's hand in his as he walked over to where Nate and Kinley were talking to Bart and some of the other players.

"Daddy, Tio Alec said girls can play polo," Penny announced as they joined the group.

"Did you tell her girls couldn't?" Kinley asked.

"No. I didn't say that. I said she couldn't because it's not safe. I even showed her a video of Zaria playing," Nate said, bending over to look his daughter in the eye. "Didn't I?"

"Yes, Daddy," Penny said. "But Beni can play."

"His uncles are teaching him. And right now, he has to ride with one of them every time," Nate said.

"But I'm a better rider," Penny said.

"Maybe so, scamp, but for right now that's the rule," Nate said, scooping her into his arms and standing up.

"I'm happy to have you ride with me, Penny," Alec said.

"Can I?"

"We'll discuss it at home," Kinley said.

Penny made a face at Kinley and looked very unhappy. "You lied about what Daddy said, girlie. You know that there has to be a consequence."

"I'm sorry, Daddy," Penny said.

As the three of them left the group, Alec noticed Scarlet watching him and realized he had no idea what she expected of him. They were strangers. It didn't matter that he knew about the birthmark on the small of her back just above her buttocks or that he couldn't forget the way her tongue felt in his mouth when they kissed. They were still strangers.

Intimate strangers.

He needed to change that. Well, *need* might be too strong a word, but he wanted to change that. He wanted to know her better and to find out why she was here.

"Ladies," he said as he approached them. "Scarlet, would you like to spend the afternoon with me so we can have a chance to talk?"

Billie stepped closer to Scarlet. Scarlet hugged her friend and then smiled at her. "Why don't you go home and I'll meet you there."

"Sure. But if you change your mind, text me and I'll come and get you."

Billie walked away but not before giving Alec a warning glance.

"I think it's safe to say she doesn't like me," Alec said.

"Yeah, I think so," Scarlet said. "So what did you have in mind?"

"I can give you a tour of the town. We have a nice Main Street with one-of-a-kind boutiques. Or we can take a drive out toward my family's ranch, Arbol Verde," he said. "Or we can go back to my place and I'll have my housekeeper make us an afternoon snack and we can sit by the pool and talk."

He thought he might be pushing it by inviting her back to his house but he wanted a chance to really be able to talk to her and clear up the mess he'd made. But he didn't want to coerce her or rush her in any way.

"Hmm… I'm not sure," she said.

"I'm not trying to pressure you but I have to go to Seattle in the morning to meet with one of my clients and I'll be gone until Saturday, so if we don't talk today… I'm not sure how long you will be here," he said.

"Fair enough. I've rented a home here temporarily," she said. "After seeing the town, it seems like a good place to invest. It's growing fast and I don't have any property in this part of Texas."

"It is a good place to invest." But something about her interest in buying here didn't ring true. She didn't have a reputation for hanging out in small Texas towns. She was more about big-city, red-carpet events. But he wasn't going to question her. He was simply glad she was here. "So should we go to my place?" he asked.

"Uh, no," she said. "I don't even know you, Alec. I mean, the first time we met you lied about you who you were."

"Fair enough," he said. "I just thought someplace private might be better so we could talk and get to know each other. But I don't want you to feel uncomfortable. I really screwed up, Scarlet, and if there's anything I can do to make this better, I want to fix it."

"Where is your house?" she asked. "A conversation someplace where we have our privacy might be good."

"I have a house in the newer section of the Five Families neighborhood. I just finished renovating it."

"I'd love to see your home," she said. "My house is in the Five Families, as well."

"It's a really nice community. But I'm sure I don't have to sell you on the amenities. Who was your Realtor?"

"Helena's fiancé. Small world, huh?"

"Definitely. I think I'm related to everyone in this town either by blood or marriage," he said. "And it's not just my family. All of the five families are like that."

"What are the five families?" she asked as they

walked to his car. He opened the passenger door of his Maserati and helped her in as he told her about the members of the original five families who'd founded Cole's Hill. His ancestor Javier Velasquez had been a rancher in the area thanks to a land grant from the Spanish king before Jacob Cole, for whom the town was named, settled here with his stepdaughter, Bejamina Little. The other three families were the Carutherses, whose ancestor Tully Caruthers and his sister, Ethel, had built a house where the Five Families clubhouse stood today; the Abernathys, who'd been rustlers before settling down and becoming ranchers; and the Grahams. Their ancestor had been the undertaker, and his descendants had turned their old ranch on the outskirts of town into a microbrewery.

Cole's Hill had history and charm, and as he drove through the small town toward the Five Families neighborhood she saw families walking together on Main Street. She wanted that for her child. This kind of slow-paced, ideal life. And Alec, even though he'd lied to her, seemed to be a decent guy after all.

The kind of a guy who might even be a good father, but was she simply fooling herself again? Seeing what she wanted to see in him? She wasn't going to take a chance on her child's future. Alec Velasquez was going to have to prove to her the kind of man he was.

Scarlet walked around Alec's pool while he spoke to his housekeeper about preparing some food. Apparently he hadn't had a chance to eat at lunch, either, because his family had been questioning him about her. As far as she was concerned, that was his own fault, so she couldn't muster much sympathy for him.

She took her strappy sandals off and walked barefoot on the pool deck, which was smooth and warm under feet. She took off the hat she'd been wearing at the polo grounds as well, tossing it on the coffee table in the conversation area of the patio. There was a solid stone fireplace, surrounded by a love seat and large armchairs. There was even a dining area in the shade of some large oak trees. The pool was magnificent; it had a two-tiered water feature that kept the water flowing and a separate hot tub in an elevated corner nearby.

The yard was lush and looked like a lush, landscaped paradise nestled right in the heart of southern Texas. She wasn't sure what she'd expected of Alec… Well, honestly nothing, but this still surprised her. She thought it was because he didn't seem like the kind of guy who'd lie about who he was.

She remembered Hadley's explanation. That Mauricio had been violently ill… And she wanted to believe that was the truth. But she was still hurt. And it didn't explain why Alec hadn't come clean once they'd been together.

It was just one example of the universe having a laugh at her expense. She knew that she was being melodramatic but hey, she was pregnant by a stranger in a town where she really knew only two people, so she felt justified.

She glanced at her watch, wondering what she was doing here. Usually she followed her whims, and though Tara had said that it was the same as following your instinct, Scarlet had never truly believed that. She always felt like she was jumping from one extreme situation to the next.

And this calm and tranquil backyard didn't feel right. It was actually too serene. Too…weird. She needed to hear horns blaring, the thumping base beat of her DJ neighbor trying out some new tracks or even just the sound of Billie talking out loud to herself.

If her intent in coming to Cole's Hill was to find someone to help her decide what to do about her situation, she was pretty sure Alec was the one.

Don't ask for answers if you're not going to listen. Tara's voice danced through her mind.

She just shook her head. She wasn't in the mood to be reasonable.

It would be easier if she saw some signs of Alec's depravity or anything that she could latch on to get mad at him about so she could just leave and then make her own decisions about the baby.

She looked around the backyard. Alec had a nice house. It was the kind of place she would have loved as a child. There was a willow branch tunnel on one side that she and Tara would have loved to explore as girls. The O'Malley gardens had all been formal, laid out in the style of Versailles, so there hadn't been any hidden spots to play.

"Okay, the food is all sorted out. Sorry, but I am definitely one of those people who gets hangry and I don't want to give you more of a reason to think I'm an asshole."

Turning to face him, she noticed he'd taken off his jacket and rolled up his sleeves, revealing his strong forearms and a smart watch. She knew he worked in tech and Billie thought he was pretty much at the top of his game, but honestly that didn't matter to her. She'd met men who were at the top of the Forbes 400 list but who were morally bankrupt. Though it did ease her mind that he wasn't after her for her money, that wasn't really her concern.

What kind of man is he?

Could he be trusted with a child or would he screw it up?

"Great," she said, walking over to the large swing that faced the willow arbor and sitting down. "I guess there's nothing left for us to do but to talk."

"Of course," he said. He came over to where she sat and hesitated. "May I join you?"

"Yes," she said.

The swing dipped a bit when he sat on the wooden bench and then he leaned back, stretching his arm along the backrest. His fingers were close to the back of her neck but he didn't touch her. That didn't mean that she wasn't incredibly aware of his hand so close to her.

She remembered the way he'd stroked his finger down the side of her neck that night at the awards banquet. He'd been leaning in to make a joke about one of the people at their table who kept bringing up the fact that he'd purchased a Maserati from the factory.

She turned so that she could avoid his touch, hoping that would give her the focus she needed, but instead she realized it put her face-to-face with the man himself. He was sprawled on the seat, looking completely at ease as he set the swing into motion. He'd taken off his sunglasses; she met his dark chocolate gaze and realized at last why she wanted so desperately to find something wrong with Alejandro.

She liked him.

Or to be more precise, she liked what she saw. He moved like a man who was comfortable in his own skin, and that was appealing to her. But also, he just seemed relaxed. Except for that moment when she'd surprised him at the polo match, he'd been calm and unflappable.

She wondered if that would still be the case if he found out that one night with her had more consequences than either of them could have expected.

Alec felt like he hadn't acquitted himself very well with Scarlet. Looking back on the night they'd met, he realized that maybe he'd felt free to be himself because he knew he'd never see her again. There had been no reason to try to impress her or to be anything other than how he really was. For one night it hadn't seemed to matter that he wasn't good at relationships or any of those other things. He could just be himself and he had been. Of course, the irony was to be himself, he'd had to pose as his brother.

Now that she was here at his home, he struggled a little bit to relax. Part of it was that she'd gotten even more beautiful since the last time he'd seen her. He wanted her, and each breath he took just reminded him of the scent of her perfume and how it had lingered on his skin after their night together.

"I guess the best thing to do would be to tell you why I was impersonating my brother," he said, unsure of where to start. But the truth was always a good place.

He applied a lot of the same principles he used in his business in his life. Getting all the facts down helped him focus on what steps he needed to take to solve the problem.

"Hadley caught me up on Mauricio being sick and you helping him out. Neither of us could figure out why two grown men wouldn't just mention the fact that they'd switched places," she said.

There was an edge to her tone that he couldn't ignore. She was pissed and he didn't blame her.

"Honestly, it just seemed easier since it was so last-minute for me to show up and accept his award without alerting the organizers," he said at last. It had been easier; that way he didn't have to answer questions about his company or talk about his own work. Being Mo was like wearing a mask. His brother was known for his gregarious personality so it had been a chance for Alec to let his guard down.

In fact, Scarlet might not have noticed him at all if he'd been there as Alec.

"I get that. But why didn't you say anything to me?" she asked.

He took a deep breath and looked away from her toward the pool, watching the sun dance on the water for a few minutes before he finally answered. "It just never occurred to me after the dinner. I didn't expect to have that connection with you, and by the time I realized you didn't know who I really was, it would have been ridiculous to tell you."

"Why ridiculous?" she asked. "Because I was just a hookup?"

No, but he wasn't about to tell her the truth. That

he'd started to like her and didn't want her to be disappointed. He hadn't wanted the night to end and it would have if he'd mentioned he'd been lying about who he was.

"To be honest I wasn't really thinking that night and it wasn't until we were in your hotel room… Anyway, I'm sorry. I should have told you as soon as things started to be more than just two people at a banquet table chatting."

She arched her eyebrow at him and then crossed her arms under her breasts, which looked fuller and larger than he remembered from that night.

"Yes, you should have," she said. "So… Why didn't you call me the next day?"

"I was pretty much trying to keep my brother from killing me and then you'd checked out of the hotel and I wasn't sure how to word an email."

She didn't say anything else as she took her sunglasses from the top of her head and put them back on her face. She shifted on the swing and he felt the brush of her hair against his hand. He wished he could go back in time and start the evening they met with the truth. She had him tied in knots. They were strangers. Strangers with anger between them, and he couldn't blame her for being mad.

He did seem to really suck at personal relationships. Give him a computer keyboard and an empty room and he could wow anyone via videoconference or online chat but this face-to-face interaction he always managed to screw up.

"I have to tell you something," she said.

"Okay," he said.

"It's probably not something you are going to want to hear but you need to," she said. "What do you know about my family?"

He knew a little bit thanks to online searches. He'd also run an algorithm to compile some of the results of a deeper search but he hadn't had a chance to read them. And he knew it would be better to hear about her family from her rather than to read about it online.

"Some. I mean I know you're part of the O'Malley Brewing family. I know that you have banking interests here and in Europe. I think you have a sister—"

"Had. She died eighteen months ago," she said.

"I'm sorry for your loss," he said.

"Thanks," she said. "Do you know anything about my dad?"

He shrugged. He wasn't sure what kind of relationship she had with her old man but there was no way Alec was going to say that he seemed to be immature and selfish from the press reports. The man was on his fourth or fifth wife and Alec was pretty sure he'd read that the latest Mrs. O'Malley was eighteen.

"It's okay. You can say it. He's got an eye for younger women," Scarlet said. "My family isn't like yours, Alejandro. I was raised with nannies and in boarding schools. I'm used to doing everything by myself and being on my own."

Alec wasn't sure where she was going with this. "There were times I wished I wasn't a twin."

"I can imagine. Your family does seem very comfortable getting into each other's business."

"That's true," he said.

"I'm sure you're wondering why I brought up family, and there is no easy way to say this…" She paused, and the look on her face made him brace for the worst. "I'm pregnant. And my family isn't the nurturing kind. I thought the man I'd slept with was Humanitarian of the Year and maybe he'd be a good parent but now I'm not sure."

He put his foot down, abruptly stopping the motion of the swing, and looked over at her not sure he'd heard her correctly. Pregnant? He wasn't ready to be a father. He didn't even know Scarlet. Sure, he wanted to get to know her…but a baby?

His baby?

Someone like his sweet nephew, Benito. A child who could be the best parts of the both of them.

A baby.

A baby!

"Are you sure?" he asked.

"Would I be here if I wasn't?" she asked.

"No I guess not. I'm… I have never thought of having kids other than in the abstract. In fact, we only slept together that one time—are you sure it's mine?"

Five

Was she sure it was his?

What the f—

Did he honestly think she'd come to Texas just to trap him? "Honestly, I've never been so insulted."

"Fair enough, but as you said it's not like we know each other or that we were even in a relationship."

He sounded so reasonable and she knew he was justified to ask questions. But she'd been dealing with a bunch of crap and she wanted just once to have a man step up and not look for an out. She shook her head.

"I don't have a DNA test in my bag but I'm happy to take one," she said. "It's odd that you think of all the men I know you'd be my first choice to approach with my news if I weren't absolutely certain."

He shifted back against the seat of the swing and she noticed how his jaw tightened. She braced herself for an angry outburst. She'd read about his twin and that he was known for his hot temper and inability to control it.

"You're right. You weren't even coming to see me, were you?" he asked, standing up and walking a few feet from the swing. He put his hands on his hips and stared across his large backyard; and she noticed his head was bowed slightly.

He was complicated, this twin whom she didn't know. And she realized she had been a bit touchy about the paternity of the baby, but it was one of her hot buttons. She got up and went over to him, putting her hand on the small of his back.

"A lot of the more salacious reports about me like to paint me as a carbon copy of my father—someone who's insatiable when it comes to the opposite sex, jumping from bed to bed—but there isn't much I can do about it. Still, it does bother me," she said. "To be fair my re-action to the news of this pregnancy was very similar to yours. It was only one time. But as my doctor said, that's all it takes."

"Yeah, I know. I never meant to insult you," Alec said. He turned to face her and one side of his mouth quirked in a tentative smile. "Seems I owe you another apology."

"Apology accepted," she said. He wasn't what she expected. There was a humbleness and sincerity to him that she'd seldom encountered.

"Alec, would you and your guest like something to eat?" his housekeeper asked.

"Are you hungry?" he asked Scarlet in turn.

"I'm not, but if you are, please eat," she said.

"I always have a snack after a polo match," he said. "Please bring it out to the dining area, Rosa."

"*Si*, Rosa," he said, then spoke to her in Spanish.

Scarlet had only a rudimentary knowledge of the language, but she understood as he thanked Rosa for the food and told her that she could take the rest of the afternoon off to enjoy with her family.

Rosa smiled at him and put the tray on the table in the dining area under the trees.

"I asked Rosa to bring drinks for us… O'Malley's Blonde Brew. But now I'm thinking you'd prefer juice or water?"

"Water would be great," she said.

He gestured for her to go and have a seat at the table while he went to the bar area and opened a small refrigerator that had been built into the river stone.

As she sat down, she realized that this pregnancy situation was more complicated than she'd considered. Obviously, her first priority was to make sure that the child had a parent who loved her and put her first, but now there was more that she hadn't thought of.

She'd never considered he'd suspect she was lying about him being the father. She supposed his suspicion was fair enough, but it raised more questions. She would have to be careful where she had the test. She wasn't ready for the public to know about this pregnancy, not until she decided what she was going to do. The tabloids would have a field day with this story.

She didn't want her child to grow up with the stain of all the mistakes and tragedies that had dogged her life. She wanted a more protected upbringing for the child. The kind of childhood that a place like Cole's Hill and a family like the Velasquezes could provide.

She wanted the baby to have the kind of family that

Alec seemed to have. But she knew firsthand that appearances could be deceiving.

"You look very pensive," he said.

"Wow. That's not a word I usually hear applied to me."

"I expect you're more used to *sexy, glamorous, trend-setting*," he said.

She shrugged. She'd cultivated an image for herself and a lifestyle to fill the emptiness left by the death of her mother and her father's distance.

"Maybe. What words would describe you, Alec?" she asked. It was time to stop dwelling on what she knew— she wasn't an ideal candidate to become a mother— and find out if he had the qualities to be a good father.

"I want to say dangerous, sexy—of course—and I'm… That's where it breaks down. Honestly, I'm reliable. And tenacious—I can't let things go. Also, according to my brothers, I'm a sore loser."

She laughed at that. "I am, too. I don't see the point in pretending I'm okay with losing. If I compete I'm doing it to win."

He nodded, moving the cloche off the tray and pulling his plate toward him. She noticed that it was nachos. "Do you mind if I eat? Are you sure you don't want anything?"

"I think you better. Don't want to see you hangry. I'm okay," she said, realizing that she sort of liked this man. She wasn't going to rush to judgment because there was a lot about him she didn't know. But he'd been honest with her today, and after the big lie that had started their…well, relationship…she needed that.

She sipped her water while they exchanged opinions

on books, music, TV and movies. He did everything digital—watched it all on apps.

"But I do have a library in my house," he added. "As much as I prefer the convenience of digital, I like seeing books on my shelves."

She did, too. She was surprised at how much they had in common. It gave her hope that he might be the solution she'd been searching for.

"What else do you prefer?"

"Not lying to you," he said.

"Me, too," she said. "I'd like to see more of this place."

"I'm done here," he said. "Let's go."

He offered her his hand, and when she took it, a shiver went up her arm. She wanted to be smart about this thing with Alec. Keep it all about the baby. But a part of her liked him and still wanted him.

After he ate, Alec took her on a tour of his gardens. His mind was roiling with so many different thoughts it was hard to focus.

He'd never been so careless in his dating life. But to be honest there was something about Scarlet that was different from any other woman. There had been a spark when he'd first been introduced to her at the gala and it hadn't lessened at all over time.

"Scarlet isn't a typical Irish name, is it?" he asked as they strolled down a path lined by rosebushes in full bloom.

"No. Not at all. My mom picked our names. She loved *Gone with the Wind*. She loved how it was the strength of the women that kept everything going. She wanted my sister and me to have that same strength. So she named Tara after the plantation and me after Scarlett O'Hara. She never really liked Melanie so that wasn't an option."

"I love that. I've never read *Gone with the Wind*," he admitted.

Scarlet shook her head, her long blond hair brushing her shoulders as she smiled over at him. "Me neither. But I have seen the movie numerous times."

Suddenly, the smile left her face and he realized that there was more to the story. Should he push or just let it be? He wanted to know more but he was actually enjoying not being in constant conflict with her. He didn't want to have to apologize again.

"My brothers and I are all named after our ancestors," he said.

"That's nice," she said. Then, without missing a beat, she blurted, "What are we going to do about this baby?"

This baby.

Not our baby or her baby. This baby. Was she trying to figure out what kind of man he was before she included him in her life and the baby's life?

Was he reading too much into her word choice?

"I don't know. I think if you aren't opposed we'll have a DNA test," he said.

"I'm not opposed. It will make my lawyers happier, as well. I'm not scheduled to start shooting my reality show again until late October," she said. "I'd like to keep this quiet until then."

"That suits me. I do have to go to the West Coast in the morning. It's not something I can put off. Will you be here when I get back? I don't mind coming to New

York to see you. Mauricio and Hadley have a place there that I can use as my base."

"I think I'll stay here," she said. "For now."

"I'll leave you the numbers for my sister and Hadley, so you aren't alone," he said.

"I have Billie and another friend here with me, and Hadley already gave me her number," Scarlet said.

"That's good," he said. She realized he was mentally going through some list and he'd switched from being relaxed into some sort of business mode. It was interesting to watch.

"Also, I was invited to book club with Hadley and her sister so I have that to look forward to," she said.

"Book club? You know they just go to a bar and hang out, right?"

"I do." She waited to see if he was going to try to tell her not to go.

"I guess that sounded a bit judgy."

"Yeah, just a bit," she said. "One thing you should know about me, Alec, I'm not stupid. I play a role for my reality show and social media but that's not really me."

"I get that. I sort of clean up the online profiles of large companies and people in the public eye who stand to lose a lot if their image doesn't jibe with the expectation of who they are," he said. "I never thought you were stupid, Scarlet."

"What do you think about me?" she asked. "You've never said. I mean I know I shocked the heck out of you by showing up here, but beyond that, I don't know what you think."

"That's a loaded question," he said, stopping in the middle of the willow branch arbor and turning to face her.

The scent of jasmine was strong here; she realized that someone had woven the climbing vine into the willow branches above their head.

"Is it?" she asked.

Because it seemed straightforward to her.

"Si," he said.

She noticed he switched between English and Spanish without really seeming to think about it. She liked it. She thought it happened only when he was distracted.

This close she couldn't help but notice the light stubble on his jaw, which drew her gaze to his mouth. He had firm, full lips that she knew felt just right pressed against her. She felt a jolt of desire go through her and blinked, taking a step back.

She hadn't come here to hook up again.

He was the father of her child and that was complicated enough. But she'd never been one to walk away from something she wanted, and frankly, she wanted Alec Velasquez.

She put her hand on his chest, running her finger over the skin exposed by the buttons he'd left undone at his collar. She touched his gold chain and lifted it up to examine the medallion. He hadn't been wearing this the night they met.

"Tell me what you're thinking, Alejandro," she said softly, hearing the lust in her own voice and knowing she'd made no attempt to disguise it from him.

His put his hand over hers, pressing it flat against his chest as he leaned in, angling his head to one side, never breaking eye contact with her as he brought his mouth closer to hers.

"I'm thinking that if I don't kiss you I might die,"

he admitted. Then his mouth brushed over hers as his hand tangled in her hair.

She sighed, realizing that this was what she'd been waiting for and that it had been worth the wait.

The tension that had been in his gut since he'd first seen her this morning at the polo grounds finally eased. He put his hands on either side of her neck, holding her gently, reminding himself that she was pregnant, and this kiss could be the start of something.

It was hard to keep the embrace gentle, hard to rein in his desire for her, because the kiss simply whetted his appetite for more. It made him want to lift her into his arms and carry her into the house and up to his bedroom.

Memories of their night together stirred in his mind, and now that he was touching her again he wanted more. But he was determined to keep things cool and casual. He didn't know what the future held for them. And really, he probably shouldn't be kissing her.

But she'd touched him and teased him, and he'd never really had to deny himself anything he wanted.

And damn, she tasted so good that none of that mattered. He opened his mouth over hers and their tongues clashed. She sighed as she moved her hands to his waist, holding him even closer. It was all he could do to keep from crushing her against his body. To keep from escalating this beyond a simple kiss to something hot and heavy.

His cock stirred, and he shifted his hips back so she wouldn't rub against his erection. But she pulled him closer with her hands on his waist, rubbing her center against him, and he couldn't help but thrust against her. She moaned deep in her throat and changed the angle of her head so that he could deepen the kiss.

He did, taking everything she offered him. He'd spent every moment since their night together reliving it and wanting to be back in her arms. Now she was here.

Yes, it was complicated, but that didn't seem to matter when he had her in his arms. He rubbed his finger up and down the column of her neck and felt the shiver that went through her as she wrapped her arms around his waist and cupped his butt, drawing him closer to her. She lifted one thigh and wrapped it around his hips. He groaned and got even harder, though he hadn't thought that was possible.

He rubbed himself against her as he continued the kiss. But he knew that the smart thing would be to break this embrace and step back. He was leaving in the morning. He couldn't sleep with her again and then leave.

That was a bad precedent to set. Yet backing away also didn't feel right.

He lifted his head and rubbed his lips over hers before he broke all contact. "You make me forget everything, even my name."

She shook her head. "You're too clever for that. I doubt a kiss could have that powerful of an effect on you."

He took her hand and drew it down to his erection and she rubbed her hand over him. "You have a very pronounced effect on me."

She stroked him through his pants, tipping her head back so their eyes met. "I seem to."

There was no way to talk about this. He was overwhelmed with the urge to get inside her. He hesitated, though, not wanting her to feel pressure, but then felt her slowly lowering the zipper of his trousers. Her hand slipped inside his open fly.

There was no turning back. He lifted her off her feet and she wrapped her legs around his hips as he carried her out of the willow arbor to the shaded double lounger next to the pool.

He sat down, so she straddled his lap and shifted against him, pushing her hands into his hair and bringing her mouth down on his.

God, he tasted better than she remembered. Straddling his lap made her realize how desperately she wanted to get closer to him. Wanted him close enough so she could feel him inside her. His mouth…damn those perfect lips that felt just right under hers. And the taste of him. It was addicting.

But she could control it.

She kissed him again, even deeper than before, rocking her hips and rubbing her center over the ridge of his erection. It felt so good.

She lifted her head. His eyes were half closed. Rubbing her fingers along his jaw, she felt the abrasion of his stubble, and it sent shivers through her as she shifted around and brought her mouth back to his.

He tasted so good.

She never wanted to stop kissing him. She remembered what it had been like—the sex between them. It had been hard to wake up alone and realize she'd never have him again.

Now she was back in his presence and less than a

few hours later she was straddling him, kissing him like she'd never get enough of him.

Addict.

The word echoed in her mind. She pushed herself off him, stumbling back away from him. She wasn't her sister or her mother. She was always in control of her desires.

Until now.

Until Alejandro Velasquez.

She put her hand on her mouth and turned away from him, not saying anything. She heard his heavy breathing and a few minutes later she heard his zipper as he did it up.

"I should be going. Have a safe trip," she said.

"I'll drive you," he said.

"You don't have to," she said.

"I do. It's late July in Texas and I'm a gentleman no matter what you might believe. It's the least I can do."

She nodded and went to find her shoes. As he led her to his car, neither of them said a word about what had happened. And when he pulled into the drive of her rented house, she bolted out as soon as he brought the car to a stop.

She didn't look back but didn't have to because in her mind she still saw the passion on his face when she'd straddled him and she knew that staying away from him was going to be harder than anything she'd ever done.

Six

Scarlet needed to go out and surround herself with people who just wanted her to be the edgy heiress. Alec had somehow found a way to make her remember all the things that she was usually much better at ignoring. Stuff like how much she had missed him…but more than that, how she missed a genuine connection with someone.

"Billie? Siobahn?"

Her little miniature dachshund came trotting into the foyer and Scarlet leaned down to scoop her up. Lulu burrowed into her neck the way she liked and Scarlet closed her eyes as she rubbed her dog's back. Then she set Lulu back on the tile floor and the dog dashed off for the kitchen. She followed Lulu and found Siobahn sitting at the counter, shoulders hunched, staring intently at her smartphone screen.

"Siobahn? You okay?"

"Yeah, I'm good. I can't believe this. Now they're saying it's going to be the wedding of the century," Siobahn said, scrolling on her screen.

Scarlet went over and took the phone from her friend, putting it on the counter behind her. "As if. It might be the tackiest wedding ever but that's it."

Siobahn smiled. "Probably all pink and frothy."

"Definitely. That woman has an unhealthy obsession with tulle."

"She does," Siobahn said. "Where have you been?"

She grabbed two Fiji waters from the fridge and passed one to her friend. "I was meeting with the guy I hooked up with when I came to Houston."

"That Mauricio guy?"

She wrinkled her brow. "Uh, well, it turns out that it was actually his twin brother, Alejandro."

"Ooh. Interesting," Siobahn said, moving over to the padded bench in the breakfast nook and patting the seat next to her.

Scarlet went over and sat next to her friend. She rested her elbows on the wooden table and held the water bottle suspended between her hands.

Interesting.

"Is he why we're in this town no one's ever heard of?" Siobahn asked.

"You needed to get out of the city, too," Scarlet said. She hated to make it seem like she was selfish and did things just in her own best interests. "But yeah."

"You're right. I did need a break," Siobahn agreed. "So tell me what's going on with this guy."

"I'm pregnant," she said without further hesitation,

even though the words still stuck in her throat as she said them. It wasn't getting any easier to tell people. She wondered if it ever would or if her kid would be thirty and she'd still feel this foreign, *what-the-fuck* feeling in her gut.

"What? I thought you were super careful," Siobahn said.

"I am normally but I had run out of pills. I figured I'd be fine since I've been on the pill forever and I don't hook up that much. Especially when I'm filming. I figured I'd be okay," she repeated.

"Did he use a condom?"

"Yes…well, one time," she admitted.

"Why am I just now hearing about this?" Siobahn asked. "Sounds like you had one hell of a night."

"We did," she admitted. "Then, of course, he was gone in the morning and I moved on. I like being able to do that. Not get too tied down, but then this…" She looked down at her body. How had this happened? Why now?

"Why did he bolt?"

"Turns out he was impersonating his brother who was in love with a girl, and he had to get back to Cole's Hill to make things right between them," Scarlet said.

Siobahn looked over at her.

"Seriously?"

"Yeah," Scarlet said, taking a long swallow of her water and wishing it were something stronger. If there was ever a moment she wanted to get drunk and forget everything about her life, it was right now.

"You know you're making me feel better about my

sucky life," her friend said, wrapping her arm around Scarlet's shoulder and hugging her.

"That was my main objective," Scarlet joked.

Siobahn smiled. "Do we have the suckiest taste in men ever or has the quality of men in the dating pool just gone significantly downhill?"

"Might just be karma," Scarlet said.

"It might be," Siobahn admitted. "Be nice if the universe had given us a free pass for all the crap things we'd done when we were too dumb to know better."

"It would be. Guess it doesn't work that way, though," Scarlet said.

"Girl, what are you going to do about the baby?" Siobahn asked, looking over at her with those wide eyes that had helped make her so famous.

"I don't know. You know O'Malleys make horrible parents. There isn't one in my direct line who didn't screw up their kids," Scarlet said.

"Yeah, but you're—"

"Please don't say *different*," Scarlet said. "I'm not. I just hide the ugly, selfish bits of myself better than Tara did, and my father does."

"Whatever you decide, I've got your back," Siobahn said. "So, what about Mauri—wait, not Mauricio, Alejandro? Did you tell him about the kid? Or are we keeping this just between us for now?"

"I told him but I'm not sure what's on his mind. He wants me to have a DNA test," Scarlet said.

"Bastard. He didn't believe you?"

"Karma. I have slept with a lot of guys," Scarlet admitted. Granted she'd been in her very early twenties and trying to exorcise some ghosts back then.

"Yeah, but still, why would you try to trap him?"

"I said as much. And once he realized I didn't know who he actually was when I came to town he admitted as much. I'm still going to do it. I need it for my lawyers, but beyond that… I was hoping he'd be a decent guy who would raise the kid."

"Good idea," Siobahn said. "Aside from impersonating his twin, is he a good guy?"

That was the million-dollar question. She shrugged, and luckily Billie walked in before she had to answer any more of Siobahn's questions.

"You two okay?" Billie asked.

Scarlet nodded even though she wasn't okay. She was pregnant and the father of her child wasn't who she'd thought he was. But he also wasn't a bad guy. She had no real idea what to do next but at lease she had her friends to pleasantly distract her for now.

They spent the evening playing a trivia game and not talking about her pregnancy. But when she went to bed all she could think about was how it had felt to be in Alec's arms.

Helena kept up the smiles until she and Malcolm were in the car. She was thinking about Scarlet and how someone who seemed to have it all was still struggling with her own issues. It sort of drove home how nothing in life was ever easy. It had been nice watching the polo match with her sister and her friends, but it wasn't lost on her that her fiancé had spent most of the time avoiding her. Sure, he'd been cool about it but she knew him well enough, or thought she did, to see that he was trying to avoid her.

He had started to lose a ridiculous amount of weight. She had believed he was taking steps to control his gambling addiction, but here he was hiding something from her again. It was hot in the car and Malcolm fiddled with the air-conditioning as he got in.

"That was a nice day," Malcolm said as he put the vehicle in gear and pulled out of the parking lot of the polo grounds. The parking lot was emptying out. Sometimes if they had a match on Saturday they'd have a party that went into the night but not on Sunday.

Most of the locals in Cole's Hill were still ranch people who had to get up early to care for their livestock. Even Helena had an early day tomorrow. She had to take one of her clients' books to Houston for review by a private accounting firm. It was just routine but she wasn't looking forward to the drive during rush-hour traffic. And she knew being in the car alone would give her too much time to think about Malcolm and wonder what the heck was going on with him.

She took a deep breath. Could she just sweep this under the rug? Could she just play it nice and easy? No. More like hell no. That just wasn't her way.

"Was it? Because it seemed to me that every time I joined a group you were part of you dashed away. What's up?"

"Helena. That's not what was happening," he said. But there was that edge to his voice. The one that she'd become way too familiar with ever since their engagement party. Then they'd had a few weeks of relative normalcy after he'd confessed his gambling problem and how he'd overextended his finances to try to impress her.

"Then tell me what is," she said. "Pull over here and talk to me. I can't do this again, Malcolm. As humiliated as I'd be by calling off the wedding, I will do it if you aren't communicating with me."

He cursed but she heard the clicking of the blinker as he pulled onto the shoulder and put the car in Park. He put both of his arms on the steering wheel and didn't turn to face her.

"I've stopped," he said angrily.

He was pissed. But that was okay because she was, too. "I'm not making an idle threat or trying to manipulate you, Mal. If the prospect of us getting married is causing you stress, then let's just keep living together. If it's something else, then tell me. Two heads are better than one to solve a problem, right?"

He looked over at her and she saw so much turmoil on his face that her heart ached for him. And it ached for herself if she were honest. This was the man she loved. She'd loved him for longer than he knew, and she wanted to have that picture-perfect engagement and wedding and then a long life with him. She didn't want to call things off. Not just because of her ego but because he was the man she wanted. With all his problems and fears, he still was the man who owned her heart.

"Fine. I'm struggling, Hel. It's harder than I thought not to make a bet. I keep thinking of the money we've got as our nest egg and how I could double it—I know I can't do that. I know that one bet won't be enough and that there's no such thing as a sure thing, but at the same time I wake up at two in the morning and plot out ways to increase our money by placing bets."

She sighed. "I know it's not easy for you. Would it help if I made a cost analysis?"

It helped her. But she was an accountant and liked looking at a spreadsheet. Watching the way that her investments would grow soothed her. It always reassured her.

He smiled at her, his real smile, and she felt the love she had for him swell inside. "No, honey, I don't think a spreadsheet would help, but thanks. You're so sexy I always forget what a nerd you are."

She mock-punched his shoulder. "Hey. I'm not a nerd."

"You are, but I love you," he said, turning toward her and reaching out to pull her into an awkward hug because of the seat belts. "I love you more than you know, Helena. I don't want to screw up again."

She reached down and undid both of their seat belts and then hugged him closer before putting her hands on his jaw and looking him in the eyes. "We are both going to screw up a million times during our life. The thing to remember is that I'm here when you do and I'm counting on you to be here when I do."

He kissed her then, and the passion that had always burned between them ignited. She remembered their first time, which had been in a car after the homecoming football game her senior year of high school.

Someone drove by and honked and she pulled back as Malcolm waved at the car. "Guess we should remember we aren't in high school now," he said, laughing.

"Guess so," she said, as they both put their seat belts back on.

Instead of putting the car in gear, he turned to face

her. "I'm not going to give in to the impulse to gamble, honey. It's hard and I definitely feel the struggle every day, but I never give in because I know that if I do, it's the path away from you. And I don't think my life would be anything without you."

She squeezed his hand. They'd get through this together, she thought.

As Alec drove back to his house after dropping Scarlet off, he heard the emptiness all around him. Normally that didn't bother him, as he liked solitude, but as he went into his office and pulled up the files that his algorithm had compiled about Scarlet, he realized he felt lonely.

But there was no reason for that. He texted his brothers to see if they were up for a game of pool or something but they both were busy with their women. Diego's wife was in town and since she split her time between Texas and London, Diego wasn't about to blow off an evening with her to hang out with his little brother.

Mo and Hadley were in that honeymoon phase of their relationship, so even though Mo had texted back that Alec was welcome to join them for dinner, the last thing he wanted was to spend an evening feeling like a third wheel.

Instead he sat down at his computer and started reading the files he'd collected on Scarlet. It was interesting to him how much of her life was available online. It went all the way back to her birth and childhood, as her mother had been a model and her father one of the richest men in the United States around the time she was born. He looked at all of the pictures of her online.

She had grown up…well, in a very public way and he had to wonder if she'd come to Cole's Hill to see if he was a private man.

She didn't want the spotlight to follow her child around. She knew how impossible it was to grow up that way.

He couldn't postpone his trip to Seattle. His client needed him and one of the things that Alec prided himself on was delivering what his clients required. But one of the main things he noticed about Scarlet was that she'd been left by herself a lot. And now she didn't even have her sister, who had died not that long ago. He wasn't the wisest man when it came to reading the opposite sex but he thought that spending a week away from her when she was feeling so vulnerable might not be the best idea.

He didn't want to make another mistake when it came to Scarlet. They'd seemed to really connect yesterday and she was expecting his child. They needed to find common ground.

Deciding on a course of action, he got in his car and drove back to Scarlet's house. The ride took only five minutes as they lived in the same gated community. When he rang the doorbell, he heard the sound of barking and then voices before the door opened.

Scarlet stood there with the famous singer Siobahn Murphy and Billie, who didn't look any friendlier than she had earlier. A miniature dachshund rushed forward and Alec bent down, holding his hand out to the dog, who sniffed it, then licked him and danced around his feet as he stood back up.

"Alec, I wasn't expecting to see you again before your trip," Scarlet said.

"I know. I've just been thinking that maybe we should spend some more time together and wondered if you'd like to go with me to Seattle," he said. "I have a private plane so that's not an issue."

"She has one, too," Billie said.

"Great. Either way. I have a nice house in Bellevue…" He trailed off, not sure what else to say.

"Let me think about it. When do you need to know?" she asked.

"In the next two hours. I was planning to leave in the morning," he said.

She nodded, then bent down to scoop up the little dog, who was standing on her back legs and looking up at Scarlet. He watched her closely, still wondering what had caused her to leave him so abruptly earlier. Had he rushed her? Was he rushing her now?

Alec just wanted to do the right thing for her. She was pregnant, and she said the baby was his. He was beginning to realize she wasn't the kind of woman who would have come to see him if she wasn't positive he was the father. He wanted to get to know her. His online research had helped but that was her digital imprint; it wasn't necessarily the true picture of her.

"I'll just—"

"Oh, come in," Siobahn said, holding her hand out to him. "I'm Siobahn."

"Alec Velasquez," he said, shaking her hand and stepping into the foyer. He closed the door behind him as Billie shook her head and walked away.

"Go think about if you want to go," Siobahn said to Scarlet. "I'll keep Mr. Velasquez company."

"Please call me Alec," he said.

Scarlet chewed her bottom lip. "Okay, but be nice."

"Of course I will be," Alec said.

"I wasn't talking to you," Scarlet said as she turned to walk down the hall.

"We can talk in here," Siobahn said, leading the way into the formal living room.

Friends of Alec's parents had previously owned this house and he noted that nothing had changed since he'd last been here. He sat on the love seat and Siobahn took the armchair adjacent to him.

"So you don't know if you're the dad?"

Well, she certainly got right to the point. He wasn't prepared to be grilled but given the fact that she was facing a lot of unknowns from him, maybe her friends were justified. But he still hadn't had a chance to make things right with Scarlet before he started answering questions from her friends. "Uh... I felt like it was a legitimate question to ask. I mean there was only that one night and I hadn't heard from her since then," Alec said. "But after we talked I realized that's not the kind of woman she is."

Siobahn leaned back in her chair, crossing her arms over her chest. "What kind of woman is she?"

He didn't want to talk about his feelings for Scarlet. End of story. He wasn't that kind of chatty guy. He didn't know how to put it into words. But for all her flashiness there was something sweet and, odd as it sounded, innocent about her.

He chose his next words carefully, aware that her

friend was ready to defend Scarlet if he said anything she didn't like. He would be upset about this mini-grilling he was getting from Siobahn but he couldn't fault her. He'd do the same for his brothers. He was quickly realizing that Scarlet had created a family for herself and their bond was stronger than any she had with her blood relatives.

"She's an enigma so I can't even begin to say that I know her. But she seems honest to me."

"She is. She's got a big heart, buddy, so don't dick around with her," Siobahn said.

"I won't," he said.

"Good," Siobahn said, then stood up. "Just because she looks tough doesn't mean she is."

Siobahn walked out of the room, and a few minutes later he heard Scarlet in the hall. "I'll go with you," she said as she entered the living room. "I'll have Billie drive me to your house in the morning and then we can take your plane. I want to bring Lulu. Will that be okay?"

"Who's Lulu?" he asked.

"My dog," she said.

"That's fine. I'll see you then," he said.

He left her house feeling much better this time. He didn't overanalyze it but he knew that going to her had been the right thing for both of them. Neither of them was sure about this pregnancy or each other and they needed all the time they could find together to learn to trust each other.

Seven

Alec parked his Maserati in the garage at the airport reserved for him the next morning and then got out to open Scarlet's door, but she was already standing there with Lulu on a leash when he came around the car. So he tried to be cool and pivoted to the trunk to unload his computer bag and one of Scarlet's suitcases. The others were in the car that Billie was driving.

He wasn't sure if her friend and assistant was joining them, and frankly he hoped she wasn't because he wanted to get to know Scarlet on her own. But he wasn't in a position to make demands. He knew that so he was willing to wait and see what Scarlet had in mind.

She wore a pair of moto-style leggings and a long T-shirt with a picture of Audrey Hepburn in her iconic

Breakfast at Tiffany's role. She arched one eyebrow at him and he realized he had been staring.

"You have great legs," he said. "I'm not going to pretend I didn't notice them and wasn't staring."

She shook her head. "Are you always this blunt?"

"Yes. Which is why I seldom socialize."

"I like it," she said, walking toward him with her large bag on her shoulder and the little dog walking along beside her. "Once Billie drops off my suitcase, we can leave. I have a tiny crate for Lulu to stay in during takeoff and landing. She likes to burrow in her blanket in the crate."

"That's fine," he said. "I could have taken my truck instead of the sports car to accommodate your luggage."

"It's okay. Is that all you packed?" she asked, gesturing to his computer bag.

"I have a home in Seattle so I don't need to bring clothing back and forth with me. And I keep a limited wardrobe on the jet, as well."

"I'm fascinated with your life," she said. "What is it you do that requires you to have houses all over...? Is it just the United States or are you global?"

They had stepped out of the garage and were standing on the tarmac when Billie pulled up next to them.

"Global. Just leave your luggage on the tarmac and I'll have it collected," he said. "Do you need this bag with you during the flight?"

"No," she said.

He nodded and turned to walk to the jet where the attendants were waiting. He employed a staff of five who rotated during the month. He had the two pilots and then three attendants depending on what was necessary on different flights.

"Please stow the luggage and then we're going to need to figure out the best place for a dog crate," he said. "It needs to be stabilized during takeoff and landing."

"Yes, sir. Will you be accompanied by the two ladies?" Marg, the head flight attendant, asked.

"I don't know," he admitted.

"Not a problem," Marg said. "I'll take care of everything. We have your desk set up, as well. Will you be needing us to adjust anything?"

"Thanks, Marg. That's great. Whatever you've set up is fine."

He boarded the plane and immediately went to his desk. But the last thing on his mind was work.

He wanted her. His body was still half-aroused from earlier and sitting so close to her in his sports car had made it worse. He'd driven too fast to burn off some of the adrenaline but she'd simply laughed. The scent of her perfume had surrounded him, egging him on to drive faster. He'd never been one of those men who needed to strut around a woman, but he wanted to with Scarlet. Sure, he could have taken the truck, but the Maserati was a status thing, and she came from a world of immense wealth, so he wanted her to know he wasn't after her money.

Was he after her?

He had told himself and Scarlet that he wanted to get to know her better because she was pregnant with his baby—Scarlet wasn't the kind of woman to lie about that—but another part of him knew that he did want her for himself. And he'd never been comfortable with that sort of longing. He'd grown up one of five kids. Sharing was practically in his DNA. Of course, as an adult he had things that were his, but he always felt greedy when he craved something or, in this case, someone. He wanted Scarlet and it felt so much more intense than just hooking up again.

There was something other than just lust coursing through his veins and he didn't want to acknowledge or examine it. But he was by nature someone who had to figure it out.

"Billie said to give you her regards," Scarlet said as she entered the jet. She bent over to unleash the dog and her honey-blond hair cascaded down over her shoulders. The little dog stood on its back legs and rubbed its face in her hair.

She stood up and their eyes met, and something passed between them. He felt the zing all the way to his groin. No surprise since he'd been turned on since he'd seen her this morning.

"She doesn't like me, so I appreciate you making it seem like she does," he said.

She laughed, throwing her head back. "She thinks she's subtle. Can you believe that?"

"No. She must know she comes across as a bulldog who will protect you at all costs," Alec said.

"Do I need protecting?" she asked, walking toward him. Lulu ran ahead of her and jumped up on one of the seats.

"No," he said, his voice low, gruff and huskier than he wanted it to be. "Not from me."

* * *

The thing about addictions, Scarlet thought as she sat next to Alec as the jet took off, was that they were hard to resist. She should have said no, she wouldn't come with him to Seattle. She shouldn't have agreed to be alone with him again until she sorted out what exactly the feelings she had for him were. But honestly, right now, after seeing the way he was watching her and hearing that gravelly tone of voice, all she could think about was how his body had felt against hers and how good it had felt to be straddling him earlier.

For the first time since she'd realized she was pregnant, something made sense. Sex was normal and logical. It didn't have to be complicated. And technically, if she were with Alec, it wasn't breaking her self-imposed rule of hooking only up once with a guy because she'd thought he was Mauricio the last time, right?

She'd started the rule to avoid the situation she was in right now. She couldn't take the chance of falling into the trap of commitment. She'd seen it destroy both her mother and sister.

That makes no sense, even for you. As usual, the voice of her sister nagged her.

Shut up, Tay. I don't want to be logical.

Obviously.

Lulu was curled up and sleeping in her travel crate, which meant there was nothing to distract Scarlet from Alec. He had his legs loosely crossed. When the flight attendants asked if they would like something to eat or drink, he glanced over at her with one eyebrow arched.

"I'm good," she said.

"Me, too. I'll let you know if we need anything," Alec said.

The attendants left to go to the crew quarters and they were alone.

Danger, danger, don't do something stupid.

Tara had been so irresponsible in life that Scarlet knew the voice she often attributed to her sister was simply her own subconscious warning her off. But it comforted her to think her sister might be watching over her.

How dangerous could he be?

You wouldn't be having this conversation with me if you didn't fear something about him.

Fear.

Was that true? Was that what this was?

"Are you comfortable?" he asked. "Do you need a blanket?"

No. She needed him naked and underneath her, so she could feel more in control of everything. He had surprised her and taken the upper hand… Yeah, that was it. She wanted to be on top again. It wasn't anything more than that. She didn't have to fear addiction—this was her first time with Alec. She could have him guilt-free and then go back to figuring out the baby situation.

Yeah, right.

Go away, Tay.

Fine, but don't say I didn't warn you.

"So, tell me more about what you do," she said. "Billie pulled up some information on you, but I'd rather hear your story from you."

"Hmm… I'm not sure where to start," he said. "My job is kind of boring."

She glanced around the plane and remembered his

cars and home. "But it pays well. It's nice to know that money can be made by other means than just being Insta-famous."

"Well, when I was in college… Let's just say that I didn't handle being on my own that well. Even though I got straight A's, I drank and partied way too much. I definitely enjoyed those years but when I was a junior and applied for paid internships, no one would even call me back for an interview. I asked one of the HR hiring managers about it and she said I looked good on paper, but the internet told a different story.

"That was a huge wake-up call and I knew that I needed to clean up my online presence. Some of my frat brothers were in the same boat so I wrote some code and created an algorithm that would go in and clean it up. It took a long time, my entire junior year, but once I had it and deployed it, I started getting interviews. I started to sell my services to my frat brothers. Once word got out, I had a lot of customers."

"I could have used you a few years ago," she said with a laugh. "Instead I've just embraced my more scandalous photos and videos and made them my brand."

"That works, too, but sometimes things happen that can really have a negative impact. So I went from helping college kids to helping companies and public figures. I've made a few tweaks along the way to keep up with the technology," he said.

"And it pays well," she said.

"Yeah, it does. Protecting their public image is priceless for some people and businesses. And I provide a service that no one else can," he said. "I did it for Mauricio after the photo of the two of us came out. But Hadley, of course, had already seen it. I monitor all of my family's mentions but it's a soft surveillance. So I just get an alert. I haven't had to use hard surveillance since my brother-in-law, Jose, passed away."

She liked when he talked about his business; she could see his passion for the work he did, and how much he liked it. "Who was Jose and why did you have to monitor him so closely?"

"He was the famous Formula 1 driver Jose Ruiz… Anyway, he wasn't faithful to my sister and there were always lots of photos of him partying with other women. I did it to keep that information private. No one needed to know that he wasn't the perfect husband that he had pretended to be," Alec said. Alec had built his business around a proprietary code that he used to search the internet for any references to Jose and then replaced the salacious stories with a cleaned up reference that focused on his career and not the affairs.

She nodded. He was a protector, she thought. That was another plus if he was going to raise their baby. Add that to the fact that he had a big, incredibly nice family—if her afternoon with them was any indication—a good job and an understanding of the power of reputation.

Now if she could only keep focused on his sterling qualities. But there wasn't anything that could pry the image of his naked chest from her mind. In fact, going back to bed with him, no matter how wrong, was all she could think about.

Talking about work was leveling him out and taking the edge off his desire for Scarlet. It was still there but not as intense as it had been when they'd first boarded the jet. He felt a bit more in control of himself. It had been a long time since he'd discussed the origins of his company with anyone.

In fact, he'd forgotten how out of control he'd been those first two years of college. He had pretty much decided that he'd say yes to everything. It had been fun but he'd been so irresponsible. It was only in his junior year that he'd started to become the man he was today. Someone who understood that following every impulse led to destruction.

But that didn't stop him from wanting Scarlet. He'd like to say he was a twenty-first-century man who could have a conversation with a woman and get to know her without thinking about sex, but he couldn't deny the primal instinct that she brought out in him.

His mom had raised him right and he had a sister so he knew how to treat women. But that didn't mean that there weren't times like this when all he wanted to do was say to hell with being polite and see if she wanted him as much as he wanted her.

"What about you? You said your brand embraced scandal, but I'm not that familiar with your story," he admitted. "Is scandal part of your business plan?" His plan was to keep talking. Then maybe he could get through the flight without making a move on her. If her earlier retreat had sent any signals, it was that she wasn't ready for anything more between them.

"I'm not surprised you don't know my brand. Basically, I have a lifestyle company that is all about embracing your inner... Well, Billie says *bitch* but we don't market it that way. It's called Get-It-Girl. It's just about not apologizing for being yourself. So I have makeup that is very flattering but might also be too bright for some people. But if that's what you like, then you can wear the red lippie and the glitter eye shadow. I also have two clothing lines—one's 'naughty' and the other's 'nice.' It recognizes that everyone is a little bit of both," she said.

"I love that. I think that Penny exemplifies that split every time I see her. To be honest, Benito does, too. It's funny that as children we can embrace these different sides while we learn the limits of how to behave." Penny wasn't strictly his niece but he and his brothers all treated her as if she were. Extended family was the same as family as far as the Velasquezes were concerned.

"That's true. My brand gives you a place to say it's okay to be you," she said. "I have the reality show as well where I just live my social media life and cameras follow me around. I try to show both the partying side and the business side, how you can do what you love and still make a living," she said.

He'd written her off as a party girl heiress when he'd first researched her but he saw now that she was much more than that. "How did you start out?"

He suspected that a lot of this had to stem from her relationship with her father. She'd said he wasn't a good parent to her growing up, and the articles he'd found on the web seemed to support that, even though he knew that the truth was always more complicated than news reports or social media posts.

"I had a really bad screwup when I was eighteen. A sex tape I made went viral and my sister, Tara, said,

'That's it. You're branded with a scarlet letter now.' My response was that my name is Scarlet so maybe it was inevitable and I should embrace it," she said, turning to face him and drawing her legs up on the seat. "Tay said to go for it and I did. I thought if I'm a bad girl in the media, then I could perform in character and control it in a way, even profit from it. You sort of always have to meet that expectation or they go looking for stuff that you don't want to get out."

"I wish I'd met your sister," he said. "She sounds like she was pretty savvy."

"She was, but she was also an idiot. She liked guys that were really bad for her and she never could stay straight."

He reached over to squeeze her hand. "I'm sorry. I guess it's like you were saying. Everyone is complicated."

"They are. Did you feel that way about your brother-in-law?" she asked. "Everyone is always trying not to speak ill of the dead, but you didn't sugarcoat it with him."

"No, I didn't. I really looked up to him when he and Bianca married but when I saw that first photo… I was so angry. I confronted him, and he said that Bianca knew the score. But I knew my sister. She wasn't the kind of woman who would be happy with a man who cheated on her."

"I don't know many women who would be," Scarlet said.

"I agree," he said. "Jose said that it's in men's natures to be promiscuous."

"Do you agree with him?"

"No, I don't. I think if you find the right woman, she fills that emptiness and you don't have to keep looking," Alec said. "What about you?"

"Hmm… I'm not sure. My dad certainly has never found the One, and Tara didn't, either."

"I didn't ask about them. I want to know if you think you can find it in one man or if you are always looking for something else."

Eight

His question didn't leave much room for anything other than bluntness. "I have no idea."

"Fair enough. I'm just trying to get things straight in my head. I mean a baby isn't going to wait around for the two of us to figure our stuff out, and I do better when I have time to plan," he admitted.

She fidgeted a bit before she realized what she was doing. She needed to stop letting him rattle her, but the truth was she wasn't herself. She hadn't been for a really long time…since Tara's death. But she'd been faking it pretty well until now.

Was it Alejandro who was responsible for the change or was it the baby?

Or both?

She had no idea. She didn't like to do too much introspection because frankly most days she didn't like herself… That was it, wasn't it? The truth of who she'd become: someone who put on a fake show for the media and then played that part until she fell into an exhausted sleep, haunted by her dead sister.

Damn.

She was a bigger mess than she thought.

"I don't know that we're ever going to come up with a plan that will make sense," she admitted.

"Me neither," he said. "I keep trying to wrap my head around having a baby… I'm not going to lie. It's scaring the shit out of me. I mean, I have a nephew but honestly, I don't really spend that much time with kids. Hell, I don't really spend much time with adults who I'm not working with."

She had to laugh at the way he said it. She heard the panic in his voice and it made her feel a little better that he wasn't all cool with everything, either.

"Don't worry, that part I'm good at…not kids but adults," she said, shifting in the large seat and stretching her legs. Lulu was still sleeping in her crate and would probably be content until they landed.

"We should make a list of pros and cons of us becoming parents," he said, pulling his tablet toward him.

She reached over and took it from him, then tucked it behind her on the seat. "No. We're not doing that. We have the rest of this week to spend with each other and we'll learn enough then to figure out what we should do next. Honestly, I thought I'd tell you—I mean, Mauricio— about the baby and then because you, or rather, he was Humanitarian of the Year I'd hand the baby over and he'd raise it. That way it would have a happy, well-adjusted life."

He shook his head. "I really screwed up this time."

"Hey, we both were there that night. You know I wish you'd been honest but no use rehashing that. We'll figure this out."

"I hope so. I don't want to be the reason a kid is messed up," he said.

"Me neither. As I mentioned, my family isn't the greatest when it comes to providing a happy, nurturing home but I still don't want to give up the baby unless we can't figure out a way to raise it."

"You'd give it up?"

"If it meant making sure the child didn't end up like my father or sister, then yes."

She realized that sounded harsh. It was the first time she'd actually said it out loud but in her heart she'd felt that way for a long time. She'd loved Tara more than she'd ever loved anyone on the planet but she'd been so broken, so flawed and it had been so heartbreaking to not be able to help her.

She wouldn't go through that again. She wanted her child to grow up safe and secure…whole. She'd failed Tara and had wanted to save her. Losing Tara had shattered something in her and she was afraid of doing the same thing with her baby.

"We're going to figure this out," he said, the conviction he'd had since the moment he'd found out about her pregnancy…well, after he'd determined that he must be the father.

"That's all I want," she admitted. "I want to get this

sorted out before I have to return to New York and start filming my show again."

"When is that?" he asked.

"About three months' time," she said. "I can put them off for a few weeks, but everything hinges on my show. I see increased sales in merchandise when it airs. My company employs about twenty-five people so I can't flake on them."

"No problem. I'm hoping this week will give us both the answers we want. I know I want to get to know you better and I hope you'll see that I'm not as craven as I might have seemed at first when I lied about who I was."

"I'm already seeing it," she said. No use hiding the truth from him. Billie always said she had no filter, which also meant she had no walls up to protect herself. But honestly she couldn't stand fake emotion in her real life. She spent so much time projecting an image to the world via her media channels that when she had downtime she had to be real.

"Good," he said. "I am, too. I had no idea how honest you would be about everything. I sort of expected you to think about how it would affect your follows and stuff like that."

She shook her head and shifted away from him. "I'm not like that. I mean I do have to be aware of how I look and the image I present but I'm not shallow."

"I know. That's what I was trying to say. I'm really good at putting my foot in it and saying the wrong things, but believe me, my intent is never to be an ass."

She had to smile at that. She noticed he used self-deprecation a lot to divert tension. She wasn't sure if it was sincere or if that was his way of pushing any blame away from himself. For now, she was going to take it at face value but it was something for her to watch.

"Fair enough," she said. "So what do you usually do during the flight?"

"Work," he said.

"Work?"

"Yeah," he said. "Or work out. I have a treadmill in the bedroom."

She shook her head. He was surprising. She hadn't pegged him for a workaholic but as she looked around the aircraft she could see it was set up as an office. She also noticed a client entertainment area.

"Well... What are we going to do?"

"Whatever you want," he said.

Whatever she wanted... Now that was dangerous invitation.

He hadn't expected to find himself sitting across his conference table from her with a deck of cards between them. But then everything about Scarlet was unexpected so maybe he should stop trying to anticipate what she'd do.

He, his brothers and their friends had a monthly poker game in Cole's Hill and he was pretty good at reading them. They'd played together since high school when they'd thought they were cooler than they actually had been. But Scarlet was completely different. It was harder for him to find her tells. And not just because she had a pretty good poker face, but because she distracted him.

She'd braided her long blond hair, but tendrils had escaped, with one of them brushing against the side of her face. She kept reaching up and tucking the strand behind her ear, which fascinated him. He'd seen his sister, Bianca, do the same thing, but it had never seemed as interesting as when Scarlet did it.

"I'll raise you a protein bar and two Hershey's Kisses," she said, pushing the snacks toward the middle of the table.

He arched one eyebrow at her. "That's a pretty steep bet."

"It is… Though I have heard that you should never wager anything you don't want to lose, so if you really want to keep your protein bar you should fold."

He shook his head. "No way. I'm sort of an all-in kind of guy."

"Are you?" she asked. "You seem like an I-don't-place-a-bet-unless-I'm-going-to-win kind of guy."

"Possibly," he said with a shrug. "In life, definitely, but when it comes to cards I have a different set of rules."

She nodded. "You're all about the rules, aren't you?"

He didn't think she meant that as a good thing and thought maybe he should hedge his answer. But when she'd been brutally honest about her family, he'd decided to do the same with her. Keep it real instead of trying to protect himself from letting her see too much of who he was. "I know it makes me sound like an old fart, but I am about the rules. Life is just so much easier when we all know what to expect."

"Why break them the night of the gala, then? And who called you an old fart?" she asked, laughing. "I mean I haven't exactly seen that side of you. At the gala you were definitely not acting like a stick-in-the-mud."

"My brothers and Bianca call me that. But that's just because they usually don't follow the rules and end up in trouble. The night of the gala… I don't know, I guess I just felt like I could let go because no one knew it was me. It gave me a chance to just let my guard down. And I imitated Alec the night of the gala because he needed me. I can't turn down family."

"That's sweet. I liked you at the gala," she said.

"You did?" he asked, leaning across the table. He wanted her so badly that every inhalation was almost painful. He could smell her perfume. His senses were overwhelmed with everything that was Scarlet. He struggled to keep his eyes off the curves of her body and that damned strand of hair she kept tucking behind her ear. He knew if he shifted his legs under the table he'd brush against her; he had done it twice already and had the feeling she'd catch on to what he was doing if he did it again.

He was trying but it was hard. He was hard, and he wanted nothing more than to forget all the rules that he applied to his life to keep it orderly, sweep her into his arms and carry her into the bedroom at the back of the plane.

"I did," she said.

He groaned.

"What?"

"You're not making this easy."

"Making what easy?"

"Just sticking to my own tips for not screwing things up with you any further than I already have," he said.

She laughed again and it made him smile. The sound was so genuine and full of joy that he couldn't help himself. Which only underscored how important it was for him to stick to his own regulations where she was concerned.

"I have to admit I like that," she said.

"You do?"

"Yes. You aren't what I expected, Alec, and I like it better when I know I'm not the only one struggling to figure things out."

That wasn't all he was struggling with. "My brothers would give me tons of shit if they ever heard about this."

"Why?"

"Because that's how brothers are," he said.

"And… You're the goody-goody in the Velasquez family, aren't you?"

"I guess. I mean, I'm not a nerdy rule follower. I just like to stay within safe limits," he said, then groaned again as he realized exactly how that sounded. "Okay, so I am a goody-goody. But I've been burned when I just let go of all my limits and I realized that I have to know which lines I can't cross."

"Fair enough," she said. "So, back to the game. Are you going to call?"

Call? No. He wanted more than her protein bar and chocolate. He wanted kisses, but real kisses. He wanted the stakes to be higher and he knew the risk. He could move too fast and push her away. But as Mo would say, you have to take a chance if you ever want the big prize.

And he wanted her…badly.

"I'm going to raise," he said at last.

"You are?"

"Yes," he said, pushing the requisite ante into the center of the table. "I call and raise you one kiss."

"A kiss? I have two in there," she said.

"No, I mean a real one. A bodies-pressed-together, mouths-fused, passion-filled kiss."

"Oh," she said, a slight flush spreading up her neck to her cheeks. "Very well, I call."

He stretched his legs, and the fabric of his trousers brushed against her. She shifted so that her calves rested against his as he slowly laid his cards on the table. She glanced at the pair of tens with an ace high that he'd revealed and then back at her own hand.

She had two pairs so that beat him. She had always been a believer that she shouldn't wager anything she didn't want to lose, and frankly, she had been craving Alec since the moment they'd been alone in the barn at the polo match. Nothing had changed since then.

Of course, she'd retreated, but that was because he was different. The type of guy she normally attracted would have pushed for a kiss or more until she either gave in or shoved him out of her life. But Alec was subtle and funny. He was carefully feeling his way along trying to get to know her better and maybe let her see the real man.

She fanned her cards out on the table and then crossed her arms under her breasts as she leaned back in the large leather chair. "Read 'em and weep."

He chewed his lower lip between his teeth and gave her a steely-eyed look. "I see I'm going to have to re-evaluate you. I was sure you were bluffing."

"I wasn't," she said.

"Obviously. But you played it so cool I couldn't tell.

Interesting. I think that means you must spend a lot of time hiding who you really are," he said.

"Dude, I said you could have a kiss, not psychoanalyze me."

He leaned across the table, reaching out to tuck a strand of her hair behind her ear. "Sorry. It's just that I haven't wanted a woman the way I want you in a long time. I'm trying to give myself a bit of time to gain some control."

Again she was struck by how he seemed to have no barriers when it came to her. She wanted to believe in him but as he'd noted a minute ago, experience had taught her that what she really needed to do was to keep her true self hidden. It was just better for her. There had been only one person she'd ever felt comfortable letting her guard down around and that had been Tara.

And she was still trying to recover from the pain of losing her the way that she had. She really didn't want to go down that dark and emotional path so she leaned forward, elbows on the table, putting her hands on his wrists. "So about the kiss I've won in this hand."

"What about it?" he asked.

"I'm trying to decide if I should take my prize and walk or keep it in the ante and see if I can win again."

He took her left hand in his, his thumb stroking her palm and sending shivers of sensation up her arm, making her breasts feel heavy.

"Up to you," he said. "You call the shots."

As if. She realized that was cynical but she'd been in too many situations like this to believe that one person called all the shots. Sex was intimate and involved so much more than power in her experience.

"I see you don't believe me," he said. "I'm not playing around with you, Scarlet. I know I lied to you the first night we met but you're pregnant with my baby. I want you more than I want my next breath and that makes me feel dangerous…out of control. I don't want to be that way. Not when so much is at stake."

Again he disarmed her with the truth. His earnestness made her want to believe him yet every experience in her life had shown her that when she most wanted to trust in another person, they let her down. And he was right: the stakes here were high. They both wanted to make sure they didn't add another screwed-up being to the planet. Both of them wanted better for the baby she was carrying.

And maybe that was enough.

Of course it is. Tara's voice sounded in her head. *Stop dithering and kiss the man. It's what you want.*

It was what she wanted so she pushed away from the table and went around to his side. She put her hands on the arm of his chair and spun it so he faced her. Then she sat down on his lap, sitting sideways so that her legs hung over the armrest and she could see his face. One of his arms came around her waist and the other one just hovered in the air over her body, not touching her.

She lifted her hand to his face, touched the light stubble on his jaw and looked into his dark brown eyes, searching for something in his gaze but not really knowing what it was. She sighed inside and realized there were no guarantees. This could be nothing more than a nice way to spend the flight or it could be the most dangerous decision she ever made.

But she wasn't someone who cowered. And Tara's voice in her head had reminded her of that.

She rubbed her thumb over his full lower lip and his mouth parted, his breath coming out in a sudden gasp. She felt him harden under her hips. She leaned in closer, taking her time because now that she'd made up her mind, there was no rush. Regardless of the outcome, she wanted and intended to make this last.

Their eyes met and she felt something shift and settle deep inside her. At least they had this one thing that made sense between them. The rest of their lives were crazy right now, but this, she thought as she leaned in and brushed her lips over his, made perfect sense.

Nine

His hands were shaking; it was all he could do to keep himself under control. But she was on his lap, her mouth so close to his that he felt each exhalation of her breath against his lips, and it served to fan the flames that were edging ever more untamable.

He put his hand on her shoulder, forcing himself to keep his touch light and not caress her skin. But the neckline of her sweater was wide, and he had brushed her naked skin as his fingers came to rest there. He wanted to stroke and caress her more, but he had promised her she was in control. That he'd settle for whatever she wanted to give him.

But he knew deep in his soul that he wanted it all. He wanted every damned thing she had to give. Her lips brushed his and sensation went through him, making his blood run heavier in his veins and hardening his cock. He shifted underneath her to try to make himself more comfortable within the tight confines of his pants.

She smiled against his mouth as she kept the kiss light. Just a mere pressing of her lips against his. Then she moved her head slightly and their lips rubbed together more intimately. The hair on the back of his neck stood up and a sensual shiver went down his spine. He moved his hand from her collarbone to the back of her neck, cupping it as he turned his head slightly and deepened the kiss.

She tasted better than he remembered... And given that it hadn't been that long since he'd last kissed her, he was surprised. Surely, she hadn't become more addictive in those few hours since their kiss. But it seemed she had. His hand tangled in her braid as he cupped the back of her head and leaned up to take her mouth more deeply. He heard the tiny moan from deep in her throat and he answered in kind.

He rubbed his hand down her back, taking his time so that he felt each curve of her spine. Then he shifted his head back to look up at her as he put both hands on her waist and lifted her until she could straddle his lap.

She clutched his shoulders and settled her thighs on either side of his hips. He inhaled deeply, smelled the slight hint of roses and something spicier, a more sensual scent that he remembered from the night of the gala.

He slipped his hands under the hem of her sweater and held her against him as he looked up at her. She smiled, just the tiniest lift of one side of her mouth, before she leaned down, resting her forehead against his. Then he felt the brush of her tongue against his lips.

He groaned, and got even harder. He wasn't going to be able to live up to his word and take just a kiss if she kept this up. Already he wanted more. He wanted her leggings off and her naked body pressed against him.

He wanted this sweater gone and them both naked with him buried deep inside her. But he knew that he had to temper that desire. Had to make this last. He'd given his word and if he didn't live up to it, she'd always remember.

He slipped one hand up her back and used the other on her waist to draw her even closer to him, until their groins were pressed together. She rocked her hips against him and he tore his mouth from hers, tipping his head back as exquisite sensation shot through him.

She shifted farther forward, grasping at his sides, and he held one of her arms lightly in his hand as he deepened the kiss. Their tongues tangled as he rubbed his hand up and down her arm, pulling the edge of her sweater down so that her collarbone was exposed. He touched her there, caressing her; her skin was softer than he remembered.

He pulled his mouth from hers, dropping nibbling kisses down the column of her throat and then sucking lightly on the pulse that beat under her skin. She shivered in his arms as he moved his mouth along the line of her collarbone to her shoulder. She put one hand on the back of his head, her fingers burrowing into his hair and holding him against her. He breathed deeply, the scent of her more potent now that he held her in his arms.

He closed his eyes, reaching deep inside for his control, but it was slipping so quickly through his grasp. The hand he had on the small of her back slipped down to cup her butt, rubbing over the spandex fabric of her leggings and drawing her ever closer to him. She shifted, still holding his head against her as she arched her back and rubbed her center over him. They both groaned out loud and he turned his head, using his nose to push the collar of her sweater down farther, kissing his way down her chest following the line of her bra. The straps were lacy, contrasting with the smoothness of her skin. He moved lower, still following the seams of her lingerie, tasting the sweetness that was Scarlet. He knew that he wasn't going to be able to take it slow for much longer, yet at the same time he wanted this to last. Wanted to keep her in his arms for as long as he could.

He buried his face between her breasts. His hand was on her butt urging her closer to him and her hands were in his hair, one fingernail tracing the shape of his ear. When the plane hit turbulence and they were jolted, he wrapped his arms around her, holding her close to him until the aircraft leveled out.

Her heart raced from lust, and the dipping of the plane. She should get off his lap, but she'd decided she wasn't doing that. This wasn't an unhealthy addiction. This was something natural between the two of them and she wasn't going to deny herself. Also, she felt like she needed to treat him as she would any other guy. How else could she judge this situation that was so far out of her experience?

"Are you okay?" he asked.

His voice was raspy, scraping over her already aroused senses and confirming her desire to have him. Now.

"Yes. That was jarring, though," she said.

He reached around her and pressed a button in the arm of his chair.

"Yes, sir?"

"Will we be encountering any more turbulence?" Alec asked.

"No, sir, we haven't heard reports of it. That was an anomaly and we should be fine," the pilot answered.

"Great. Thank you."

"No problem. Do you need anything?"

"We're fine and do not wish to be disturbed," he said.

"Yes, sir."

He put his hands on her waist over her sweater and looked up at her with a very serious look on his face.

"Do you want to stop?" he asked.

She felt his erection still pressing against her. His skin was flushed, his pupils dilated, and his voice still betrayed his lust.

"No. Do you?"

"I don't, but I'd never want you to feel pressured," he said.

"I don't," she returned. "Do you?"

He shook his head, slipping his hands under her sweater, cupping her butt and rubbing it. "What do you think?"

He pulled her forward, thrusting his hips up so that her center rubbed over the ridge of his cock. She let her head fall back at the exquisiteness of the feeling that washed over her.

"I think we should stop talking," she said, putting one hand on the back of his head as she brought her mouth down hard on his.

He groaned as his hands moved up to the waistband of her leggings. He pushed beneath it to touch the naked skin of her back, his fingers feathering downward until he was cupping her butt, this time without any fabric separating them. He ran his finger along the bottom of her butt cheek and lifted her higher against him.

He pulled his mouth from hers, kissing her in the center of her chest, slightly to the right of her heart. He used his other hand to tug at the hem of her sweater and pulled it up over her head. She moved her arms to help him remove it.

He kept stroking her backside as his gaze moved over her chest. He drew his finger down her body from her neck to the V created by her bra and then up the other side of her body. She felt the goose pimples rise and her nipples tighten as he continued to trace her skin. She wanted more of his touch and yet enjoyed the feel of just his fingertips on her skin.

"You have the smoothest skin I've ever touched," he admitted, licking his way down her body. "It's one of the things I couldn't forget about you after our night together. I thought I'd imagined how soft you were…"

His words were whispered against her skin as he moved his mouth down her neck. She shifted around, her braid coming forward to brush over her shoulder, the end of it brushing against his nose.

She'd always been the girl to take a risk but this time, with Alec, it felt different. The first time they'd been together hadn't been all that risky or bold. Not really. It had just been a bit of fun with a guy she thought she'd never see again.

This time it was different. She was consciously choosing to be with a man she was connected to through this baby, a situation that she still couldn't really wrap her head around.

He reached up to tug off the elastic that held her braid in place and dropped it on the table next to them. He pulled the plait apart and then ran both hands through the long strands of her hair, drawing it forward until the ends draped over her shoulders. Her hair was long enough that it reached the top of her breasts. He reached behind her, undoing her bra, and then she shrugged it off, setting it on the table next to them.

He continued to run his hands through her hair. "You smell like spring, fresh and flowery. After our night together, I couldn't get your scent out of my mind. I made my housekeeper crazy trying to figure out the smell by ordering different bouquets of flowers."

"Did you figure it out?" she asked as he leaned forward and brought a strand of her hair to his nose.

"No."

"It's a mix of strawberries, magnolias and freesia. Sounds like it shouldn't work but for some reason it does," she said with a laugh, realizing that she was nervous. She was talking to him during sex and that made it more intimate than their one-night stand. They hadn't talked, just kissed and touched and made love.

But this was different. It was deliberate. And that both excited her and scared her.

He felt a pulse of desire between his legs and realized he couldn't take his time. He was too hot for Scarlet but then had been since the beginning.

He tongued her nipple, then scraped his teeth gently over it. She arched again, grinding her hips against his. He tugged at the waistband of her leggings and she shifted position, drawing them down her legs and standing up to take them off. She stood next to his chair totally naked and he couldn't think. Couldn't breathe. Couldn't do anything except lift her into his arms and carry her to the bedroom at the back of the jet.

He opened the door with one hand and then kicked it closed behind him as he entered the room. He set her on her feet next to the bed, and she reached for the buttons on his shirt, slowly undoing them and distracting him from the urgency of getting his pants off.

The red haze that had fallen over him lifted as he slowly wrested control back. He could do this. Still be cool and not fall on her like a man enflamed with lust and passion…maybe.

He kicked off his loafers and shoved his jeans and underwear down his legs as she pushed his shirt off his shoulders. As soon as he was naked, he felt better. This was how they should both be.

She touched his chest; her fingers were slightly cold as she drew them over his pectorals. She ran her nail around the edge of the muscles and then slowly back up to his neck. Her touch sent shivers down his body and he felt like he was on the verge of losing control once again. He truly wasn't sure how much longer he was going to be able to let her touch him.

He wanted to draw this out so it felt like making love and not a hurried coupling. They'd had sex twice the night of the gala and he'd still woken up hungry for her again. Would he ever be able to satisfy that hunger?

She was so pretty and feminine. He traced her curves from her shoulder down to her hips, trying to be cool like he wasn't dying to caress her, to taste her intimately. But he knew he was.

He slowly moved his fingers up her thigh to her hip bone and then down to the cradle of her womanhood. He ran his fingers along the neatly trimmed pubic hair and then lower as she scored his chest with her nails.

She rocked her hips forward as he touched her, tapping lightly on her, and she moaned. As she was stroking him, he couldn't help but rub the length of himself against her. She wrapped her arms around his shoulders and he put his arm behind her as he tipped her back onto the bed, coming down over her.

She arched her back as he caught her nipple in his mouth and suckled it. At the same time, he palmed her body and thrust the tip of one finger inside her, drawing out the wet tip, bringing it to his mouth and licking it.

He sat back on his knees and looked down at her. Their eyes met, and he knew that he was never going to be the same after this.

"I'd forgotten how good you are."

He leaned down to taste her again, used his tongue to seek out the tiny bud between her legs, flicking it again and again as her hands held his head to her, her hips lifting into each flick of his tongue. Her legs tightened around him as he continued to eat her.

She clasped him tightly to her as her hips rose frantically, her legs scissoring around him. Then she called out his name and felt her orgasm roll through her body.

Her body was still buzzing and pulsing from her climax. It was nice but she needed Alec inside her.

She pulled him up and over her, lifting her torso so she could find his mouth and take it in a deep kiss. She took in the salty taste of her own passion on his tongue, as she felt him enter her. She held on to his broad shoulders and arched her back, pushing up against him to drive him deeper.

He groaned and called her name as he pulled back and then thrust into her, taking her even deeper than he had before. He was big and solid and filled her completely. She let her head fall back as he drove himself into her again and again. She felt the tingling in her body, and each time he thrust into her she craved more.

Twisting his hand in her hair, he held her head so her neck was exposed and dropped a light bite against her there. It sent off a chain reaction inside her, and her second orgasm took her by surprise.

She clutched him to her as she rode her orgasm, and he lowered his head, taking one of her nipples into his mouth and suckling her. His hips were moving faster and faster until she heard him grunt as he emptied himself inside her. He kept thrusting until he was completely empty and then rolled to his side, taking her with him. He tucked her up against him and stroked her back.

She refused to let herself think about anything other than this moment. She was in the arms of a man whom she'd slept with before. She was going to have a relationship with him whether she wanted one or not, and instead of it making her want to get up and run away, she curled closer to him. He fumbled around for the edge of the comforter and drew it over her.

"Are you okay?" he asked.

"I'm good," she said.

He kissed her forehead and held her lightly in his arms.

Something had changed inside her and she pretended it hadn't.

Ten

The week in Seattle had cemented a bond between her and Alec that had been unexpected. In the last six weeks or so since they'd returned, she had balanced between Cole's Hill and trying to get to know Alec and his family and her commitments in New York. She was still having some morning sickness but it had started to settle down. She'd tried to make sure she was in Cole's Hill for the "book club" on Friday nights with Hadley and Helena and their friends. She'd taken Lulu for walks around the neighborhood and enjoyed how quiet it was. A part of her sort of liked it here.

Now she was sitting by his pool under the shade of an umbrella on a lazy Saturday afternoon. Lulu was sleeping in the sun on a cushion that Alec had set up on the patio close to a bowl of water. Music was already blaring from the speakers. She noticed that Alec liked Drake and Childish Gambino but occasionally something from Pitbull would pop up.

His family was coming over later for a cookout and tomorrow they were going to a baby shower for his sister, Bianca.

Lying on the sun lounger with her shades on, she felt like she could be a woman who would fit in here. Her baby was growing, and she had a doctor's appointment next week in Cole's Hill just to make sure things were still on track. She'd flown her doctor in from New York for her last monthly checkup, but Alec had suggested she see someone local just to be on record as a patient.

She stretched her legs out and placed her hand on her abdomen. The baby wasn't big enough for her to feel it move yet, but she knew it was in there.

Alec's shadow covered her, and she glanced up. "Do you mind if I sit down here?"

She shifted her legs to give him room to sit next to her on the chair. He handed her the bowl of strawberries that he'd gone to get for her. To be honest, Alec spoiled her and she liked it. All she had to do was mention she was hungry or that the strawberries they'd picked up at the market looked good and he was off making her a bowl.

He put his hand on her thigh and that familiar buzz of desire and lust started humming through her body. He caressed her inner thigh and then she noticed him watching her.

"What is it?" she asked. "Thanks for the strawberries by the way."

"No problem. Do you mind if I touch your stomach?" he asked. "It's hard to believe our child is in there."

She set the bowl aside and took his hand in hers, placing it on her stomach. She had a slight pooch there now, but really it wasn't easy to tell from just looking at her that she was pregnant. Alec, being the superefficient man he was, had researched the different stages of pregnancy and had sent her a pdf containing all the information. It had made her smile when she'd received the text.

Other men might send flowers or expensive gifts, but Alec Velasquez was too practical for that.

"Yes, it is. Now that the morning sickness is over, I'm not really that affected by the child…except for these," she said, gesturing to her boobs, which were already half a cup size larger than usual.

"I noticed that," he admitted.

"Given that you couldn't keep your hands off me last night, I'm not surprised," she said with a smile. "I have a doctor's appointment this week. Do you want to come with me?"

Each step in her pregnancy, she was starting to see how good Alec was at adapting to the situation. There were moments that had clearly taken him by surprise but there were also many that seemed to show he was in his element.

"I'd like that. Do you have the details?"

"I'll text them to you later," she said.

He leaned over and kissed her before standing up and moving back to his own chair. "Are you okay?"

"I don't know. I'm still trying to adjust to you being pregnant and I'm not sure I'm doing the right thing. I mean I want you but I'm not sure that I should… I mean you're pregnant."

"Dude, I was pregnant on the jet and in Seattle and last night and that didn't stop you," she said.

"Maybe it should have," he said. "I mean pretty much we're still strangers and you're having my baby…which makes me think of my *abuela*'s favorite show, *I Love Lucy*, and that episode where Ricky sings… I'm losing it. I don't know how to act anymore. I mean I can't be the guy I was because I'm going to be a dad. I don't know if I'm ready."

She swung her legs to the side of the chair and leaned forward to touch his hand. "Hey. I'm not ready. That pdf you sent said that the nine months of pregnancy are supposed to help you prepare for the child."

"I don't know if nine months is going to be enough," he admitted.

"Me, either," she said. It was the first time they'd really talked about the baby. She felt like that was partially her fault because she'd been trying to make things between herself and Alec just feel normal instead of… like this. "I've never had a relationship with a guy before that's lasted this long."

"We've barely been seeing each other six weeks," he said.

"I know. It's just the way I normally am. I don't know how to do this," she admitted.

"Well, the sex seems to be good between us," he said, smiling and tangling their fingers together.

"It does… But is that all there is to a relationship?" she asked, moving over to sit on his lap. He wrapped his arms around her waist as she cupped his jaw.

"No. We also have to get to know things about each other," he said.

"Like what?"

"Well, I know you like strawberries," he said.

"And you like Lone Star beer," she said.

"We should probably learn a few more things about each other before we call it a relationship," he joked.

"You like Drake…a lot."

"I do," he admitted. "What about you?"

"Well, of course I like Siobahn's songs but my comfort listen is jazz standards from the thirties and forties."

"What? The brand influencer likes old-timey music?" he teased.

"I do," she admitted. "And you're the only one who knows."

"I'm honored," he said.

"You should be," she said, stretching up to kiss him as she put her arms around his shoulders. She pressed herself against his naked chest and in this moment she didn't let herself worry over what she was going to do when the nine months were up and her baby was here. Instead she just enjoyed the afternoon in the sun with her lover.

Alec shifted on the sun lounger made for two so that they were lying side by side and he was cuddling her from behind. Their bodies fit together perfectly, her curves settling against his angles. His hand was warm on her hip as he caressed her. His head rested on her shoulder as he continued to ask her questions about things she liked and didn't like.

This was like nothing she'd ever experienced before

and a part of her wished that it wasn't happening. She had that weird feeling again. It was warm and almost comforting. She associated it with Alec but she couldn't say for sure what it was. She thought she might be starting to care for him.

She didn't want that.

Sex was one thing. But if she let herself start caring… She admitted to herself she was afraid that she might not be able to control herself with Alec if she cared. She was trying to get to know him without allowing herself to need him. She couldn't need him except as a father for her baby. She knew that she wasn't facing the fact that she was going to have make a decision about the baby's future and she was starting to care for Alec. But she couldn't allow herself to feel anything other than lust for him.

She turned in his arms. His hands stayed at her waist and when she faced him, seeing the stubble on his jaw and the intensity of his gaze, she knew that lust was definitely a big draw for both of them.

He leaned down to kiss her and she caught his bottom lip between her teeth, sucking on it. Then he shifted his head and his mouth was on hers, his lips firm as he slowly kissed her. He moved his head back and forth, until her lips parted and she felt the exhalation of his breath into her mouth. He tasted of lime and tequila and something that she associated only with Alec. She opened her mouth to invite him deeper.

She shivered as she wrapped her arms around him and draped one thigh over his hips, trying to get closer to him. The taste of him always made her hungry for more.

"I'm having another craving," she whispered against his jaw.

"What is it for?" he asked, his hands moving up and down her body.

"You," she admitted.

She squeezed his shoulders, then moved her hands up his neck to cup the back of his head. His hair was thick and silky under her fingers. God, she wanted him. And it was okay to admit it because sex was safe. Not like hearing him talk about her having his baby. This made sense. This she understood.

He caressed her back, his fingers tracing a delicate pattern down her spine. Then he pushed one of his hands beneath her bikini bottom to cup her naked flesh. She rubbed her backside against his hand, liking the feel of it.

He ran his other hand up the curve of her waist and around to her chest. She shifted back and their eyes met as he moved his hand up to her breasts, which were almost too big for her bikini top now that her pregnancy was advancing. He traced his finger around the triangles of fabric, then slowly dipped one under it to brush over her already aroused nipple.

Delicate tremors went through her entire body. He kept one hand on her butt and one fingertip idly circling her nipple. She shifted in his arms, trying to get closer to him.

He lowered his head, his lips gliding down the column of her neck. Then she felt his teeth on the bikini tie at the back of her neck. He twisted his head and the bow came undone, then he caught one strap between his lips and drew it forward until one of her breasts was exposed…the one he wasn't caressing with his finger.

"Oh, hello," he said, lowering his head and circling that nipple with his tongue. Her head fell back, and she clutched at his shoulders as he took her into his mouth and sucked eagerly. Every nerve in her body seemed to constrict with desire and her center was damp and aching for him.

He shifted her suddenly so that she was lying on her back underneath him as he knelt over her. His mouth continued to drive her mad and all she was aware of was the delicious feelings he was pulling from her.

His muscled thigh pushed between her legs, nudging them apart, and she felt the ridge of his erection rubbing against her. She lifted her hips, moving her body under his until he rubbed her in just the right spot.

She ran her hands down his back, reaching the point in the small of his back that made his hips jerk forward against him. He eased down her body, kissing her from her midriff down to her belly button. He eased even lower, nibbling at the skin of her belly where he'd touched her earlier.

He kissed her there and whispered something against her stomach that she couldn't hear before he dipped his tongue into the indentation left by her belly button. She felt an answering pulse between her legs. She gyrated underneath him and he pushed back, his erection thrusting against her leg.

His mouth went lower on her, his hands roaming to the waistband of her bikini bottoms and slowly drawing them down to her thighs. She wanted to push them lower, but she felt his moist breath against her stomach and then the scratchiness of his stubble as he rubbed his jaw against her.

"Lift up," he said.

She planted her feet on the sun lounger and did as he asked. He shoved her bikini bottoms the rest of the way down her legs. Their eyes met and he held her gaze as he put his hand on her feminine center. Her skin felt too sensitive and her blood felt like it was boiling in her veins. She was on fire for him. She had never expected to still want him just as badly over so much time. She thought that their lovemaking wouldn't be as intense after all these weeks.

She was wrong.

He spoke against her skin, telling her what he was going to do to her, how much he loved the feel of her naked body under his. Then he lowered his head again, his chin brushing her center as he twisted his head back and forth. The movement put pressure on her, causing her clit to swell and become more sensitive.

He parted her using both of his hands and she felt the brush of the cold air against her most intimate flesh. Then he warmed her with his mouth, breathing over her. She squirmed against him hungrily.

She felt the rasp of his teeth against her and everything inside her clenched, almost making her come. But Alec lifted his head at the last minute, leaving her yearning for more.

"I want to make this last," he admitted.

She put her hands on the back of his head and directed him back to her clit. "Later we can make it last. I need you now."

She felt one of his hands go lower, tracing her opening. Those large knowing hands of his made her push up against him with need. Everything in her body was on the edge. He pushed his finger—just the tip—inside her and she felt the first ripples of her orgasm rushing through her. He pulled back, lifting his head to watch her as she undulated beneath him.

"Alec…"

"Yes?" he asked.

"I need you inside me."

"Perfect. That's what I need, too," he said, lowering his body over hers so the warm flesh of his chest rubbed against her breasts. Then his thigh was between her legs brushing against her engorged flesh, and she wanted to scream as everything in her tightened just a little bit more.

"Alec!"

She twisted underneath him, clawing at his shoulders as he thrust up and inside her. He drove into her again and again until she was crying out his name, and he shouted hers against her shoulder. They came long and hard and then afterward he held her in his arms, shifting to his side to hold her. She looked up at him.

And that funny feeling was back, even more intense this time. *Oh, God.* She wasn't sure she was ready to admit that she liked him this much.

"I guess we know something else about each other."

"What's that?" he asked, tucking a strand of hair behind her ear.

"We both don't have a problem getting naked in the great outdoors."

He started laughing and then shook his head. "Very true."

Eleven

The longer Scarlet stayed in Cole's Hill, the deeper the bond grew between her and Alex. His family and friends had accepted her into their circle and she was feeling for the first time in her life that it might be okay to let her guard down with more than just a select few people.

A couple of hours in, Bianca's baby shower was in full swing. All of the Velasquez brothers were in attendance, which was a big deal since Inigo had come fresh from a Formula 1 race to make it. Benito was proudly wearing a shirt that said I'm the Big Brother and because he was close with Nate and Kinley's daughter, Penny, Penny had a shirt that said "I'm the Big Cousin." The two of them were thick as thieves and it made Scarlet smile to see the way Alec's entire family embraced Bianca's baby.

Alec had been locked away in the den for several hours discussing something with Inigo, but she hadn't missed him. She was seated on the couch with Helena, Hadley and Kinley, and honestly, she'd never had more fun.

She'd sent Billie back to New York to get ready for the launch of her newest lifestyle box, a quarterly subscription that included trendy products, and Siobahn was still lying low at the house that Scarlet had rented. She'd started writing music again and Scarlet felt her friend was finally moving on from the heartbreak that had been dominating her life for so long.

Being surrounded by so much domestic bliss today brought her to an idea she'd been toying with for a while. She'd never really been able to crack the market of women who were older and maybe settling down. Her audience members were young and single and pretty much interested in working hard and partying hard. But spending time with Helena and Kinley made her think of maybe curating a wedding/bride subscription box. As the demographic of her audience was maturing, this might be a logical next step.

"Are you two available tomorrow to discuss a new project I'm working on?" Scarlet said. "I'm sort of known for my monthly lifestyle boxes and I'd love to do one with a wedding or bridal theme. Kinley, maybe I can partner with Jaqs if you think she'd be interested and include some exclusive content. Helena, as a bride-to-be, it'd be great to get your input on what to include."

"I love this idea," Kinley said. "I'll text Jaqs after the party. She's always looking to expand into new markets. We've been working on an exclusive tiara collection with Pippa and House of Hamilton. Maybe we could bring her into this as well with some bridesmaids' gifts."

"Sweet," Scarlet said.

"I'm happy to help but honestly the things I'm interested in might be out of step with most brides. Like I've been majorly stressed by things that aren't necessarily planning related," Helena said.

"Hmm… Maybe we could include some tips from meditation experts, too. So it wouldn't just be actual wedding products but wellness items, too. So will tomorrow work for you two to discuss the details?"

Kinley nodded, and Helena pulled out her smartphone, glanced at her calendar and then back at the two of them. "I could do early afternoon, but I have to combine it with lunch. Maybe around one or one thirty."

"That's fine with me," Scarlet said.

"I'm good with that, as well. Tomorrow I'm working on Helena's wedding, so I can move around a few things," Hadley said.

"Mom won't like that," Helena warned.

"Your mom's going to Vegas to meet with Jaqs. She and Jaqs have become closer after their blowup," Kinley interjected.

Alec knew there had to be more to the story and she was interested in hearing it, but the main festivities of the baby shower were starting. She realized she'd never been to a party like this one. It was multigenerational, and almost everyone at the party had known each other for most of their lives. There was a lot of joking and reminiscing.

She looked over at Mr. Velasquez and tried to imagine her father ever attending a baby shower but frankly couldn't. He wanted nothing to do with babies because they'd make him seem older or settled.

She already knew he wasn't going to be a doting grandfather... Why would he be? He hadn't exactly embraced fatherhood.

Just then Alec entered the room holding a plate of food from the buffet and a glass of sparkling water. He came over and handed them to her. "Figured you'd be getting hungry."

"Thank you," she said, taking the plate and drink from him. They'd discovered while she was in Seattle that if she ate something every hour she didn't get sick.

"Looks like someone has broken Alec," Mauricio said as he joined them.

"Mo, he's not a horse," Hadley said.

"What is he?"

"A gentleman... In fact, you could take lessons from your twin. I don't think you've ever brought me a plate of food."

"I give you other things," Mo said, drawing his fiancée into his arms and kissing her, much to the delight of everyone in the room.

Helena got up and Alec took her spot next to Scarlet. "I like your family," she said to him.

"Me, too. They are a bit of a pain sometimes because everyone feels like they know best but at the end of the day they'll always be there for me," he said, stretching his arm along the back of the sofa and wrapping it around her shoulder.

Alec was turning out to be an even better man than she'd expected to find, and his family would be exactly what her child needed. She felt better and better about the prospects for her baby, and that made her decision easier. She knew that if things didn't work out in her relationship with Alec—and frankly, she wasn't expecting them to, because she'd never been able to make one last more than six months— at least her child would still have a decent family to raise it.

Sometimes she started to think that they might be able to be a couple and raise the baby together. But there were times when she woke up sweating and scared thinking about the possibility that the baby would grow up and be in the place Tara had been toward the end of her life She had failed her sister and she didn't want to fail her child.

Helena wasn't too sure if she should bring up Scarlet's request to Malcolm, but she wasn't hiding anything from him. They were doing pretty well but she had been careful not to do anything that would rock the boat. She knew that wasn't a healthy way to treat him but she'd been afraid of doing something that would drive him back to gambling. So as soon as he got home from work after picking up takeout from Taco Heaven, she decided to talk to him about it.

"Scarlet asked me if I would contribute to a project she's working on," Helena said.

"Really? That's interesting. Is it budgeting tips? You're really good at that," Malcolm said.

She smiled as he passed her a Dos Equis from the fridge.

"Thanks, babe, but that's not it. She wants me to help her curate a wedding planning subscription box to go out to her mailing list and talk about stress and how to deal with it," Helena said.

"Oh," he said, looking over at her. She knew that his gambling and how he'd dipped into their wedding fund to cover his losses were still shameful for him and hoped that she wasn't striking a nerve. "Well, I have to say you're good at that, too."

"I won't mention any specifics… Actually, I was going to suggest that we write the text for the insert together. We have to just talk about why we chose the products. Maybe talk about how pretending nothing is wrong leads to a bad situation or something like that," Helena said.

Malcolm was her partner in life and even though they weren't officially married yet, the two of them had a strong bond—even stronger since everything had come out about his gambling and they'd taken steps to deal with it together.

"I'd like that," he said, pulling her into his arms, lifting her up onto the kitchen island and stepping between her legs. "You're still much too good for me."

She laughed. "Don't worry, I won't let you forget it."

He kissed her and one thing led to another. Ultimately they had to reheat their tacos in the microwave before they ate them but neither minded.

Monthly poker night was a tradition in his group of friends. Until Scarlet had come along, it had been his only activity outside of polo that wasn't strictly work-related. He'd always looked forward to it. It was a traveling game, and everyone took turns hosting it. Malcolm was supposed to host tonight but since he had been dealing with overcoming his gambling addiction he'd dropped out of the game. It made him feel better and it definitely reassured Helena, according to Bianca, who had given Alec an earful when he'd mentioned his view that harmless betting with friends wasn't the same thing as gambling huge sums of money.

He hadn't realized how insensitive the comment was until she'd pointed it out. Betting of any kind was too much of a temptation for Malcolm. Alec felt like an awful friend for not recognizing that so he'd suggested pool tonight at the Five Families Clubhouse instead. That way Malcolm could join them. The rest of their group had agreed to pool instead of poker, so Alec was heading up there to spend the evening with the guys.

"Are you sure you don't mind me going?" Alec asked Scarlet as they were sitting on the couch in her house. Siobahn had taken over the large armchair catty-corner to the sofa and looked over at him shaking her head.

"She doesn't mind, dude. We're planning girls' night," Siobahn said.

"She's right, we are having girls' night and I'm fine," Scarlet said.

She had her legs draped over his lap and he rubbed her calf. She'd gone to the local pediatrician earlier and her visit—the first he'd accompanied her on—had revealed slightly elevated blood pressure. The doctor had advised her to stay off her feet so Alec had come to her house tonight.

It was hard to reconcile his feelings for her, which were more complicated than any he'd experienced before. And let's face it, he thought, he wasn't the most touchy-feely of men. He preferred to be in his dark office, with three computer monitors running different codes and algorithms to actually trying to decipher what his emotions meant. But he couldn't stop thinking about Scarlet. He'd cut back on some of his client meetings to stay closer to her as she transitioned from the first trimester into the second.

He hadn't told his parents about the baby yet because Scarlet wanted to wait. In fact, he'd mentioned it just to Mo because his twin was the only one he trusted to keep it quiet. Not that Bianca or his other brothers would intentionally spill the news. But he wasn't sure he was ready for anyone else to know about the baby. Right now it was their little secret. Just between him and Scarlet and the few people they trusted. If he told his parents, his dad was going to ask what their plans were. Were they going to get married or live together? His mom… She was always pressuring his brothers and him to settle down, so she'd push hard for him to make this permanent.

And he had no idea if that would work.

Her friends still weren't sure about him. And while Billie had gone back to New York, Siobahn was still here and had made it clear she still wasn't certain he was good enough for her friend. Given that Siobahn was still recovering from her breakup, that made a bit of sense. She was hiding out while she recovered from her broken heart. And he was doing everything possible to assure Scarlet and her friends that he was a decent guy.

But he also knew that he was afraid of how he could fit into her life. That if they were a couple he wasn't going to be able to avoid her high-profile lifestyle.

White lies had always seemed like something that

weren't really harmful. He thought about the number of times he and Mo had pulled the switch before and they'd never thought about the consequences, but this time it had impacted both of their lives in ways neither of them had anticipated. He never wanted to put anyone through that again. He'd hurt Scarlet and Hadley, something he never would have thought he'd do.

He always prided himself on being a gentleman, so it had been difficult to see himself as the bad guy.

"Fair enough. Who's coming over?" he asked.

"Bianca, Helena, Hadley, Kinley and maybe Ferrin. She and Hunter are driving home tonight. It's the start of the term break." Lulu was curled up on Scarlet's lap but then jumped down and trotted across the room to her chair, where Scarlet kept a cashmere blanket for her.

"Sounds like fun. Are the kids coming?"

"No. Derek is babysitting," Scarlet said.

Alec chuckled at the thought. The onetime most eligible bachelor and notorious playboy had certainly changed a lot since he'd married Bianca. Alec liked the change for his sister's sake. She'd been burned badly once by love so it was nice to see her so happy now.

"Do you need me to do anything before I leave?" Alec asked.

"I think lending me your housekeeper to cook meals for us and to keep me company is enough," Scarlet said.

He shifted out from under her legs and leaned over to kiss her. As always when he touched her, he felt the tingling of desire burning through him. "If you need me, text me."

"I will," she promised, touching his jaw with her finger. "I'll be fine."

"Good."

"Bye, Siobahn," he said, as he straightened and walked out of the room.

She waved in his direction but didn't take her eyes off the notepad on her lap. Scarlet had explained that her friend was busy writing lyrics for a new album. Scarlet thought it was an improvement over partying every night so Siobahn could forget her ex.

"See you later," Scarlet said.

He nodded, not sure he could trust his voice. Because for the first time he had someone he wanted to come home to. It should have been nothing, really. This was a normal, everyday thing for people everywhere but for him it was different.

He drove to the clubhouse thinking about the future and realizing that he was starting to see himself with Scarlet. That the idea of having a family was no longer something foreign that made him feel like an impostor. And he wasn't sure what that meant.

Scarlet stood in the doorway of the family room watching Siobahn laugh with Helena and it made her smile. Of course she hadn't intended to get pregnant but it had led her to something that she never knew existed. It wasn't just this Texas town. It was a lifestyle she'd never realized she'd actually like. As good as it had been for her, she could see Cole's Hill working its magic on Siobahn, too. Her friend was recovering from her heartbreak in a healthy way and Scarlet had to wonder if it would have helped Tara to be in a place like this, too.

For once her sister's voice was quiet in the back of her mind and she wasn't sure if that was a good thing or not. One of the hardest parts about losing someone she loved was trying to hold on to that person. Trying not to let the memories fade. Her therapist had said she should just accept whatever felt right, but a part of her didn't want to ever let go of Tara.

"Hey, you okay?" Bianca said, coming up next to her.

"Yes. How about you? Your due date is getting close, isn't it?" Scarlet asked.

Bianca's stomach was large on her small frame and though she smiled easily, there were moments when Scarlet thought she noticed fatigue in her new friend. "Not soon enough."

"I'm not sure what I'm going to do when I get to that stage," Scarlet admitted.

"I don't want to alarm you but I haven't seen my feet in weeks and they are constantly swollen. Last night Derek had to help me get out of bed to go to the bathroom. I'm just so big now," Bianca said. "I don't remember being this big with Benito."

Scarlet felt panic rising in the back of her throat as Bianca talked about her late-stage pregnancy. She felt a little queasy and started to see spots dancing in front of her eyes. Damn. She was going to pass out if she wasn't careful.

"I have to sit down."

Bianca's eyes widened, and she put her arm around Scarlet, leading her to one of the armchairs. "I'm sorry. I shouldn't have said any of that."

Bianca used her foot to push a small footstool over toward Scarlet. "Prop your feet on here. I'm going to get you a damp towel for your neck. Put your head back and breath. I'm so sorry."

"You okay?" Hadley asked, coming over to Scarlet.

"Yes. Just not adjusting to the Texas heat as well as I'd hoped," Scarlet said, seizing on the weather as an excuse.

"I was going to get her a damp towel," Bianca said.

"I'll get it, Bia. You stay here."

Scarlet closed her eyes and put her head back. She had been so busy thinking about what she should do once the baby was born she hadn't even considered the actual birth. Damn. She wasn't sure she could do it. Frankly, what Bianca had described wasn't something she wanted to experience…ever.

"I really shouldn't have said anything. I'm so miserable that I didn't even think… God, someone gag me. I just can't stop talking," Bianca said.

Scarlet had to laugh at that. She reached over to squeeze Bianca's hand. "It's okay. I mean I'd rather hear the truth than think it's going to be some dreamy perfect feeling."

"Me, too. The first time… Well, Jose wasn't around, and it was much harder on my own," Bianca said. She sat down in the chair next to Scarlet.

"I hope you don't mind but Alec did tell me the reason why," Scarlet said.

"I don't mind. I mean, at the time I was horrified. I had that big, televised wedding… I'm sure you know what that's like. Everyone saw it and I was really embarrassed by how fake it had become."

Scarlet definitely got that. "I try really hard to think of all my social media stuff as a job. When I film, I think of it as getting dressed up for the day. I'm still me but I'm playing a part. Then when I'm home I'm the real me… But if I had a wedding like yours, it would have been hard. I loved it, by the way. My sister and I watched the entire thing. It was a gorgeous wedding."

"Thank you," Bianca said. "I had hoped to transition into doing more lifestyle modeling after it, you know, a prettied up version of my real life, focusing on being a new mother and all of that, but with my marriage breaking down and the baby, it just never happened."

"I'm working with Kinley and Helena to do some subscription wedding boxes… Would you be interested in sponsoring a month? You would be perfect for a fairy-tale wedding planning one and then maybe you could keep it real by talking about living in the actual world after all that fantasy," Scarlet said.

Hadley came back and handed Scarlet a glass of water and the damp towel, which she placed on the back of her neck. "I love the wedding box idea. I hope it's ready before I get much further into planning mine. Do you have one for dealing with moms who want to take over the entire thing?"

Bianca and Scarlet both laughed at that. Hadley's mom was definitely having a moment with two engaged daughters and enjoying planning both of them.

"Not yet," Scarlet admitted. "We will have to do one."

She continued talking to the other women and started to feel sort of normal again, but in the back of her mind was the reminder that no matter how much she was enjoying her time in Cole's Hill, it was just a short interlude before she was going to have to return to her real life. Bianca's comments tonight had made her realize she needed to make a decision about Alec, so she could start figuring out the pregnancy and childbirth part.

She liked his family and his hometown. So, if they weren't going to be together, the thought of asking him to raise their child was becoming harder because each time she pictured that future she imagined herself with him. And she wasn't sure that she'd fit in. Right now when she was out of control and adrift it was easier to think of letting Alec raise their baby alone, but she had started to change and she only wished she could trust herself and believe that she could be a good mother. But had she ever been good enough at anything except scandal?

Twelve

The Five Families Club house was adjacent to an eighteen-hole golf course, tennis courts and the community swimming pool. Growing up, Alec had spent most summers at the clubhouse, charging things on his family's account and playing with his brothers and the friends he still had today. The area was named after the five families that had originally inhabited Cole's Hill. Wanting their town to be different from the others in the area, they'd established a close bond and had often driven their cattle up to Fort Worth Stockyards together back in the frontier days.

"You're looking…different tonight," Mauricio said, coming up to him and handing him a Lone Star beer.

His brother had always seemed like he had too much energy, like he was going to explode if he didn't keep moving. Their mom had often said that they were yin and yang to each other. But since Mo and Hadley had gotten engaged, his brother was calmer. Alec wanted to know what had made the difference but tonight wasn't the time to ask.

Alec took a long swallow and then glanced around to see if anyone was close enough to hear their conversation. The coast was clear; Mal and Diego were off in a corner discussing the upcoming polo match on Sunday and new strategies for the game. "It's Scarlet. Her blood pressure is a little high. I'm worried about her. I had been thinking of the—" he dropped his voice lower "—baby as something that we had time to adjust to and had completely forgotten that pregnancy can be complicated. And things between us are just starting to gel, you know?"

Mo clapped him on the shoulder and squeezed. "I get it. That's how I continue to feel with Hadley and she's even worse than I am. We both want this perfect version of life but it's not that way… It's messy and complicated. I don't want to sound like a sap but do you feel like you two are a team?"

"A team?"

"Yeah, like sometimes when things get really stressful I know I can turn to Hadley and just vent or other times I don't have to say it, she can see I'm on the verge of losing it and she helps me destress. I do the same thing for her."

"I don't know. It's hard to really tell. We are getting closer, but you know me… I'm not really good at reading people," Alec said.

"I am. And she watches you like she cares about you," Mo said.

"I think we like each other. How did you know things were different this time with Hadley? I mean, you broke up after high school and then got back together, and did it again after graduating college, and then again when she moved to New York."

Mo shook his head. "I didn't, bro. I was just winging it and trying like hell to control my temper. Then I started to realize instead of being angry…that part of me, well, Hadley calmed me down and was exactly what I was missing in my life."

"I don't have the anger you always did," Alec said.

"No you have a different kind of thing… Maybe emptiness?" Mo asked.

He shrugged. But his twin was right on the money. There had always been an emptiness inside him that he didn't know how to fill. But Scarlet was starting to fill it… Maybe that was what had him so off-kilter. Because she hadn't indicated that there was any reason for her to stick around after the baby.

"What are you two talking about?" Diego asked, coming over to them with Malcolm on his heels.

"Relationships."

"So it's getting serious with Scarlet?" Malcolm asked.

"Yes, but I know she's only in town temporarily. I mean, we've only been together for six weeks," Alec said, rubbing the back of his neck and taking another long swig of his beer. This discussion wasn't what he'd intended for the evening.

"Six weeks can be a lifetime in some relationships.

Helena and I dated a long time before we got married but I knew on our second date that she was the one," Malcolm said. "Then I had to figure out how to up my game so that when I asked her she'd have no choice but to say yes."

"How did you up your game?" Diego asked. "Pippa and I started out with lust and then, well, things sort of happened."

"Things sort of happened?" Mo asked, jokingly. "You're such a romantic, bro."

"You know what I mean," Diego said. "Some women don't care as much about the words. It's action that matters."

"You have a point," Mo said, laughing.

Actually, his older brother did have a point. Was he worrying this entire situation to death? Trying to make something out of it that wasn't there? She was here and she was pregnant and they were together.

"I agree, but I want to add one thing, Alec. Helena didn't need me to up my game. She'd been ready since that second date, too. She'd just been afraid to tell me," Malcolm said. "Sometimes in love you have to take a risk."

"Wow, I'm a few minutes late and I walk in on a therapy session," Bart said as he approached.

"Hey, not all of us can rely on an accent to charm women," Alec said, going over to give Bart a one-armed hug.

"It's not just the accent, *mi amigo*," Bart said. "I can try to teach you boys, but I think it might be something you're born with."

There was a lot of good-natured ribbing as they

started playing pool. Alec realized that despite the fact that he hadn't really told them the entire situation with Scarlet, his friends had given him some solid advice.

Now if he could figure out a way to charm Scarlet into staying in Cole's Hill. Into believing that he'd make a good father for their baby and that he was worth the risk of staying here.

He went to take another swallow of his beer and realized it was empty. The clubhouse kept the bar and the fridge behind it fully stocked in the pool rooms so he went and grabbed another drink. He had a lot to think about and the answer wasn't that hard to figure out. He needed to ask Scarlet to stay or at least to stay in his life.

Scarlet was surprised when she opened the door and saw Mrs. Velasquez standing there with Lulu at her heels two days later. The dog barked once and then when Mrs. Velasquez leaned down to pet her, stood up on her back legs and just watched her. Alec's mom was a morning news presenter in Houston and commuted to the city every day. So on her days off—according to Alec—she usually spent her time chilling out. But here she was on Scarlet's doorstep. Though the two women had met before, they really hadn't spent much time alone talking.

"Hello, Scarlet. I'm sorry for the intrusion. I was wondering if you could spare a few minutes to chat with me."

"I can," Scarlet said as her dog danced around her feet. "I was actually about to take this one for a walk. Would you like to join me?"

"That would be nice," Mrs. Velasquez said.

"Come on inside while I get her harness and leash, Mrs. Velasquez," Scarlet said, stepping back into the foyer.

"Please call me Elena."

"Of course," Scarlet said. "Is everything okay?"

"Yes… It's just I haven't had a chance to get to know you and I know you and Alec have been spending a lot of time together…"

"And?"

"And I wanted a chance to just chat with you. Bianca said you're funny and smart and I think I was a bit jealous," Elena said with a laugh.

Scarlet realized that Alec's mom was here to see what kind of woman she was. How she would suit her son. And it was interesting—she didn't think she'd ever been in a situation like this before.

She got the dog's leash and they started out on their walk. The weather today was a bit cooler but not really cold.

They made small talk about the town and the upcoming open-air movie night in the park and then finally Elena stopped walking and sighed. "My husband said don't go over there, you'll make things awkward, and I hate to admit it but he was right, wasn't he?"

Scarlet shrugged. "I think so. I'm not sure what you want to know about me."

"I don't know, either. I miss out on what goes on in the daily routine of my kids and my husband because I do the morning news show and I'm gone a lot. And I didn't get a chance to know you at the polo match. It just wasn't the right time. I should have invited you to lunch or something," Elena said, tucking a strand of hair behind her ear.

"I pretty much grew up without my mother, so I have no idea how to deal with situations like this," Scarlet admitted. Talking about her mom always made her feel hollow and empty.

"I'm sorry to hear that," Elena said. "I did know your mom had passed away… I read your bio online, and am familiar with your TV show. Seems like you've had your share of tragedy."

Scarlet wasn't sure where this was leading and she didn't really want to talk to Alec's mom, but she wasn't going to be rude. Plus, she and Alec had had a paternity test just to resolve the issue and make sure there were no lingering questions, so she could speak with absolute assurance if the subject came up with Mrs. Velasquez.

"I have, but I'm sure that's not why you wanted to chat," Scarlet said. She wondered if Elena knew she was pregnant. Scarlet had the tiniest belly but it wasn't visible beneath the baggy top she had on.

"It isn't. Bianca shared your news with me and, of course, I know I should wait until Alec wants to tell me, but I've been a career woman who has been pregnant and I know that there are other considerations… Anyway, I just wanted to let you know I'm here if you need someone to talk to. I realize you don't have a mom and I know you are very capable but… Oh, Lord, I'm rambling."

Scarlet was upset that Bianca had told her mother. She turned to face the older woman and saw the concern and worry on her face. She'd felt attacked a moment earlier but now she realized that Elena was concerned.

"It wasn't Bianca's news to share," Scarlet said.

"I know. I tried to pretend I didn't know but frankly that's not the way I'm wired and after I realized you didn't have your mom…well, I thought you might need someone. And I know you don't know me but I want to fix that."

Scarlet also thought she saw a bit of joy. Elena might be the first person to see this baby just as a source of joy. Unlike Alec and her, who had been busy trying to figure out what to do next.

"It's okay. I was trying to keep it quiet as I'm not sure I'm ready for it to get out on social media."

"Bianca swore me to secrecy, but I just couldn't keep away," Elena said. "I want us to try to have a relationship. It's different with Bianca because I can just show up at her house and boss her around, but I won't do that with you."

Elena Velasquez was funny, Scarlet realized. And really sweet. "I'd like that. I'm not sure how long I'm going to stay in Cole's Hill. I sort of just came to give Alec the news… Well, I actually thought he was Mo at first."

"My boys really can be dumb sometimes," Elena said. "Would you like to have lunch? Maybe once a week. We can do it my house or wherever you like."

"Okay," Scarlet said. "That sounds nice. Thank you, Elena."

"No, thank you. I know I came over unannounced and then proceeded to be a meddlesome mom but I'm not someone who can just sit by and wait… But I won't be too pushy. Well, I am pushy, but you can always tell me to back off," Elena said.

Scarlet nodded. Her mom hadn't been around since she was a child and she had very few relationships with women who weren't her age or just a few years older, so this was different. They started walking again and Elena was more relaxed talking about current events and life around Cole's Hill. She admitted to being glad she worked in Houston, so she could sometimes escape from the bustle of small-town gossip.

After Elena left, Scarlet tried not to let the feeling of melancholy bother her. If her father had been a different sort of man, if he'd married a woman like Elena... But he hadn't. It was nice to have Elena now, but she didn't need a mom. Her child would have a grandmother who wanted to be in the baby's life, and that was something she'd never thought was a priority before.

But did Scarlet have what it took to be the baby's mother?

Alec had asked his housekeeper to make sure the garden and pool area looked like something out of a romantic fantasy tonight. She'd sent him several pictures from which to choose and she'd hit it out of the park. The entire backyard had been lit with fairy lights in the trees and bushes. There was music playing through the landscape speakers and a thick carpet had been laid in the sitting area under the portico.

He took one more look at everything before he left to go and pick Scarlet up. Mal had been right the other night when he'd said that waiting sometimes wasn't the answer. Alec had been letting his fear dictate his silence with Scarlet. He wanted them to be a couple, and while he was the first to admit that there was no way they were going to have everything sorted out before the baby came, they were certainly on the path to that.

So he'd done it. Pulled the trigger and gone to the jewelers in Houston to buy her a ring. He'd planned a night that would show her how much she'd come to mean to him. He could work from anywhere in the world. Unlike his brother Diego, who had to stay in Cole's Hill because of the ranch and his horses, Alec's job was pretty much online. So he could be wherever Scarlet needed to be.

He knew his parents might not like that; his mom especially preferred that they all lived in Cole's Hill. But she also was realistic. He'd stopped by his parents' house the night before to talk to them about it. Though it would be embarrassing if she said no, he couldn't ask a woman to share his life without telling his parents about her, the baby and how he wanted a life that he might have with Scarlet.

He ran his hands down the side of his dress pants, felt the ring in his pocket and realized his hands were shaking.

He had also given Mo a heads-up about his plans, but his twin said he'd already seen it coming. Alec wasn't sure if that was true or not.

He took his time driving to Scarlet's house to pick her up. He parked in front and fiddled with the in-car audio system so that when they got back in the vehicle, the song that had been playing the first time they danced would come on. It wasn't a particularly romantic song—"Hey Ma" by Pitbull and J Balvin—but it was their first song.

He flipped down the mirror to check that his hair

was in place and then got out of the car. He'd never felt so nervous. Then Scarlet opened the door and he saw her standing there in a cocktail dress with her hair up. Simply put, she was the most beautiful woman he'd ever seen.

She was everything that he hadn't realized he'd been looking for and suddenly he understood what Mal had meant when he said he needed to up his game. When he stood there staring at Scarlet, he had to wonder if he was good enough for her. Most of the time he was a good man but there were days when he did what he had to in order to get by. He could improve…not that she'd asked him to.

"I've never known you to be so quiet," she said in greeting.

"You're gorgeous tonight. I just can't believe that you're mine," he said at last.

"Am I yours?" she asked with an arched eyebrow.

"I hope so. I like thinking of us as a couple," he admitted. And frankly, if she didn't, then this entire night was going to go downhill fast.

"I like it, too," she said. "You're looking very dashing tonight. Who knew you owned a tux."

"I was wearing one the night we met," he reminded her, putting his hand on the small of her back as they walked down the steps that led to the driveway and his car.

"It was your brother's," she reminded him.

"You're never going to let me live that down, are you?"

"Never," she said with a smile.

He opened the door for her and couldn't help but let

his gaze linger on her legs as she swung them into the car. He went around to the driver's side, got behind the wheel and started the engine. "Hey Ma" started playing and she looked over at him.

"Wasn't this the song that was playing at the gala?"

"It was. I know it's cheesy, but I think of it as our song," he said.

She smiled over at him. "You're a closet romantic, Alec."

"I have my moments," he admitted.

"You sure do," she said, as he put the car in gear.

She put her hand on his thigh as he drove through the neighborhood and he started to relax. The nerves that had been dogging him since he'd shown up at her front door were starting to dissipate.

When they got to his house, he escorted her to the front door and then swung it open and stepped back for her to enter. He'd lined the floor with rose petals, something Hadley had promised him looked romantic, and had his housekeeper light candles in Scarlet's signature scent, which he'd tracked down via her assistant, Billie, who'd been surprisingly helpful.

"Alec... This is so romantic."

"Well, I wanted this night to be special," he said. "We've been seeing each other for a while now and I wanted to show you how much you've come to mean to me."

He closed the door behind himself and she turned toward him, putting her hand on his chest and going up on her tiptoes. Their eyes met.

"You mean a lot to me, too."

Thirteen

Scarlet had never had a man try to romance her like this, and it touched her. She felt that warm sensation in her stomach that made her wonder if she loved him. Love was the one thing she'd always tried to avoid. She'd loved Tara, of course, but that was it. Tara been the one person she'd been unable to keep herself from caring too much about.

Alec was different. There was no reason to love him. They weren't related, and they didn't have any bonds between them other than the child and the ones that they'd created over the last six weeks as they'd gotten to know each other.

She slowly followed the path of roses toward the back of his house and caught her breath when she looked out at his patio and garden. It had been transformed.

He made you an Eden, Tara's voice whispered through her mind.

The Princess Diaries had been their favorite movie to watch and she knew immediately what her sister meant. He'd made this ordinary suburban backyard seem otherworldly. And she knew in her heart of hearts that she cared deeply for him. More deeply than she'd ever cared for anyone before.

She almost wished she didn't. That she could enjoy the fantasy of this and go back to pretending that she was addicted to him because addiction was dangerous and unhealthy. Looking at it that way, it would make sense to want to escape this. But romance… Well, it would make her look silly if she turned and ran away.

If she let the panic rising up inside her have free rein.

"I had my chef prepare dinner for us," he said, holding out a chair at the table for her.

Dinner. It was just dinner, she thought as she sat down. She could handle this.

He sat next to her and poured her some sparkling water over ice, adding some fresh strawberries the way she liked it. He was the kind of person who noticed details. She liked that about him.

"Your mom stopped by to see me," she said when they were eating. She'd been unsure of how to bring it up to Alec. He hadn't mentioned a future together and she'd been trying to keep the baby and them separate. And once she'd met his mom, it had been even harder to think of not being a part of her baby's life. "I meant to text you earlier but she knows about the baby."

"Oh, well, I was going to tell my parents soon but

wanted to figure out what we were doing first," he said. "I know they're going to have a lot of questions that you and I haven't really been ready to answer."

She nodded. "Yeah. She said she knew I didn't have a mom and wanted to get to know me."

"You can tell her no," Alec said. "She's a bit—"

"Pushy," Scarlet said. "She told me. But honestly she was so sweet I liked it."

"Good. My parents, as you've seen, are the type to get involved in everything."

"Yeah, it's kind of funny but I noticed they sort of parent all of your friends, too," Scarlet said. Her father was more the hit-on-her-friends type, which was kind of what she thought the norm was until she'd come to Cole's Hill. Of course, she'd seen families like the Velasquezes on TV and in the movies but they'd never seemed real to her.

"They do. Mainly I think it's because we all grew up around here and they've known all of my friends since they were little kids," Alec said.

"I like it," she said. "I think Tara would have liked it, too."

"I wish I'd met her," Alec said. "She was very important to you, wasn't she?"

"Yes."

"What was the craziest thing you two did growing up?" he asked. "Mo and I were always in trouble so our kid is going to get the mischief gene."

Our kid.

Like they were a couple.

Panic started to rise in her, laced with a bit of hope that she didn't even acknowledge.

Tell him about me, Tara's voice whispered.

"She was always good at surprising me with something fun. We went to different boarding schools and the year after our mom died, I was pretty miserable. One night I was lying in my bed at the dorm when I heard this scratching at the window.

"I opened it up and glanced down to see Tara standing down below. She had this large branch in her hands and had been scraping it across the glass."

Scarlet took a sip of her drink.

"She waved at me to come out and I sneaked down to meet her. She took my hand and we ran as fast as we could to a taxi she had waiting and she ordered him to take us to the beach. It was the middle of the winter, freezing cold, because my school was in Massachusetts. But when we got to the beach, we went and stood on the sand and waited. And I asked her what we were waiting for and she said we'd see Mom's angel at sunrise."

"That sounds wonderful," Alec said. "I wish my brother were so thoughtful. Instead, Mo smacked me on the head with a pillow until I woke up one time so I could hand him his stuffed dog, Scratchers, who'd fallen out of the top bunk."

"Poor baby. Mo is such a bully," Scarlet said, jokingly.

"Yeah, he was. But Tara sounds like she took care of you," Alec said.

"Sometimes. She had her own problems, too. One time she deliberately crashed her sunfish sailboat into mine to keep me from winning a Fourth of July regatta at our yacht club."

"That I can relate to. Inigo was always superfast

on bikes or go-carts or even golf carts so we'd sometimes crash into him to keep him from winning... But
it hasn't hurt him. It probably made him even better at
racing," Alec said.

"I'm sure."

"Have you ever thought about having more kids?" he
asked. "Or do you think this one will be it?"

He had a right to ask her that question, she thought,
but at the same time she didn't want to answer. She
wasn't even sure what she was going to do about the
baby she carried right now. "I haven't. I'm not at all
ready to think about that."

"Fair enough. I'm not, either. I just didn't know if
you dreamed of a big family," he said, clearing away
the dinner dishes.

"I didn't dream of a family at all. I figured I'd be
doing my thing by myself forever," she said.

"Ready for dessert?" he asked because he wasn't
sure how to react to her answer.

"I'm good for now," she said.

"Okay."

He sat back down and they both sort of stared at each
other. She wished she could read his mind. Know what
he was thinking. This dinner he'd asked her to dress
up for was more than just their usual get-together. And
he was coming to mean more to her than she wanted
to really admit.

"You really outdid yourself tonight," she said.

"I know it's over the top but you're the first woman
I've ever wanted to do this stuff for," he said. "You mean
a lot to me, Scarlet."

She nodded. What was she going to say? She had to

think and fast because she was starting to want to stay. Here in Cole's Hill. Here with Alejandro Velasquez. Here with this family she'd always secretly craved.

He might not know it but he was offering her everything she'd always believed she'd never find. And it was harder than she thought to keep her cool. She swallowed hard, feeling the tears burning in her eyes as he opened the French doors to the patio and she heard the sound of jazz music playing. She'd told him she loved jazz and he'd remembered.

He's good for you, Tara's voice whispered again. *Don't mess this up.*

Don't mess it up.

That was exactly what she was so afraid of doing.

"Thank you," she said as she stepped onto the patio. She saw that he had new carpet in the seating area, a thick Berber rug that looked really soft. She toed off her shoes and stepped onto it.

The smell of roses and jasmine mingled in the air. She turned to check on Alec and noticed he was watching her. She held her hand out to him as "'S Wonderful" started playing and he came to join her, drawing her into his arms, singing under his breath as he danced them around in a circle. His hands against her back were warm and strong, his touch turning her on the way it always did.

His slightest touch was all it took to inflame her senses and make her forget everything but his dark chocolate eyes and his rock-hard body. He dipped her as the song ended and she clung to him, confident he wouldn't drop her because Alec was strong. He was always there for her. And as much as she didn't want to depend on him, she realized she already did. Whether she wanted to admit it to herself or not, she already felt deep affection for him.

Affection? Tara's voice jeered. *Why can't you admit you love him?*

She pulled herself from Alec's embrace and turned away from him—and from the voice in her head. No way was she going to admit it, but the truth was there echoing in each beat of her racing heart.

She wasn't lovable.

She never had been.

Her mom had left her.

Her sister had disappeared first into addiction and then died.

Her father couldn't even be bothered to speak to her unless he needed her signature on a document.

How was she going to believe that she could love Alec and be loved in return?

"Scarlet, baby? Are you okay?" he asked.

The concern in his voice made her feel dumb. She wasn't reacting the right way. She never knew how to behave in this situation. Give her a bunch of paparazzi standing outside her front door trying to catch her in an embarrassing situation and she could handle it. But a guy who'd planned a romantic evening—no dice.

"I'm not," she said, shaking her head. "I just realized that I've been pretending all this time that you and I could be a real couple."

"What? What do you mean? I wanted to make this night special… I'm not like this normally."

She shook her head. "I know. That makes it even worse. I want to be the kind of woman you deserve,

Alec. Someone who can see all this and feel safe en-joying it, but I'm not. Nothing in my life prepared me for this. I'm chaos and ruin. I'm running from one hot mess to the next and I don't think I can change."

He shook his head, holding his hands out toward her. "You don't have to change. I'm not asking you to."

But he was. He might not have said the words, but he wanted something permanent between them, and that scared her more than anything else. She had to get out of here, out of Texas before she forgot the truth of who she was. That she was Scarlet O'Malley of the hard-drinking, always fighting O'Malleys. Not the woman who could settle into domestic life.

That wasn't her scene.

He had no idea how things had gotten so far out of his control. "Let's go inside."

She didn't budge, just stood there with her arms wrapped around her body, and he realized she was scared. He went over to her and hugged her, careful to be aware if she was resistant to his embrace. But she sighed and rested her forehead against his shoulder. Her breathing was ragged and rough as she stood there.

He rubbed his hand up and down her back.

"I have no idea what I've done to upset you. But I'm sorry. I'll try not to do it again," he said, remembering that first afternoon when they had been on the patio and she'd run away from him.

"I'm not that guy who lied to you the first night we met. I've been trying to show you that I can be so much more than you first thought I was. But I know I still have a long way—"

"Stop. Alec, you're so much more than I ever expected you to be. Even when I thought you were Mo, Humanitarian of the Year, I couldn't have guessed at how perfect you really are."

He shook his head. "That's definitely not true. You don't have to spare my feelings, Scarlet. I know I'm not anyone's idea of a hero."

She lifted her head and their eyes met. "Stop. This is more about me than it is about you. I'm not this kind of woman. One who settles down."

She gestured to the table and the carpet, then to the speakers and the house. "But this makes me want to believe I am. All my life I've been pretty damn sure of who I am. I know I'm not everyone's cup of tea, but that's fine. I'm an O'Malley and I get by. This is different. This is changing my life to something that I've never had. I only ever had one-night stands before you. And it didn't bother me. I liked being unencumbered."

He nodded. He understood where she was coming from. "Everything changed the moment you got pregnant. We have to change to."

She nodded. "I don't know if I can. I don't know if I can be a mom. If I can be…whatever this is you want me to be. I was just starting to get used to sleeping with you and being here in your town, but this… It's too permanent. Things don't last, Alec. They never do."

Her words made him ache for her and angry at her at the same time. "I'm not your dad."

"I'm not saying you are," she snapped back at him.

She was full-on defensive, the way she'd been when he'd first seen her at the polo match. He had no idea what to say to diffuse the situation. How had he read it so wrong? He wasn't good with people, but this was a big misstep even for him.

"Don't be like that," he said. "I'm not attacking you."

"I know," she said, turning away from him. "This is how I get when I'm scared."

"What's scary about this?"

"Everything. Every. Damn. Thing."

He waited, hoping she'd continue, but she didn't.

"I can get rid of it all," he said, gesturing toward the candles, the rose petals, all the romantic trappings of the evening. "Will that help?"

"No, but mainly because I want it. I want to believe all of this and you. I want to have this feeling inside when I look at you and think about you and not be afraid that it's going to disappear."

"Then do. I'm not going anywhere…unless you want me to come to New York with you."

She gave him the saddest smile he'd ever seen and just shook her head. "I don't think you'd like it. My life isn't at all what we've had here in Cole's Hill. And I've stayed too long. I forgot what I was here to do."

"What was that?"

"Find out if you were a decent guy who could raise my child without screwing it up or if I would need to find another family to do that," she said.

"What?"

"Don't be like that. It was a one-night stand, we didn't know each other at all," she said. "My family is completely f'd up and I don't want any child of mine to grow up the way I did. I wasn't sure what to do. I didn't know what I was going to encounter when I got here."

He took her hand in his, rubbing his thumb over her

knuckles. He understood her fears, but surely they'd gotten past that. "But we do now."

"Yes, we do. And like I said earlier, you're more than I expected. And your family is a great support network. This baby will have everything I never did."

"So then why does the romance bother you? Do you want us to be more businesslike in how we are with each other but still sleep together?" he asked, because he thought he'd been moving them toward what she was describing.

She shook her head and walked back over to her shoes and put them on. "I am not going to be part of the child's life after I give birth."

"I'm not following," he said. "You want me to raise the child alone?"

"Yes. You're a much better person than I am. You know how to be a part of a family. You know how to raise a child. I'm—"

"Hell, no, I'm not," he said. He couldn't do that. Not on his own. He had thought they could do it together because they each brought something to the partnership that was different. But his raising the kid alone? What was she talking about? "I work late nights all the time. I can't be a single dad."

She nodded.

"Fair enough. I just want this child to have everything I can't give it. And, Alec, you are a very caring man. You'd be a great dad."

"You'd be a great mom, and I don't want to do it on my own. Won't you please consider doing this with me?" he asked. "Together I think we make a great team."

She didn't say anything and he realized that he had

read her wrong. That whatever it was she'd been doing with him the last six weeks, it hadn't been establishing a relationship so that they could raise a family together. He was the person she saw as taking care of the child while she went back to New York, back to her social-media-driven life and away from him.

He didn't blame her for thinking that at first but they'd gotten to know each other. She had to realize that he wasn't going to be okay with that. Or maybe she didn't?

"I want us to try living together," he said. "I know you weren't thinking in those terms so I'm not in any hurry for your answer."

"I can't."

He was starting to get angry. "Make me understand this. I know you're not the kind of woman who would just walk away."

"I can't trust myself," she said at last. "What if I'm like my dad?"

"What if you're not?" he asked.

"I won't take a chance with our baby," she said.

Fourteen

"What do you mean? Alec, I'm not going to be this woman," she said, gesturing around the patio. "Our lives are very different. I came here because I needed to know if the father of my baby was a decent guy—"

"You keep saying that. But we've moved beyond that. You've become an important part of my life and I think you feel the same about me. We aren't two strangers figuring out a problem. We are two people who care deeply about each other."

Care deeply... The words echoed in her head and for once Tara's sarcastic voice was silent. And the panic that she'd mostly managed to forestall since the moment she'd found out she was pregnant started to rise inside her. A tsunami of doubt was swelling and making her aware of how ill prepared she was to have this conversation with Alec.

"I can't. I can't do this. I'm sorry. I'll be in touch in a few days. I need you to think about whether you want to raise this child without me or if we should look for another option," she said.

She walked around him and toward the house. Again, the smell of roses and jasmine surrounded her but this time it made her sad. This patio had been the place that had cemented their relationship and it was probably fitting that it was here that she was ending it. She had never been good at relationships and she wasn't truly sure why she'd stayed here so long.

The novelty of it?

Don't be daft, Tara's voice whispered through her mind. *You liked it and you love him.*

Love.

No way. She didn't love him. She wouldn't allow herself to. Everyone she'd ever loved had died.

"Scarlet!"

She glanced over her shoulder and she saw the agony and pain and anger in his eyes. In the way he stood there with his hands clenched in fists just watching her. There was a knot in her stomach and she just wanted to get far enough away from him that she could stop feeling this. She hated this.

"Don't go. Not like this," he said.

"I have to. You want something from me that I can't give you and I should never have allowed myself to let this happen."

"You didn't allow it," he said. "There's a bond between us whether you want to admit it or not, and no matter where you go and what decisions you think you're making that bond will still be there."

She shook her head. That couldn't be true. She'd never been in that position before and she highly doubted that once she got back to New York and her old life that she wouldn't be able to move on from him.

She'd been playing a game while she was here. Pretending all along that she was someone like Mia in *The Princess Diaries* but knowing it was a fantasy she'd never be able to have in real life. This Eden wasn't for her. Not really. It was for some woman Alec thought she was.

"Thank you, Alec," she said at last. "Our time together was unexpected, and I enjoyed this while it lasted."

"Yeah, whatever," he said. "I'll drive you home."

"You don't have to," she said. She didn't know what she'd do if they were in the car together. She needed to get away. To be alone.

"Sorry, but you're pregnant with my baby and I'm not going to let you walk back to your house alone," he said. "I can call someone to pick you up if you'd prefer."

She debated it. If she stayed any longer, it was only going to make this worse on both of them. The car ride would be over in minutes. She nodded.

"I'd appreciate the ride," she said.

"No problem. I was raised to be a gentleman," he said through clenched teeth as he walked past her and held open the French doors that led to his living room. She walked into his house and straight to the front door. She heard his footsteps behind her and then the rattle of his keys as he took them from the bowl on the foyer table. He reached around her to open the door and his arm brushed her shoulder.

She felt that delicious shiver of desire go through her and she turned to step away at the same time as he did. They bumped into each other, and when their eyes met, her heart broke. She knew that she was making the right choice for the baby but also for Alec. Everyone in her family had a major self-destruct mode when it came to love, and she knew she wasn't any different. She hated to see the pain on his face, hated to feel this heaviness in her own heart, but there was no other way.

This was bigger than herself. This was the only thing she could do to make sure her child didn't grow up like her. And that was the important thing. The pain would pass and fade despite what Alec had said.

"I hope…" She trailed off. What could she say? There weren't words to express what she wanted to say because the truth was, she hoped he could find happiness without her and she was pretty sure he would.

"Yeah, whatever," he said.

She realized that was his way of hiding his hurt. She also noticed as they walked to his car in the driveway that he'd never lashed out at her. He'd been angry but the meanest thing he'd ever said was that their bond was strong, and she might not get over it. Which was hardly mean. He was a great guy. The kind of man she wanted for her own but was too afraid to claim.

That just made her love him more.

Damn. She did love him.

Which made it all the more important that she get away from him. For both of their sakes. Whenever she wanted something she turned destructive. He drove her home in silence and when he pulled up to her house, she opened her car door herself, putting her hand on his arm to stop him from coming around to help her out.

"Goodbye, then," she said.

"Yeah, goodbye," he replied. She closed the car door as she got out and then stepped away as he gunned the engine and disappeared into the night.

Alec knew he wasn't in the best shape to be attending a family dinner. It had been six weeks since Scarlet had left Cole's Hill. She'd instructed her attorney to contact his attorney, Ethan Caruthers, to keep him informed of the baby's progress. She had also conveyed via letter that she hoped he'd reconsider and raise the baby on his own, or she'd have to consider other options like adoption. Ethan had counseled him to think of the child but Alec was convinced. He wasn't the kind of man who could raise a child on his own. Other options worried him and he didn't want to give up his child any more than he thought that Scarlet did.

But his mom wasn't happy with that decision and so he wasn't surprised that his dad was waiting for him on the front porch in one of the rockers when he arrived at his childhood home. His father had a bottle of tequila sitting on the table between the two chairs on a bar tray that also had salt, wedges of lime and shot glasses.

"Dad," Alec said by way of greeting.

"Son, take a seat."

"I really don't want to," he said. In fact, he should leave. He wasn't ready to talk to his family or anyone else. He wished he could say he was mad because that at least would make sense. But instead he was hurt and he still woke up every night reaching for Scarlet even knowing she'd never be next to him in his bed again.

"Tough shit," his father said. "Take a seat, Alejandro."

"Dad—"

"I'm not asking," he replied.

Alec sat down in the empty chair and refused to look at his father. Over the course of his life, he'd had exactly five conversations with his father on this porch. Three of them had occurred when he was under the age of eighteen. One of them took place after he'd screwed up royally in college, and then there was this one today. He knew his father saved the porch talks for stuff that he didn't want to bring into the house. The messy stuff that needed to be said.

"I'm not ready to talk about this," Alec said.

"That's fine. You just need to listen. But first, pour us both a shot," his father said.

Alec opened the bottle of tequila and poured two shots. His father licked his hand at the same time that Alec did. They took turns with the saltshaker, then picked up a wedge of lime each and then their shots. Alec licked the salt off his hand, downed his shot and then chased it with the lime. He put his glass down and then sat back in the Kennedy rocker.

"I don't know what's going on with you and Scarlet," his father said. "But your mom told me she's pregnant and you told me you were going to ask her to marry you. And she's gone so I'm guessing something happened."

"Yeah, she doesn't want this. She said she's not cut out for this kind of life and she wants me to raise the child on my own. That's why she came here."

"To check you out?" his father asked.

"Yes," he said, turning to face his father. He felt overcome with emotions and blinked because he really didn't want to lose it. Not now. "And we passed her test. She thinks our extended family would be great to raise the child. Yay for us. But I didn't pass her test."

His dad reached across the table and put his hand on Alec's shoulder. "What makes you think you didn't?"

"She left. She made it clear that she's not into me," he said. "I sound like a complete dumbass, right? I should be able to say I've moved on. It's been six weeks, Dad, and I'm still not over her."

"Love's not like that. You don't get over it," he said. "Especially if it's real. Look at your brother and Hadley."

"I can't. Dad, I'm turning into a really nasty person on the inside. I hate that everyone else seems to be able to find happiness and I can't."

His father nodded. "You will find it."

"Not with her," he said at last.

"Not with her. Your mom told me a little bit about her family and it seems like she has her own issues to sort out," his dad said. "And you'll figure out how to move on. But your mom and I think you should raise the baby. We will help you. Your brothers will help you. And that child will probably help you, too."

Alec leaned forward, putting his elbows on his knees and then his face in his hands. Raise the baby? That's what Scarlet wanted and he honestly had been so consumed by her rejection he hadn't spent much time allowing himself to think about the baby. But now that his father said it like that, he hated the thought of a Velasquez being raised by anyone else. He wasn't sure what he was doing but he'd figure it out.

"Okay," he said at last. "I'm not going to pretend I know what I'm doing but I'll let Ethan know I want custody."

"Good. Now about the girl," his father said, pouring two more shots of tequila. "What can we do there?"

"I don't know, Dad," Alec said. "She said she's not good at relationships. Hell, I'm not a poster boy for them, either."

"No, you're not. Maybe you need to show her what it would mean, being in a relationship with you."

His father had a cagey look on his face and Alec wasn't sure what his father had in mind.

"How?"

"Your mom's going to kill me for suggesting this, but why don't you move to New York and make sure she knows you're there."

"I don't know. I don't want to seem like a desperate loser," Alec said.

"Don't, then. Be there for the pregnancy and the baby. That's it. Once she sees you, she'll change her mind."

"I'm not so sure. I love her but is that enough to convince her?"

His dad smacked him on the back of the head. "Dammit, Alejandro. Love is the most powerful thing in the world. You just keep loving her until she realizes she loves you back."

"You think that will work?" he asked his father. Though he had seen firsthand how Diego and Mauricio had both won the women they loved.

"How do you think I won your mom over? She wanted

a city slicker, not a horse rancher. Not even one who played polo. But I wore her down. Just kept asking her to marry me until she said yes."

Alec shook his head. It wasn't a bad plan, he thought. If he'd learned anything in the last six weeks, it was that his feelings for Scarlet had grown, not disappeared.

So that was it, then. He had a plan and some hope for the future. His dad had been right about being closer to Scarlet, but not in New York. That was her turf. He'd agree to raise the child but only if she came back here until she delivered. That would give him the home-field advantage, and hopefully the remaining time in her pregnancy would be enough to convince her that they were stronger together. He didn't allow himself to lose hope. He loved her too much for that.

Scarlet wasn't feeling it today but her film crew was due to arrive any minute. Since the shows were all filmed six months before they aired, she'd asked the crew and the film company to keep her pregnancy under wraps. And they agreed. She needed to figure out the situation with her child, and she needed to keep her pregnancy private to do that. Alec still wanted them both to be involved in the baby's life, and the longer she was carrying her child the harder it was to think of letting anyone raise the baby but Alec. In the middle of the night she sometimes pictured herself and Alec with the baby, but then the dreams twisted into that lifeless image of Tara when she'd died.

Her partners in the subscription box business loved the idea of a wedding/bride theme, but since she was pregnant they were pushing for her to do an expectant-mother-themed one, as well. The only problem was she didn't want to concentrate on that. The almost seven weeks since she'd left Cole's Hill hadn't been easy. Each day she missed Alec—and how was that even possible?

She'd left friends and homes and family a million times in her life and just moved on without looking back. Now all of a sudden she couldn't stop thinking about him. She had decided to communicate only through lawyers and by letter because she was afraid if she heard his voice she'd change her mind and run back to him.

And if it was just the two of them, she might risk it, but there was the baby to consider.

She put her hand on her stomach, which was definitely getting larger. She'd taken to wearing clothes in her apartment that showed off her baby bump. She liked the thought of the child, which was its own kind of torture. Billie had recommended that she reconsider giving the child to Alec. And the truth was she was reconsidering a lot. Life wasn't any easier now that she was back in New York.

"The film crew is here. Do you want to go down and get them?" Billie asked. "I think they want to do some outside shots."

"Will you go for me and tell them I can't do it today?"

"Sure, but you should probably leave the apartment. You're going to have to at some point."

"I know, but not yet," she admitted. She'd been hiding away, trying to make sense of her feelings. She didn't know what love should feel like but the way she longed for Alec, the way she missed him, made her believe this had to be something pretty close to it.

Scarlet bent down to scoop up Lulu, who was dancing around her feet. The little dog buried her face in the curve of Scarlet's neck as Scarlet petted her.

"How about if we go for a walk in Central Park when I get back?" Billie asked. "The weather isn't too bad today. It's supposed to snow, which you love, and you can put a coat on so the baby bump won't show if any paps snap a photo of you."

She looked at her friend and assistant and saw the concern on Billie's face. She'd also heard from Bianca, who had her baby—a little girl she'd named Aurora. Kinley, Hadley and Helena had all emailed and texted as well, just saying they missed her.

She missed them, as well.

You don't have to miss anyone, Tara's voice whispered through her mind. *Go back to Texas.*

Go back to Texas.

Was it that simple?

She stood there staring at Billie for a long minute and then nodded. She wasn't happy here. She knew she was due to start shooting, but for once in her life she wasn't going to share this with the world. Not until she won Alec back... If he'd still have her. She was in love with him and being apart wasn't really making her feel any better. She had absolutely no idea how to raise a child but with Alec by her side she'd feel a lot better about trying.

"Uh, that's a no on the park, Billie. How about if we go to Cole's Hill instead?" Scarlet said.

"About damned time," Billie said. "You have been miserable since you came home, and I think it's because you love Alec."

"I think I do, too," Scarlet said. "Go and deal with whoever is downstairs while I call the film company to reschedule shooting and call the pilot—"

"How are you going to deal with any of that? I'm the one with the numbers," Billie countered.

"Text them to me. Billie, I think I'm going to be a mom."

"You are going to be a mom," Billie said, coming over and hugging her. "And you're going to be great. Be right back."

Billie left the apartment and Scarlet picked up her phone and looked at the text messages. She hadn't heard from Alec since she'd left him that night. What was she going to say?

Tell him how you feel, Tara's voice whispered. *That's the one thing we never did in our family.*

Her sister was right. It was time to do the opposite of everything that she'd learned to do in order to protect herself from being hurt. It was time to be honest about her emotions and admit she needed Alec in her life. That she wanted the family that fate had dropped in her lap.

Fifteen

Ethan's law offices were in one of the new towers that had just been completed on the outskirts of town near Hadley's loft. Normally he took care of all of his business with Ethan at the Five Families Clubhouse or the Bull Pen. But Ethan had insisted that to get everything he wanted in the new deal with Scarlet, he was going to have to come into the office.

So he'd postponed a trip to Michigan to see one of his new clients and was now on his way to the lawyer's office. It had been three days since his conversation with his dad and Alec had been working nonstop to get everything in order so that when Scarlet came back to Cole's Hill he'd be able to focus on her. That was why rescheduling the client trip wasn't ideal. What if she was able to come back sooner than he thought? He definitely wanted to be here when she arrived.

But when he got to Ethan's office, Hadley was waiting in the parking lot and she looked upset.

He couldn't ignore his future sister-in-law, and Ethan would understand if Alec was late.

"You okay?"

"No, I'm not. Thank goodness you're here. I think there's a mouse in my loft," Hadley said. "I've texted Mo, but he said you were on your way to Ethan's. Could you go and check it out?"

"Sure," he said. "I thought you weren't living there anymore."

"I'm not but I've been working to get it ready so I can rent it out, and I have someone coming to look at it in like thirty minutes," Hadley said. "I swear, I can handle anything but a mouse. They are small and fast and I'm getting the heebie-jeebies just thinking about it."

"I got this. I'll go check it out and then figure out how to catch it," Alec said.

"Thank you," she said. "Should I tell Mo to still come?"

"Yes. He's going to have to figure out how to humanely dispose of it. Also, if there's one in the loft you should check your studio."

"I didn't even think of that," Hadley said. "Here are my keys. The front door code is 0322."

He nodded, taking her keys and walking toward the entrance to the lofts, which was around the side of the building where Hadley had her art studio. There was also a coffee house and a martial arts dojo. Ethan's offices were in the new high-rise adjacent to the lofts.

He keyed in the code and as soon as he stepped inside he saw the rose petals on the floor. They stirred memories of the night he'd been planning to ask Scarlet to marry him. He still couldn't believe it had gone so wrong. He followed the trail to the elevator. Obviously one of Hadley's neighbors had the same idea that Alec had and he hoped it worked out better for them than it had for him.

He took the elevator up to the residential area and when he got off he noticed the trail of rose petals continued down the hall ending at the door to Hadley's loft. He was starting to worry that his brother might be waiting for Hadley, and if there was one thing he didn't want to see it was his brother trying to be sexy for his fiancée.

He knocked on the door. "Mo? You in there? Uh, Hadley is downstairs. She thinks there's a mouse up here."

The door opened slowly and he saw that the petals made a path through the entire loft to form a giant heart in the middle of the floor. He stepped inside and turned as the door closed behind him.

His heart raced as he saw Scarlet standing there watching him. She wore a flowy dress that fell to her knees and had a V in the front. She looked so good it was hard to not go right to her and pull her into his arms. He noticed the tiny changes that pregnancy had made to her body and he smiled at her as she stood there.

"So... Turns out I'm not Mo," she said.

"I'm so glad. I wasn't looking forward to seeing my brother trying to be romantic with Hadley," he answered. He had a feeling that this was a good thing. Her being here in Cole's Hill before Ethan had even sent back his counteroffer seemed like really good news to him.

"Me, too. That would have been awkward," she said, twisting her fingers together, and he realized she was nervous. "But I wasn't sure you'd come if you knew it was me. Seems that I'm the kind of girl who likes this stuff."

She gestured to the rose petals and the heart she'd made in the middle of the empty loft. Inside it, spelled out in rose petals, was a message.

Do you believe in second chances?

"I do," Alec said, gesturing at the rose-petal message and answering her question. "I never got to say it that night but I love you. I have absolutely no idea how to raise a kid but my folks did a pretty good job with my siblings and me so we can call them for advice. And Bianca has a new baby so you'll be in good company… I just want a chance to do this together. That's what you're saying, right?"

"Yes. That's it. I love you, too, Alec. I've been so afraid to admit it because love and I aren't exactly on good terms so there might be times when I might panic and freak out but I want you to know I'm always coming back."

He could live with that. "I'm going to follow you."

He walked over to her and pulled her into his arms, kissing her with all the pent-up desire and emotion that had been building inside him for the last six weeks. "God, I missed you."

"I missed you, too," she said.

He patted his pocket and the ring box that he still had in there. He'd been carrying it around as if by doing so he'd bring Scarlet back to him. "I want to ask you to marry me, but there's no hurry. I know it's going to take time for you to feel safe living with me and our child, but know that's what I want."

"I'm going to say yes, but not today," she promised him. "I want to say yes when we both can believe that I mean it."

"I'll believe you," Alec told her. "You'd never make a promise you couldn't keep. Isn't that why you left?"

She nodded and then let her breath out in one long gasp. "Yes. I'll marry you!"

He carefully lifted her in his arms and hugged her as tightly as he could. "Thank you."

He took the ring box out of his pocket and put the ring on her finger. He'd picked out a princess-cut diamond and then had two smaller stones put on either side of it. He wanted to take her home and make love to her but it turned out his entire family was waiting outside Hadley's building when they exited.

"So, did you catch anything upstairs?" Mo asked.

"Just the love of my life," Alec responded.

Epilogue

One year later

Alec was sitting on the patio of the new home they'd had built just outside Cole's Hill, holding his tiny daughter, Tara Maria, in his arms while Scarlet lay next to him on the sun lounger. It was a gorgeous morning and the baby preferred to be outside so they spent most of their time outdoors.

Scarlet had decided to continue filming her reality TV show, and her fans were completely over the moon at the pregnancy and the baby. Alec was always monitoring their online footprint to ensure their privacy. He had been careful so that he and the baby were only filmed in the periphery. She had successfully launched her wedding subscription box, along with one for expectant mothers, and was planning one for new moms later this year. He was proud of how hard she worked and that her public seemed to be accepting her new, more mature persona.

"So are you ever going to set a date for the wedding?" she asked him.

He glanced over at her. Since that day he'd asked her to marry him, he'd never brought it up again, knowing when she was ready she'd say the word. They'd been dividing their time between New York and Cole's Hill and probably would until Tara Maria was ready to start school.

"Are you ready?"

She nodded as the baby started to cry for her feeding. Scarlet breastfed her while he watched. His wife and his daughter. He'd never seen anything more beautiful and he'd never expected that having a family would enrich his life as much as it had.

"Then let's set a date. Kinley is dying to plan it," Alec said. "She pestered Nate into asking me about it last night at the Bull Pen."

They continued to discuss the details, and when Tara was fed and sleeping they took her into the nursery, which Scarlet had decorated in a soft floral theme. Then he carried his soon-to-be wife to their adjoining bedroom and made love to her, knowing he'd achieved a happiness he'd never dreamed he'd find.

* * * * *

COMING SOON!

We really hope you enjoyed reading this book. If you're looking for more romance, be sure to head to the shops when new books are available on

Thursday 14th November

To see which titles are coming soon, please visit

millsandboon.co.uk/nextmonth

MILLS & BOON
A ROMANCE FOR EVERY READER

- **FREE** delivery direct to your door

- **EXCLUSIVE** offers every month

- **SAVE** up to 25% on pre-paid subscriptions

SUBSCRIBE AND SAVE

millsandboon.co.uk/Subscribe

MILLS & BOON

THE HEART OF ROMANCE

A ROMANCE FOR EVERY KIND OF READER

MODERN

Prepare to be swept off your feet by sophisticated, sexy and seductive heroes, in some of the world's most glamourous and romantic locations, where power and passion collide.
8 stories per month.

HISTORICAL

Escape with historical heroes from time gone by. Whether you passion is for wicked Regency Rakes, muscled Vikings or rugge Highlanders, awaken the romance of the past.
6 stories per month.

MEDICAL

Set your pulse racing with dedicated, delectable doctors in the high-pressure world of medicine, where emotions run high an passion, comfort and love are the best medicine.
6 stories per month.

True Love

Celebrate true love with tender stories of heartfelt romance, f the rush of falling in love to the joy a new baby can bring, and focus on the emotional heart of a relationship.
8 stories per month.

Desire

Indulge in secrets and scandal, intense drama and plenty of si hot action with powerful and passionate heroes who have it all wealth, status, good looks...everything but the right woman.
6 stories per month.

HEROES

Experience all the excitement of a gripping thriller, with an in romance at its heart. Resourceful, true-to-life women and stro fearless men face danger and desire - a killer combination!
8 stories per month.

DARE

Sensual love stories featuring smart, sassy heroines you'd want best friend, and compelling intense heroes who are worthy of
4 stories per month.

To see which titles are coming soon, please visit

millsandboon.co.uk/nextmonth

JOIN US ON SOCIAL MEDIA!

Stay up to date with our latest releases, author news and gossip, special offers and discounts, and all the behind-the-scenes action from Mills & Boon...

 millsandboon

 millsandboonuk

 millsandboon

t might just be true love...

MILLS & BOON

MODERN

Power and Passion

Prepare to be swept off your feet by sophisticated, sexy and seductive heroes, in some of the world's most glamourous and romantic locations, where power and passion collide.